LIES

© THE KILLION GROUP INC.

SECRETS AND LIES

Jacki Renée

*I dedicate this book to my two amazing and talented daughters,
Jai'Lauren and Jos'Lynne. Your love, support,
and words of encouragement feed my soul.*

ACKNOWLEDGEMENTS

NO ONE CAN ASK FOR a better cheer squad than the one I have in my family and friends. They understand and support my need to write the kind of stories I like to read. Leading the cheer squad is my mother, Jacqueline Miller and dear friend, Joan Goldman. Thank you for your critiques, input, keen eyes for consistency, and debates (wink @ Joan).

My deepest gratitude to iProofread And More for your continued guidance in helping me grow as an author. Thank you for understanding my need to be myself and providing services that make my voice shine.

A big thank you to the wonderful team at The Killion Group, Inc. for your outstanding customer service. Everyone there is a joy to work with.

A special thank you to the book clubs who read *Necessary Lies* and *Lies You Tell* and invited me to a meeting to get to know me better. I know you've been anxiously awaiting the release of this book. You won't be disappointed.

IAMJACKIRENEE.COM is maintained by the very talented Kenward Romero. I can't thank you enough for your services.

Finally, thank you all for the follows, likes, views, and comments on my social media pages. Please keep reading and responding to my posts.

Website: iamjackirenee.com
Twitter @iamjackirenee
Facebook /iamjackirenee
Instagram /iamjackirenee

CHAPTER ONE

BRYAN

Colorado, Present Day

"Hawk!"

"Hawk, are you all right?"

"BRY!"

"Mmm." My eyes creep open. Above me is the moonless ink-black sky. The left side of my face feels like it's too close to the flames. Underneath me, something round and hard presses into my back. Pointy blades of grass prick the back of my neck. My right arm is pressing against something hard and unforgiving.

"Hawk is down!" My best friend's anxiety is magnified by the earpiece in my ear. Dr. Ignacio Acosta Jr. does not panic in the field, but because of the extreme ways we're going about taking down our enemy, we're all a little anxious.

I manage to groan again and find my voice. "I'm good, Acosta."

"What the fuck, Hawk! You trying to do Langford's job for him? Another second and you'd be dead."

Slowly, I move my head and look to my left. Ig's Camaro is on fire. The heat it's giving off feels like hell. The odor of explosives mixed with heated metal and burning rubber makes my nose wrinkle.

"Dani held on to me a second too long." I had to pry my wife's fingers from my arms. Even running as fast as I could, I still only made it a foot outside of the safe zone when the second blast knocked me back, slamming my body against the brick boundary wall. I landed between the wall and the thick cover of bushes and shrubs and sprinklers.

"Is anything broken?"

I exhale and do a mental assessment of my body. Confident nothing's broken, I slowly roll onto my stomach. "No, just got the wind knocked out of me. What kind of explosives did Tony use?"

"You told him to go all out. I'll cover you then head to the airport."

"The keys to Dani's Range Rover are under the driver's seat."

"Stay safe, Hawk."

"See ya when I see ya, Acosta."

I use my elbows to military crawl through the wet grass to get to the edge of the bushes. The outside lights on this side of the hospital are out, but the ones inside of the lobby are still shining bright. The entrance is filled with medical staff and visitors looking and pointing.

The loud sound of a helicopter's rotor blades slicing the night air from the rooftop circulate with the sirens and horns of the fire engines racing down the street toward the hospital. Hawkeye Personal Protection's helicopter is taking off with my daughters onboard.

While the looky-loos hanging outside of the hospital are focused on the helicopter, I climb to my feet.

Sticking to the shadows, I round the boundary wall.

Camouflaged by darkness, parked cars, and foliage, I creep my way through the parking lot. Ig is watching from his hiding spot underneath a parked car.

At the rear of the hospital I find the dark corner where my motorcycle is hidden. I mount it and wait for the next important person in my life to leave the hospital.

Our enemy knows us. Everything I thought I knew about Willis and Marie Langford is a lie.

They played me.

They played us all.

Because they are knowledgeable about Phantom's tactics, we had to do something an entire Elite Special Operations Team has never done. We faked our deaths. Langford hired a hitman to take us out. Why not let them think they succeeded?

The darkness my monster thrives in is slowly seeping from its cage. I'm still in control, but the monster's pleasure in being the silent dark hooded executioner who gets to carry out the death sentence of Willis and Marie Langford is slowly becoming my pleasure too.

Until it comes time to pull the trigger, I visualize my light—my wife— to keep the man separate from the monster. Dani is the only woman who can touch me on a level I never knew existed until I met her.

———◆———

Arizona, Nine Years Ago

This is it. My first up close interaction with the girlfriend of Army Sergeant James Andrew Edwards, the traitor who managed to uncover a one-hundred-year-old United States secret.

"Recover that information by any means necessary, Hawk," Colonel Willis Langford's command rolls through my brain as Danielle Lauren Tatum greets me.

"Hi, you must be Hawk." She smiles and opens the screen door. "James left a message on the voicemail while I was in the shower. There was a lot of background noise and I had to listen to it a few times. He said to expect you." She gestures for me to come in.

I cross the threshold into the small living room and something pleasant in the air that I can't identify welcomes me.

The walls are the color of hazelnut coffee creamer and match the blinds covering the windows. The carpet is light brown. None of the pieces of furniture match, yet everything fits together. They look second hand.

On the coffee table is a big glass bowl filled with multicolored, dried flower petals. Next to it is an expensive bottle of champagne—no glasses. I still don't see the source of the pleasant scent.

"You must be Danielle, Edwards's girlfriend." I hold out my hand.

Danielle's eyes drop to my feet and travel up, pausing for a long second on my thighs then the fly of my jeans. The forward motion of her right hand freezes. Her lips part, and she slowly exhales.

I reach out and take her hand, and her assessing gaze continues up my torso and stops at my eyes.

"I… I'm… I'm his wife." She shows off the simple gold band on her ring finger.

My grip on her hand tightens. *Why would she marry that asshole?* "Edwards never said anything about… Are you *even* old enough…?"

Danielle snatches her hand back. Those pretty brown eyes darken as they go from welcoming to frosty. "I'm of consensual age—*Mr. Hawk.*"

The way she said my name makes me sound like an old man. And judging by her defensive stance, I'm guessing that's exactly what she intended. I do have seven years on her.

I raise my hand, surrendering. "Sorry, that came out wrong."

Her shoulders relax a bit and she waves me off. "I'm used to being questioned about my age. It's just today I'm not feeling well, so my temper is quick. Have a seat." She gestures to the sofa and loveseat.

I walk around to the loveseat, drop my duffle bag, and sit. Right away I spot the wedding photo on the coffee table. It takes everything in me to not rip it in quarters. In an attempt to divert my stare, I turn away and my eyes catch on two opened shiny black foil condom wrappers under the sofa. Edwards got him some before he left. Too bad it'll be his last. They don't allow conjugal visits where he's going.

To give the appearance of friendly and approachable, I rest my arms along the top of the loveseat, place my right foot on my left knee, and get comfortable by keeping my breathing normal and even.

Her stare zeroes in on the tattoo partially showing under the short sleeve of my shirt. The profile written on her says she seems to be attracted to guys with tattoos. My lion tattoo is different from the other guys on Colonel Langford's Elite Special Operations Team.

"I talked to Edwards last week. He didn't say anything about getting married."

Danielle walks across the carpeted floor to the square wooden dining table, with four mismatched chairs.

The light gray slacks she's wearing hug her firm thighs and nice round ass. The Bahama-ocean-blue dress shirt curves to her round breasts and athletic waistline and disappears behind the gray belt. She left the top two buttons open. Nothing shows, but that makes it sexier on her. Today her curly brown hair hangs down to the middle of her back.

She packs her backpack. "James and I got married yesterday afternoon. It was sort of spur of the moment. We didn't call any-one."

That's unfortunate, Mrs. Edwards. Your husband will be in a federal supermax prison soon and you'll be guilty by association. Forever known as the wife of a traitor.

She looks over her shoulder at me. Her mouth turns down in a slight frown.

Did I slip and say that out loud?

Frowning or smiling, Danielle is an attractive woman with curves in all the right places. For my country, I will break a personal rule and fuck another man's wife to get what I came for—the Phantom file.

"Where's your husband? I thought he'd be home from the base by now."

Her eyebrows scrunch together, and her head tilts to the side. "James deployed this morning for a tour in Iraq. He didn't tell you?"

My arms drop, and I plant both feet on the carpet. "No."

"Huh, that's weird. He's known about it since last month."

I get to my feet and reach for the handles of my duffle bag—all for show. "I can't stay here if Edwards isn't around. I'll find a motel for the night, then hop on a bus and go visit my parents in Colorado Springs." To be a good liar, a small part of the lie has to be the truth.

"It's graduation season. All the decent hotels and motels are booked up."

"I slept in a six-by-six hole in the ground for three months. I'm sure I can handle one night in a less-than-stellar motel."

"James wouldn't say to let you crash on the sofa if he didn't trust you. I picked up some extra hours at work because we need the money. So, I'll be out of the apartment most of the week anyway."

Either she's clueless to her husband's activities or she's an award-winning actress. It's part of my assignment to find out which.

"I'm only going to be here for two nights. Let me pay you…"

"That wasn't a hint for you to pay to stay here." She interrupts. "I don't feel right charging you anyway. You're too tall for the sofa so I doubt you'll be comfortable." Her eyes travel my body again.

The corners of my mouth turn up. "I'm good with my hands *and* I can cook. If you won't take my money at least let me earn my keep in other ways."

I hold her gaze for a minute longer than what is considered friendly. It borders on a sexy challenge.

A playful smile lights up her face. "The handle on the toilet is broken and the garbage disposal isn't working in the kitchen. DIY or call the manager. I guess I'll know how good you are with your hands when I get back."

The confident smile I paint on my face is my way of extending the challenge. "Shall I have dinner waiting for you, too?"

She picks up her backpack and heads to the door.

I drop the duffle bag and follow.

"No, thanks. If my stomach can take it, I'll get something from the cafeteria. There isn't much to eat in the fridge but help yourself to whatever's in there. If you need to go out, the spare key is hanging on a nail in the cabinet over the sink. My cell phone number is on the calendar on the refrigerator in case you need to get in touch with me." Danielle steps one foot out of the door but pauses and turns to face me. "You're the only friend of James's that I've met. For him to say it's okay for you to stay here says a lot."

I nod, acknowledging her subtle meaning: *but I reserve the right to kick you out, friend or not, if you cross the line.*

Damn if her independence isn't a turn on.

Through the screen door I watch Danielle walk the pathway to the garage. The cell phone in my front pocket starts to vibrate— not the best time for something to be moving in that area. I pull the phone out before it fully wakes the hawk.

"How long we got?" My best friend, Anthony Jonathan Paul asks.

I check my watch. "Roughly nine hours. Eight in case she leaves work early."

"Did she question the message on the answering machine?"

"Why would she? That spliced-together recording of Edwards's voice I made was convincing. The background noise I added hid the flaws."

"If I hadn't watched you do it, I'd think Edwards left the message too."

"Hey, on your way can you stop at a hardware store and pick up a toilet handle and a garbage disposal?"

"Dawg, what were you and Danielle talking about?"

"I'm just rising to the occasion of a challenge."

"Are you sure you don't want me to bring your laptop?"

"No, leave it at the hotel. I've already got it logged in and set for you to monitor while I'm here. I'll use Danielle's desktop computer."

"Colonel Langford wants you to report in once you get set up. And Ig said to call Amelia."

My stomach tightens at the mention of Amelia Goodman. I can't deal with her right now, but if I don't at least send a text, she'll hound my friend.

The call to Colonel Langford is brief because I have nothing significant to report other than Edwards and Danielle got married.

I type out a short text to Amelia: "I'll get back to you later." I hit send and pocket my phone.

Before I start removing the surveillance cameras I installed a few weeks back, I retrieve the condom wrappers from under the sofa, pick up the empty champagne bottle off the coffee table, and dump them in the overflowing kitchen trash can. What they represent makes me sick to my stomach.

By the time Tony gets here, I have everything ready for us to swap out the faulty cameras with the ones I modified.

Tony opens the cardboard box. "Bry, we hanging out tonight? I found this steakhouse I want to try out."

"If we find the file after we finish installing the cameras, you can head back to Colorado. I know your girl is pissed you canceled on her again."

Tony hands me a camera after I get up on the stepladder. "Nah, she was chill. Told her I have training."

I glance at him over my shoulder with a raised eyebrow.

Tony's nonchalant shrug means he told his girl as much of the truth as he's allowed to tell. I *am* teaching him the ins and outs of the surveillance system I designed.

We move from spot to spot around the apartment. Me instructing. Him learning.

I ask him the one question we've never bridged since his girlfriend moved in with him a year ago. "Is she the one you'll tell about Phantom?"

"Yeah. One day. Maybe after we're married."

I climb down the ladder and move it to the next spot. "You really want to be tied to one woman for the rest of your life?"

"Charly's my do-right-girl. I *love* her."

"Man… here we go. Love is just a four-letter word people use to explain the need to fuck as much as you want for as long as you want without judgment."

I use Danielle's antiquated computer to log on to the site to access the camera feed while Tony climbs the ladder to replace one of two cameras in the kitchen.

"You have a twisted view of love, considering how long your parents have been together. I hope I'm around when you meet that one girl who knocks you on yo' ass."

"Not happening, bro," I grunt. "Angle the camera a little more to the right."

No girl paid attention to the kid with glasses who got straight A's in math and science without opening a textbook. Then puberty hit. The muscles started forming, facial hair started growing, and thanks to advanced Krav Maga tournaments, I started wearing contacts. Freshman year of high school, I learned the hard way about opportunistic females. Never again will a girl "knock me on my ass."

Tony makes the adjustment to the camera and I tell him how to hide the wires along the molding.

"Is Danielle as nice on the eyes in person as she is in a photograph?"

"Better." The word slips before I have a chance to censor myself. For Tony, that's all he needs to start the parade of jokes and innuendos.

While I'm on Danielle's computer, I search the hard drive and the browsing history. From what I can tell, Edwards hasn't used her computer for acquiring stolen top-secret information or contacting his brother.

It takes Tony and me three hours to finish the installations. I can now view every area of the apartment again. This new system will not fail like the first one did. I'm using Phantom's satellite system. Each camera has an internal back-up battery that will last twelve hours. The old ones relied on hardwired electricity and when the neighborhood experienced a blackout, the cameras malfunctioned and didn't come back online.

Tony and I divide the apartment and start searching for the Phantom file or anything that will lead us to it. Edwards couldn't take anything with him except what the Army allows. And he's smart enough to know not to leave anything on base. I'm confident what we're looking for is in this apartment.

I search the papers and computer parts on his desk. Nothing on it contains what I'm looking for, but I bag and tag a few pieces to examine once I get back to headquarters. My next destination is the bathroom.

The tampon wrapper in the trash stands out. I don't know too many females who are into period sex.

The process of a thorough manual search includes checking for loose bathroom tiles, removing the medicine cabinet from the wall, disassembling pipes to the sink and toilet. My mini-flashlight aids the search.

I move to the bedroom and start with the closet. First, I snap pictures with my phone so I can put it back the way I found it once I'm done. Then I start removing the clothes, shoes, and boxes.

In a corner in the back of the closet, I notice frayed carpet strings along the base of the wall. I pull them, and a big square piece of carpet comes up.

The floorboards are scratched and chipped.

"Hey, Tony. I got something!"

He rushes in the room wiping the sweat from his forehead with his arm and dusting the front of his shirt with his hand. I lean to the side to give him a better view of the floorboards. He slaps me on the shoulder.

I wedge the head of a flathead screwdriver between two planks. One lifts with little effort. The other one takes a little wiggling and a lot of tugging to lift out.

"Jackpot," Tony says and reaches for one of five stacks of stamped, letter size envelopes that were hidden underneath the floorboards. "It looks like they're all postmarked from Hayward, California."

Tony and I take the envelopes to the dining table. We lay them out by postmark date. There are hundreds of letters, the earliest dating back to before they graduated high school. The latest dated two weeks ago.

Each letter reads like a couple in a long-distance relationship.

Then it hits me.

I go back to the bedroom closet with the flashlight and screwdriver.

"What are you looking for?" Tony stands in the doorway of the bedroom.

"A key?"

"What kind of key?"

"Words or a phrase written on a separate paper."

"Huh?"

I huff. "It looks like the brothers used a version of the Playfair cipher technique to pass information. You need the key to decipher the letters."

"Man, are you sure girls found your nerdiness hot when you were in high school?"

Yes, and they used me because of it. He already knows the answer to that question, so I keep searching the small space under the floorboards.

It's empty.

"Did you bring the scanner?"

Tony nods. "It's in the truck. I'll go get it."

On my hands and knees, I test the carpet along the baseboards throughout the room, then venture to other parts of the apartment.

No other pieces of the carpet have been cut out.

Tony gets the scanner set up on the dining table. We scan each envelope and the letter that came in it. By seven thirty, we have the letters copied and put away. I help him get the kitchen cabinets back in place.

I replace the garbage disposal and the toilet handle.

We clean up and I go around the apartment dumping the waste baskets into a large trash bag and take it down to the dumpster. My stomach growls and Tony laughs. When I'm on to something, I tend to forget to eat.

Danielle doesn't even have the basic foods a household should have in case of an emergency. Considering how much money Edwards is raking in on selling government secrets, I can't believe his meager lifestyle. One-bedroom apartment. Mismatched second-hand furniture and appliances. Older model cars. His girl is working extra hours to make ends meet while Edwards is stacking his cash. Danielle can't possibly know what her husband is up to. How many women would agree to living like this when their man has millions tucked away?

"Hey bro, let's go grab something to eat and then I'll take you to the grocery store before I head back to the hotel."

"Call Vin and Ig and have them come to Arizona and you can go home to Charly before she dumps you."

"I'll make the call, sir, but I'm staying. We stick together." Tony takes his role as my wingman literally. We've been best friends since second semester of freshman year at CU.

Twenty minutes after midnight, Danielle walks through the door looking like she's ready to fall over. I take her backpack and guide her to the sofa.

"Still feeling sick?"

She nods with her eyes closed and her head resting on the overstuffed cushion behind her.

"The toilet and garbage disposal are fixed." In my ears I come off like a little kid who proudly announces the accomplishment of a big boy's job.

The smile on her face makes me smile too even though she can't see it with her eyes closed.

I slip her shoes off. Danielle tucks her feet under her butt and mumbles something that sounds like thank you.

"Have you eaten today, Danielle?"

Her mouth turns down and she shakes her head. "My stomach's been queasy."

The back of my hand touches her forehead. That's how Mom and Grandma checked for a fever. She's not warm. *Can a woman be pregnant and on her period?* I'll have to ask my sister.

"Want some soup and crackers? You need food in your stomach before you take anything."

"We don't have any in the apartment."

"I went to the store earlier." I lean over about to kiss her forehead, then stop myself. *Where did that come from, Hawk?*

I go to the kitchen and grab a can of soup out of the cabinet. "How much did you drink last night?"

"Just a glass of champagne."

"The bottle was empty. Did you guys have friends over?"

"No. I remember feeling sleepy after drinking the glass James poured me. Next thing I know James is waking me at five in the morning. I'm on the loveseat still in the white dress I wore for our wedding, and he's running out the door. I guess he finished the bottle."

Edwards had sex with her while she was unconscious? That dirty bastard!

"He drinks like that?"

"Normally he doesn't. But two weeks ago, I noticed he'd been drinking more than usual."

"How so?"

"Out of nowhere, he asks me to marry him. I told him we weren't ready. He got upset and left. When he came back, I could tell he had been drinking. He stopped talking to me. Each night after that he'd come home stumbling. Then night before last, James came home and I could tell he had been drinking, but he wasn't drunk. He started listing reasons why we should get married and I said okay."

"Why?"

"I think he's scared. This is his first overseas tour and it's to an area where there is actual fighting. Deep down I knew I'd marry him someday, so why not now?" Danielle yawns. "After we left the chapel, his anxiety got worse. This morning he wasn't even mad that we didn't consummate our marriage."

What?! But I found two condom wrappers.

Somebody was fucking last night. If it wasn't her and Edwards, then who?

I make a mental note to go get the bag out of the dumpster and have Tony sort through it. Danielle was drugged last night and whatever sedative was used didn't set well on her stomach.

I keep an eye on her while I doctor up the soup and put crackers on a plate. My mind is going through a bunch of different scenarios as to what went down here last night. If the cameras had been working, I wouldn't be imagining the worst.

When the soup is done, I pour it into a bowl, pick up the plate, and do a balancing act with a glass of water as I carry them to the living room. One by one, I set the bowl, plate, and glass on the coffee table.

Danielle cracks an eye open, then closes it. "Nice touch with the cucumber slice in the glass of water."

I pick up the bowl and sit next to her. I scoop up a spoonful of soup and hold it up to her lips. "Open."

Her lips part and I tip the spoon and watch the liquid dish flow into her mouth. She chews and swallows. "Is that from a can?"

I laugh and offer her another spoonful. "I may have added a little sumthin' sumthin' to it."

She takes the second spoonful quickly and opens her mouth for another. I switch up and put a cracker up to her lips instead.

My eyes fixate on her lips. Their sexy. They fit her face. And their kissable. The tint of her full lips is their natural color.

When she opens for another bite, my mind starts to drift in explicit territory. Like her lips wrapped around the hawk as she takes me deep in her mouth. Or my name slipping past her lips as I make her come.

Her eyes open.

Curiosity staring at me.

Shit! She knows what I'm thinking.

Her stare drops to the spoon dangling over the bowl.

In the depths of my fantasy, I stopped feeding her.

The spoon taps the ceramic lip of the bowl when I miss the opening. I manage to scoop up another spoonful. She accepts it and closes her eyes.

Danielle's blindly allowing me to take care of her; the least I can do is keep my fantasies at bay.

She finishes the soup and I leave her munching on the last cracker while I take the bowl and plate back to the kitchen. Until I know what drug was used on her last night, I can't let her take any medication. Hopefully the soup and water will settle her stomach.

"Thank you, Bryan."

A foreign sense of protectiveness steals my reply. I sit close to her on the sofa and pick up the TV remote, prop my feet up on the coffee table, and turn down the volume.

Danielle drifts off to sleep and cuddles into my side, laying her head on my shoulder. The soft strands of her curls brush my cheek. I'm surrounded by the unidentifiable pleasant scent from earlier. It's coming from Danielle. It's not manmade. It's natural and pure.

She exhales, and her body completely relaxes.

Careful not to wake her, I give in and run my fingers through the curls of her long hair. They're soft. Danielle's hair is one of the first things I noticed the first time I saw her in California walking across the big college campus. Then those striking brown eyes dominated my camera lens and demanded my attention. And when she smiled, I wanted to be the one who put it on her lips.

A soft snore escapes her parted lips and her hand rests on my chest.

This is such a couples' thing. I don't do "couple things" with any woman.

My cell phone buzzes right when I'm about to remove her hand. I ease the phone out of my pocket and read the text from Tony.

I look straight into the camera ahead. Smile. And flip him off.

CHAPTER TWO

DANIELLE

Colorado, Present Day

THE HOSPITAL ROOM DOOR CRACKS open and a wide-eyed James slithers through. His gaze searches the room. The fitted black shirt, black cargo pants, bandana, and black military boots mirror the clothes Bryan and his friends wore when they fought off the intruders who invaded our home hours ago. James is now working with Phantom to defeat the people behind the homeland terrorist group trying to start World War III. The ones leading the threat are my long lost grandparents, Willis and Marie Langford.

James has the backpack I left in the other room in his hand along with a plastic bag, a familiar red and white store logo on the front of it. Another black backpack is strapped on his back.

Marie's gasp echoes around the room.

He tosses the store bag on the bed. "Let me guess. You thought I was dead. Didn't they teach you to shoot the undead in the head to make sure they don't get up again?" He sets my backpack at my feet.

I stand there frozen, Bryan's words replaying in my mind. *Willis and Marie Langford are your maternal grandparents and they're the leaders of RAGS. James is alive and working with us; you can trust him. If you come across Malinda Williamson, shoot her in the head. Her real name is Amelia Goodman. And she's not to be trusted…*

James snaps his fingers and waves his hands in front of my face. He's disconnected Marie's IV line and is working on the wires to the heart monitor.

I realize he is waiting for me to respond to something he's said.

"Help her get dressed. We need to go before Langford comes back." James steps away from the bed. The curtain rings scrape along the curved metal rod as he pulls it closed to give my grandmother privacy.

Marie peels back the covers and swings her legs around. Her pedicured feet dangle a few inches above the floor. I rifle through the bag and lay out its contents.

She and I don't speak, yet her eyes stay on me. Studying my face. Carefully assessing me. I focus on the task at hand and keep my thoughts from showing on my face. There will be enough time to process once we're somewhere safe and secured.

On the other side of the curtain, I hear the medical supply cabinets opening and closing while Marie and I work together to get her into a pair of jeans, a short sleeve button-down shirt, socks, and no-lace shoes without busting a stitch in her arm. Every item fits her perfectly.

I use scissors from the mobile tray to cut the hospital's pillowcase and make a sling for her injured arm, then open the curtain.

James is waiting by the door. Gun in hand.

"What about the girls?" Marie asks.

There's a faint click in my right ear. *"Stare her straight in the eyes. Take a deep breath and when you release it, say your line. Don't divert your gaze."*

I inhale. "They left with Jessica a while ago. It was part of Bryan's plan. She doesn't know he's dead."

"Call her, I want my great-granddaughter with us."

"Ladies, we don't have time for this. We need to get moving." James opens the door. He gestures for us to follow.

I slip my arms through the straps of my backpack. It's lighter than it should be.

My grandmother and I hold hands. We keep up with James's fast pace toward the elevator. As we approach, the up-arrow flashes, the chime dings, and the door slides open.

The guy I know as Mills stands inside the elevator. The silver hawk pin catches the ceiling lights in the cab. Slowly, the corners of his mouth turn up. He raises his arm, pointing a gun at—Marie.

James steps in front of me and raises his gun hand. He doesn't stop moving. He backs into me. We're so close I see the tension in the back of his stiff neck.

With his other hand, James reaches behind and guides my free hand to the gun in the holster at the small of his back hidden by the backpack.

Zero time to panic, I let go of Marie and take hold of the weapon like Bryan taught me for maximum control.

I release the safety.

The walkie-talkie in Mills's other hand squawks. The voice of Willis comes through. "Does anyone have eyes on Danielle?"

"Stairs," James whispers.

Mills lifts the talkie, his eyes locked on me.

"Now!" James says as a loud pop, fire, and scent of gunpowder leave his gun.

I don't look to see if the shot hits its mark; I turn and use my shoulder to herd Marie toward the door to the stairs.

We duck as we run.

My heartbeat keeps time with the sounds of bullet casings bouncing on the tile floor. Projectiles flying around us. Embedding in walls and doors. And shattering glass.

Marie shouts out but keeps moving.

I reach the stairwell entrance first and push the crossbar hard enough for the door to fly open, leaving a dent in the wall.

The painful howl and thud from a body dropping to the floor halts my feet.

Hoping for the best—yet my defensive mind comes up with an alternative plan for the worst—I turn and raise my weapon. Ready to fire at Mills.

"Keep moving," James yells.

I grip Marie's hand and pull her down the stairs with James sprinting to catch up with us.

Three sets of rapid pounding footsteps descend the concrete stairs.

Flight after flight, landing after landing, we flee with James chanting, "Keep moving."

My grandmother is struggling to keep up. I'm pulling her more than she's following under her own weight. As my eyes focus on the steps, my ears strain to hear sounds of pursuers.

"We'll take the service elevator from the second floor," James commands.

When we reach the second-floor landing, he takes the lead. He checks to make sure the area is clear before Marie and I follow.

The single-door elevator slides open. James is ready. Arm raised. Finger on the trigger. Feet moving him forward.

The elevator is empty.

He lowers his weapon.

We rush inside.

I bend at the waist to catch my breath. All the running I've been doing today cannot be good for my son.

There's a faint click in my left ear. *"Ask her if she's okay. 'Granmé, to bon?'"* The female translator says.

I reach out and squeeze Marie's hand and repeat the question.

Marie nods, unable to speak. She's breathing hard too.

My gaze sweeps over James. As far as I can tell, he wasn't hit by gunfire. The signature Phantom armored vest under his shirt protected him.

James disengages the magazine from the gun. He unzips the side pocket of his cargo pants, pulls out another one, slaps it in place, and stands in front of the door.

Marie and I become life-size posters plastered to the shiny metal side walls. The red loading dock symbol flashes on the digital monitor above the door.

I brace myself as our sole means of exit slowly comes in to view.

Four anxious heartbeats, then James declares, "We're clear."

I take Marie's hand and walk-jog behind James, fifty-feet to a set of double doors. He holds one open and gestures to the red four-door car with the familiar bow tie emblem on the grill backed into a stall with paper plates.

Marie and I cross the lot with James covering us.

A soft breeze rustles the debris on the ground and I'm momentarily wrapped in a distinctive scent. Power. Strength. Spicy. Confidence. Soap. Comfort. Warmth. Sandalwood. Everything rolled up into one Mr. Tall-And-Sexy.

From a dark corner somewhere in this lot, his hazel eyes are on me. I can't stop to search for him or run into the safety of his arms. Bryan was adamant about sticking to this plan, and after what I pulled back at the house, I dare not push his buttons again for the rest of the night.

Another breeze sweeps the debris and brings with it the overpowering smell of Ig's burning car polluting the night air. I cover my nose with my hand and walk faster.

The car's headlights flash two times followed by the clunk sound of the four doors unlocking.

"Danielle, you drive. The GPS is programmed for the Goldman Hotel and Resort. Elijah Hopper reserved the North penthouse suite." James relieves me of my backpack and takes Marie's hand and guides her to the front passenger seat.

I secure my gun, then climb into the driver's seat and strap myself in. James climbs into the back. Marie struggles with her seat belt for a second. James huffs, reaches across her and snaps the buckle.

I pull out of the stall and head toward the exit. Our collective heavy breathing is the only sound in the car.

Halfway up the driveway, a sheriff is directing cars away from the emergency vehicles and crew working to extinguish the flames coming from the burning car. From the looks of it, neither the driver nor anyone within two yards of the explosions survived.

Once I turn onto the street, I follow the directions of the automated voice of the GPS.

Marie groans and holds her injured arm. James unzips his backpack, then hands her a small bottle of water.

"Is Jamal also immune to bullets?" She twists the cap off and drinks.

"Naw, he's the mortal twin." James perches on the edge of the back seat and fills the gap between the passenger seat and driver's seat. He passes an opened bottle of water to me over my shoulder.

Marie continues to face forward, staring out the windshield. "You and Hopper will have to explain things to me," she says, the threat made clear by the tone of her voice, body language, and lack of eye contact. This chilled air of authority is a side of Marie I am unfamiliar with. "Your parents have gone missing from the prison they've been in for twenty-eight years." She leaves the unspoken question dangling in the air.

James does not reply. Instead, his fingers gently squeeze my shoulder.

The miles pass as I navigate the road. Marie continues to sip water from the bottle while James remains wedged between the seats like a barrier. Every so often his fingers tap out something like Morse code on my headrest. It's getting annoying. I'm tempted to smack his hand.

I exit the highway. According to the automated voice of the GPS, we are seven miles from the turn off to the mountain resort. The car starts the climb up the dark winding road. My grip on the steering wheel tightens and I go the exact speed limit.

When the headlights reflect off the sign for Little Hawk Mountain, I chuckle to myself and think back to that day in March when Bryan, our daughters, and I were in the limousine on this very road. Heading to our celebration reception after the wedding and adoption ceremonies. Kourtney read the sign aloud and asked Bryan if he owned the mountain. He laughed and said no, then told her there is a Bryan Mountain too.

Our little girl was so happy that day. We all were. We publicly became the Hawk family. Between then and now, something changed. At first I thought Kourtney was having a difficult time adjusting to our new family dynamic. But as I reflect on our time in Boulder, Kourtney has not been herself since she and I drove away from our home in Tucson, Arizona, almost a year ago.

I have witnessed our daughter angry, but tonight was different. Kourtney was seething and inconsolable. Once this is over, Bryan and I will sit down and talk to her. Yes, the conversation will be difficult, but the words she used to express her anger demand it. I won't let him take the blame. I too play a role in keeping the biggest secret that affects our family.

I follow the final directions given by the automated voice and pull into valet parking at the Goldman Hotel and Resort. James jumps out and opens my door while the attendant opens the passenger door for Marie. James carries my backpack along with his.

My grandmother wobbles on her feet. I rush around the car and take hold of her elbow. We walk through the resort's entrance and lobby with James slightly ahead of me. No doubt following orders to protect me with his life.

In the elevator, James inserts the keycard that will allow the cab to go up to the penthouse.

Click. *"Danikins, now that you're at the resort you have to make Marie think James is your enemy. Go with your gut reaction to make it look real. Just don't incapacitate him."*

James turns and smiles at me. Without thought, I strike. My right hand closes over his throat. The left seizes his genitals. I shove him against the doors. "You could have killed my son and me at that hotel."

Caught off guard, he grips my left hand. James's eyes widen and knees waver.

"*Arêté!*" Marie commands.

Click. "*She said, 'Stop.'*"

I release him.

James drops to the floor of the cab coughing and covering himself with both hands. The elevator stops and the doors open. My grandmother steps around him. I step over him and walk into the open floor plan of the penthouse.

My eyes sweep over the elegance of the room before I look over my shoulder at James.

He strains to pull himself up to his knees and round up the backpacks at the same time. He is really selling this with the turtle crawl out of the elevator before the doors close on him. His performance includes collapsing on the cool marble floor.

Marie sways even more on her feet. That sedative in the water bottle has kicked in fast. I take her by the elbow and guide her to a bedroom on this level.

I pull back the covers, and she sits on the bed with her eyes closed. I slip the shoes off her feet and help her lie back.

"*Mèsi, shè.*" Her words are slurred.

Click. "*She said 'thank you, dear.' Answer 'padkwa. It means you're welcome.'*"

My grandmother should sleep until late morning. I turn off the lights and close the door behind me.

James is sitting on the sofa, earpieces on the coffee table, a cell phone to his ear. He's using a sheet of the resort's stationary to write on. He tips his chin up and gives me a big smile.

It took a lot of self-control to not really choke and squeeze him for real.

Click. "*Danikins, go get some sleep. James has eyes on you. If anything goes down, leave him behind and get yourself out of there. I'm signing off now, my plane is about to land.*"

"Thanks, Maxie. I don't think I'd have been able to fool Marie without you coaching me, and the person Bryan has translating for me." Bryan is right, Maxim Li Chen is good at coaching someone to tell believable lies.

Click. *"Be safe, Danikins. Premium spa day when this is over."*

"It's a date."

My friend's flaming flamboyance is a front for the badass Super Soldier he really is.

I pick up my backpack and unzip the center compartment. "Where's the laptop?"

James pulls his mouth away from the phone. "Hawk said to leave it for that traitor Langford to find. It's how he can track Langford's whereabouts." He puts the phone back in place and continues his conversation.

I yawn. My body is tired. If Bryan hadn't blocked me from doing my normal exercise routine I wouldn't be this physically drained. My feet feel heavy as I slowly make my way up the stairs to the second floor.

The lamp on one of the two nightstands is on in the master room. The bed is already turned down. I take out the earpieces from my ears and put them on the nightstand. I drop the backpack and sit on the side of the bed and undo the laces on my shoes. They fall to the plush white carpeted floor. I turn off the lamp and crawl into bed.

As I settle on my side, hugging a pillow, my son starts to kickbox. My hand circles my stomach and I hum a tune I loved a long time ago.

—◆—

Arizona, Nine Years Ago

"Ouch." An unfamiliar male grunts. My elbow crashes into flesh and bone as I stretch and yawn.

I sit up, frozen and lost. Eyes wide open. Trying to place the voice of the person next to me in the shadows of my living room.

It's not James.

The soft glow of light from the courtyard isn't enough to tell me who is in the apartment with me.

Please don't let it be Mr. Tucker. The frightened chant plays over and over in my mind.

The warm male body shifts. I catch a whiff of his scent before the lamp on the end table provides enough light for me to see James's friend Bryan.

A fresh red mark is growing on his cheek. My eyes zero in on the big wet spot on his shoulder.

"Sorry." How embarrassing. Self-consciously I wipe my mouth with the back of my hand. I fell asleep on Bryan's shoulder and drooled. To top it off, my mouth is dry, so I'm pretty sure I was blowing my bad breath in his face. Scooting away from him won't make this any less cringeworthy.

Bryan's unique hazel eyes sparkle with his smile. Boy, he has the longest eyelashes I have ever seen on a man.

"Don't apologize." His shoulders rise and fall in a carefree shrug.

Bryan took care of me. My inner me smiles. James always managed to avoid me the first day of my period. The cramping is too much for him. This time I have a queasy stomach too. I'm sure if Bryan knew what was really going on, he'd tuck tail and run too.

"What time is it?"

His arms stretch to the ceiling. He twists his torso side to side, then turns his wrist to look at his watch. "Two thirteen."

I know I should be ashamed for admiring the way the cotton T-shirt hugs his muscles and the way his jeans mold around his thick thighs. He probably has a girlfriend, not to mention I'm a newlywed. But to be perfectly honest, shame is the last thing I am feeling. And that's dangerous.

Before my imagination goes a step too far, I hop to my feet and walk to the hallway closet where I keep the linens.

Two pillows, a set of sheets, and a lightweight quilt should make a good pallet.

"The carpet may be more comfortable than the sofa." I drop the bedding on the coffee table.

He stands. "I'll manage, Dani."

No one has ever called me Dani. He makes it feel like the intimate caress of a man who knows me in a way no one else does.

James always calls me Danielle.

Bryan walks to the kitchen and I become mesmerized by the flex of his thigh muscles with each step he takes.

In my human sexuality class study group, we asked questions about what attracts us to someone. The first thing that attracts me is a man's thighs. The second thing that attracts me is a man's eyes. The third thing I notice is the difference in length between a man's index finger and ring finger.

Everyone thought my answer was funny until I explained the old wives' tale. One girl asked if it's true. Another wanted to know how many guys I tested the tale on. My reply sparked a whole different battery of questions that evening.

Bryan opens the refrigerator and brings out the water pitcher. From the dish rack, he flips over a glass, then pours himself a tall glass of cold water. He is no guest in this apartment.

His Adam's apple bobs up and down as he drinks the water in one breath. I find myself swallowing with him.

Just watching him makes me—thirsty. And water is *not* what will quench my dehydration.

Bryan catches me watching him. An eyebrow arches and he holds up the glass.

I look away before my eyes tell him it's not water I want to drink.

"Goodnight." I hurry to the bedroom, grab my pajamas, then go across the hall to the bathroom.

Behind the closed door, I take slow deep breaths. Mrs. Franklin's voice echoes in my mind, "Your body is a gift; make sure the man you give it to has earned the present. You'll know if he's worthy because the heat between your legs will come from the care of his touch, the worship in his eyes, the respect he shows you publicly and privately, and his willingness to relinquish control to you." My foster mother has a "real" way of explaining things.

I turn on the shower and strip out of my clothes. As I pull the tampon string, I notice the trash can is empty. Now that's something James never did—empty the trash—even if it wasn't my time of the month. I'm meticulous about keeping the apartment clean. James would have it looking like a place where electronic equipment and parts went to die. It took some time to get used to overlooking his desk, but now I hardly notice it and I certainly do not go near it if I can help it. When we buy a house, his man cave will be in the basement where company won't be subjected to his clutter.

Bryan's girlfriend is lucky. He knows how to make a simple can of soup taste pretty good. He fixes things. And isn't squeamish about emptying a trash can with feminine product wrappers inside.

Yes, it's unfair to compare the two men. James grew up in a boys' group home. Nothing I say or do will get him to change. I don't know Bryan's history, but I'm guessing it wasn't like the way James and I grew up.

In the morning, I'll make breakfast to thank Bryan for taking care of me and find out how long he plans on staying. James's message said a few days. How long is "a few days" in men-language? It's funny, as James was running out the door this morning he told me to be cautious and trust no one yet forgot to tell me about his friend visiting.

I don't linger in the shower. It's late and I have to be at work at eight in the morning. Now that the spring semester is over, I can work the morning shift, which makes it possible for me to work with my favorite therapist at the clinic.

I quickly moisturize my damp skin with an organic body butter made of aloe vera, sweet almond oil, coconut oil, pure vitamin-E oil, grated beeswax, and vanilla essential oil. According to my foster mom, even though Black don't crack, we still need to take care of our beautiful skin. She taught me how to make the body butter.

When I open the bathroom door, Bryan is sitting on the arm of the sofa with his duffle bag dangling between his legs. We make brief eye contact. He stands and walks toward the hallway. I go to the bedroom and crawl into bed on James's side.

I'm not sleepy. The nap I took on Bryan's shoulder was the best sleep I've had since the night I fled my own apartment, having fought off Mr. Tucker's attempt to rape me. I know that pervert is across town and can't find me, but I don't really feel safe even when James is in the bed next to me. Falling asleep on Bryan's shoulder, I had no trouble letting my guard down because I felt protected. Like if Mr. Tucker were to kick down the door, Bryan would stop him from getting to me.

Knowing Bryan is sleeping in the living room tonight, I forgo stashing defensive weapons throughout the apartment and sleeping with a knife in my nightstand and a baseball bat next to the bed.

The soulful melody of a saxophone starts to flow from the bathroom. I don't have to look at Bryan's playlist to know "Silhouette" by Kenny G. I have dreamed of making love to this sensual, instrumental song for a long time. The knobs squeak and the music notes blend with the waterfall sound in the tub. I close my eyes and let my imagination go.

The choreography is already scripted, and the moves memorized by the lovers.

One: James and I exchanging subtle touches. I undress him. He undresses me. Our eyes lock in an unspoken conversation. The plastic shower curtain rustles as it stretches out around the tub to keep the water in. Then the sound of water drops kissing fine muscled flesh heightens the smooth notes from the saxophone.

Two: I wade through the steam and join him. My fingertips swim against the rivers of water rushing down Bryan's bare, thick, wet thighs. His muscles tighten and flex as he makes room for me. My fingernails go with the current's flow down his chest, over the wedges of his defined abs and through the bush of pubic hairs; then my fingers wrap around his hardened penis.

Three: we move to the bedroom, our bodies still dripping wet. I climb in first and he follows. His eyes trace the outline of my body followed by his fingers. My hips circle on the wet sheet. Bryan kisses me, and I feel it in places I never knew could be stimulated indirectly.

Four: Bryan settles between my legs. Our unbreakable connection is formed. The rhythm set to the sultry tempo of the saxophone: unhurried, loving, and intimate. At the height of the sequence of notes, we climax together like the couples in romance novels. Bryan and I stay united long after the saxophone fades away.

Oops! Did I just think, Bryan?

I roll over onto my stomach and cover my head with the pillow.

At what point did Bryan replace James? And when did my choreography change to a shower scene?

A groan leaves my chest. Man, I need to get it together.

The knobs squeak and the flow of water stops. Another instrumental song is ending. A violin I think. The final note lingers in the air. I wait for the next song, but Bryan's vocals take over.

I roll onto my side and listen to the sounds of him moving around in the bathroom and softly singing.

He has a nice voice.

Finally, the bathroom door opens and a little steam drifts into the hallway. I'm rewarded with a glimpse of shirtless Bryan in cut-off sweats that hang so low on his hips it barely covers the point of his abdominal V or the line of wet pubic hairs that disappear under the waistband. My gaze gravitates further south and can't miss the outline of his penis. Bryan isn't wearing underwear.

He reaches out. Before the bathroom light goes out, I get to see the lion tattoo on the inside of his upper arm.

The apartment isn't completely dark, thanks to the lights in the courtyard. I watch Bryan's easy stroll down the hallway to the living room. For a tall muscular guy, he doesn't make any noise as he moves around.

As innocent as it seems, my attraction to James's friend can be labeled emotional cheating. I don't want to start off my marriage like that. Yes, the minute James put the band on my finger, I felt we'd made a mistake. The psychological unease of getting married too soon manifested in the pain in my ring finger this morning. But I took a vow to stay faithful to my husband and I will. When he gets back from his tour in Iraq, his virgin bride will be waiting.

"Hope my music isn't the reason you're still awake," Bryan says from the living room.

I swear I hear the knowing smile on his face. "Nope, I liked the music."

He yawns. "Then it must be my terrible singing."

"That could be it."

He chuckles.

"I know it's pretty warm in Tucson. I can turn on the air if it gets too hot."

"I'm good for now but will let you know if my body temperature rises."

"Are you purposely messing with me, Mr. Hawk?"

"No, but if you want me to, I will."

Unwanted flirting usually put me on edge, but his delivery is different. More like a challenge of who can out quip whom.

"Beware of what you're offering, Bryan. You may find yourself with more than you can handle."

He groans. Bryan concedes the battle to me with stunned silence.

I will not gloat this time because next time he may call my bluff.

CHAPTER THREE

BRYAN

Colorado, Present Day

DANI IS SECURE FOR NOW and James is guarding her. Once the sedative kicks in, Marie isn't a threat. Langford has the laptop and he's conducting a floor-by-floor search of the hospital trying to find her and Dani. Hopper has decoys running around the hospital to keep Langford and his crew occupied. I can track Langford's whereabouts from my watch as long as he has the laptop on him.

The helicopter my girls are on should reach Colorado Springs in thirty minutes. Instead of leaving the country as originally planned, the girls are being taken to my parents' house.

Mom and Dad are going to be pissed that I'm not the one explaining what's going on. President Hart insisted on contacting them.

Jessi is at the house packing suitcases for Dani, the girls, and a bag for Trevor. She'll drop off a change of clothes to the front desk at the resort for Dani, then be on her way to Colorado Springs to prepare for the arrival of the air medical helicopter carrying James's wife and son.

Prince Jawad is on standby at a private airport seven minutes from my parents in the event it becomes necessary for my family to leave the country. He will remain there until the threat is over.

I'm heading back to Boulder riding a magnificent piece of machinery. You haven't ridden a bike until you ride a Tomahawk. I am Super Hawk and this is my super mode of transportation.

On the highway I push the bike to its maximum speed. The

scenery is a blur as I zip around the other vehicles moving at the posted limit.

Man, this is almost as good as a HALO jump.

The Watchers in The Nest are focused on the sky and the rest of the world, not the streets of Boulder. I'm using that knowledge to get me to my building unnoticed. All of Phantom believes the Elite Special Operations Team is dead. The first twenty-four hours after the death of Second Command, certain protocols are to be followed by each Ghost no matter their location.

Hawkeye Personal Protection Officers have a different set of protocols.

Two miles out, I pull off the highway and take the streets. The clubs in the area are jumping tonight. Long lines of people are waiting to get in. They have no idea that their way of life is in danger of changing. At times like this, ignorance is a blessing.

I turn into the twenty-four-hour parking garage a block from my building. It's the one we use when transporting prisoners to and from the facility.

I park the Tomahawk near the elevator and take it down to the lowest level where a scanned keycard gives me access to the passageway into the facility.

Kimberly Baryshnikova is still detained in a cell. She is in the maximum-security section. And has had minimal interaction with anyone for five months. It's punishment for knocking Dani out the night of my company holiday party. Tying Dani to a table in a deserted warehouse. And threatening to hurt Dani in order to get information.

If I had the time to find and kill Amelia myself, I'd do it. I'm hiring Kimberly to handle Amelia for me.

Amelia has been off grid and Kimberly is the perfect person to locate her. Everything about Edwards's story of how he was found in Ethiopia points to Kimberly being behind it. Who hired her to do it I've yet to uncover. Langford is my number one suspect.

Reputation is all a for-hire-operative has regardless of what team they're playing for. Kimberly has a reputation for executing the task exactly as it is specified in the terms of the contract. Nothing more. Nothing less. Not only do I have to present the job in a way that piques her interest, I also have to convince her that completing the job guarantees her freedom. Freedom that I have no intentions of giving her. Kimberly is on our list of loose ends that need to die by the time this is over.

As I approach her cell, I see Kimberly sitting on the cold tile floor meditating. A tactic I'm familiar with. When I was put through anti-interrogation training, Chen taught me a similar method. Isolation will break you. Meditation will save your sanity.

My knuckle taps the glass three times.

Kimberly's eyes open.

"Ready to reenter society?"

She stares at me. No emotion on her face, but her eyes show signs of interest.

"I have a job offer, two-mil. You in?"

"Who do I get to kill?"

"Amelia Goodman."

"She's already dead."

I unzip my backpack, get out the eight-by-ten color photo, and press it against the glass. "The new Amelia."

"Who are you, Hawk? You're not CIA."

"You in or not?"

Kimberly unfolds her legs and stands and covers the distance to the glass that separates us. "In."

I reach in the backpack again and pull out a bottle of top-shelf whiskey and two paper cups. Kimberly smiles as I pour a hefty shot in each cup. She can't see my hand when I return the bottle to the backpack and grasp a sleeping pill between two fingers.

I walk around to the locked slot in the door. Along the way, the pill slips from my fingers into the amber liquid. I make it seem like the lock is giving me trouble, but I'm really giving the pill time to dissolve.

The flap on the slot opens and I set the cup inside, then close it. Kimberly opens her side to pick up the cup.

We toast by touching cups against the glass, then toss back the expensive whiskey.

She closes her eyes and licks her lips. When she stares at me again, excitement stares back at me. "Tell me the specifics."

Seven.

Six.

Five.

Her eyes crinkle as she waits for me to respond.

Four.

Three.

Kimberly collapses to the floor.

Moving quickly, I use the keycard to open the door and enter the cell. The backpack falls from my hand as I squat and roll her onto her stomach. I retrieve the small syringe with the microchip from the side pocket and an alcohol wipe. I lift Kimberly's left foot, clean her big toe and implant the grain-of-rice-size tracking chip into the pad of her toe.

Next, I scoop her up off the floor, toss her over my shoulder, grab my backpack, and leave the cell, walking back through the passage to the elevator. It begins to rise. I shift Kimberly to better distribute her weight on my shoulder.

The elevator stops on the level where I left the Tomahawk.

I put Kimberly behind the wheel of a compact Chevy that my best friend Vincenzo Ricci parked here earlier this evening.

On the passenger seat are the clothes Kimberly wore the night we subdued her, twenty-five thousand in cash, a laptop, a Glock outfitted with a silencer, and extra ammo.

On the dash I place a letter outlining the specifics of the job.

I close the door and hide in a dark corner and wait for her to wake up. If Kimberly follows the last item on the outline she gets to live long enough to find Amelia. If she disregards it, I'll put a bullet in her head and go with plan B.

Ten minutes in, Kimberly starts to wake. She cranes her neck looking around the empty garage. I watch her pick up the single sheet of paper off the dash. The interior light turns on. She's reading the note.

When the driver's side door opens, and Kimberly touches the edge of the paper to the glowing orange-red car cigarette lighter, I nod to myself.

The light from the burning paper highlights the smile on her face. The flames devour my written instructions, turning them to ash. Right before the flames reach her fingers, Kimberly releases the paper. The burning sliver of paper floats to the concrete and quickly burns itself out.

Kimberly sheds the jumpsuit, gets into her own clothes, then starts the car. Quickly she backs out of the stall and points the car toward the exit.

I step out of the shadows, recover the jumpsuit, and climb back on my Tomahawk.

This time I mind the posted speed limit as I head to the next destination.

It doesn't take me long to get to the self-storage facility. Our unit is in the center of the complex.

I press the remote fob attached to the left handlebar of the bike. The unit door lifts and the ramp in the center of the floor drops. Once I clear the door, I press the fob again for it to close. I guide the Tomahawk down the steep ramp to the underground passage.

The tunnels are pitch-black, but the bike's headlights and my familiarity with the city street-wide path makes it possible for me to navigate the way.

The roar of the bike's engine echoes in the deserted concrete passageways.

My bunker is hidden under the manmade pond at my house. The storage unit is one of three entrance points.

Much like the Presidential Emergency Operations Center, my bunker is built to withstand a nuclear attack. In its entirety, it is the size of an average city block, although the pond isn't as big.

Construction of the bunker started a month after I bought the land—nine years ago. One of the things I considered when looking for property to build Dani's house on was how long it would take me to reach the bunker from underground in case of an emergency.

Langford didn't have a bunker this extensive. His basement-size bunker, located under the floors of Phantom's old headquarters, is no longer connected to the White House or any military networks. It's more of a hideout. I'll make sure he can't access it in our current state of emergency. If RAGS is going to start a war, Langford for damn sure is going to be one of its casualties.

Coming up on the outer entrance, I shift both thumbs over the scanner on the handlebars. Up ahead, a concrete wall swings open. I fly through the opening and the wall slides back into place.

Half a mile out, I decrease my speed as I get closer to the main entrance.

Through the Bluetooth in my modified helmet, I speak my code. The sound of the automatic entrance door unlocking echoes in the cavernous underground passage.

The motion lights turn on around the room. I guide the Tomahawk to a spot in the area we call the garage. Every military armored vehicle the Elite Special Operations Team uses is parked here.

The layout of the bunker is broken up into four sections. Living quarters. Command Center. Medical Ward. Power station. I go to the Command Center.

"How's my wife?"

Fontenot looks up from the monitors around her. "They arrived at the penthouse. She helped Mrs. Langford to bed. I won't need to translate until the drug wears off. Is there anything I can help you with until then?"

"Go grab some shuteye. Things are going to move quickly. You're our Watcher and we need you sharp."

"Yes, sir." She pushes back from the desk. Head held high and lots of tension in her shoulders, Fontenot walks out of the door.

She has been monitoring the activities of Phantom since we stormed into my house to rescue my wife and kids. Before that, she was in The Nest monitoring the extraction of Edwards's wife and son in Fallujah.

Fontenot's notes are detailed. It doesn't surprise me that two of the three Watchers who were eyeballing Fontenot the day I visited The Nest aren't at their station keeping watch on military movement in other countries. Rosemond and North are at the hospital searching with Langford.

The investigation into the department moles was spot on. Rosemond, North, and Mills are the culprits.

Chen believes Mills was flipped *after* his promotion to my security detail. I'm fighting for our country; I don't have time to fight the bad guy who is supposed to have my back.

The moles are under the misconception that the consequences of treachery do not apply to them. Ending their life is nothing to me. A dead Ghost can't tell secrets.

The eyes of the virtual image of my wife follow me to my station. Riley is in hibernation mode.

"Wake up, Riley."

"VRS identification."

"Kilo. Zero. Two. Alpha. One. One. Zero. Six. Hotel." My daughter has no idea how much she's a part of my everyday life. My identification code is a variation of Kourtney Allison Hawk and February 11, 2006.

With Riley back online, I track Phantom's Elite Special Operations Team whereabouts. Paul, Acosta, Ricci and Porter are on their way to Yemen. Their task is to waylay the convoy of missiles in the possession of the Islamic Liberation Army. Initially we thought they only had surface to air missiles. Satellite intel showed intercontinental ballistic missiles too.

Rumors are starting to spread about an international RAGS threat. World leaders are gearing up.

No president wants this to happen during his term in office. President Hart has given me carte blanche in my role as Second Command. That is why I'm busting my ass to make sure his last term isn't tarnished.

Phantom is a myth.

Wraiths described in scary stories.

Glorified scary ghosts played out in Hollywood blockbusters.

CIA operatives wish they were as good as us, but then again, they don't know we exist. Phantom is real. Exposure will cause a rift in foreign relations. The United States will no longer be viewed as a civil ally. In the eyes of the world, we will be the bloodthirsty country with a sovereign mentality that needs to be slayed for the greater good.

Chen's encrypted message pops up on my monitor. It was sent fifty minutes ago. He's letting me know he just touched down in Washington, D.C. He's there to question Nora Owens, the presidential cabinet member who got caught in our round up of smoke bomb carriers. She is being particularly stubborn about giving up information. I'd hoped it wouldn't come to sending Chen, but we're on the verge of a war.

It's now zero two hundred hours. I go to the bathroom and shower off the dirt and sweat, then reenergize my body with food. I set up a cot in a corner of the room and lie on my back staring up at the ceiling.

Today, we either end RAGS or RAGS ends us.

Arizona, Nine Years Ago

I didn't need to have sex with Danielle to find the letters, but I do need the key. I'm just not so sure sex is the best approach with Danielle. Yes, she's attracted to me, her body language shows it. But there's an innocent sophistication about her that's different from other females I've come across. I'll back off for now. We know where Edwards is. We've got eyes on his brother in California too.

My cell phone buzzes from an incoming call. I exhale and pick it up off the coffee table. Amelia's name flashes on the screen. I send the call to voicemail, then toss the phone back on the table. I'm not avoiding her. I just haven't had time to process the bomb she dropped.

"I'm pregnant and it's yours." The words rolled off her tongue effortlessly.

"The hell it is," was my first response. *"Bullshit,"* the second.

I always use a condom when I fuck, and *I* dispose of it when I'm done.

There is no way Amelia's pregnant. I know condoms aren't one hundred percent, but in all my years of being sexually active I've never had a female claim to be carrying my child.

If Amelia is pregnant with my baby, I will take care of my child. That still doesn't mean we're a couple.

I exhale and sit up, resting my elbows on my thighs and covering my face with my hands. I can't think about this here. In this apartment. The last thing I want is to bring my personal drama into Dani's already complicated life. Nor can I continue to snub Amelia's attempts to get in touch with me.

The stubble on my chin sounds like sandpaper scraping the palms of my hands as I scrub my face. I reach over and get my running gear out of the duffle bag and change right here in the living room. The way Dani's been checking me out, I'd change right here even if she were awake.

I'll jog over to the hotel and call Amelia. Plus, Ig and Vin got in this morning. Edwards was screwing someone in this apartment and I want to know who. Once Dani leaves for work, the four of us will sweep the place for DNA fingerprints.

I fold the covers, stack the pillows on top, and leave everything in the corner of the sofa, including my duffle bag. In the bathroom

I rinse my mouth, then put in my contacts.

The light snores coming from the bedroom across the hall draw me to the doorway. One foot across the threshold into the bedroom, the other one out, I stare at the woman sleeping on her back.

Danielle's scent is strongest in here.

Her foot kicks the covers off her lower half and she rolls onto her side. I have an unobstructed view of her in too short shorts. Those long, toned legs are making me drool. And that ass I picture my hands gripping while I'm taking her from behind. If I put the other foot across the threshold I know I'll use everything in my arsenal to fuck her. A pinpoint-size burn forms in my stomach chasing away my explicit thoughts.

Danielle has all the qualities a man like me is attracted to—beauty, brains, and independence. But can she do the "no strings attached" thing? That is the other quality she needs for me to lie down with her, outside of the job.

I step back and close the bedroom door. My grandmother would say it's a move only a true gentleman would make.

When Dani wakes up, I don't want her to freak out wondering if I leered at her while she slept. A person is most vulnerable when they are asleep. By closing the door, I'm building a trust between us.

I write a quick note to let her know I've gone for a run and stick it on the refrigerator with a magnet next to the calendar filled with reminders, weekly work schedules, and a red circle around yesterday's date with a slash through it.

Tony texts me while I'm doing warm-up stretches in the middle of the living room. I reply, "you're on."

I strap my cell phone and ID to my arm, holster my gun under my T-shirt, grab the spare key, and leave the apartment. Locking the door behind me.

Out in the open, I'm aware of my surroundings. I keep my head up and eyes sweeping as I set an easy pace.

The hotel is three miles away.

The weather is warm for zero-five-thirty. Mid-eighties I think. It's not uncomfortable and I'm not in danger of heat stroke.

One mile in and the sweat is already dripping from my chin. If I weren't strapped, I'd shed my shirt.

I nod the customary greeting to the other morning joggers I pass on the sidewalk.

Two miles in and my shirt is sticking to me. The image of Danielle's legs drifts into my mind, making me smile.

I head east on the final leg of the third mile.

The hotel's entrance is coming up. I start to slow down.

At the light, I jog in place while I wait for it to turn green, then cross the street walking.

The driveway to the hotel is active with people getting into taxis. I walk through the turn-style glass door. No one pays attention to me as I stroll through the lobby to the bank of elevators. A young couple is exiting one. I step in and press the button for the ninth floor.

"Is she up?" I ask when I let myself into the room.

Ig hands me a water bottle. "Yeah, she just got up." He goes to the opened box on a bed filled with evidence kits. The other bed in the room is unmade.

Tony looks up from the monitor and tosses me a stack of cash rubber banded together.

I slip off the rubber band and fan out the ten crisp hundred-dollar bills in my hand. "Told you she wouldn't go through my stuff while I was gone." I lick my thumb and count out the money. "I'll use this to take her out to dinner tonight. What's the name of that steakhouse again?"

"Burt's." He leans back in the chair, balancing it on two legs.

Vin steps through the door connecting the two rooms with a towel in his hand. He tosses it to me. "Amelia just left the condo building."

"Why is she stalking you?" Tony sets the chair back on all four legs.

I take a deep breath before I tell them. "She says she's pregnant."

"What!" echoes around the room and ricochets off the walls, hitting my ears three times.

"Yeah." I wipe the sweat off my face and neck. "I don't know what I'm going to do other than call and see what she wants. Can I have the room?"

We don't keep secrets. They know I'll fill them in later.

"Another rack says Danielle will go through your bag before you get back."

Tony likes losing his money. "You're on."

Ig opens the door. "We'll meet you at the apartment after Danielle leaves for work."

I nod.

Vin closes the door behind them.

I unstrap my phone, sit in the chair Tony vacated, and call Amelia. It rings once on my end and she answers.

"Where are you? This is important. Why are you just now getting back to me?"

"I'm not obligated to give you the details of my life."

"Are you with somebody else?"

"No." My eyes shift to the monitor in front of me. Danielle is in the kitchen wearing a green robe. The note I left is in her hand.

"Can we meet at the park, Bryan?"

I watch Danielle go to the stereo and turn on music. She starts rocking her hips and swaying side to side. "I'm in Vegas. I'll be back tomorrow. As soon as I touch down I'll come over."

"You promise?"

Danielle dances her way over to the refrigerator and starts pulling things out, laying the items on the counter.

"I will be there, Amelia."

She hangs up without saying goodbye.

I turn up the audio volume to hear the song she's dancing to. "The Way You Make Me Feel." Damn, any woman who can roll and rock and sway like that has got to be exquisite in bed. This is the one time I'll allow myself to envy what Edwards has.

I like watching this uninhibited side of her. The need to get back to the apartment is strong. Instead of giving in to it, I minimize the screen and open another to access my email.

I skim through the messages in my inbox. Two-line replies are sent to the ones from Colonel Langford. Some I flag to reply to later. The rest can wait until I'm back in Colorado.

Reading emails does nothing to distract me from this pull to be with Danielle. There's no point in fighting it any longer. I leave the hotel, setting a faster pace.

My route back to the apartment is different. It'll take me a mile out of the way, but hopefully I can rein in this craving I'm developing for Danielle.

The scenery is a blur.

By the time I walk through the complex entrance, my calves and thighs are burning and I'm breathing hard. I ran—not jogged—back.

I stick the key in the lock and find that the apartment door is already unlocked. "I know I locked the door before I left."

Danielle is dressed for work and standing in the kitchen. A welcome smile on her face.

"Did you unlock the door?"

The smile on her face transforms to a frown. "No. Why? Is something wrong?"

"Everything's fine. Maybe I forgot to lock it when I left. I'm sorry. I'll be more aware next time." *I locked that door!*

"No worries. This is a safe neighborhood. You have time to shower before breakfast is ready. Do you drink coffee?"

"Yes. Thank you." I grab my duffle bag off the sofa and take it to the bathroom with me. The lock thing is going to bother me until I rewind the recording from the camera facing the front door.

I store my gun in the side compartment of the bag, shed my sweat-soaked clothes, and hop in the shower without waiting for it to warm. I duck my head under the cool water pouring from the showerhead as the intensity of the magnet eases up now that I'm back in the apartment. It has nothing to do with the extra mile I ran.

The water's temperature finally reaches my ideal level, but I'm already rinsing out the shampoo and getting out.

I wrap my towel around my waist and stand in front of the mirror visually doing a self-inspection. I start my newly acquired grooming routine. Never have I paid this much attention to how I looked until I started preparing for my face-to-face interaction with Danielle Lauren Tatum.

Satisfied that I look good for her, I get dressed and leave the bathroom.

Danielle is seated at the table sipping orange juice. "Thank you for closing the bedroom door this morning."

The sincerity of her tone both warms and twists my gut. I'm earning her trust even though I don't deserve it. Chen wrote the profile on Danielle. I'm sure his suggestions for getting close to her would work if I followed them as written. But I'm choosing to go on instinct.

"Thank you for this." I gesture to the steaming cup of coffee and the hot breakfast waiting for me on the table. Two biscuits with something on top and covered with gravy sit in the center of the plate, potatoes on one side, eggs on the other. Grits in a bowl on the left and melon spears on a small plate on the right.

Dani is watching me. "Bayou biscuits. I didn't have everything I needed to go all out, so this is my modified version. Those are creole breakfast potatoes. The rest I assume you know what they are."

"Do you and Edwards eat like this all the time?"

She frowns and takes a sip of orange juice. "No. With school and my work schedule and his extra trainings at the base or out of state, I don't get to cook for him as much as I'd like to."

I want to yell, *he's not at the base training,* but I keep that to myself. I pick up the knife and fork and start with a biscuit.

Mentally I quote Tony, "*She can burn in the kitchen.*"

"I've never had Bayou biscuits, but damn, these are good. Who taught you how to cook?"

My words put that big smile on her face. "Mr. Franklin, my foster father."

"What happened to your parents?"

"My mother died when I was young. Didn't know my father."

"How was it—growing up in a foster home? Am I being too personal? Edwards never said his girlfriend was a foster kid too."

"The typical reaction to learning someone grew up in the system is to think they were mistreated, are ill-educated, and low achievers. Not all foster homes are like that. Mr. and Mrs. Franklin didn't allow me to be pigeonholed by the title foster kid. They didn't object when I wanted to emancipate myself at age seventeen because I was a junior in college."

"Edwards said you guys were a couple in high school."

She chuckles. "Yeah, but we were friends first in middle school. When he found out I was taking boxing lessons, he'd tag along with me to the gym. We hung out so much that by ninth-grade year of high school we fell into the 'couple' category."

I feign a shocked face by making my eyes wide and lifting my eyebrows toward my hairline. "You box?"

She nods. "Being the youngest in a classroom of students two or three years older made me a target for bullies. Mr. Franklin taught me to box to give me confidence and a way to protect myself. I started kickboxing two years ago."

"Have you ever had to use your skills?"

The pulse in her neck speeds up and a shadow crosses her pretty brown eyes. She picks at her food and glances at the front door.

When the silence becomes uncomfortable, I break it. "These potatoes are really good too."

"There's more in the skillet. Help yourself. How long are you planning on staying in Tucson? Not that I'm kicking you out or anything."

"Actually, I'm catching a flight out tomorrow afternoon. But I'd like to take you to dinner tonight as a way of saying thank you for letting me crash on the sofa. What time do you get off?"

The shine in her eyes is worth the invitation.

"You don't have to do that, Bryan. I appreciate you fixing the garbage disposal and the handle on the toilet. James doesn't like for anyone he doesn't know on a personal level to be in the apartment. And that includes the building's manager."

"I'd still like to take you to dinner, Dani. What time do you get off? I want to call ahead and get us a table at Burt's." I toss her my winning smile.

She spittles in her juice glass. "That place is too expensive."

I set my knife and fork on the edge of the plate. Cock an eyebrow and fix her with a pointed stare. "What time?"

"Six."

"I will meet you at your job at six sharp."

"You don't know where I work."

"Then you'll just have to tell me." I don't let up on the stare until she stands and retrieves the note I left her this morning. She scribbles down the address on the back of it, then brings it back to the table.

While we eat breakfast, Danielle asks questions about my friendship with Edwards. The lies roll off my tongue without hesitation. I ask questions about her relationship with Edwards and toss in a few about her childhood. So far, she hasn't strayed from the truth. She asks about my childhood but does not ask if I'm in a relationship.

I walk her to the door with the promise of a fun evening.

The guys arrive at eight fifteen. I tell them about the unlocked door. We view the recording and see that no one entered the apartment while I was gone.

Vin does a security assessment of the apartment, then goes about improving the areas that make Danielle vulnerable. He even installs a security screen door. The building's owner had no problem with it after a face-to-face conversation with Vincenzo The Tank Ricci.

Tony, Ig, and I run single use lint rollers on every surface of the apartment to pick up DNA fingerprints and dust for physical fingerprints. Ig picks up strands of red hair on the carpet between the sofa and coffee table.

Late afternoon, we start round three of rock-paper-scissors to see who is jumping in the dumpster to retrieve the garbage bag I dumped yesterday. Then we hear the rattle and rumble of a trash truck rolling down the street. All four of us jump in.

I ride back to the hotel with the guys because I have a full suitcase of clothes there to properly prepare for my dinner date with Danielle.

On the way to her job, I tell Vin to pull over at a flower shop.

At exactly eighteen hundred hours I stand on the steps of the mental health clinic wearing dark-colored chinos and a button-down shirt and holding a single pink thornless rose that is unassuming yet powerful like Dani.

CHAPTER FOUR

DANIELLE

Colorado, Present Day

THE BABY SETTLES DOWN, BUT I'm too wired to sleep. My brain won't shut down from processing all the things Bryan told me before he took off running for Ig's car. The simple days back in Arizona seem like a lifetime ago. They hold some of my most memorable moments even though the last four years were my loneliest.

Here in Colorado, we are trapped in a power struggle that is surrounded by too many secrets and held together by a web of lies.

To get a better perspective, I step behind the camera lens and focus on Bryan. Our time spent together. The conversations we have had. The events that led up to today. And why I dreamt of running in the dark toward Bryan's voice with Kourtney clutched to my breasts.

My body jerks like I was yanked by the arm and made to sit up in bed.

Now that I have all the information, the light of understanding forces away the dream's darkness.

How did I miss it?

How did I miss the tactical moves to obscure his ultimate weakness?

It's been right there all this time. Bryan used darkness to hide us even though the weight of separation hurt him. I didn't think it possible to love him more than I do right now. Falling in love with Bryan has been the easiest part of this—conundrum.

There must be something I can do to ensure his victory.

I think about it for a while then scooch to the end of the bed.

My feet sink into the deep plush carpet as I stand and rush out of the bedroom.

The lights are still on downstairs. James is lying on his back on the sofa. Feet crossed at the ankle and dangling past the armrest. He sits up when he hears me on the stairs.

"Is something wrong? Is it the baby?"

The alarm in his voice and wide-eyed worry confirms what I suspected earlier.

I chuckle. "What was Bryan's threat?"

James scratches the back of his head with his finger and gives me a sheepish smile. "Your husband promised to gut me like a fish if I let anything happen to you or his son."

I sit on the coffee table in front of the sofa. James turns to face me.

"He doesn't make idle promises. But rest assured I'm fine."

"Then why are you up? You are supposed to be off your feet."

"I can't sleep. I need answers."

"To what? Hawk said he was going to tell you everything."

"He did, but he didn't tell me why RAGS is after you."

James exhales deeply. "Jamal and I weren't just selling Phantom information. We were also selling the identity of RAGS's leader."

"Who is Elijah Hopper? How is he involved in this RAGS-Phantom battle?"

"I'm not quite sure how he's in the mix."

"Who is he to Marie?"

"She gives orders, he carries them out."

"Are they lovers?"

He shakes his head. "No."

"Who is Willis's go-between?"

"For a while we thought it was Hawk?"

"Bryan? Why him?"

"Phantom only brings in military people for key positions. Langford pulled him in straight out of high school, then let Hawk bring in other non-military people. Two are from other countries."

"Does Bryan know about Elijah Hopper?"

"I told him everything. What are you getting at, Danielle?"

"Look, I know Bryan told you not to let me deviate from the plan, but I need to talk to Hopper. Can you get him here first thing in the morning? Before the sedatives wear off on my grandmother?"

"I'm not so sure about this. Hawk told me what happened at the house. Since when have you become reckless?"

"It wasn't recklessness. I was in survival mode. Come on, James, this is important to me."

His frown deepens. "I'll call him." He goes to pick up the cell phone, but I stop him by placing my hand over his.

"You were in Ethiopia all this time?"

"Yes."

"Were you happy there?"

My question surprises him.

"Yes, I have a wife and a four-year-old son. They are my life. Like you and your girls are Bryan's life. Are you happy?"

It's my turn to be surprised. "Very happy. Bryan and I have something that most people won't get." I chuckle. "Sometimes even I don't get it."

"It's called unconditional love. My wife taught me that." He stares me in the eyes. "I'm sorry, for everything."

The genuine sincerity in his voice and repentance in his eyes earns my heartfelt forgiveness.

"How were you recruited into RAGS?"

James slides his hand from mine and exhales, heavily. He sits back on the couch. I move from the coffee table to sit next to him.

"For as long as I can remember, three things were drilled into my head. Become the very thing the leader of RAGS covets. The blood of my enemy is my stepping stone to the top of RAGS. Danielle will suffer if you fail." He recites it like he's checking them off a list.

I squeeze his hand, encouraging him to keep talking.

"I didn't know who Danielle was until I was transferred to the Thompson's house. On the first day of middle school, I was given a picture of you before I left the house. I didn't just happen to strike up a conversation with you—it was my assignment to."

I listen to the man I referred to as my childhood best friend tell me how he trained to complete his missions and when he found out he had an identical twin brother his focus changed. James goes into detail about the three-way game of chess between the Edwards brothers, RAGS, and Phantom with me as the queen. I'm not a chess player, but I know the queen is the most powerful chess piece. They never found out why it was so important to protect me, but they knew it had to do with the game they were playing.

The brothers tried to use hidden audio messages in the CDs he gave me to condition me to their will. They realized it didn't work when I refused to live with James when I initially moved to Arizona. He apologizes for bringing Derek Tucker into the game, but my refusal put their victory in jeopardy. He hired the lowlife, wanna-be actor whose real name was Stephon Greene to torment me. Deep in my soul, I know Tucker's predatory nature was no act. That man was going to violate me that rainy night in the underground parking garage. James says he went looking for Tucker the next day to kick his ass, but learned the animal was already dead.

When their game was exposed, the brothers plotted their last move. Their checkmate—per se. Sell the information to the highest bidder.

James slipped a strong sleeping pill in my glass of champagne on our wedding night and Jamal implanted the microchip in my ring finger. To them, Amelia was just an expendable player—a pawn. As was Deidra, aka Madelyn Brooks.

After the raid, James made it to Ethiopia. Hopper sent him forged passable papers to get a job as a clerk at the U.S. Embassy in Addis Ababa. He met Selam when he accompanied an ill coworker to the hospital.

My heart goes out to him when he describes how his wife and son were taken. My friend is not a bad person. I'm happy Bryan's people rescued Selam and Solomon and are bringing them to Colorado.

I sit up. "Thanks, James. I think I can sleep now." I rise from the sofa. "Good night."

"Night, Danielle."

"Friends call me Dani." I go back upstairs and climb into bed. My eyes close immediately as my mind and body relax.

◆

Arizona, Nine Years Ago

This is not a date. Even though he showed up at my job and handed me a beautiful pink rose, this is not a date. Married women do not go on dates with their husband's friends.

Bryan pulls out my chair and waits for me to sit.

He is a gentleman.

I try not to gawk at his thighs as he walks to his seat across from me. We're seated at a small table for two.

Burt's Steakhouse is busy for a Wednesday night. I'm happy our table is on the second level next to a window, out of the way of the hustle and bustle of the wait staff and customers, yet we still have a view of everything around us.

The host hands us menus, recites the specials, then leaves us.

The aroma of grilled beef makes my mouth water. I ate a light lunch this afternoon in anticipation of a heavy dinner. Missing a kickboxing class tonight is worth it for a meal at Burt's. The establishment doesn't accept coupons; therefore this isn't somewhere James would take me for dinner.

"I hope you're not one of those salad-eating girls." Bryan says from behind his menu.

"Nope, I'm a carnivore with a big appetite and not ashamed of it."

"Anything look good to you?"

"Everything," I laugh.

Bryan lowers his menu and laughs too.

Our waiter appears and introduces himself. He places a wooden board holding a small loaf of honey wheat bread and whipped butter, and two glasses of water on the table. "Can I get you anything from the bar?"

Bryan flips the menu pages to the selections of beer.

It's times like these when being nineteen sucks. I hide my irritation behind the open menu in my hand. "Iced tea for me."

"Make that two," Bryan says.

I peek around the menu. "You don't have to do that. Go ahead and order a beer."

His eyes tell me his reply before the words pass his lips. "I don't feel comfortable drinking if my dinner companion can't."

Mrs. Franklin would say Bryan has been taught well.

My husband would have ordered the beer.

Leaning forward, I use the menu to hide my batting eyelashes from the waiter. "I dare you to order me a Long Island iced tea and tell him to put it in a regular glass."

Bryan cocks an eyebrow.

I cock a challenging one.

He leans to the side and reaches in his pocket. I can't see what he pulls out because he keeps his hands under the table. He gestures to the waiter. Bryan quietly speaks to him and then the two men shake hands.

The waiter nods and slips his hand into the pocket of his half apron before walking away.

My menu hides the victorious smile that spreads across my lips. "I can't believe he did it," I whisper under the guise of the noise in the restaurant.

"That makes two of us," he replies from behind his menu loud enough for me to hear.

Once I decide what I want, I close the menu and glance out the window. The view of the sky is beautiful. If this were an actual date, I'd say it is romantic. I look around to see if anyone else notices the blend of orange, yellow, and red in the pale-blue sky.

An older couple is looking our way. They are cute together. Both with salt and very little pepper hair. She is wearing a flowy summer dress and simple gold jewelry. He's wearing a crisp white dress shirt and dark colored tie.

I wonder how long they've been together. Is this date night or perhaps an anniversary? Were they high school sweethearts like James and me? Do they have children and grandchildren? What kinds of troubles did their relationship face through the years? What kind of advice would they give a young couple like James and me?

I offer them a friendly smile.

Immediately her top lip curls and he leers.

Taken aback, my gaze shift to the window to peek at whatever or whoever displeases them. The only thing in the window is the beautiful backdrop of sky and my reflection.

An uncomfortable feeling starts to hover over me. I look back at the couple.

The woman's eyes roll so hard I'm afraid they won't stop, and she will get a three-sixty view of the dining room without ever turning her head.

What could I have possibly done to them in the short amount of time I've been in the restaurant?

The man's leer shifts to Bryan and then he says something to his wife. She too looks at Bryan and nods. I can't read lips, but I can read body language and it appears their displeasure stems from who I'm dining with.

The menu in Bryan's hand hits the table so hard both water glasses and I jump. The skin along his strong jawline is taut like he's clenching his teeth. The greenish gold brown hue of his eyes is gone, replaced by a dark anger. He turns in his chair to stare at the couple. The muscles in his arms flex, stretching the material of his dress shirt to its limits. Bryan looks like he's about to take flight and land on the couple's table.

Our waiter returns with our drinks and a sample platter of appetizers. "Is everything okay, sir?" He follows Bryan's stare. When Bryan doesn't answer, our waiter then approaches the couple's table. "Can I get you folks anything else?"

Bryan turns and leans toward me. "Do you trust me?"

Why wouldn't I trust him? "Yes."

Bryan reaches for my hand and brings it up to his lips for a lingering kiss, then intertwines our fingers. He looks back at the leering couple. The inquisitive side of me wants to know when he noticed them. The romantic side of me doesn't care.

The old couple scurries from their table.

"Have you ever dated a Black woman?"

Bryan untangles our fingers. "I've gone out with women of different ethnicities. Attraction doesn't have a color. Have you ever dated a White guy?"

"No. James was my first and only boyfriend. Now he's my husband."

"Let me rephrase. Would you date a White guy if you weren't married?"

"Yes. Love has no color. It has a soul." My answer makes him smile. "Will your girlfriend be mad that you took me out to dinner?"

For a quick second, his eyes widen. "I don't have a girlfriend and even if I did, she'd know me well enough to know that I don't play games and I'm not a cheater."

"Why don't you have a girlfriend?"

He does not shift in his seat nor avert his eyes like most men who value their single status would do.

"Relationships take up a lot of time that I do not have."

"What do you do, Bryan?"

"I used to work for a landscaping design company, but I've started my own personal security business and I'm hiring ex-military personnel. Edwards is helping by giving me the inside scoop on military life."

"You're not Army?"

Bryan shakes his head and the lines of confusion form across my brow.

"You have this—military aura about you."

"I take that as a compliment. I have much respect for the men and women who serve our country."

"Yesterday, you said your parents are in Colorado Springs."

"Is there a question in there?"

"Is that where you're from? Do you have a big family?"

"Yes, I'm from Colorado Springs. I have one older sister, JP1. She calls me BK4."

"They sound like names of sci-fi characters. What does JP1 and BK4 mean?"

"I'm Bryan Kendall Hawk the Fourth. I hated being called little Bryan so my sister came up with BK4. She's the only Jessica Paige in the family."

"You and your sister are close?"

The smile reaches his eyes. "Yes, even though we're four years apart. I've learned a lot from her. Do you have any siblings?"

"I'm an only child."

"What about foster sisters and foster brothers?"

"Nope. I'm the only one the Franklins took in."

"What is it like not knowing your family roots?"

My gaze shifts to the window. No one has ever asked me that question. Not even James. I look back at Bryan and summons the courage to say the word I've never said out loud. "Lonely."

Bryan takes my hand again. The gesture is not just comforting, it somehow makes the word untrue from this point on.

I ease my hand from his to wipe my eyes with my napkin and deflect to a different, less personal topic. "What did you do today?"

"Installed locks on all the windows in the apartment and added a security screen door."

"I apologize in advance because I don't mean to sound unappreciative, but you just met me. Why would you care how secure my apartment is?"

His shoulders rise and fall in a nonchalant shrug. "This may sound cliché, but you bring out my protective side."

"Wow, okay. Not sure how to respond. Thank you does not cover my gratitude."

Our food arrives.

Bryan and I talk about hobbies. Turns out he's a technology geek—his words not mine. Mentally I correct him—he's an easy on the eyes technology geek with thick thighs, index fingers shorter than his ring fingers, and the longest eyelashes I've ever seen on a man.

We talk about the pros and cons of living in Tucson versus Los Angeles, or Colorado Springs versus Tucson.

After listing our favorite movies, we find that we both like high action-packed movies. I love romance movies. He hates them but loves horror flicks. I love erotic romance books. He doesn't have time to read, but if he did, it would be psychological thrillers. His favorite children's story is the one told mostly at Halloween about the headless horseman. Mine is about a mischievous little boy whose imagination takes him to an island of rambunctious beasts.

I could blame it on the Long Island ice tea, but honestly, Bryan is the source of my buzz more than the drink is.

We decide to take dessert to go.

Our shoulders accidently brush as we walk through the parking lot to the car. He took a cab to the clinic and I drove us here. I hand over the keys and let him drive us home. He doesn't mock my old car like James does.

The minute I walk through the door, I put my rose in a vase and set it on the dining table, then go change into shorts and a tank top.

Bryan shows off the security improvements he made.

We sit on the sofa with our feet propped up on the coffee table and eat our dessert while we watch an action movie with a female lead.

He makes fun of the way the actress handles the weapons in her arsenal. Once he starts critiquing her fighting abilities, the quips fly back and forth between us. He's winning.

I stand up and turn off the television.

"Don't make me embarrass you, Mr. Hawk."

"You don't want none of this, Mrs. Edwards."

"Push back the furniture and show me what you've got." I pause for dramatic effect. "That is if you don't mind getting knocked down by a girl."

"Bring it."

I go to my gym bag, get out the tape and start wrapping my wrists and hands. Bryan grabs clothes out of his duffle bag and carries them to the bathroom. When he comes out, he's wearing the cut-off sweats from last night, a wife beater, and a cocky smirk.

I work off that New York strip steak, loaded baked potato, steamed broccoli, corn on the cob, and the New York-style cheesecake by showing Bryan my kickboxing skills. Thankfully my apartment is on the ground level; otherwise the manager would be knocking on the door telling us to settle down.

Bryan is quick. He blocks each hit and kick and knee I throw at him. I can tell he's holding back on his counter attack. Every time he knocks me on my butt, he explains where I went wrong. With my years of training and his coaching, I manage to get a few surprising hits in. At one point, he sweeps my feet and I grab hold of him, using my full weight to bring him down to the floor too. Bryan shifts, and I land on top of him.

He doesn't make a move to get me off him. Our bodies rise and fall as one with our rapid breathing. I become trapped by the unspoken words filtering through his hazel eyes.

He's conflicted.

As am I.

Can I get up and pretend the gravity does not exist between us?

His hold around my waist tightens and my gaze drops to his kissable lips. Of its own accord, the pad of my thumb skims the outline of his bottom lip.

Bryan closes his eyes and stops breathing.

This intrigues me.

I trace his lip again.

A sex-filled groan escapes his mouth as he exhales. His eyes open and their usual hazel color has a wondrous shine that reveals he's a virgin to intimate touching that reaches his soul.

I'm his first.

Bryan's eyes now tell me he will follow my lead.

All the reasons why this is wrong fade to the background. Knowing he won't make the first move, I lower my head until our lips touch.

Soft.

Giving.

Warm.

Those are the words that come to mind to define the feel of his lips. I kiss him again.

Bryan's hand cups the back of my head and he takes over. His tongue skims my lips and I open for him. Our tongues touch and dance and stroke one another. His mouth tastes like cinnamon mints and hunger.

This kiss is more than an attraction. It is about exploring the realm of intimacy with someone who connects with you on a level you never knew existed. It's scary and sensual and sexy.

I pull away.

"I'm sorry." I climb to my feet. My heart is pounding so hard it's making me dizzy. I put some distance between us.

Bryan sits up. "No, Dani. I'm the one who should be apologizing."

"No, it's on me. I'm married. I know better."

I make it to the linen closet without running. The pillow and sheets he used last night are in there. I take the bundle back to him. Bryan is still sitting on the floor in the middle of my living room.

"Thank you again for dinner. Good night, Bryan."

Tonight, I close the bedroom door and curl up on James's side of the bed. I wait for the guilt to weigh me down, but it does not come.

I dream of the boy I grew up with and the anxious man who ran out of the door on his way to fight for his country.

In the morning, I linger in the room for as long as I can. Unsure of the etiquette for the morning after kissing your husband's friend. The best way to squash the awkwardness is to talk about it. I open the bedroom door and walk into the living room.

The apartment is empty, but I find a note on the refrigerator.

> *I made you an omelet and left it on the stove.*
> *If I'm not back from my run by the time you*
> *leave for work, thank you for letting me stay here.*
>
> *B*

I read the handwritten note again. This is not how I wanted to leave things between us. We need to talk about what happened last night, but if I don't leave now, I'll be late for work. I scribble a thank you reply on the back of his note and stick it back on the refrigerator.

Today, not even the fact that I'm working with my favorite doctor can chase away the sad gray cloud hovering over me. One of the other interns, who is also a study group partner, tries to pry answers from me about the hot guy who I met on the steps yesterday.

I take a late lunch and sit by the window in the air-conditioned cafeteria and stare at the sky. Realistically I know I won't see him on the airplane, but there is nothing wrong with wishing I can.

The rest of my work day is spent typing doctor's notes in patient files. At the end of my shift, I decline an invitation to grab a bite and head home to my empty apartment.

I go to set the mail on the table and freeze.

Sitting in the middle of the table is a vase overflowing with long-stem pink roses. Stuck in between the prongs of the clear plastic stick is the business card for Bryan K. Hawk IV. A message is written at the bottom: *I stocked the refrigerator and cabinets.*

CHAPTER FIVE

BRYAN

Colorado, Present Day

I GIVE UP TRYING TO GO to sleep. Knowing I can't get to my wife and daughters right away if RAGS is successful in firing the first shot that starts World War III is keeping me awake. I get up from the cot and go to the desk. All monitors are still on. I use one to log into my home security system. I start watching archived footage from the time I left for work yesterday morning to the present.

Langford tampered with the interior garage door. He also let Ross and Madelyn Brooks in through the laundry room door. The others he let in through the garage before Dani locked down the house.

There has been no movement in my house since Jessi went back to pack.

Once I give the go-ahead, a special cleaning crew will remove any traces of our home being invaded. This is also the best time to make a couple changes before we move back in. Dani needs her own home office. Mine is large enough to add a wall and a door, giving us equal-sized home offices. We'll stay with Mom and Dad until the house is ready.

"Sir, you have an incoming message from Hollis," Riley announces.

I switch screens.

It's an update on the airplane heading to South Central Asia. On board are three hundred passengers who think their RAGS leader rescued them from federal custody and is whisking them away before they can be tried and convicted of treason and other crimes against the United States.

The plane took off twelve hours ago. The person operating the remote controlled aircraft is the infamous blogger slash hacker slash gamer slash mathematician slash conspiracy theorist, Braxton Hollis. He now works for Phantom—under close supervision.

Hollis is letting me know that the airplane's cabin is filling with the odorless gas from the confiscated smoke bombs RAGS intended for the terrorist attack on the DC Metro system. All passengers on the airplane will be dead within six hours.

Four hundred miles from its destination, the plane will explode over the highest summit of a mountain in Nepal.

It does not bother me to orchestrate the death of three hundred men and women. I will sleep just fine at night. Those people made the conscious decision to betray their country.

The computer monitor at my station starts ringing with the presidential seal icon flashing in the center. I move over to it and tap the icon.

The man on the screen looks like he hasn't slept in days. "I spoke to your parents face to face. The kind of information they needed to know could not be given over the phone, that's too impersonal."

"Thank you, Mr. President. I can imagine how they took it."

"About as well as any parent would be considering they were told their son is off saving the United States."

"I bet my mom spewed a string of cuss words that turned your ears red and my dad paced back and forth asking question after question like a prosecuting attorney."

"You know your parents."

"I really wish you'd go underground, sir."

"If I go into hiding, heads of state may react negatively. Military intelligence reports show most already have ten to fifteen percent of their armed forces on combat readiness. Because of that, the United States is at DEFCON 4. I've sent my sons to a secured location. My wife refuses to leave my side. Vice President Forrester is secured. After Chen interrogates Owens I'll know which men and women in line of succession to send to the bunker. I need to stay visible. And Hawk."

"Sir?"

"*I've* got eyes on you."

The significance behind his words makes me admire him even more. We don't get the publicly recognized Presidential accolades, but to First Command, we are heroes just like every man and woman who serves our country. "Thank you, sir."

The video call ends.

Fontenot enters the room dressed in a standard Phantom Watcher uniform. She looks like she got more rest than me, which is a good thing.

"Ready to help me get into the suit?"

"Yes, sir."

My monster smiles. This is the final showdown between me, Willis Langford, and the woman who has mothered me since the day I met her. His wife, Marie Langford, who managed my household, cared for my wife and children. But it wasn't care; it was infiltration. A clever maneuver pulled off by the woman who is Antoinette Marie Toussaint. The daughter of the tyrant who founded RAGS, Dominique Elian Toussaint.

<hr>

Arizona, Nine Years Ago

The minute I sit in the chair in the first-class lounge, the guys start in with the jokes. I knew they would, especially since they were at the steakhouse too and most likely glued to the monitor when Dani and I started sparring.

I'm still trying to make sense of what I felt when she touched my lip. Something good passed through me and I don't understand why.

"More pink roses?" Vin hands me a beer. "Poetic romance or subliminally letting her know you'll be gentle?"

Chen suggested I leave her roses on the table. I thought it was a stupid idea until I remembered how big Dani smiled when I handed her a single one last night. I walked a little taller knowing *I* put that smile on her lips.

"So, is Jessi right? Is the back of a woman's hand an erogenous zone? From where I was sitting, I couldn't gauge her reaction." Ig leans forward waiting for my reply. Sometimes I forget my friend isn't as experienced as us.

"I wasn't trying to turn her on. It was a knee jerk reaction to hearing that old man utter loathsome words about Dani and me. I couldn't call him out on his racist shit the way I wanted to."

"Apparently Bry's lips are an erogenous zone. The pillow stayed balanced on his lap most of the night," Tony jokes.

I tried to control my body, but the memory of Dani on top of me, and the feel of her lips, and taste of her mouth kept me hard all night. It was a high I'd never experienced. I would have kissed her longer, deeper, but she pulled away and I let her. She is married to the man I intend to have put away for life.

I slouch in the chair, beer in my hand, and stare out the window. The note she left me made me smile. I did more things for Dani in two days than Edwards has done for her since she's known him.

"Ten says she's his do-right-girl." Ig holds out his hand.

He's going to lose his money. I don't believe in romance and love. They know that, but hey, if he wants to pay up ten grand on a bad bet, who am I to tell him how to spend his money? I shake his hand.

"Why do you think you're gonna win?" Vin asks.

"He's already calling her Dani," Tony answers.

Our flight is called.

Mentally, I flip the switch from what I'm leaving behind in Arizona to what's waiting for me when I touch down in Colorado.

My fuck-buddy is pregnant.

I won't give up my platinum membership to bachelorhood for anyone. But I will be an active parent in my child's life. That is nonnegotiable. Amelia and I will have to work out the details on shared custody.

Once the seatbelt light is turned off, I pull out my laptop and work on the real-time super computer I'm going to build.

When we touch down, a Phantom sedan is waiting for us. Langford wants to debrief now instead of in the morning. We give each other the "is he serious" eye and walk with the Shadow to the car. During the ride to Boulder, we text each other about the report we'll give.

The outside of the main building of Phantom's headquarters reads Langford's Landscaping and Design. It is the colonel's cover for the secret military organization. A few months ago, Colonel Langford instructed me to start my own cover, hence Hawkeye Personal Protection. I already have three meetings scheduled with foreign dignitaries who are interested in doing business with me.

Face wiped of any emotions, Colonel Langford stands at the podium in the conference room waiting for us. "Did you find anything useful?" He skips the pleasantries and gets straight to the point.

Since I'm lead on this assignment, I respond. "Paul and I found letters hidden under a floorboard. We cut the trip short so I can utilize Phantom's resources to analyze the content and ascertain their relevance to the case."

"It would be a great learning tool for *you* to figure that out without tapping into resources."

What?! "Roger that, sir."

"And the girl?"

"Doesn't appear to know about his activities."

"You've drawn this conclusion based on what?"

"One-bedroom apartment. Two student loans. Less than a grand in her bank account. Basic wardrobe. Late model car. Basic cable. Old computer. Working extra hours to make the rent and pay bills."

"That could all be a cover. Is the equipment working now?"

"Yes, sir. Fully operational."

"Good, stay on her. By the way, Hawk, what was the purpose of summoning Acosta and Ricci to Arizona?"

"I believe there were others in the apartment the night before Edwards deployed. I asked Acosta to sweep the apartment. To further gain Danielle's trust, I asked Ricci to assess the safety of the apartment and make improvements."

"Acosta, I'll give you until Monday to give me your report. The rest of you, I expect your reports in the morning." He nods his dismissal.

We stand and head for the door.

"Hawk?" Colonel Langford calls out.

While I stop and turn around, the guys keep walking.

"I have reason to believe RAGS is sending someone to get close to you. Get them before they get you. Do you understand?"

"Yes, sir."

He steps down from the podium and exits out of a side door. I catch up with the guys in the hallway. We do not speak until we leave the building and are miles away from headquarters with me behind the wheel of my own car.

"Langford is a pussy," Tony says. "Get them before they get you. What kind of shit is that? Why doesn't he have more information on this RAGS person?"

"We'll just have to watch Bry's back twenty-four seven," Vin says.

"The prototype for the chest armor is ready. You can test it out, Bry," Ig offers.

I pull up in front of the condo building that is in the housing complex for Phantom. "Can we talk about this when I get back? I'm heading over to Amelia's."

"Cool. I can say a proper hello to my girl." Tony opens the passenger door and climbs out.

Vin and Ig climb out of the back seat. My friends get their luggage from the trunk.

I pull away from the curb and head toward Loveland. At this time of day, I'm going with the flow of traffic. It will take me over an hour to get to Amelia's apartment. But it's plenty of time for me to think.

I'm trying to remember the last time we fucked. We were at her place. I opened the new box of condoms I brought. I rolled it on. And the condom was intact when I pulled out. I took it with me when I left and tossed it in my trash. That was a couple of months ago. We've hung out a few times since then, but nothing sexual.

The closer I get to Loveland, the more I want to turn around and go home. But I can't. My dad is big on owning up to responsibilities. Amelia didn't make this baby by herself and if it's mine, she will not raise the child by herself. Forced child support isn't something I want hovering over me for eighteen years. I'd never hear the end of it from Dad.

I exit the highway and drive another two miles. When I turn the corner onto Amelia's street, I see the circling red and blue lights of two police patrol cars in front of her apartment building. My eyebrows touch in the middle of my forehead and my eyelids narrow. I pull over and park and get out of the car.

An officer is talking to one of Amelia's neighbors when I approach. "Excuse me, officer. My name is Bryan Hawk. Amelia Goodman lives in this building. Can you tell me…"

"How do you know Ms. Goodman?" The officer cuts me off.

"We're friends. We had plans to go out tonight. Has something happened to her?"

The officer steps away from the neighbor and pulls me aside, out of earshot from the other bystanders. "When was the last time you talked to Miss Goodman?"

"Yesterday morning."

"We were called by Ms. Finkleston. She heard shouting and a commotion coming from the apartment above her. When she went up to see if Miss Goodman was okay, she found the door wide open, the living room trashed, and drops of blood trailing from the door down the back steps."

I pull out my phone and call Amelia.

The call goes straight to voicemail.

I call the number again and get the same results.

"Mr. Hawk, where were you between the hours of three and five?"

I pull out the stub from my checked bag at the airport. "My plane landed at fifteen hundred hours. I went straight to the office for a meeting with my boss. Here's my business card, you can call the front desk. I have to clock in and out of the building."

The officer takes the card. "Thanks. If I need to get in touch with you is this a good number to call you at?"

"Yes."

"If you hear from Miss Goodman, please have her contact me." He hands me his card.

I go back to my car and call the guys while I'm driving.

We come up with a list of her regular hangout spots, divide it, and each go looking for her.

I check the hospitals and urgent care centers too.

Nothing.

After hours of searching, we conclude she's in the wind. I'll just have to wait for her to contact me.

Once I get to my condo, I grab a beer out of the refrigerator and go sit out on the balcony. My phone is in my hand and I'm calling Dani. As an afterthought I check the time.

"Hello." Her voice is soft and raspy from sleep.

"Sorry we didn't get to say goodbye, but I hope the flowers made up for it."

"They are beautiful, thank you very much." I hear the smile in her voice. She's happy to hear from me. "You have to let me pay you for the groceries."

"Not a chance."

There is a rustling sound on her end. "How was your flight?" She sounds more awake now.

"It was good. How was work?"

"I got through the day."

This conversation sounds too *couplish*. I need to reset the tone. "Have you heard from Edwards?" It wasn't a question. It was a reminder that she's married and we're not a couple.

There's a moment of dead silence. "Not yet. He said it might be a few days before he can contact me."

"Make sure you tell him to get in touch with me."

"I will, Mr. Hawk. Is there anything else you'd like me to relay to my husband?" And there's that feisty tongue I like so much.

"No, nothing else."

"Great. You forgot to leave the spare key. Please mail it back to me. Have a great evening." She ends the call before I can say anything.

I drink down the rest of my beer and decide to turn in. I have a session with Major Chen in the morning. There's no telling what he has cooked up for me.

Before I turn off the light, I try Amelia's number again. It goes straight to voicemail. I leave a message. "Call me."

A week comes and goes and still no word from Amelia. The story about her missing was on the local news. She hasn't used her credit card or pulled any money out of the bank. The guys and I swept her apartment late one night. Something serious went down there.

I work on deciphering the letters to keep me busy. If they were alphanumeric anagrams, I'd have cracked them by now.

I need the key.

Langford doesn't want to send them to an FBI specialist. He says he's confident I can decipher them on my own. Yes I can… *if I had the key.*

As a last resort, I spar with Chen to help me come up with possible words or phrases that Edwards may have used.

At two in the morning, an unfamiliar number comes up on my caller ID. I answer. "Hawk."

"Bryan?" Amelia whispers.

I sit up in bed.

"They're after me."

"Who's after you?"

"I can't tell you over the phone."

"Where are you?"

"Around the corner from Misty's Diner."

I jump out of bed. "Meet me in the parking lot in twenty minutes."

I throw on some sweats and tennis shoes, text the guys, and run out of the door.

It's only because I'm in a hurry that the elevator wants to take a long time to get to the garage. My finger hasn't let up off the G-button since I stepped in the cab.

My stall is closest to the elevator.

I don't give my car time to warm up. As soon as the engine turns over, I shift the gear in reverse and back out of the stall. The scent of burned rubber and a cloud of smoke left in the building's garage is a testament to how quickly I exit.

It's a straight shot from my condo to Misty's. At this time of morning, there is little traffic on the streets.

I get to the parking lot of the twenty-four-hour eatery with seven minutes to spare, thanks to the red lights I plowed through.

There are at least a dozen cars in the lot. Three of them are police patrol units. I keep my foot on the brake and the car in drive while my eyes search the deserted lot. The low rumble of the idled engine drowns out the occasional laugh coming from inside the diner.

A single light flashes near the trees in the back by the dumpsters. I grab my gun from the door holster and slowly pull closer to the stalls in the back.

Amelia dashes out from behind a blue dumpster and sprints toward the car. I hit the unlock button and she jumps into the front passenger seat.

"Did anyone follow you?" she pants.

"No." I speed out of the parking lot.

Her arms and legs are bare. The tank top and jean shorts she's wearing are filthy. And she stinks.

Neither one of us talks, as I navigate the streets above the speed limit while Amelia breathes heavily. She twists and turns to look out the windows and ducks down if we pull up alongside another car.

Even though my friends are on the same floor, I can't take her back to my place. I need somewhere to stash her until I know what's going on.

The entrance to the highway is coming up and I get on heading south.

Amelia shivers, wrapping her arms around herself. My thumb presses the button on the steering wheel to turn on the heat.

Every few miles I glance at the woman sitting in the passenger seat with scabbed-over scratches on her face and arms, finger-size bruises on her neck, and a busted lip that looks infected. Her hair is matted, and boy, does she smell unladylike.

I'll wait until we get to the hotel to question her. She's alive. She's safe. And she doesn't have to look over her shoulder. I will protect her.

An hour into the drive, Amelia leans the seat all the way back, turns on her side to face me, curls up, and closes her eyes.

Her feet are bare and caked in dried mud.

My cell phone rings. I put the Bluetooth in my ear and answer.

"Where are you heading?" Tony asks.

"Buena Vista."

"What do you need?"

"Ig and Jessi to come to the hotel."

"Done. Ig is getting his medical bag together. I'll have him bring your overnight bag and backpack. I'm calling Jessica now."

"Thanks, Tony."

"I've got eyes on you. Text us the room number when you check in."

I turn on the radio to keep me company for the rest of the drive. The hotel I'm going to is tucked away in the small community. The guys and I have gone river rafting around there a few times.

Amelia whimpers something incoherent in her sleep.

I get off the highway and continue straight on the street until I pull into the hotel's parking lot and find a parking spot near the rear exit. Amelia wakes up.

"Wait for me."

She nods.

The lobby is empty. I'm greeted by the night manager at the registration desk. I request a room near the exit on the first floor. She's all smiles and hair flips when she gets me registered and hands me the envelope with the key card inside.

"Let me know if there's anything I can do to make your stay pleasurable, Mr. Osborne."

When hiding someone, using your real name is just plain stupid.

I open the envelope to look at the room number, a phone number and the message *call me* is written next to it.

Not interested.

I go to the room and grab one of the thick white robes from the bathroom and complimentary slippers, and the trash can liner. Then I go out the back exit.

Amelia is wide-eyed and tense in the front seat of my car.

"Take off your clothes and put these on." I hand her the robe and slippers, then turn my back and wait for her.

The car rocks.

Amelia grunts.

She cusses.

And huffs in frustration as she changes.

"I'm done."

Together we enter the rear of the hotel and go to the room. Amelia drops the liner with her clothes on the floor in front of the bed before she goes to the bathroom.

I sit at the small table by the window and pull out my phone and shoot the guys a text letting them know I used the Osborne identification and credit card. Tony replies right away: *Jessi will be there in the afternoon, she's on duty at the hospital.*

Vin's text says he's got the blueprints for the hotel and a map of the area and will send escape routes to my email. I tell him to hack the hotel's security camera system and erase anything that can positively identify me or Amelia.

The bathroom door opens and Amelia steps out looking much better. The scratches and bruises don't appear to be as bad as I first thought, but I still want Jessi and Ig to check her out.

She sits on the edge of the bed in the belted robe with a fluffy white towel wrapped around her hair.

"Who's after you, Amelia?"

"Rebels Against Government Suppression."

"Why?"

She exhales, and tears start to roll down her cheeks.

Tears?

Really?

Amelia doesn't cry.

I move to the bed and sit next to her but leave some space between us.

She takes a deep breath. "I'm from RAGS, Bryan. I was sent to get you to join us."

"I'm not a terrorist."

"We're not terrorists, Bryan. The country's current state of government is detrimental to the American people. We can make it better. You can help make things better. You own a company that is getting government contracts not just here in the U.S., but other countries too."

Her words come across like a rehearsed sales pitch.

"There's no way I'd join RAGS. And how do they know about the contracts I'm negotiating? That's classified information."

"RAGS has people everywhere."

"Why are they after you?"

"Because I was stupid and fell for James Edwards and believed he was going to give me a cut of the money he and Jamal are getting for selling some important top-secret information to Islamic Liberation Army."

My fingers curl into a tight fist. "Explain yourself, Amelia."

"A little over a year ago, the assignment came up to get you to join RAGS. The payout was too big to pass up. I came to Colorado. Getting you to open up to me was a challenge."

I cock an eyebrow.

"RAGS said I was taking too long to bring you in and if I couldn't they'd give the assignment to my girlfriend. I did the only thing I could think of. I took the brand-new box of condoms out of your bag while you were in the shower. Opened it, poked tiny holes in the packets, then resealed the box."

"You did this on purpose?" My eyes shift to her stomach, then back to her face.

She nods.

I suck in a deep breath of air and release it. "You're giving me information without telling me why RAGS wants you dead."

"They found out I've been helping James gather information on them. I've seen them torture and murder people who were sent in undercover by the government or law enforcement."

"Where is he meeting up with the buyer?"

Amelia reaches for her shorts in the bag of dirty clothes on the floor. "Since both James and Jamal left the States, I think Iraq." She sifts through the pockets of the shorts, then pulls out a folded piece of paper and hands it to me. "I went to Arizona to tell James I found a way to finish my assignment and get the money. I walked in on him and his brother fucking *my* girlfriend while some random bitch slept on the couch across from them. We got into a fight. When they weren't looking, I took that off the table and ran out."

I open the paper and stare at the map and the phrase written across the page. It's the key! This is what I need to decipher the letters. Excitement makes my heart beat faster. If we leave Colorado in the next couple of hours we can stop Edwards. I need to call Colonel Langford.

"Bryan, I don't want this baby. Will you come with me to the clinic to terminate the pregnancy?"

I jump to my feet and kiss her cheek. "Amelia, I have to go. *Do not* leave this hotel room. *Do not* contact anyone, not even your parents. *Do not* open that door for anyone. The two doctors I send will have their own key card. Wait for me to get back before you do *anything* about the baby." I run for the door. "Order as much room service as you want." The door slams behind me.

CHAPTER SIX

DANIELLE

Colorado, Present Day

"DANIELLE." JAMES KNOCKS ON THE door.

"Huh?"

He knocks again. "Dani, are you up?"

"Yeah, give me a second," I groan. It feels like I just went to sleep. I squint at the red numbers on the clock. Six thirty.

I kick the covers off and roll out of bed. My bare feet sink into the plush carpet as I walk to the door. Sometime in the middle of the night, I kicked off my socks. I open the bedroom door.

James lifts the strap of the overnight bag in his hand. "Hawk's sister dropped this off. Hopper said he'll be here at eight. What do you want for breakfast?"

"Buttermilk pancakes, scrambled eggs, and lots of bacon. Oh, milk and grape juice too." I take the overnight bag from him. He turns to walk away. "James, when did you marry Kimberly Baryshnikova? Was she your first?"

He turns around with his eyebrows rise midway to his hairline.

"It was in the file Bryan let me read."

James scratches the back of his head. "I married her when I graduated boot camp. She needed citizenship. I needed someone with connections to black market buyers. Ashley Hudson was my first, but I'm not the one who got her pregnant. And for the record, every girl I dealt with back then was jealous of you."

"Why? We weren't sleeping together."

"Exactly, and I still wouldn't leave you."

After our talk last night, I realized the change I saw in him before we graduated high school was because of the demons he literally had to fight. James took a risk by coming to Boulder to warn me. And he's now working with my husband to protect me. Our friendship wasn't a waste of my time when I think of all the things he has sacrificed for me.

The strap of the overnight bag dangles from my hand as I wrap an arm around his waist to hug him.

We reconnect as friends.

Real friends this time.

"I'll be down after I shower." I close the door after he leaves and carry the bag into the bathroom.

My calves are a little sore from the running I did yesterday. I wish I had time to soak in the bathtub.

When Bryan and I had this room, we did some fun stuff in that tub. That's one thing I love so much about him, from our first time to now, Bryan encourages me to explore sex freely. Never turning me down. Always open to experimenting.

I set the overnight bag on the counter and unzip the center compartment. My toiletry bag and two sets of clothes and underwear are inside. The small zipper compartment on the side holds my prenatal vitamins and iron pills. Good, she remembered my body butter.

The bathtub is calling me, but I turn on the water in the small walk-in shower instead.

The warm steam from the shower starts to fill the bathroom. I stand in front of the mirror over the sink and twist my hair into a lopsided ponytail, then cover it with the shower cap.

I step under the stream of water and close the shower door.

The hot water feels good. I make an adjustment on the showerhead, so the water pulsates like tiny fingers massaging me all over. I inhale the steam and stand there for a second, then exhale and embrace the feel of tension easing from my muscles. I'm ready to face the day.

I quickly wash up and rinse off, then turn off the water. My feet welcome the feel of the fibers in the bath matt. I love it so much, I put one just like it in every bathroom in our home.

I spread my body butter over my body and get dressed.

Part of my attire today includes a gun holstered at my side, hidden by the loose-fitting shirt. The earpieces are safely in my pocket.

I was told to keep them in my ears. But for now, I'm choosing not to. That little part of me that I call defiance is poking her head out of the closet. She's been in hiding since the morning Bryan tied me to the bed to keep me from fighting Vin. I need her sassiness to help me stack the odds in Bryan's favor.

I shake my vitamins onto a tissue, then give myself a mental pep talk before I leave the master suite and go downstairs for breakfast.

James has the table set at the six-seating, Cherrywood dining table in front of the floor-to-ceiling window. Sunlight reflects off the sterling silver plate covers. I don't know which I like more, the mountains in the winter or the mountains in the spring. Both are breathtaking.

He pulls out a chair and waits for me to get settled before removing the covering from the dishes in front of me.

That is new. He rarely displayed gentlemanly manners in informal settings.

James sits across from me and uncovers his plates. I watch him bow his head and close his eyes. He silently prays over his food.

My eyes grow wide. The James I knew never prayed for anything.

He catches me watching him and shrugs with one shoulder before picking up his fork and spearing the pile of country potatoes on his plate. "My wife insists we give thanks for our blessings before we nourish our bodies."

He must be quoting her verbatim. James doesn't talk like that.

"You changed because of a woman?" I swallow my prenatal pills with a grape juice chaser.

He cocks an eyebrow. "I can say the same about you."

His words give me an opening to test something out.

I toss an eye dagger across the table. "For real, James? You really want to go there with me? *I* was the faithful one in our fucking relationship, but apparently, I had no reason to be." The use of profanity is not in my everyday vernacular. I don't need to cuss to get my point across. I hold my breath and wait to see if he calls me out on my foul mouth.

"Jeez, Danielle. I was just pointing out that you of all people should understand love changes you. I wasn't implying you did anything wrong. I'm happy you have Hawk. When I followed you, I saw how much you guys are into each other. That's the kind of love I have with Selam."

Good, I sound natural cussing.

I pour maple syrup on my pancakes, cut off a piece with my fork, and take a bite. "Tell me about your son."

"Solomon is good. And smart. And talkative." His eyes shine with pride as he talks about his son. "I'm worried my past will scar my son for life."

"I'm afraid of what all this is doing to my girls. I'll research child psychologists who specialize in post-traumatic stress counseling. Kourtney, Emma, and Solomon will need therapy."

"Thank you for including him. I want you to meet my family."

I reach for his hand across the table. "I'd like that."

"Tell me about your girls."

I laugh. "This could take a while." The words flow easily. "I'm the proud mother of two very talented, very different daughters."

James and I exchange funny stories about our children.

When the elevator doors open we stop talking and I look that way.

The air stops flowing through my lungs. The chair I'm sitting in skids on the marble tile like a jolt from an electric shock rolled through my body causing me to stand, pushing it back.

Mahogany cane.

Sharp creases in his dark-colored trousers.

Crisp white dress shirt.

Dark tie.

Customary cardigan sweater.

Page-boy hat on his head.

The man I've known as my patient of eight months, Terrance Brumfield, steps off the elevator, his eyes locked on me.

He isn't the reason I'm on my feet though.

The other gentleman stepping out of the elevator I recognize from years ago. Time has aged him, but not his features. He came to the boxing gym once when I was in the ring with Mr. Franklin. The stranger stood on the sideline watching me until my foster father noticed him. The two glared at each other like old friends still harboring a grudge.

Mr. Franklin called over one of the other trainers to work with me; then he and the mysterious man went into his office. I could see them through the window. It looked like they were arguing.

That was the only time Mr. Franklin allowed another trainer to spar with me. The two men were still in the office when I climbed out of the ring. James was waiting for me near the office door with a strange look on his face. I hadn't seen the mystery man since that day, but I never forgot him.

James stands and greets the men with handshakes. "Good morning, gentlemen."

"Is Antoinette still asleep?" Mr. Brumfield asks.

James checks his watch. "If what I was told is correct, we have two more hours before the drug wears off."

The stranger pats James on the shoulder. "Leave us, son. She'll be all right."

"Yes, sir."

James walks past and squeezes my hand before he goes upstairs.

Brumfield removes his hat, then slowly shuffles across the floor with the aid of his cane. He slides my chair back behind me, grasps my elbow, and guides me to sit.

"That old coot over there is one of my oldest friends, Elijah Hopper." Brumfield sits in the chair adjacent to me and leans the cane against the table. "You want to know how this involves you."

I manage a jerky nod.

Hopper takes the seat James vacated. He pushes the dishes aside.

The seed of doubt in my ability to pull this off is planted. There are just too many of them for me to keep up with.

Brumfield nods to Hopper, then looks at me. "You already know I was a high school chemistry teacher. What you don't know is that I worked for Phantom too. Your father was my favorite student. He was focused on his future, got straight A's, but he was also a little uptight. Your mother, Elizabeth, was the opposite. A rabble-rouser, and barely passing her classes. She was also the daughter of a friend and I felt compelled to watch out for her. I paired Elizabeth with Daniel for tutoring.

"In the beginning, those two were like winter and summer. Over time, Elizabeth started to settle down and Daniel started to loosen up. Daniel changed toward the end of his senior year. He maintained his grades, but he started missing school a lot. The week before his graduation Elizabeth stopped coming to school. Daniel came to me. He wanted to know how well I knew Elizabeth's father. When I said Willis was one of my closest friends, he handed me the plans for a deadly attack on the United States by Rebels Against Government Suppression.

"Daniel stood tall and looked me in the eye and said, *'I'm taking Elizabeth far away from here to keep her and our baby away from those people.'* I begged him to give me a couple of days to come up with a plan. As soon as he left my classroom, I called Elijah."

Hopper clears his throat. "I am a Phantom Field Agent who has been on a Top-Secret assignment, undercover in RAGS for decades. Neither Daniel nor Elizabeth knew how dangerous it was for them to have those plans. It made me, Terrance, and George look differently at our friend Willis. I went to POTUS to get clearance to bring them in on the assignment. We agreed we had to get Daniel and Elizabeth out of Boulder."

"We gave Elizabeth and Daniel new IDs, cash, keys to a car, and a number to a secured line where we could pass messages to one another," Brumfield says. "Elizabeth insisted Daniel give his valedictorian speech at his graduation before they left. I told them not to pack anything, but Elizabeth wouldn't leave her journals and jewelry box behind. The two left right after Daniel walked across the stage. Every month we moved them to different states and gave them a different car. The last place they moved to was Los Angeles, California. The plan was for them to stay there until she had the baby, then move again.

The evening of Valentine's Day, Elizabeth called the secured number in a panic saying she thought they'd been found. The message was forwarded to me. We'd been over what to do in case of an emergency. I was already in LA with George. By the time we arrived, Elizabeth was being loaded into the ambulance and Daniel was dead behind the wheel of their car. I told the police I was Elizabeth's father and they allowed me to ride with her to the hospital. George stayed behind to pack up their apartment and wait for Elijah. Elizabeth was conscious and in active labor. The doctor told me once the baby was born I had to leave the room. As they prepped her for an emergency delivery, I held Elizabeth's hand and prayed you and she would make it. Then you were born, and the doctor placed you on your mother's stomach. She made me promise to hide you from her family. She said to name you Danielle Lauren Tatum, after your father." His voice quivers. Tears glimmer in his sad eyes. "Then Elizabeth stopped breathing." Mr.

Brumfield pulls a handkerchief out of his pocket and hands it to me.

I hadn't realized tears were flowing from my eyes.

"When I arrived, the coroners were just getting to Daniel. George and I swept the surrounding area and a little before sunrise, we found a revolver wrapped in a plaid shirt in a trash can five blocks away. I used my level of security clearance to cover up Terrance's presence at the hospital and I kept Daniel's and Elizabeth's identity out of the news even though they had aliases. Willis had Watchers monitoring all news feeds for stories about teenage couples. George resigned as Willis's Lieutenant Colonel. I falsified documents for him and my sister Katherine to be certified foster parents, then manipulated the court system so they were granted guardianship of you. We prevented you from being adopted. I kept my ears open around RAGS to see if any of our hitmen bragged about a job in Los Angeles."

Mr. Brumfield reaches for my hand. "I had Daniel and Elizabeth buried side by side. Their belongings are in boxes in my basement."

A sob rakes through my body. For twenty-eight years I knew nothing about my parents except my mother died in childbirth. Now, all this information is coming at me and I don't know what to do with it.

"We couldn't figure out how they were found or who murdered them, but it was a RAGS hit," Hopper says.

"How do you know that?" I dab at a stream of fresh tears.

"The gun belonged to Dominique Toussaint. It was also the gun that killed him."

"How were Willis and Marie able to hide their identities for so long?"

"I hid Antoinette," Hopper says. "Willis wasn't involved in the day to day operations of RAGS. He aided and abetted the cause. Antoinette allows her half-brother to think he has a voice in how things are run."

"She has a half-brother?"

"Yes, but they aren't the heirs to RAGS."

"They're not?"

"The way Toussaint set up his will. He gave the heir the documentation needed to take control of RAGS."

"How did we end up here?"

Hopper wipes his brow with a handkerchief. "Willis has been making noise about getting out of RAGS for years. He even made a major play after finding out James and Jamal knew about Phantom. Antoinette sucked him back in by having the woman he truly loved murdered, the threat of more making him stay put. Dental records were the only way Carolyn's body could be identified. We think all of this is because Willis is trying to make moves to get out again."

Doubt is a weakness I can't let paralyze me. I wipe the last of my tears and restore my self-confidence. Bryan isn't going to be happy that I've gone off script, but I'm going to find the heir of Dominique Toussaint and get him to stop my grandparents.

———◆———

Arizona, Nine Years Ago

It's been almost two weeks since Bryan called. Our conversation started off fun and friendly, then he got all serious and brought up James. I demanded that he return the spare key, then hung up in his face and turned my phone off. As soon as I did it, I knew my reaction was childish and uncalled for.

Part of me is hoping he'll call. I could call him, but I do not want to be the one to make the first move again.

The pink roses are fully opened now. If I have time, this week I'll pull off the petals and make potpourri.

I say a prayer for James, put the baseball bat between the stacked pillows and headboard where it is within reach, and turn off the light. Tonight, I sleep on top of the covers in the middle of the bed. I could turn on the air, but while James is gone, I'm watching the household expenses. I also spent the week precooking dinner meals so I have no excuse for eating out. James sold his car to an Army buddy for seven hundred dollars and gave me the money to go toward next month's rent. With the extra hours I'm working at the clinic, I'll have enough to pay a little extra on the bills to get ahead.

My eyelids get lower, and I roll onto my side, snuggling with the pillow. I feel my mind crossing the realm of reality into the world of dreams.

James and I are hiking at Patagonia Lake on a sunny spring Sunday. We are holding hands as we walk the nature trails. He is the one who suggested we take the two-hour drive up here to get away from the city. I'm not much of an outdoor person, but this isn't so bad. It's a good day to be outside.

Up here, James is relaxed, and remnants of the boy I first met in middle school are coming out. His laughs are belly deep. He is getting a kick out of me ducking and dodging and batting away anything that flies too close to my ears.

We stop at a secluded spot by the creek. James unpacks the blanket and our lunch from his backpack. He prepared everything. We eat listening to the zoom of boats and the hoots and hollers of water skiers off in the distance.

After lunch, I lie in his arms and enjoy just being with him. I'm too happy to pay any mind to the insects flying near us. One day, I'm going to marry this man and have his children.

"I'm leaving for training next week." James kisses my forehead.

"Another one? I thought you were on thin ice with the Army."

"Oh, I am, but I was chosen for this training. If I pass, I'll be gone for a year, maybe two."

"Of course I want you to pass, but two years is a long time."

"I'm doing this so I can move up and make more money. I don't want you to be in debt when you graduate as Doctor Danielle Tatum-Edwards."

I tilt my head back and let him see my smile. "Why are you so sure I'll marry you before I graduate?"

James flashes one of his confident smiles before leaning in to kiss me.

Beep.

Beep.

Beep.

My alarm goes off. I reach out and hit the snooze button and try to get back to my dream of that day at the lake with James.

Ten minutes later, the alarm goes off again. Instead of hitting the snooze button one more time, I climb out of bed and get ready.

The eight-week accelerated summer course I enrolled in starts today. The professor is the toughest in the Psych Department. A's are hard to come by in his classes.

My day starts at the clinic. I'm facilitating a group session with teens who were adopted.

After the meeting I type my notes in the case study file, then eat my sack lunch in the cafeteria before heading over to the university.

I get to class fifteen minutes early to claim my usual spot in every class. Middle seat second row. Other students file in. I talk quietly to the ones I know. We take out our calendars and make plans to get together to study. For one person, this is her second time taking this course with this instructor. He's the only one who teaches it.

At two o'clock, Professor Bullock hands out the twelve-page double-sided syllabus. I skim through it, happy I waited to take this class in the summer because of the high academic demands. It is the only class I'm taking this summer.

Professor Bullock announces that lectures start promptly at two and will end exactly at six. He warns us not to open his classroom door if we are late and do not leave until dismissed, it is inconsiderate of the other students and offensive to him.

Next, he informs us that the campus book store still does not have one of the required books, it's on back order and will be here later in the week, but the circulation desk in the school's library has five on the shelf. He will not excuse us from any material covered or assignments due from that book.

Great, I was going to pick up toiletries and laundry detergent after class.

He begins the lecture. My notes are written with my version of shorthand.

At the end of class, I walk across campus to the library. I do the assignment and copy the next few chapters of the book, so I won't have to come back to the library.

I walk back across campus to the parking lot.

It takes two turns of the key to get my car started. I pull out of the lot and head home. By leaving school this late, I miss most of rush hour traffic.

I'm tired, hungry, and still need to prepare for tomorrow's lecture.

My car jumps and jerks when I put it in park in my spot. I know my car is old, but the mechanic didn't mention any major issues when I took it in for routine maintenance last month. I'll have to block out some time to take my car in.

At the apartment building's mailbox, a woman paces back and forth near the secured entrance.

"Is everything okay?" I ask.

Her friendly smile adds youth to her face. "Everything is fine. I'm watching out for my son and his friends in the moving truck. He wouldn't let me hire a moving company. I'm starting to think I should have followed my first mind. I'm sorry"—she holds out her hand—"I'm Yvon Wright. I'm moving into 112, recently divorced."

I reach out to shake her hand. "I'm Danielle. My husband James and I are in 105."

A big rental truck pulls up and double parks in front of the building with its hazard lights flashing.

"There they are," she huffs and opens the security door.

We wave goodbye and I walk the walkway past the pool to my apartment. Yvon is the first neighbor I've said more than hello to.

I lock the door behind me once I let myself in.

As I shuffle through the bills and sales papers, I toss my backpack on the table, then walk into the kitchen and open the freezer. The choices of precooked meals do not look appealing. I close my eyes and grab the first thing my fingers touch.

Meat loaf, rice, and cabbage it is.

Knock.

Knock.

Knock.

I put the mail on the counter, the dish in the microwave, set the timer, and go to the door.

I peek through the peephole.

Coldness spreads over me like my body was doused by a bucket of ice water. Frostbitten fingers fumble with the locks. The ice on the palm of my hand makes it impossible to grip the door handle, but somehow, I manage to get it open.

A fog rolls in, obscuring my brain as I stand behind the security screen door staring at the men in Army uniforms on the other side.

One speaks. "Are you Danielle Tatum?"

If I tell him no, then this won't be happening. Like getting a notice in the mail. If you don't open the envelope, then the notice doesn't exist.

"Yes."

Who said that?

Their words of identification are warped and distorted because everything around me is happening in slow motion.

"May we come in?"

I already know why they are here, but I don't want to hear the words because it makes this real. I want to slam the door in their faces and go back to that day at the lake.

Someone unlocks the screen door and allows them to come in. Perhaps I did, but I'm so numb I can't say for sure it was me.

In the background, the joking voices of men fill the courtyard along with Yvon giving instructions as to the best way she thinks the sofa will fit through the door.

I don't remember telling the Army men to have a seat or how I made it to the love seat, but across from me on the sofa are the chaplain and a man whose name and military occupation I can't recall.

The microwave signals my dinner is heated. It will have to wait. These people are here to personally deliver a notice.

I disconnect from reality and travel back to the last peaceful time I spent with my best friend. I'm lying on the blanket in James's arms listening to his heartbeat and the easy inhale and exhale of his functioning lungs.

The people in front of me are far away. In the tunnel, their words do not penetrate my peace.

When I come to, I'm on the sofa, still in my clothes. The pillows and sheets Bryan slept on support my head and cover my body. It's three fifteen in the morning.

The memory of my lost time comes to me in bits and pieces in reverse order.

I lie on the sofa and cover my head with the sheet blocking out everything.

A loud crash of glass shattering on the stone walkway followed by the laughing voice of a man saying, "Sorry, Ms. W. I'll buy you another one."

Running around the apartment turning on the lights.

Engaging the locks after they leave.

The grief therapist invites me to a support group he facilitates for spouses and significant others.

What woke me up?

Is there someone you can call to be with you? The chaplain's question is what woke me.

I run to my backpack and toss books and papers and supplies out until I find my wristlet purse. The zipper opens with a yank of the tab. I grab my phone. My hand shakes as I search the call history. I find the number I need.

Ring.

Ring.

Ring.

"Hawk." His greeting sounds official. Commanding.

"I need you."

"Dani, what's wrong?"

"Bryan, I. Need. You."

A century of dead silence passes. "I'm on my way."

The call lasts twenty-seven seconds.

What do I do now?

My stomach growls a loud answer. I was warming dinner when the messengers of bad news knocked on my door.

I get the dish out of the microwave and take it to the table. A lump lodges in my throat making it difficult to swallow, but my stomach growls again and I feel light headed.

I use my fingers to break off a chunk of meatloaf and put it in my mouth. It tastes like— air. I grab a handful and shovel it in. Cheeks stuffed, I chew, and smack, and chew, and swallow. And repeat the process until I get it all down.

More of the air-filled food is shoveled into my mouth. I chew, and smack, and chew, and swallow until my stomach no longer growls out of hunger. It now growls in protest. I keep shoveling until all of the food in the container is gone.

I burp, then push back from the table and sprint to the bathroom. Before I can get the seat up, the contents of my stomach hit the floor, missing the toilet bowl.

My throat is on fire.

The acidic taste makes me gag.

My body strains as my stomach continues to roll and expel the food I forced down.

When I'm given a reprieve, I take slow deep breaths and stay on my knees just in case.

My stomach hurts. My throat feels like sandpaper. My soul aches.

Splatters of vomit are stuck to my slacks, blouse, and hands. I force myself to get up from the floor and turn on the water in the shower.

To focus on something other than my pain, I count as I get undressed. Letting the soiled clothes pile on the floor.

I step into the tub, under the flow from the showerhead. The water is hotter than I normally like, but I'm so cold and need to warm up.

Steam fills the bathroom, coating the mirrors and floating out into the hallway. Water ricochets off my body onto the floor mat, mixing with the mess on the floor.

The one bit of memory I've suppressed for as long as I could, comes to me concealed in a mental envelope. Demanding to be opened.

I inhale the steam and steady myself for the pain that is sure to incapacitate me. My metaphoric finger slips under the flap of the envelope and slides across. Managing to get a mental paper cut. A prelude to more pain.

The flap flips back, and the chaplain's words tumble out. "It saddens me to inform you that on the eighteenth of May two thousand and five, Sergeant James Andrew Edwards was killed in action."

My knees give out and I fall to the bottom of the tub. I draw my knees to my chest, lock my arms around them and let the hot water batter me. I give in and cry.

CHAPTER SEVEN

BRYAN

Colorado, Present Day

THE GRAY AND WHITE CARGO van moves along with the morning traffic. On the outside, the armored vehicle reads Asbestos Inspection & Removal. Inside I'm hauling enough explosives to reduce a one-story building to rubble.

Langford's warehouse is on a lot with a series of other warehouses that used to house Phantom. He condensed his landscaping business to one warehouse after I moved Phantom's headquarters to the building I purchased. The fact that Kimberly held Dani captive in one of the vacant warehouses makes sense now.

The fat suit I'm wearing is more comfortable than the body-heat concealing combat fatigues we wear when executing covert missions. It was designed and made by Ig. The synthetic skin feels real to the touch and can adapt to the temperature of its environment. The suit itself is hollow and lightweight but adds the illusion of thirty pounds to my body frame. The full round belly and man boobs make me look like the stereotypical beer drinking, junk food eating couch potato. The prosthetics on my face and hands complete the package. I'm also wearing a blond wig, blue contacts, and the eyeglasses we used for the DC Metro operation. Getting into the suit took several hours even with Fontenot's help. It's not a one piece that I could easily step into.

I doubt my own mother would recognize me. Dani, on the other hand, has a knack for knowing when I'm around. Like at the hospital, I saw her slight pause in step as she walked toward the car. It was like she knew I was there, watching her.

My thumbs drum on the steering wheel in time to the music on the radio. The station is on the Reese Shore Morning Show, a radio host in LA. Tony is the last person to use the van, no doubt listening to the man who is now engaged to his ex. I don't get why he bothers to keep up with what's going on in Charly's life. We've helped each other out of some heart-hurting situations over the years, but my best friend had the most difficult time getting over his do-right girl. Or maybe he isn't over her.

A driver makes a right turn into my lane on *her* red light. I brake and so does the car behind me. I lay on the horn, roll down the window, and let loose a long stream of cuss words with hand gestures to match.

She waves an apology. My tirade stops.

The traffic inches along past my building. Everything looks normal on the outside. The men and women are preparing for the visit from POTUS. They think he's coming to announce the new Second Command. He's actually not coming, but a credible lie always includes the small details.

"Sir, I have that update on the ESO team." Fontenot's voice comes through the two-way earpiece in my ear. "They are on the ground moving toward the convoy."

"Any activity at the resort?"

"Nothing out of the ordinary. Mrs. Hawk is in the car behind you. She's turning into the parking garage at headquarters."

"Are her earpieces in?"

"No."

"Is Edwards with her?"

"She's alone."

"Give her clearance to be on the premises."

I hear the rapid ticking of the keys on the keyboard.

"Done, sir."

"That's all for now, Fontenot."

"Roger that, sir."

I knew Dani wouldn't stick to the plan. Her leaving the security room at home in the face of danger just about guaranteed she'd go off script today. Whatever it is that made her leave the resort on her own and go to my building must be important. At least she's close enough for me to get to in a matter of minutes should anything go down.

Once I get past downtown Boulder, the traffic lightens.

I turn into the main driveway of the warehouse complex and park in a visitor's stall in front of Langford's Landscaping and Designs.

The big belly gets caught under the steering wheel and honks the horn when I try to get out of the driver's seat. I laugh out loud, push the seat back as far as it will go, then roll out of the van.

I laugh at myself all the way up the steps, through the glass doors, into the reception area.

"How may I help you?" the receptionist asks. Her gaze drops to the computer screen in front of her.

My Watchers are better trained; they know not to look at the screen when the subject is facing them. Plus the Facial Recognition Software *I* designed identifies the person and gives detailed information *before* guests get to the desk.

The name Jake Weber should be flashing on her screen now.

"I'm here to do an asbestos inspection."

"My boss didn't request an inspection." She finally looks up at me.

"Here's the work order, ma'am. You can call the office if you'd like." I unclip the papers from my clipboard and hand them to her, then turn around feigning nonchalance. If she calls the number on the letterhead, Riley will answer and transfer it to Fontenot.

"What areas of the building do you need access to?"

I turn back and fix her with an annoyed glare. "It's on the paperwork, Ms."

Cognitive training alerts me to how fast her eyes flow left to right. She's just skimming the words on the pages. The movement is too fast for her to be truly reading and retaining the information. She's only focusing on words unfamiliar to her.

"Let me make a copy of the work order, then I'll buzz you in."

"Once I'm done, you'll have to sign it and then I'll give you a carbon copy. It's how I get paid. But you can keep the copy of the description of how I go about completing the inspection." I reach over and retrieve the paperwork from her fingers, rifle through them, then hand back what she needs. "I'll start with the roof." I turn and walk out of the door.

Arizona, Nine Years Ago

My plane touched down five minutes ago. I flew commercial. I'm running through the airport terminal with my field backpack in hand to get to the exit and catch the shuttle to the offsite parking lot. Tony left the truck there for me.

He was able to rent the vacant apartment across the street from Danielle's building. Tony brought my clothes with him. I need to change out of my Phantom field uniform before I see her.

I get to the curb just as the shuttle is about to pull off. There are less than a handful of people on the shuttle. I sit in an empty seat in the front.

Dani's distress call came right on time. I needed to take a step back from Langford. The mindfuck bomb he dropped on his wife had me reeling. I know we lie for a living, but what he did went beyond our training.

I *want* to believe Langford used that part of Dani's story to help ease the sting of telling his wife he is Second Command of Phantom, but I watched him as he informed his wife their missing daughter is dead and they have a granddaughter who is mixed up in this Phantom case. Langford got off on Marie's pain.

We don't know who Dani's parents are. But to watch Marie breakdown made me think of my mother and how she'd feel if she were told one of her children had been killed. I thought about how I'd feel if Amelia terminates the pregnancy. I'm not ready to be a father, but I'm also *not* ready for a life I helped create to end either.

The shuttle pulls to a stop in the parking lot.

I locate the truck. The keys are on the back driver's side wheel. I keep my cell phone in my hand and set my backpack on the passenger seat. The number to the burner phone Ig gave Amelia is stored in my phone. I call it as I start the truck and drive out of the lot.

"What did the doctors say?"

Amelia huffs. "*He* treated the cut on my lip. *She* examined me. Drew blood. Swabbed my mouth. Not sure why she took a hair sample. Told me to stay off my feet. And left vitamins and some other pills."

"When I get back, we'll talk, Amelia."

"Raising a kid is not what *I* want."

I purposely soften my tone despite my anger at her for putting us in this situation. "Let's talk about it, please."

"When?"

"I have a business emergency so I'm not sure. But as soon as I get back we'll talk. Do you need anything?"

"No."

"I'll call you tomorrow."

"Okay."

The next call I make is to Vin. I tell him a list of things I need for him and Ig to get from my cubical and the condo and bring to Arizona.

I call my sister. She starts off cussing at me for having her go to a hotel to examine a pregnant woman instead of the woman coming to the hospital. When my sister lets me get to the reason for the phone call, I'm already pulling into the assigned parking stall of the apartment building where Tony is keeping an eye on Dani.

"Is Amelia healthy?"

"Her lab work came back normal. Even though you didn't ask, I checked for drugs and STIs. Results from genetic tests take longer. And I need a blood sample from you."

"Why?"

"To do a paternity test."

"You can do that before the baby is born?"

"She's coming up on the end of the first trimester, I can analyze the fetus's DNA in her blood stream."

"It's my baby, Jessi."

I pull the phone away from my ear. JP1 is threatening bodily harm for just now admitting to being the father of the baby. I tell her the short version of how Amelia ended up pregnant. That starts my sister off on a new tirade. Jessi is just looking out for me, so I let her get it off her chest.

"Thanks for going to the hotel, JP1. I'll call you when I get back to Boulder."

"Where are you? You're acting Second Command now. You should be in Boulder running Phantom until the colonel comes back."

"By tomorrow afternoon I'll be linked to the Phantom network and can oversee things from where I am. I'm following up on some leads."

"Be careful, BK4."

"I will. The guys will be with me."

"See ya when I see ya, little brother."

"See ya when I see ya, big sis."

I climb the stairs to the second floor of the complex and walk the few steps to the back apartment.

Tony opens the door and stands at attention and salutes. "Everything's good so far, sir."

"Don't start. It's temporary." I push past him into the apartment.

Except for two card tables holding computers and surveillance equipment, and an air mattress set up in the middle of the living room, the place is vacant.

The apartment is the mirror image to Danielle's except it's a two bedroom.

Tony closes the door and drops the model soldier act. "If we're lucky, he'll be forced in to a medical retirement and you'll get the position permanently." Tony's never really cared for Langford. He says Langford is shifty.

"Do you know how much shit it takes to lead a secret military organization? I don't want that."

He tsks. "Dude, you're already doing the work for him. You might as well have the title, pay, and privileges that go along with it."

I stare at Dani on the monitor.

"She's been curled up on the sofa since sunrise."

I wonder if she'd still need me if she knew I was the one who ended her husband's life. And was happy to do it. "Where's my bag?"

"In the bedroom to the left. While you're across the street I'll go out and get some furniture. We can't live like squatters in here." He gestures to the emptiness of the apartment.

"Keep it simple though," I tell him as I walk down the hallway to the bedroom to get my duffle bag.

I waste no time showering and getting dressed.

Tony and I walk out together. I take my bag with me across the street and use the spare key to let myself into Dani's apartment.

Every light in the place is on.

Dani jumps up from the sofa and sprints toward me, wearing

pink sweats and an unflattering yellow shirt. No bra. Her brown-red puffy eyes shine with fresh tears. Her hair is a tangled mess on her head.

A jacks' ball-size spot in my gut starts to burn.

I release the straps of my bag to catch Dani in my arms because she launched herself at me.

I squeeze her. "Shh. I'm here. I've got you."

"He's… he's dead," she stutters.

I hate playing the ignorant role, but I have to. "Who's dead?"

"James."

I force my eyes to widen and let my mouth drop open, then lean back to look at her. "What happened?"

"They said"—she hiccups—"he died in action." She pulls me to her and cries. "He just got there. How could he already be in the fight?"

I scoop her up in my arms and move us to the sofa.

Dani's fingernails dig into my shirt and her arms tighten around me like I'm her tether to keep her from drifting too far in the undertow of grief.

I let her cry it out.

Once again Dani trusts me to take care of her. And I will. If anyone wants to hurt her they'll have to kill me, but after me, they'll have to get through my best friends.

A mixture of her snot, tears, and slobber collect on my shirt. I hold her tight until she cries herself to sleep.

Rising from the sofa is a bit of a struggle with Dani in my arms, but I manage to do it without waking her. I carry her to the bedroom and put her to bed, covering her with a warm blanket.

This time I don't close the bedroom door when I leave. As I pass the bathroom I can't help but notice the pile of clothes and chunks of vomit on the floor by the toilet. It looks like she swallowed her food without chewing. With everything she's had to deal with, this is one thing I can spare her of.

I get the cleaning supplies from the kitchen cabinet.

The sight and smell of dried vomit doesn't repulse me. I lived with three guys for three years. We partied hard on the weekends I wasn't training with Chen. Sunday mornings the four of us rolled out of bed, hungover, ready to clean up vomit, urine, dirty underwear, and other things we promised to never talk about.

Once I get the bathroom cleaned, I bag up her soiled clothes. I'll find a cleaners to take them to tomorrow. I put away the cleaning supplies then go around the apartment turning off the lights.

Since the sofa is already made up, I toe off my shoes and lie on my back and stare at the shadows the setting sun is making on the ceiling. This is the first time I've had a moment to exhale in ninety-six hours. Everything happened so fast. I keep reviewing the details because something about how the raid went down bothers me.

On the flight to the Middle East, we mapped out our mission using satellite images of the mosque and its surroundings. We prepared our weapons. Once we were on the ground, we did a physical reconnaissance of the building and tweaked our plans.

Langford was snapping pictures of the buyer entering the building from the front doorway, carrying a briefcase too small to hold millions of dollars. Then Edwards entered with his Army issued assault rifle and a laptop.

Without warning, Colonel Langford tossed in a flash bomb and charged into the building. Edwards got off two shots. The first one hitting Langford in the abdomen; the second one hitting the buyer in the head.

I returned fire, hitting Edwards once in the chest and once in the head.

While the team went to the colonel's aid, I grabbed the laptop and stored it in my pack. We gathered materials for a makeshift backboard and carried the colonel out before Edwards's unit entered the building looking for him.

My mind is on overdrive and I'm overlooking an important detail.

The cell phone clipped to my belt vibrates. Only one person has this number. I push the accept button. "Sir."

"I understand you're in Arizona. How will you oversee headquarters from there?"

"Ricci and Acosta are traveling with my laptops. They will arrive late this evening. Both computers have the capability to monitor Phantom and all government networks."

"How can I help?"

"I'd like to have Edwards in the ground as soon as possible and see if anyone from ILA or RAGS shows up. Also, if you can get the university to grant Danielle bereavement so she won't lose her place in the summer class, that would be helpful too."

"I will arrange everything."

"Thank you, sir."

"Hawk, I read your report. Good job."

I didn't put the part about the laptop in the report. "Thank you, Mr. President."

I clip the phone back to the belt holder, take my gun from the side holster and slip it between the pillows. I do a few deep breathing exercises to empty my mind until I fall into a dreamless sleep.

In the morning, my neck and shoulders are stiff from sleeping in one position on this little sofa.

Dani is sitting at the table, the house phone in her hand and a note pad in front of her. "Good morning." Her voice is soft and raspy. "I just got off the phone with the coordinator at the military cemetery. We went over the arrangements for a graveside service Monday morning. I didn't think it could be done that fast. His body will arrive tomorrow afternoon."

"Are you okay with the services being on Monday?" I go to the kitchen and pour myself a cup of coffee. It smells strong.

"Yes. I just need to get James's dress uniform to the mortuary."

"I can do that for you. I didn't come prepared for a funeral. I need to buy a suit."

"While you're out, do you mind going over to the university? I called my professor to let him know why I'm missing classes. He's giving me time to get things settled and will give me audio copies of the lectures I miss. I can turn in the assignments when I return."

"That's good news, isn't it?" I sip the coffee without squinching my face. Dani isn't a coffee drinker and therefore not a good coffee maker.

"I was expecting Professor Bullock to drop me. He isn't the most lenient instructor in the department."

"Maybe his hard exterior is a front to discourage lazy students from trying to get by with frivolous excuses for why they've missed class or haven't turned in assignments."

"Speaking from experience?"

I eyeball her over the rim of the coffee cup. "I've seen it happen."

Dani stands and crosses the floor into the kitchen. She slides her arms around my waist. I set the coffee cup on the counter to return the hug.

"Thank you for coming, Bryan." Her voice is soft and full of emotion.

"I wouldn't be anywhere else. I've got you, Dani."

She takes a deep breath, then steps out of my arms. The back of her hands swipe away the tears. My thumbs finish the job.

"Do you need me to make calls to his friends and family?"

"No, I can do that. He didn't have family, and you're the only friend I met."

"When's the last time you've eaten?"

Her shoulders rise and fall in a sad shrug.

"Think you're up for one of my omelets?"

Her brown-red eyes shine with the big smile and her head nods with an enthusiastic shake. "Thank you for cleaning the bathroom."

"You're welcome." I open the fridge and inspect the contents. She has everything I need to make a Spanish omelet.

Dani returns to the table. She starts calling people.

I put slices of bacon in a frying pan, then start cracking eggs.

Her conversations are kept short. I listen as I cook.

The last call she makes is to Edwards's foster home. This call is more emotional than the others. She tells the person on the other end of the call that she doesn't need anything.

I set a plate in front of her when she ends the call.

"This looks good. What else can you cook?"

"A lot of stuff. My mom and grandma taught me. Just don't ask me to bake anything." I sit down with my own plate and another cup of strong coffee.

She lifts her fork to her mouth. Her eyes close and she hums. I like that Dani is a foodie. We trade cooking trial and error stories while we eat breakfast.

When we finish, I wash and rinse the dishes. Dani dries and puts them away.

I get dressed, grab the bag with Dani's vomit-soiled clothes inside, pick up Edwards's uniform off the back of the love seat where Dani left it, and leave the apartment. She's sitting on the sofa with her class book open.

In the apartment across the street, I set up my laptops and once I'm logged in to Phantom's network, I work on things that need immediate attention. That includes sending a team of Field Agents to the Middle East to see if there's any buzz about the botched sell. Captain Holly Valentine is leading the team. She is the best linguistics person we have.

The update I get on Colonel Langford's condition is promising. Mrs. Langford is staying by his side.

When I finish with Phantom business, I check in with Amelia. I assure her we will talk about what to do about the baby, but I want us to do it face to face. I hurry and get her off the phone before she protests.

Vin lays out an aerial view of the cemetery on the table and we go over how we're going to protect Dani at the funeral. As of this afternoon, Edwards's burial plot is marked.

I tell them about Amelia being RAGS and giving me the paper with the key for the letters I'd found under the floorboards. I also give them a play-by-play of the raid. And the laptop I stashed.

Tony comments on how out of character it was for Second Command to break protocol by being the first to enter the room and not fire his weapon.

And there it is, the detail that has been bugging me.

When Langford charged in, his firearm was not in his hand.

After our meeting, Tony offers to take Dani's clothes to the cleaners and stop by the university to get the class recordings. Ig and Vin leave to go to the cemetery.

I open the file containing the scanned letters. With the key, it takes me three hours to decipher the letters. Next, I turn on Edwards's laptop. It is password protected. The question—*Who are the boys that are the men in the mirror?*—is the hint. That's easy. Lamaj and Semaj. If standing in birth order in the mirror, the men's reflection is reversed as is their names. James is older than Jamal by two minutes.

The second hint is not a question: *when my brother dies I will share with him my immortality to keep us together.* After some research, I figure out the password. Gemini. It references the mythological twins Castor and Pollux. Edwards and his brother were born in November though.

The screen goes black and then a message pops up. It's neither a riddle nor a question. The message on the screen reads: touch the key to the lock to open the slot. I get out the paper with the Playfair cipher key on it and type it in, then hit enter.

The message on the screen reloads: touch the key to the lock to open the slot.

Maybe I made a mistake when I typed in the key. I take my time entering it again, then hit the enter key. *Touch the key to the lock to open the slot* reappears.

My finger hammers the enter key. The message just keeps reloading.

"What the fuck? What key? What lock? The USB ports and disk drive don't work." I'm yelling at something that can't answer me.

I shove away from the table before I pick up the goddamn laptop and throw it across the room.

My fingers leave a trail in my hair. "Fucking Edwards!"

Ig and Vin walk through the door carrying bags from the burger place near the hotel.

"What did he do now?" Vin asks.

"The first two were easy. A question. A riddle. But this third one is about a key, a lock, and a slot. The cipher key was for the codes to the anagrams for their listings on the black market. This shit is something different."

"You're speaking tech-geek. Dumb it down a bit." Ig sets two bags on the dining table.

"I used the Playfair cipher to crack the letters Edwards and his brother sent to each other. They contained a bunch of dates, times, amounts and the codes to the anagrams they used to post what kind of U.S. government information they were selling. What is needed to unlock the third security measure on the laptop isn't in the Playfair cipher. It's a key for a lock."

"Discourage Danielle from going to the airport tomorrow. Vin and I will be there to accept his belongings on her behalf. Or, we do have his brother in custody, Vin and I can go question him."

"We'll see what comes back with the body." I take the bag Vin holds out to me and go back to Danielle's apartment.

While we're eating, I offer to go to the airport for her. She smiles a sad smile and tells me a heartfelt thank you.

In the morning, the guys and I are there to sign for the body and the box. We wait until we get back to our apartment to go through the contents of the box.

Nothing that can be used as a key is in it. But there is a letter written to Danielle. It's not like the ones under the closet floorboards. The pairs of letters do not follow the same pattern. She will not get this letter until I decipher it.

The day of the funeral Dani is somber and reserved.

Dressed in a dark blue suit, I stand by the front door waiting for her to come out of the bedroom. We are getting to the cemetery early; she requested a private viewing before the services.

Dani steps into the hallway wearing a navy-blue dress that doesn't hug her curves nor hide them. The heels on her feet add length to her legs. She's chosen to hide her pretty brown eyes behind dark lens sunglasses with navy-blue frames. Her hair is pulled back off her face. Dani is naturally beautiful without makeup and as far as I can tell she isn't wearing any. Her cheeks are already sporting tracks of dried tears and her nose has a slight red tint.

I open the door, put on my own dark shades, and follow her out.

We ride in the truck in silence. Even the air around us seems to be quiet this morning.

When I turn the truck into the entrance of the military cemetery, Dani starts to wring the handkerchief in her hands and her knee bobs. I follow the signs along the two-lane road and stop behind a black-colored hearse parked in front of the mortuary.

I get out and come around and open her door.

Ten o'clock in the morning in Arizona in May, the weather is warm yet bearable. In the distance the peaceful sound of water flowing from a fountain accompanies the chirping of the birds in the tall treetops.

I intentionally stay one step behind Dani as she walks toward the doors of the mortuary. She's greeted right away and shown to a small room off the foyer.

"I'll wait out here," I tell her.

She grabs my hand, silently asking me to come in with her.

The American flag is folded back over half the mahogany casket. The shell of Army Sergeant James Andrew Edwards lies inside. I stay back and let Dani approach.

She stands there looking down at him with her arms wrapped around herself.

Several minutes pass before she moves. Dani's hand visibly shakes as she reaches out, to touch his face. She lays her hand over his heart.

When she leans in and whispers something, then kisses his forehead, I avert my gaze. The only thing I feel sorry about is that she is grieving for a man who doesn't deserve it.

"I'm ready," Dani whispers.

The representative from the mortuary closes the lid and locks it.

Two service men enter the room and unfold the flag so that it covers the entire casket. Dani and I walk behind them as they wheel it out of the building. We stand aside and watch them load the casket into the hearse.

I help her into the truck, then get behind the wheel and follow the procession to the gravesite where a white canopy is set up with chairs underneath. This time, I let Dani walk alone behind the casket.

A little over a dozen people are in attendance for the funeral.

Tony, Ig, and Vin are strategically scattered around the grounds out of sight. I unbutton my suit jacket to make the gun holstered at my hip easily accessible. Neither RAGS nor Islam Liberation Army have made any attempts on Dani's life so far, but we're prepared just in case they choose today to try anything.

The base's chaplain begins the services.

Back straight, shoulders squared, Dani sits in the chair showing no emotion throughout the short ceremony. I stand behind her on watch.

At the close of the services, Dani clutches the folded American flag to her chest as the attendees file past her, conveying their condolences. The chaplain is the last to speak to her before he leaves.

It's just Dani and me at the gravesite.

I do not rush her.

When the casket is lowered into the ground, she stands and grabs my hand squeezing it. She steps closer, pulling me with her. Endless tears roll down her cheeks.

And when the casket stops inside of the burial vault, six-feet below, Dani loses it.

Sobs bow her body as she stares down into the grave. I wrap an arm around her waist to keep her from toppling over.

My friends hover closer because my full attention is on the woman in my arms.

Dani's mournful cries and sobs rip through the cemetery. I do not let her watch the men cover the vault with the lid and shovel dirt into the grave. I guide her to the truck and block her from looking back.

The drive to the apartment is stifling silent and oppressively somber.

I carry her from the truck to the apartment to her bedroom and lay her on the bed. I slip her heels off her feet. With her back to me, I unclip my holster and set it in the seat of the chair, then drape my suit jacket over it. I take off my shoes and climb into bed with Dani—spooning her.

While she grieves, I hold on to her and watch the day through the window. A song my grandmother used to sing to me floats in my head. I find myself humming and softly singing it over and over.

We ignore the ringing of the landline. And callers calling her cell phone.

The sunlight moves from one side of the room to the other; then it disappears and the streetlights outside come on. We have not changed positions.

I don't have to be looking at her to know Dani's tears have dried up. Her ribcage expands and releases as she takes in a deep breath.

In one smooth move, she rolls over to face me. Her hand cups my cheek.

"Why do you call me Dani?" Her voice is hoarse.

I use my fingertips to brush the hair off her face. "Nicknames are how I show someone I care about them. And I do care about you, Dani." My answer is not part of some necessary lie to gain her trust. I'm speaking the truth.

It's not so dark in the room that I can't see her pretty brown eyes peering into mine like she's searching for something.

Dani runs her thumb along my bottom lip. Just like the first time she did it, I stop breathing. The unfamiliar spark of completeness starts in my heart and travels with the flow throughout my body. Touching every inch of me. From her, the gesture is—personal.

She kisses me.

One.

Long.

Peck.

I tell myself, *"Don't be the monster. Not with her. Not right now."* Before things go too far, I pull back and get out of the bed. Turning on the lamp on the nightstand.

Dani sits up. Her twisted dress is showing off her toned thighs. Another couple of inches and I'll know the color of her panties.

"Bryan, I'm fully aware of what I'm doing."

"*I'm* not so sure this is a good idea."

She gets to her knees and crawls to the edge of the mattress. "Bryan Kendall Hawk the Fourth, you care about me in a way I've never known. You make me feel—safe and alive. That's what I want. Life. This is not grief talking. It's me, Bryan. All of me." She climbs off the bed, takes my right hand, placing it over her heart. "I need you, Bry."

I capture her face in my hands and kiss her. Unabandoned. Unreserved. I claim Dani's mouth because I need her too.

My tongue twists around hers. Finding more of that unchartered completeness only she gives me. Her greed is like mine.

Dani undresses me with single-minded determination. Leaving me no chance to overthink this. But I watch her for signs she's changed her mind.

As I kiss her neck and unzip her dress, I remind myself to pay attention to her words, not the sexy sounds from her throat.

I ease the dress off her shoulders and let it fall to the floor.

The way Dani is standing before me in her dark blue panties and bra is the signal that she is a willing participant in where this is going. And she wants it. But I still need to hear the words.

Her thumbs hook in the waistband of my boxer briefs. Tugging them down to my feet.

Dani lifts my hands, pressing her smooth palms into my rough ones. The spark hits me in the back of my knees and makes the hawk jump. I keep my feet planted and hold my breath.

She smiles and presses her palms against my chest. Her fingers glide down my torso, tracing the abdominal muscle low on my abs. My hawk dances, trying to get her attention. He's impatient for the personal touch of her energy.

Her fingers spend a lot of time on my thighs. Running up and down them, front to back like a sculptor gaining inspiration from lumps of clay.

Dani sits on the edge of the bed and pulls me closer. She takes my dick in her hands. I feel the skin tighten in the warmth of her touch. Before I can stop her, Dani takes me in her hot mouth, fisting what doesn't fit.

My head drops back. Eyes close. Thighs and ass clench to suppress pushing myself in deeper.

Her mouth starts slowly sliding up and down my length while the hand fisting me mirrors her action. Her tongue circles the hawk's head. The pleasure of her unhurried speed only brings me to the edge of release faster. Dani's skills are beyond her nineteen years.

I step back. Breathing hard. Trying to regain control. The hawk protests. But I ignore him.

Dani looks me square in the eyes as she reaches behind her. The straps of her bra slacken, then slide down her arms. She lets it fall to the floor.

I break the eye contact to stare at her breasts. They are exquisite, and her coffee-brown nipples look ready to be worshiped by my mouth, teeth, and tongue.

She stretches out on her back in the middle of the bed with her head on a stack of pillows.

Dani is watching me.

The unspoken invitation to join her is in her eyes.

My feet move on their own or maybe the hawk told them to move. It doesn't matter at this point. I stretch out beside her.

Dani is so beautiful.

I kiss her in a way I've never kissed a woman before. It's personal. Her arms circle around me.

I palm her breast. Circling the nipple with my thumb. Her hips rock and roll against my thigh. I temporarily vacate kissing her to lean down and draw her nipple into my mouth. Sucking it in deep. Branding her nipple with my tongue.

Dani cups the back of my neck. Her moans growing louder and more urgent.

I move to the other nipple giving it equal attention.

She takes my hand, guiding it inside the front of her panties. I feel her heat before my fingers touch her flame.

Oh Damn! She's hairless.

I leave her breast and reclaim her mouth, using my tongue to convey what it wants to do between her legs, at the same time, my palm presses down on her clit as a single finger slips inside her. I hook it and starts rubbing the roof of her pussy—using the beckoning motion to coax her to the edge of an orgasm.

When she gasps, stealing the breath from my lungs with her mouth, I break the kiss to slide down her side and ease her panties down her legs as I go. She parts her thighs for me. An invitation I gladly accept by settling between them and licking her with one, slow, long, swipe of my tongue.

Dani's hips buck and her fingers grip my hair at the roots. I ignore the pain and taste more of her by slipping my tongue inside.

She rocks and rolls her pelvis against my mouth and tongue.

I start tracing a figure eight around the smooth lips of her pussy and the hood of her clit over and over at the same pace of her hips. She holds me captive between her legs.

Her movement stops, and her body tightens.

My name fills the sexual air in the room as Dani comes. Her natural flavor spreads out over my taste buds. And an instant addiction is formed.

We're at the point where penetration for our pleasure is the next step. I get to my feet and put some distance between us to give Dani the physical space to make the final decision.

"If you don't want to do this, I'll walk out of the room, but not out of your life."

Panting from the aftermath of an orgasm, Dani reaches out to me with both hands. "I want to do this with *you*, Bry."

My heartbeat drums in my ears and in my toes. I should be thinking about the job and not my own pleasure, but being Phantom does not belong in this bed with us.

I crawl back between her legs, positioning the hawk's head at her opening, then tangling our fingers and palms together. I peck her lips and rest my forehead on hers.

Slowly my hips move forward, my tip opening her wider. A tight barrier is met.

I ease in a little more and Dani's fingers cut off the circulation in mine. Her entire body is stiff.

My head jerks back like she struck me.

I stare down at her.

My brain yells, *"You have not earned this gift."*

"Please don't stop," Dani whispers.

I close my eyes. *I should stop.* Plus, I don't have a condom on.

Dani untangles a hand and cups my cheek. "It's okay, Bry. I'm okay." Her thumb brushes my lip. "Only you," she whispers.

I can't deny it. I want to *know* her sexually. It gives my soul pleasure to be her first.

Dani's too tense. I want her first time to be nothing but pleasure.

I recapture her hand and explore her neck with my lips and tongue, finding a spot behind her ear that makes her purr. I tickle it with the tip of my tongue and her knees open wider. My teeth capture her earlobe and I bite down as I ease past the barrier.

Inch by inch I ease deeper into her heat. Her walls expand, then mold around me. Dani's face is a mixture of wonder and emotion.

When I'm in as deep as I can go, I give her a minute to adjust to the feel of being fulfilled in the most sexual way. *And* give me a minute to regain some control—she's so goddamn tight I'm ready to come.

I kiss the corner of her mouth. "Breathe, Dani."

She releases the air and her body relaxes, allowing more of me in, and giving my fingers a reprieve.

I ease out half way and ease back in, deeper. I keep the movements slow and unhurried.

I focus on her pleasure by paying attention to the way her body moves. I want Dani to enjoy every bit of this new experience. Hell, I want to enjoy every bit of being inside of her.

Each stroke of the hawk binds her to me. Dani is mine, and I like how that declaration makes me feel inside.

I stare into her eyes and find they mirror my own. She's claiming me. And I want it.

Her pants and moans of pleasure are in time to each stroke. Her walls have my dick in a grip so tight the pleasure hurts. Her pussy is getting wetter.

Dani lifts her head off the pillow. Her body trembles underneath me. Her nails dig into my shoulders and she coats the hawk with her slick, hot come as she orgasms.

In reaction, my balls tighten and draw in closer. I stroke her faster. Harder. First my body tenses as I orgasm, then my mind and body let go. Each squirt of my release brings me pleasure while leaving my mark inside Dani forever.

I put most of my weight on my arms and elbows. We catch our breath in between affectionate kisses. Dani smiles up at me and it makes me happy.

I ease out of her, roll to the side, and pull her into my arms with her head on my chest. We don't talk; that can wait until tomorrow. Tonight, we just live in the moment. Celebrating life.

This is how we sleep, arms and legs tangled. Neither one of us dares to break the connection.

Tonight, I don't dream about the raid. I dream about my first time with the woman in my arms.

My buzzing cell phone wakes me early in the morning. Regrettably, I leave Dani's bed to tend to Phantom business.

When I'm done, I hop in the shower to get the scent of sex off me.

Dani meets me in front of the bathroom door. She looks sexy with her swollen lips and messy hair. I control the impulse to take her back to bed, but I look over her shoulder and see that she's already changed the sheets and made the bed.

Is that her way of letting me know she regrets what happened? Is she subliminally telling me I'm no longer welcome in her bed?

This is new to me. I don't sleep in women's beds. I don't have "the morning after experience."

She looks me up and down like I did something wrong and doesn't respond when I say, "Good morning." Dani walks around me and closes the bathroom door behind her.

I go to the kitchen to make breakfast. Neither one of us ate yesterday. Maybe Dani is hungry and that's why she's acting funny. I start taking ingredients out of the cabinets and refrigerator to make French toast. At the same time, I keep an eye on the bathroom door, waiting for Dani to come out.

The clock hits the three quarter-hour mark and breakfast is ready, but Dani has yet to come out of the bathroom. Is she waiting for me to leave? Is that why she's taking a long time in there?

I make my plate and eat breakfast in front of the television watching the news.

The bathroom door opens an hour after she went in.

Dani makes a plate and joins me on the sofa. No eye contact. No words for me.

I know my reasons for being silent. I don't know hers.

When she finishes eating, she takes our plates back to the kitchen, then pulls out her books and sits at the table.

What the fuck!

My cell phone buzzes from an incoming text message. It's from

Vin.
What's up with you! It reads.
I reply, *will be over in a minute.*

CHAPTER EIGHT

DANIELLE

Colorado, Present Day

"JAMES, I DON'T CARE WHAT your orders are, I'm not going with you."

He is pacing the floor in the master suite. We have been arguing since Mr. Brumfield and Mr. Hopper left the penthouse. It's not like I can call Bryan and tell him what I am about to do—well actually, I can put the earpiece in my ear and tell the person who has been translating to pass along a message.

"You want Hawk to end my life? That's what'll happen if you don't get your ass in that car so I can drop you off at his folks'. He said you're too damn stubborn for your own good."

"What you guys call stubborn, I call standing up for myself."

"He told me if it came down to it, to pick you up and carry you out of here."

I pull the gun from the holster at my side and tap it against my thigh. I keep the safety on and the muzzle pointed at the floor. I am serious about not leaving Boulder until I've found the heir. "You can try."

James stops pacing. A menacing smile creeps across his lips. "I know how to disarm an opponent."

I chuckle humorlessly and make a show of releasing the safety. "Five military certified marksmen trained me on the use of firearms. Go ahead and take that step in my direction so I can show you how well I can hit a target advancing on me."

James and I are in a stare-down.

Him weighing the truth of my words and actions.

Me, on the outside, daring him.

Me, on the inside, praying he doesn't call my bluff. I'm mouthy when I'm being defiant. It's not in me to intentionally harm someone just to get my way. But I need my attitude and body language to put up a good front.

He huffs and resumes his quest to leave his footprints in the plush carpet. "Danielle, please. I'm meeting my wife and son at the hospital. If I don't drop you off at his parents' house, do you really think they'll let me see my family?"

"You had no qualms about putting me in the middle of this. When I don't play nice, it's an inconvenience." It doesn't feel good to say that to him, but I need him to get on board with my plan. "I have errands to run so I'm taking the car."

James takes a step toward me, then his gaze drops to the gun in my hand and he stops. "Put yourself in my shoes. If your husband and children were taken and held captive…"

"My husband and children *are* being held captive, maybe not physically, but we are separated because my grandparents endeared themselves to us and they are the enemy. Look, James, if they win, do you really think your family will be safe? I'm doing this so we can all live without having to look over our shoulders. You are not going to stop me."

I gesture for him to walk out of the room ahead of me. I flip the safety on and holster my gun, grab my backpack, and follow him.

His body is stiff. And his fingers are balled in skin-tight fists, but he walks down the stairs without saying another word in protest.

As if on cue, Marie stumbles out of the bedroom in her sock-covered feet.

"*Bonmatin, tit-fiy…*"

My raised hand halts her speech. "I can't keep up the charade with you anymore, Antoinette. I don't speak nor do I understand the Creole language. I had a translator communicating through an earpiece last night. Damn thing was uncomfortable so I flushed it down the toilet. If you want to talk to me, it'll have to be in English like we've been doing since the day we sat on the patio and watched the girls play in the leaves."

I don't know who I have shocked more, my grandmother, or the man glaring at me.

"James, dear," I tease, "please order my grandmother's breakfast.

And, Grandmother, please behave yourself. James's life already hangs in the balance. Don't make it worse for him." I pick up the keys to the car and exit the penthouse through the elevator doors.

The car is waiting for me. I'd already called down to the front desk and asked for it to be brought to the front and to charge the customary tip to the room. The valet opens the car door for me.

I input the address to Bryan's office building in the GPS system, slip my sunglasses on, and follow the instructions of the automated voice.

The estimated drive time to downtown Boulder is forty-five minutes with traffic.

Hopefully Bryan didn't block my access to his building and computer because the one place I can learn more about the maternal side of my bloodline is at Phantom headquarters.

Once I get there, I will have to play the part of the grieving widow. It won't be hard. I was one nine years ago. The emotional pain was real. My memory of the day the Army chaplain told me James was dead still makes me feel like the air was punched out of me.

I make it to the bottom of the road and merge onto the highway. If I had my phone I could sync it to the radio and listen to music as I fight the morning traffic.

I use the controls on the steering wheel until I find a radio station. It's the sister station of a popular one, based in Los Angeles. The early morning host is Reese Shore. I read on the internet that he and his fiancée, Charly, are getting married at the Goldman Hotel and Resort here in Boulder next fall. Their wedding budget is rumored to be eight figures. Charly is a dessert chef with a specialty high-end shop on Hollywood Boulevard.

On the radio, Reese and his morning crew are cracking jokes about the cheating public official in Kentucky whose wife hired a private detective to follow him. She publicly humiliated him with the picture of him with his mistress at a town hall meeting yesterday. It is all over the news. Now his constituents are demanding he step down from his seat.

The way she did it makes me laugh so hard, tears are running down my cheeks and my son is kickboxing.

I exit the highway onto the surface streets still laughing. In between songs, listeners call in to lend their opinions—cracking jokes too.

Downtown traffic is moving at a snail's pace. Reese's show keeps me distracted until I turn into the garage of my husband's building.

A guard is posted at the entrance. I stop and roll down the window.

"Good morning, ma'am. Do you mind removing your sunglasses?"

Thankfully the laughing-crying tears linger on my eyelashes. I pull the sunglasses off my face and stare the guard in the eyes.

"My apologies, Mrs. Hawk. We have to positively identify anyone entering the building."

Remembering the tips Max gave me about making a lie credible, I inhale deeply, then exhale while saying my line without breaking eye contact. "I won't be here long. There are some papers I need from my husband's office to start making arrangements."

"Of course, ma'am. If you would place your hand on the scanner, I can log you into the building from here. And you can take the elevator from the garage."

He presents the tablet-size scanner. I hold my breath while I wait for the screen to turn green. When it does, the guard signals to the two men inside the garage holding assault rifles.

"You're logged in, ma'am. Do you want me to send someone up to help you retrieve the papers?"

"Thank you, I know where they are." I pull in and park in Bryan's spot.

The first time I visited this building I was anxious about my meeting with Bryan. I remember the sound of my heels echoing in the garage as I walked to the entrance. Today, my boots do not make a sound. The elevator doors open without me placing my hand on the frosted black shield.

The voice of Riley does not ask what floor when I step inside the cab. Since I'm already logged into the building, the elevator automatically stops on the fourth floor.

No one is sitting at the desk to receive me. The fourth floor appears to be physically deserted, but the spirit of the men who normally occupy it cannot be exorcised.

I walk to Bryan's office and close the door behind me.

It feels strange being here without him. His presence is everywhere in this room. The last time I was here, I didn't notice the family pictures hanging on the walls. Bryan even framed the first ultrasound image of our baby. Next to it is the ultrasound picture taken in the emergency room after I fell down the stairs. Emma's artwork decorates the walls too.

I sit at Bryan's desk. The monitor turns on and a hawk glides onto the screen, talons out, ready to strike. I use my code to log in, then click on the documents tab and type Dominique Toussaint.

A large file begins to load. I grab some paper out of the printer and a pen from the holder to take notes.

I skim through the document only picking up certain details.

My great grandfather was left on the steps of Toussaint House—an orphanage in Opelousas, Louisiana—with the umbilical cord still attached, December 28, 1900. He was named by one of the nuns. Labeled a troubled youth. Rarely attended school. Ran away to Vernon Parish, Louisiana, in 1914 and worked as a day laborer at a mill. Lied about his age to join the Army in 1916. Went to France and started speaking out against the American government and its treatment of Coloreds. Dishonorable discharge in 1919. Returned to Louisiana. Married Savannah Watson. Four sons. 1921, Dominique Jr., county judge. 1924 Mathias, family doctor. Twins 1930, Savinien, college professor; and Emilien, editor and chief of *Black* magazine. Resumed speaking out against the United States. Wife and sons moved to Alabama in 1935. Toussaint moved back to Opelousas. Unknown mistress and possible son. Started Rebels Against Government Suppression in 1937. Blinded in right eye after brutal beating on February 20, 1940. Started receiving support from radical groups in other countries. Government wire-taps and surveillance began. Jailed twice. 1943 home set on fire in Lafayette, Louisiana. 1978 found executed in his home in New Orleans, Louisiana. Killer unknown.

Nowhere does it say Dominique Toussaint had a daughter.

I skim through the document again to make sure I didn't miss it.

The next person I research is Willis Percival Langford. Born November 24, 1936 on a small farm in Tensas Parish, Louisiana. Parents Horace and Louisa Langford. Father killed in farming accident. Mother remarried to Joseph Baptiste. Two half-brothers: Joseph Jr. and Clement. One half-sister, Josephine. Joined the Army in 1953 with high MEPS score. Started boxing—more wins than losses. Had to stop boxing after being knocked unconscious in the ring for several hours. In 1958 engaged to Carolyn Lowe. Entered into Phantom. Earned certificate in explosives. Successful completion on Pierre Dupree assignment. Assigned to Marie Beaudry. Cleared Beaudry of RAGS affiliation in November 1959. Married Marie Beaudry in December 1959. Highest number of completed assignments. List of successful missions. Promoted to Major in 1963. Started landscaping business after appointment to Second Command after death of Colonel Eugene Murray in 1968. Daughter Elizabeth born in 1969. Medical retirement in 2005. Onsite Watcher for Colonel Hawk in 2009.

I can't find a file for Antoinette Marie Beaudry or Antoinette Toussaint. I try Marie Beaudry and the document opens. Born June 15, 1941 in Lafayette, Louisiana. Father Thaddeus Beaudry, a reporter and activist, the great-grandson of a Creole who had been living in France. Mother Bernadette Beaudry an activist who'd been living in France was also of Creole descent. Both parents met and married in France, then moved to the United States. Father killed in protest in Clarke County, Mississippi, before daughter was born. Marie was the debate team captain in high school. Played basketball. Worked part-time as a nanny for the children of the mayor of New Orleans. Valedictorian. Enrolled in college. Married Willis Langford December 19, 1959. Associates of Arts degree in political science. Moved to Boulder, Colorado with husband in 1967. Worked as a housekeeper and cook for the Campbell family. Mother moved in, in January 1969. Daughter Elizabeth born March 10, 1969; went missing in June 1985. Mother died of a stroke in March 1986. Part-time housekeeper and cook for Hawk in 2006, became live-in full-time housekeeper and cook in 2009.

There is no mention of a fiancé.

The last file I open is the one on Amelia Caitlyn Goodman born October 22, 1979. I stare at the pictures of her as a teen sitting on horses. Emma looks just like Amelia. The other pictures say before: Amelia Caitlyn Goodman and after: Malinda Williamson. Her face was completely reconstructed and her body surgically enhanced to hide her real identity. I can't believe all this time Emma's biological mother was in our lives and Bryan never said anything. After taking a minute to regroup, I turn my attention back to the monitor. I skip over the basic information and get to when Amelia moved to Colorado in 2004. Worked as a teacher's aide at an elementary school in Fort Collins. Yada, yada, yada. I keep skimming the file until I come across a scanned news article dated June 16, 2005. The body of Amelia Goodman was found seven miles from Dillion Reservoir, death from an apparent suicide. Goodman had been missing for over a month. Loveland police were called to her apartment building in May after a neighbor reported hearing fighting and glass breaking. An unidentified man showed up at the scene claiming to be a friend of Goodman. After being questioned by the police, the friend was allowed to leave. I stop reading and go back to the date of the article. It was written in June. Emma was born December 7, 2005. Bryan hid Amelia, but why?

I close my eyes and try to remember everything he told me before he went running for the burning car. He was talking so fast, and after he said Willis and Marie are my maternal grandparents, it was hard to concentrate on anything else.

When I open my eyes, the screen has timed out. The nature photo of a hawk with piercing eyes stare at me. The left eye is different than the right one. I touch it and the hawk disappears, replaced by a familiar image.

***

Arizona, Nine Years Ago

Today, my soul does not ache. I do not feel weightless and disconnected. My first time was planned to include music and romance. What Bryan and I shared surpassed all the silly fantasies I conjured up by my young self.

He showed respect not just of my body, but of my frame of mind too. Bryan gave me more than the physical act of sex. He made love to me. We made love to each other.

The words he whispered in my ears touched my soul. I do *not* regret giving up my virginity to Bryan last night.

I'm alone in bed but not disappointed. His scent is on the bedsheets and all over me. I know exactly where he is. The shower is running in the bathroom. I should join him. Maybe we can try having sex while we share the shower. We can wash each other with our soapy hands. I smile and open my eyes and kick off the covers. The instant soreness between my legs makes me pause and inhale deeply.

Instead of sex in the shower, maybe we can just wash each other's bodies. I loved running my hands over his thick thighs and wouldn't mind doing it again this morning.

I ease to my feet, ready to join him in the shower.

Wait! Do I knock first and wait for an invitation to join him?

Do I just walk in, pull back the shower curtain, and get in with him?

What *is* the protocol for the morning after?

I look back at the bed as if the answer lies in the rumpled sheets. The slight stain of blood on the spot in the middle of the bed stands out.

I slip on an old T-shirt that barely comes mid-thigh, then go about pulling the covers off the bed. I drop them in the laundry basket. I'll do laundry this afternoon. Shoot, I didn't get detergent. The knobs squeak and the sound of the shower is gone. If Bryan goes out today, I'll ask him to pick up some detergent for me.

I get fresh sheets from the linen closet and make the bed and straighten the bedroom.

On my way across the hall, the bathroom door opens, and Bryan walks out dressed in basketball shorts, T-shirt, and running shoes. He mumbles something that sounds like good morning, then looks over my shoulder like he's anxious to get somewhere. I step out of his way into the bathroom and close the door.

What was that about?

I fill the tub with hot water and add drops of lavender oil.

The image in the mirror over the sink makes me chuckle. My hair is a tangled mess. My lips look like they were injected with an enhancement drug. My eyes are puffy from crying all day. My neck and chest are sporting evidence of being kissed and loved last night. And I smell like sex and Bryan. Okay, I understand why he couldn't look at me.

Swirls of steam hover over the water. I get in, lean back, and close my eyes. The soreness between my thighs starts to go away.

My mind drifts to James.

Seeing him in the casket at peace gave me some closure. He was not himself the days before his deployment. My torment was that he suffered before taking his last breath. But his face was relaxed just like it is when he sleeps.

I whispered goodbye and thanked him for being my best friend.

The most difficult part of all this was watching the casket lower into the ground. It made everything final. James is never coming back. My roots in this world are gone forever. A different kind of pain ripped through me. The desolation was too much to bear. The only thing keeping me from giving in was Bryan's warmth surrounding me.

He held me while I cried. I felt the comfort of his beating heart against my back. At one point, Bryan softly sang to me while he stroked my hair and the darkness started to give way to the light.

I made the conscious decision to tuck away my grief, and live life by sharing my body with the man who genuinely cares about me. It shows in the depths of his hazel eyes and in the care of his touch and in the way he relinquished control to me.

The water is now cold. *How long have I been soaking?*

I pull the stopper from the drain and stand. The knobs squeak when I turn on the shower. While Bryan is here, I'll ask him if he can do something about the sound the knobs make.

I quickly wash up, then get out.

While my skin is damp, I moisturize my body and wrap a towel around me.

The smell of bacon and coffee greet me when I open the door. Bryan is sitting on the sofa with a plate in his hand and coffee mug in front of him.

I get dressed. Comb the tangles out of my hair. And go eat breakfast.

Bryan is intently staring at the television. The morning news is on. The violence in Iraq is growing. Suicide bombers are wounding and killing innocent people.

I'll give him space even though I want to pull his shorts and underwear down to his ankles, get on my knees on the floor between his legs, and orally pleasure him. There is no way I'd ever tell a man I've read case studies on fellatio and practiced on cucumbers.

Bryan is still watching the news when I take our plates back to the kitchen then sit at the table with my books and a recording from Professor Bullock.

Instead of concentrating on the lecture, I stare at Bryan. His eyes are focused on the screen, but they do not move like someone who is actually watching television.

I rewind the recording and start again.

Twenty seconds into the lecture, my eyes go back to Bryan.

His cell phone buzzes on the coffee table. He picks it up, then his thumbs drum on the keyboard. He stands and walks out of the door.

Irritated by his abruptness, I shove back from the table, ready to go after him and demand he talk to me. Professor Bullock's voice stops me just as I'm about to take the headphones off. "Grief and how people react to it," Professor Bullock begins.

The hue of my wrath evaporates as I sit back down and listen to the entire lecture.

It did not occur to me that Bryan might be grieving too. From the talks we've had, I didn't think he and James were all that close. But I can't assume they weren't.

Grief isn't the same for everyone.

People may not see my actions as a part of *my* mourning process. They would question why I slept with James's friend the same day I buried him. There is no one-size- fits-all 'To Do' checklist for anyone experiencing a loss.

I stop the recording and put away my books. Homework can wait until later. Getting out of the apartment to exercise will do me some good. I change into my workout clothes, grab my gym bag, and head out.

Yvon waves to me on my way to the garage. I press the button on my alarm remote and the car's headlights do not flash. I do it again as I get closer to my car. The headlights still do not flash. I try the driver's side door and it opens.

I must have forgotten to lock it the last time I was in it. *Which was when exactly?*

It takes four turns of the key for the car to start. I'll call the mechanic's shop and see if I can bring my car in this week.

According to the schedule on the flyer I keep in my car, an advanced kickboxing class starts in forty-five minutes. The instructor whose class I usually take isn't teaching this one.

I make it to the gym in time to go through my warm-up routine, then walk in to the exercise room with the others taking the class.

The workout is brutal, and I know I'm going to pay for it in the morning. It's a class of ten, predominately men. Sean, the instructor, keeps singling me out. This is my first time taking his class and, apparently, he thinks I can't handle it.

The fighter in me perseveres through the hour and thirty minutes of intense kickboxing. The last twenty minutes of class time, we each have a two-minute one on one with Sean where we get to execute three combinations.

My first combination, I intentionally go easy.

The second one, I give it all I've got, and Sean drops to the mat with a wide-eyed glare tossed my way. While my classmates hoot and cheer, I bow and curtsey at the applause, then offer my hand to help Sean up—which he ignores.

He moves on to the next person. I guess he doesn't need to see my third combination. Mr. Franklin would be proud.

I float out of the gym with Sean's annoyed glare following me.

"Hey, Danielle."

I smile up at the six-foot, ex-professional kickboxer standing in front of the glass doors, about to walk inside.

"Hi, Rodrick."

"You coming from Sean's class?"

My smile grows bigger. Rodrick knows what I'm capable of.

"Yeah. I don't think he likes me much."

Rodrick's loud belly laugh draws the attention of people inside and outside of the gym. He holds up his hand and I have to jump a little to high five him.

"It's against company policy to badmouth a fellow instructor." He waves goodbye and goes inside.

I weave my way through the parking lot to my car and get behind the wheel.

It won't start.

Not even four turns of the key and a plea to get it to the shop this week will get the engine to turn over.

Just perfect!

I open my wallet and get out my membership card and reach for my phone to call a tow truck. The customer service representative tells me it's an hour wait time. There is no way I'm sitting in the car for that long.

I weave my way back through the parking lot and go inside the juice bar next to the gym. I get a peach-flavored drink, then walk over to the super discount department store a few doors down. Now is as good a time as any to pick up the things I was supposed to last week.

An hour and fifteen minutes later, the tow truck shows up and my car is hooked up to it. I ride with the driver to my mechanic's shop.

The mechanic says she won't be able to get to it until tomorrow morning, but will call me before she does the work.

I walk home in the dry Arizona heat at two o'clock in the afternoon carrying four bags plus my gym bag. I didn't think things through when I went shopping.

The apartment is empty when I make it back. I guzzle down a cold glass of water, turn on the air, then go to the bathroom to take a lukewarm shower.

Standing under the spray, I let the water consume me. I chuckle to myself when I think about the look on Sean's face when he hit the floor. Many sparring partners underestimate me—that's a good thing.

The front door opens, and I hear Bryan belting out an old Ginuwine song. Since I left the bathroom door open, every note carries to me.

I peek around the curtain and stare at his reflection from a corner of the mirror. He is walking toward the bathroom. The cords from his earbuds cut across his shirtless torso, stopping at the band around his well-defined bicep. Just outside the door, he bends at the waist and one at a time, sheds his running shoes and sport socks.

He attempts a two-step but can't pull it off. I clamp my hand over my mouth to stifle my laugh.

Thumbs hooked in the waistband of his basketball shorts, Bryan walks into the bathroom and freezes, mid note.

The air in the bathroom takes on an unexpected life of anxious buoyancy.

He takes the earbuds out.

I peel back the shower curtain and bare myself to him completely. "I won't apologize for what we did, Bryan. It was special. What I will apologize for is being selfish and not taking into consideration how you were feeling about burying your friend." I step out of the tub and reach for my towel.

Bryan places his hand over his heart. "I genuinely care about you, Dani. What we did meant a lot to me. But you were quiet this morning and I thought you were regretting it."

I get closer to him and take his hand, intertwining our fingers. I cup his cheek with my other hand and look him in the eyes. "No, Bryan. I'm happy that my first time was with you. And I'm sorry I didn't tell you I was a virgin."

His hazel eyes shine with his smile. "That was a first for me too."

"You were a virgin too?"

We laugh together and the air shifts between us.

"No. I meant it was my first time with a virgin."

"If I had my wish, we would have done it in the shower this morning."

Bryan brings our entwined fingers up to his lips. "If I had my wish, we'd do it right now."

I drop my towel and step into the tub. He unwraps the band around his arm, dropping it on the counter, and steps out of his basketball shorts and underwear. I admired his body by lamplight last night. But in the light of day, I get to see all of him. I commit to memory everything. The light dusting of chest hairs. The number of packs in his abs. The trail of pubic hairs from his navel down to the thick nest around his penis. Those magnificent thick thighs and long legs and decent male feet. From the mirror I see the muscles in his back, the curve of his butt cheeks, the back of his thighs and defined calves.

He joins me in the shower.

We soon learn that the space is too small for two people, but with a little creativity, we manage to use our hands to cleanse each other's bodies.

He turns the water off. I lead him into the bedroom letting the cool air surround and dry our wet bodies.

With Bryan on his back, I climb on top and straddle his hips.

I start by taking my time kissing his neck. His erection dances between my legs, brushing my clitoris. I rock back and forth on him because I love the way it makes me feel.

His fingers dig into my hips, halting the motion. The throaty sounds of him maintaining self-control are intoxicating.

The exploration of him with my mouth continues in a southern direction. Bryan is not a research subject. I turn off the case study details floating through my head and just go on instinct based on *his* responses.

I grip his penis in one hand. The flat of my tongue glides up the length of him. I settle on my knees between his legs and lick him again. Bryan's chest rises and falls rapidly, and his sexy bottom lip is caught between his teeth. Over and over, the tip of my tongue traces the rim of his penis lingering on that bundle of nerves just under the head.

He moans, "Please, Dani."

Bryan supports himself on his elbows. Our eyes connect. I open my mouth, sheath my teeth, then take in as much of him as I can without gagging.

"Shit," he sings.

My mouth slides up and down the smooth skin of his erection. Stroking him. Pleasuring him.

"This feels *so* damn good." He cups the back of my head with one hand while the other overlaps my fisted hand around him. I relax my throat and take him in deeper.

I relinquish control and increase the pressure of my suction. Bryan urges me to go faster by directing my head and my hand. He's guiding me on how to orally please him.

This is for his pleasure and the heady feeling it gives me is echoed between my thighs.

The sounds he's making and the explicit words he's whispering are making me wet with a craving to be filled by him.

"Dani, I'm about to come. If you don't want it in your mouth, please stop right now!" He relaxes his grip on my head only.

I continue to suck him.

His hold around my fisted fingers tightens.

I watch his face.

Bryan hisses. His body grows taut. Mouth twists. Eyes squinch. He chants as my first full taste of a salty treat coats my taste buds.

We keep stroking until he's no longer using my uvula for target practice and his body is limp.

"Come here, Dani," Bryan says in between each breath. He grips my shoulders, helping me to climb up his body.

I straddle his hips. He brushes the hair out of my face and kisses me, deeply.

There is an unspoken emotion that he is expressing through this kiss that makes my heart happy.

His finger hooks under my chin to lift my head so that I'm

looking at him. "You… are so beautiful." He kisses me again. This one coming from deep within him. A place I don't think he even knows exists. His arms snake around me and he holds me tight, like he wants us to become one person.

He rolls me onto my back and orally gives me two orgasms before he enters me.

We explore each other's bodies until the sun sets. Then Bryan and I get dressed and go out.

For the week he is in Arizona, we make love every morning before I leave for work, go out in the evening after I finish my homework, make love before falling asleep in each other's arms.

I take him to the gym. He embarrasses the hell out of me by taking over Sean's class and telling the poor guy he wouldn't last one minute in a real kickboxing ring with me. To emphasize his point, Bryan comes after me. With space and opportunity, I go full out on showing off my kickboxing skills.

The afternoon he leaves, Bryan promises to call every evening.

True to his word, he does.

I vent about my summer school class or the lazy therapist at the clinic. He listens.

He vents about the pressures of getting a business up and running. I listen.

We have phone sex.

We have friendly debates over my refusal to allow him to pay for the repairs on the car because it seems every week I am getting something fixed.

Bryan and I get into an argument over me not letting him put a down payment on a new car for me.

"We're almost in July. You live in *Arizona*, Danielle. It's a hundred and two at night. I can imagine how hot it is during the day. You need a reliable car, with air conditioning, to get you around. Why are you being so stubborn?"

"Why can't you accept that I have to do this on my own? My summer school class is ending soon. After that, one bus gets me to work, to the gym, and back home. If it comes down to it, I'll find a cheaper apartment and get a new car. Until then, I'm driving *my* car 'til the wheels fall off."

We hang up without saying good night.

The next afternoon, I'm off from work and Professor Bullock's assistant calls to say class is canceled today. I sit at the table with the bills, the calendar, unopened bank statement, and my checkbook in front of me. There is an envelope for James from a bank that is not the one we have a joint account with. I set it aside and sort the bills by due dates, then start writing it on the calendar. The red circle around a date in the beginning of July sends a chill through my body.

I flip back to June and see the same red circle. I flip back to May and see the X through the red circle around the date. I flip all the way back to the beginning of the year before returning to the June calendar.

"Stress," I tell myself. "Stress from James's death, the summer school class, and the car. That explains why my period is thrown off and I did not have one this month. It's because of stress."

"Or you could be pregnant," defiance whispers. "You and Bryan haven't used protection.

"Stress!" I rebut, not wanting to think of the possibility that I am pregnant.

When defiance doesn't object, I pick up the envelope addressed to James and open it. The statement inside is for a savings account.

I unfold the statement and drop it. "No way," I whisper as I stare at the balance.

Without touching the bank statement, I read the balance again, then pick up the phone and call the customer service number. Of course, they can't give me information about the account over the phone. I write down the list of things I need to bring with me to the closest branch.

From a dresser drawer, I pull out the documents and lay them on the bed while I get dressed.

I take the bus downtown to the bank.

My knee bobs up and down as I stare out the big window and wait for my name to be called.

"Danielle Tatum," the accounts representative calls out.

I stand and shake her hand. She introduces herself as Mele Vain-ikolo. She offers me a small bottle of water, which I accept, and then we go to her desk.

She smiles. "How may I help you, Ms. Tatum?"

Her friendly demeanor immediately puts me at ease.

"My husband, James Edwards, died in May. I received this statement for a savings account he supposedly opened. I want to verify that he is not the victim of identity theft. Here are all the documents I have as proof of kinship along with his death certificate."

Mele reviews the papers and asks to see my driver's license. Once I hand it to her, she types on the keyboard while looking at the computer screen.

"The savings account was opened at this branch with a valid driver's license and military identification card." She turns the monitor to show me the nonsmiling face of James on the cards scanned into their banking system. She moves the mouse and clicks on a tab and his signature appears at the bottom of a document.

"That is my husband and his signature. What about the balance?"

She taps another key.

Only two transactions have been made. One for a thousand dollars to open the account. The other, a wire transfer of funds into the account in the amount of one hundred fifty thousand dollars was made the day James left for Iraq.

"Ms. Tatum, are you okay?"

My head is swimming.

Where did James get that kind of money?

I drain the bottle of water in my hand and ask for another. Mele jumps up from her desk, returning with four more bottles. I drain them and take deep breaths until I start to feel better.

"I'm sorry," I tell her. "This is… I am… What are my options?"

"A copy of a letter regarding his living trust is on file. We can open an account for you, transfer the money, and close this one. We can also issue you a cashier's check and you can deposit it into an account you already have with another bank. I can see if the investment consultant is available to speak with you. Our bank has various types of retirement investment accounts you may want to consider."

I exhale. "Thank you, I think I will speak to my tax person before I do anything."

Mele hands me a business card. I thank her for her time and leave the bank.

The bus stop across the street from the bank offers shade from the sun and a bench. The next bus is coming in twelve minutes.

My knee bobs again, but not from nerves. With all the water I drank my bladder is full. I look around for a public restroom. I can't hold it until I get home.

Behind me, green letters outlined in white advertise free pregnancy tests in the window of a family planning clinic.

"Why not prove me wrong?" defiance challenges.

"I know it's stress. But to rule out the possibility, I'll take the pregnancy test."

There are two pregnant women in the small, air-conditioned waiting room when I walk in.

"I'd like to take a pregnancy test, please."

The receptionist smiles and hands me a clipboard. "Fill this out, please."

It asks the basic questions. I stand at the window and complete the form, then hand back the clipboard.

"Come on through." The door by the reception window buzzes. When I'm in the office area, she hands me a clear plastic cup with a red cap, and two packets of feminine wipes. She directs me to the restroom down the hall.

My feet move fast down the tiled hallway to the unisex restroom. While I struggle with the toilet seat cover dispenser, I do a little variation of the pee-pee dance.

It is a close call, but I manage to get the seat cover on, my pants down, and keep my panties dry. I fill the specimen cup.

I'm shown to a small exam room. A nurse takes my blood pressure and temperature, then weighs me. I'm the same weight I was in high school. Instead of recording my medical stats in a computerized system, the nurse writes them on a chart in a patient file with my name on the tab. The nurse lays out two testing sticks in foil wrappers, then leaves the room.

I don't have to wait long before there is a knock on the door and a man in his mid to late sixties, walks in. He introduces himself as Dr. Henry.

He verifies the date of my last menstrual period, washes his hands then covers them with exam gloves, and tests my urine with both sticks.

Dr. Henry asks what forms of contraception I use. Do I have multiple sex partners? I answer each question truthfully, yet I cannot tear my eyes away from the double red lines in not one, but both test strip windows.

I vaguely remember leaving the clinic with a next appointment reminder card, paperwork, pamphlets, and a small white paper bag in my hands.

Getting on the bus and off at the stop down the street from my apartment is a blur.

My body is on autopilot because my mind is on something else.

Tonight, and the next night, and for several more nights, I don't answer Bryan's calls.

CHAPTER NINE

BRYAN

Colorado, Present Day

THE FAT SUIT DOESN'T SLOW me down from climbing the ladder to the roof with a duffle bag full of explosives and wiring tools, and a backpack on my back. The belly takes some getting used to, but I make it to the top and immediately get out my laptop.

I pull up the notes Vin gave me on the location of the cameras. Langford used Vin's security company to upgrade to a web-based system last year. The cheap bastard didn't add enough cameras to give a three-sixty view of the entire warehouse.

Even without Vin's notes, I can point out two areas on the roof that make the company vulnerable to the point where the people inside won't know the enemy is on top of them. Like right now for example.

I log into the security system to keep an eye on the activity of the men and women inside. The receptionist is at her desk. I watch her, watching me. I bend to unzip the duffle bag and give her a good view of the crack of my fabricated fat ass.

Tony marked the best places to put explosives throughout the one-story structure on my copy of the blue prints. We want it to implode, not send brick and mortar flying and damaging the other warehouses in the complex.

It takes me thirty minutes to get one explosive wired and hidden. I kept referring to Tony's instructions. He's the expert. Years of watching him do it didn't prepare me for doing it on my own. But now that I've got this one done, and the solid green light is on, the others shouldn't take as long, barring any interruptions.

To keep up appearances, I move in and out of view of the camera, writing notes on the work order. I'm starting to sweat inside of this suit.

Wiring two-dozen demolition explosives on the roof of a warehouse this size takes some time. To the untrained eye, the material blends in with the anatomy of the building. Someone like Tony would spot them right away. Langford is a military certified explosive expert too. There is the possibility he may spot one or two of the boxes I just implanted, but I doubt his old ass will climb up here to investigate if he arrives before I'm done. He's the one who created the smoke bomb casings for RAGS.

I pack up and climb down.

From the van, I get the backpack of explosives and go inside.

No one pays attention to me as I move around the interior of the building. The handful of employees are sitting around gossiping about our deaths.

I climb up a ladder to the rafters—where there are zero cameras—to freely attach explosives to structural support pillars.

Over the cubical area that once belonged to the Field Operatives I eavesdrop on a phone call between Langford and Ivan Jones. If Jones was worried about discretion, he wouldn't have his boss on speakerphone.

Ivan Jones was the Delta Team Lead when Langford was in charge of Phantom. I let him go because he is a lazy sonofabitch who gossips all day instead of doing his damn job.

"Is it true Hawk and his team are dead?"

"Their bodies have been positively identified. That's what I've been doing most of the morning," Langford claims.

He's lying.

"Have you been in contact with POTUS? When is he gonna reinstate you?"

"I haven't been able to reach him. I *am* the logical choice. None of the people Hawk brought in are qualified. Too many bitches in lead positions."

Well damn, Langford, why don't you tell him how you really feel about the women in Phantom.

"Anything going on over there?" Langford asks.

"It's been pretty quiet. Some asbestos guy is checking out the building. Abigail's keeping an eye on him."

"Make sure you cover all areas he's been in. I wouldn't put it past my enemy to send someone in to see what I'm doing."

"Will do, sir. I'll see you in a little while."

A male enters the cubical. From where I am, I can't see his face. "Was that the boss?"

That's Mitchells. He was on my security detail until he requested a transfer to a different assignment. That's how Mills ended up on my detail.

"Yeah, he'll be in later. You need to talk to him?"

"No, it's nothing big. I heard from my boy Hatchett over at headquarters. He said Hawk's wife is in the building. Fool thinks he's got a shot at her. Claims he's going to bend her over Hawk's desk and fuck her 'til she forgets her own name." He laughs and so does someone else. A female I don't have a visual on. If I move to get a better view, they'll notice me.

"He should not be talking like that on the work phone."

I don't recognize her voice. She has a heavy Middle Eastern accent.

"He's ballsy, but that's what we need. Couldn't convince nobody else to be our eyes and ears over there after Hawk got shot," Mitchells comments.

"Fontenot," I whisper.

"Already on it, sir."

Sounds like they've been busy haunting my house.

Hatchett is a damn good Watcher. Realistically, I can't go around gouging out the eyes of every man who stares at my wife's ass— she's got a nice ass—but telling someone he's going to fuck her on my desk—I can't give him a pass on that.

When I'm finished here, I'll deal with him.

Being the youngest Second Command in the history of Phantom, I've come to accept no matter how much I put into building a strong organization, there will always be someone trying to tear it down because they think I didn't deserve the position.

When I moved headquarters from this warehouse, I started going level by level weeding out the weaklings to bring in more skilled men and women. Some Ghosts didn't cross over quietly.

I set the last device in place and climb down out of the rafters.

I intentionally walk past the trio in the cubical, touching the frame of my glasses to snap photos of the woman.

Abigail is on her feet and apparently waiting for me if I'm judging her body language correctly. I hand her the invoice to sign while I make a show of storing my equipment in my bag. She keeps her copy and hands me back the original.

"Someone from the company will be in contact once they've had a chance to read over my findings."

"I will let my boss know," she says.

I bring my hand to my mouth and blow her a kiss goodbye. Her wide-eyed, mouth-drop expression follows me out the glass entrance door.

Although the countdown clock is ticking, I keep my pace down the stairs and to the van casual. When I slide the side door closed, I catch a glimpse of Abigail pressed against the warehouse entrance door in my side eye. I walk around the front of the van and ease into the driver's seat.

The van's engine turns over and I rev the engine. Abigail now has both hands on the glass, about to push the door open.

The timer on my watch beeps. I give a little smile and wave and shift the gear in reverse; peeling out of the stall. Quickly, I shift into drive and the van speeds away.

I glance in the rearview mirror in time to see the warehouse collapse like it was made from toothpicks, flour, and water. The mushroom dust cloud shoots toward the sky, temporarily obscuring my view.

I'd planned on going back to the bunker to get out of the fat suit. Hatchett is the reason I turn left onto the street, heading to my building.

Lunchtime traffic is light, and it takes me fifteen minutes to get there.

I reach the parking garage. The van takes up two spaces because of the haphazard way I park it. I leave the wig, glasses, and contacts in the van.

For the second time today, I access the underground passage to the first floor facility in my building.

I set up Edwards's cell, then shut down the lights in the section and set off the emergency sensor.

"Fontenot, act as the Watch Team Leader and send Hatchett to the first-floor to investigate a sensor alert in section C. Disable the elevator he uses once he's down here."

"Copy that, sir."

I sit and wait.

It's not long before I hear Hatchett's footsteps echoing as he walks. No one except for the Elite Special Operations Team has access to this section of the facility. He is unfamiliar with the lay-out. If he goes to the left, he'll be heading in my direction. If he goes to the right, he'll be heading in the direction of the SCIF.

To make sure he comes to me, I activated the red swirling light in the cell. When he approaches, he'll see me sitting in a chair with my back to the sliding glass door. I left it opened.

Hatchett is slowly approaching now. From the angle of the chair, he won't see the gun in my left hand resting on the arm of the chair.

"Identify yourself," he commands.

The sound of his cocky voice is enough to make my monster want to jump out of this chair and kill him where he stands in the middle of the hallway.

"I said identify yourself, muthafucker." The distance of his voice sounds like he's crossed the threshold.

Hatchett's reflection goes in and out on the other glass wall.

I remain statue still by holding the air in my lungs.

Hatchett starts sidestepping a wide semicircle. "Hey, asshole. Did you hear me? I said identify yourself."

Face blank. Eyes fixed straight ahead. I teach my monster the value of patience by waiting for the prey to step into the trap.

This will be an easy kill.

Two more steps and Hatchett is now standing fifteen feet in front of me, firearm aimed at my head. His eyes locked on mine.

The glow from the red swirling light dances across our faces.

Hatchett's eyes narrow. His eyebrows become one.

I know the exact moment he realizes who is sitting in the chair.

Bang!

Bang!

Bang!

Arizona, Nine Years Ago

Dani freezes just inside the door of her apartment when she sees me sitting at the table. Flames burn on the wicks of two white candles on either side of a vase filled with different shades of closed pink and white roses. A glass of the best red wine is set by each plate. And dinner waiting for her.

My palms become sweaty, and my breathing is uneven. I stand on steady legs and go to the door, closing and locking it behind her. I relieve Dani of her backpack with one hand and grip her wrist with the other.

On the way to the table, I toss her backpack on the love seat.

She's not resisting. Maybe we can talk about whatever's bothering her while we eat dinner. Afterwards, we can have a different kind of conversation with our bodies.

I pull out the chair and wait for her to sit.

"Bryan, why are you here?"

I wait until I'm seated across from her to answer. "Every night for weeks, I've called you, just like I said I would, and every night you haven't answered my calls. I started to get worried, so I came to Arizona. I bought you roses. Made you dinner. Set the table for you. And poured you a glass of wine. Dani, if you want to tell me to fuck off, you'll have to tell me to my face." I pick up my knife and fork and cut a piece of the tender pot roast and put it in my mouth. "Not to brag about my cooking skills, but damn, this tastes good." I eat a stalk of broccoli and watch Dani. She hasn't picked up a utensil.

The skin of her knuckles tightens from the grip she has on the edge of the table. She swallows, audibly. Beads of sweat break out on her top lip. I put down my knife and fork.

Dani shoves her plate to the side so hard, I have to reach out and stop it from falling off the table.

"What the hell?"

She strains to say something but closes her eyes. When she opens them, she grabs the glass of water and take a long drink.

"Don't tell me you're not eating because I bought the food and made it?"

"No." She jumps up from the table and walks fast toward the hallway.

I jump up too and cut off her escape.

Dani tries to push past me.

I stand my ground.

"Move," she growls.

"No. Not until you tell me why you're blowing me off."

"Bryan, plea…" Dani's body lurches forward. She gags, then chunks of —I don't know what—land on the hem of my suit pants and leather shoes. This time when she shoves my shoulder, I let her go.

Dani runs for the bathroom.

I kick off my shoes and follow behind her.

She's on her knees with the toilet seat up. I wedge myself between the sink and Dani, on my knees too, and pull her hair back, out of her face.

I feel helpless watching her body strain and heave as everything in her stomach comes up. Words of comfort spill from my mouth without a thought of what I'm actually saying.

Dani's body relaxes, and she sits back on her knees. I reach for a small towel, wet it in the sink, and wipe her mouth.

She rests one hand on her stomach, the other on a knee.

"How long have you been sick?"

Her head drops back, eyes fixed on the ceiling, she takes several deep breaths. "I'm not sick."

I wet another towel and press it against her forehead. "Then what's going on with you?"

Dani ducks away from the towel and reaches for the countertop to use as leverage to get to her feet. I throw the towels in the sink and help her up.

"I'm fine."

I'd believe her if she were steady on her feet and would look me in the eyes. "Talk to me, Dani. Why are you ignoring me?"

"I've been busy, Bryan. You're not the center of my life. I've got a lot going on."

"Let me help you with whatever it is."

Tears sparkle in her eyes and she still avoids eye contact. "I don't need your help," she whispers.

"Normally I like your independence, but when it's making you sick, I find it irritating."

"Then go. Get out."

"What?"

"You can't handle the fact that *I'm* in control of *my* life so leave me alone."

"Is that what you really want? Stop calling and coming to see you? Leave you and your independence to figure it out?"

"Yes." She brushes past me, heading to the bedroom. Slamming the door behind her.

Something in me I can't explain stops me from leaving. It just seems important that I clean up first. I start with the spot on the living room floor, then the bathroom. Dani knows I'm still here. It's not like I'm tiptoeing around. I put the food in plastic containers and store them in the refrigerator, pour the wine down the drain, and wash the dishes. Dani stays in the bedroom.

Get your shit together, Hawk. She told you to leave her alone. Stop making a fool of yourself and get out.

Retrieving the stolen information is still my primary focus, and by default, so is Dani. I'll leave her alone for tonight, but I cannot leave her alone until I've completed my assignment.

Something is going on and I'm determined to find out what it is. What if Islam Liberation Army or RAGS has found a way to get to her without me knowing and is pressuring Dani for the information? I've been so busy with Phantom business, Hawkeye business, and appeasing Amelia, I haven't been monitoring Dani's activities personally.

I spend the night in the apartment across the street, watching Dani on the computer monitor.

She eats French fries with chili, pastrami, and pickles—yuck—with her feet up on the coffee table, reading a book.

After a shower, Dani picks up the suit jacket I left, slips her bare arms through the sleeves, then turns off the lights and goes to bed.

On my laptop, I open the Phantom personnel roster and filter out all the male Shadows. It's a shame the number of females in Phantom is low. For a powerful entity, the lineup of females reads like a bunch of benchwarmers. I do a wider search, then select two female Watchers that come close to what I'm looking for. I call them.

Getting any sleep is impossible. I sit and watch Dani on the monitor. She's cuddled up with a body pillow and the sounds of her soft snores filter through the speaker.

At six forty-five in the morning, Dani leaves the apartment.

With a baseball cap pulled down low to hide my face, sunglasses to hide my eyes, and a backpack, I haul-ass in the opposite direction to make it to the bus stop a quarter-mile ahead of the one Dani is walking to.

The bus pulls up just as I reach the stop. I pick a seat in the back where I have a view of the front door.

I count a dozen people already on the bus.

Dani is standing at the bus stop with five other people. One in particular, a man in blue hospital scrubs, is standing too close to her for my comfort. The two are talking, and when the door opens, his hand conveniently slips to the small of her back. I know Dani wouldn't just let a man touch her in such an intimate way, so his hand must be hovering at the small of her back. Mr. I-Want-To-Lose-A-Hand-Today steps aside and lets her board ahead of him.

I can't tell if he's staring at her ass and that's a plus for him. He won't lose his eyesight today, just his hand.

The Cozy-Duo find seats together at the front of the bus. Bits and pieces of their conversation float back to my ears. So far, it's nothing *couplish* or top secret.

By the eighth stop, the bus is filling up, and the heat coming off my body is fogging the window next to me despite the cool air flowing from the vents. This guy is too friendly with my Dani.

A passenger exits through the rear door. Warm air rushes in and Dani looks over her shoulder in my direction. I do something repulsive, I pick my nose. The gesture helps to hide my face.

Dani's forehead wrinkles and her eyes narrow. Shit, I thought for sure she'd stop looking. Normal people do.

Mr. I-Want-To-Lose-A-Hand-Today says something and Dani turns around. She waves to the female boarding the bus.

Okay, I won't chop his hand off—I'll just break it.

I get a rag from my backpack and wipe my finger.

At the next stop, a couple of passengers exit through the rear and I change seats. I make sure no one is paying attention, then shed the button-down shirt. The T-shirt underneath has the image of a 1968 Chevy muscle car on the front. I turn my baseball cap around with the bill in the back and put earbuds in my ears. My head bobs in time to a beat I make up as I go. The earbuds aren't connected to anything.

The trio holds a conversation across the aisle and the bus travels down the street.

More people get on. Less get off.

We're nearing the university area where the clinic is.

The bus gets to Dani's stop, the trio says their goodbyes. She quickly glances to the spot where I *was* sitting, then exits through the front door.

Four more stops and the guy exits the bus through the front. I go out the back. The stop is across the street from the hospital.

He joins the group of people waiting at the light. Some also wearing hospital scrubs, the rest in regular street clothes. I blend in, in the background.

The light turns green and the group begins to cross. I stay on his tail. We make it to the middle of the crosswalk and he shrugs out of one strap to swing his backpack in front of him. Mr. Too-Friendly is distracted.

We make it out of the crosswalk and head toward the lobby entrance to the hospital. He slows up still rummaging in his backpack. I walk past him and linger just inside of the doorway.

The prick isn't paying attention, so he doesn't see me. We collide. The contents of his backpack spill to the floor, scattering around us. I apologize and help him retrieve his belongings. When he isn't looking, I pocket his brown wallet.

He thanks me for my help and clips his hospital badge on the pocket of his shirt. He works in the radiology department.

I head to the exit and find the bus stop to head back to the apartment.

My cell phone vibrates on my hip. I unclip it and answer. "Hawk."

"Where are you?"

"Tailed Dani to work."

"I'm here with Cooper and Watanabe. Want me to pick you up?"

"No, I'll take the bus back. Is Vin with you?"

"He went over to the garage to have a look at Danielle's car before the mechanic gets there."

"You know how to hack a hospital security system?"

"No, but if you walk me through it I'm sure I can."

"Never mind. Go ahead and get started with Cooper and Watanabe. I'll be there in forty-five minutes."

The bus is pulling up to the stop in front of the hospital. I use the ride back to convince myself that jealousy isn't the motivation behind me investigating Mr. Too-Friendly. He could be RAGS.

Tony cocks a questioning eyebrow at me when I walk through the door, but doesn't voice it. He, Cooper, and Watanabe are seated at the table reviewing the details of a Shadow's job. I am acting Second Command and do not have time to trail Dani twenty-four hours a day. Since she is shutting me out, I need more people on the ground here.

After a crash course in being a Shadow, Tony takes Cooper and Watanabe to the clinic where Dani works to give them a hands-on demonstration. There are two vacancies for part-time receptionists at the twenty-four-hour clinic. Cooper and Watanabe are going to apply and I'll make sure they get it. While I wait for Tony to get back, I meet with the Watcher who has been in place since the middle of May. Sergeant Wright tells me Dani hasn't had any visitors and she's been keeping to herself. I tell Wright to work on getting closer to Dani.

On the flight back to Colorado, Vin shows me a list of things wrong with Dani's car. He confirms the mechanic is doing everything she can to keep it running, but it's just a matter of time before Dani will have to junk it.

"Why were you at the hospital?" Tony asks.

I take the wallet out of my bag. "I need a background check on…" I open the wallet and look at the driver's license. "Levi Phillips. He's real friendly with Dani. I want to know if he's RAGS." I toss the wallet to Vin.

Tony elbows me in the ribs. "Do right girl looks good on you, bro."

I huff and flip him a double hawk. The bet is up to thirty-five grand.

The plane touches down ahead of time. Instead of going to Boulder, I drive to my parents' house in Colorado Springs.

As always, my mom and grandmother hug and kiss me like I'm a little boy who went missing and has found his way home. Dad is away at an administrative retreat.

I sit in the family room with Grandmother while Mom is in the kitchen. Whatever she's cooking smells good. My stomach growls reminding me I haven't eaten since the two bites of pot roast.

"What's troubling you, Little Bryan?" Grandma is the only one

I allow to call me that.

"Just tired, Gran."

"Boy, I tell you all the time, your eyes give you away. Even when you try to hide them behind those glasses. Why were you in Arizona?"

"Visiting a friend."

"A friend who has touched you here"—she taps the place over my heart—"and here." She taps my temple. "Tell me about her."

"How do you know my friend is a girl?"

She cocks an eyebrow and twists her lips.

"Dani is independent and gifted. She has a smart mouth and is frustratingly stubborn." My grandmother and I are close. Talking to her is easy and the words pour out.

Except for the top-secret stuff, I tell her everything. I censor the sex part, but my grandmother is no prude.

"She's testing you."

"Why?"

"You said she grew up with no family of her own. She considered the friend to be her family and now he's gone. My guess is, she wanted to see if you'd leave her too."

I drop my head and look down at my hands. "I failed because I left."

"Not necessarily. She didn't tell you to leave her key and never come back."

"But I asked if she wanted me to…"

Grandma lifts my chin with her aged fingers. "You asked three questions—which one did she say yes to?"

"Huh?"

"Which one do you think she answered?"

"All of them."

She pats my cheek. "You are very smart, yet very clueless when it comes to matters of the heart, like your dad. My guess is that she wants you to let her solve the problem on her own before telling you."

"But whatever it is, it's making her sick, Gran."

"When she needed you, didn't she call?"

I let that soak in for a minute. My grandmother is right.

"Have you heard of a do-right-girl?"

An odd sound comes from my eighty-year-old grandmother's

mouth. Her eyes are bright and shining. I don't think I've ever heard her giggle before.

"Yes, I have. Is this young lady *your* do-right-girl, Little Bryan?"

"I don't believe in love. You know that, Gran."

"You don't just *love* a do-right-girl." Her eyebrows dance up and down.

I don't get it.

Gran smacks her lips. "You don't have sex with your do-right-girl because the pleasure you find in bed with her comes from making love."

"Love wasn't in bed with us."

"Little Bryan, I hear what your mouth says, but I pay attention to your eyes when you talk about *your* Dani. She is not like those silly high school girls who used you and broke your heart. This one has tapped into a part of you that even you don't know about. And if your Dani is as smart as you say she is, she'll know to always look you in the eyes for the truth."

My cell phone rings. Colonel Langford's name is flashing on the caller ID. "Sorry, Gran, I have to take this." I answer the phone walking out the patio door.

"Come to the house at zero nine hundred hours."

"Yes, sir. Should I bring anything?"

"Just bring yourself." He hangs up.

Langford has been a pain since they returned from Germany. But he is still officially Second Command and I have to follow orders.

Jessi and her girlfriend, Samantha, join us for dinner. Without Dad here, the atmosphere is light and friendly. Mom sends me home with leftovers for myself and the guys. I make it to my condo a little after midnight. Before I turn in, I check up on Dani. She's already asleep and I see she moved the roses to the dresser in the bedroom. I have the camera zoom in and smile. Dani is wearing my suit jacket again tonight. I'll give her some space for now, so she can work out whatever she's going through.

In the morning, I ring the doorbell at Colonel Langford's house at the requested time.

"It's good to see you up and moving around, sir." I follow him down the hallway. His gait is slow and unsteady. A few times I reach out to grip his elbow to keep him from toppling over. He shakes me off with an irritable grunt.

Langford knew what time I'd be here, yet he's still in his bathrobe, pajamas, and slippers. He needs a shave, a haircut, *and* a shower.

Usually we meet in his home office. This morning we sit in the den.

The curtains are closed and there is a stale odor in the room. His half-eaten breakfast sits on a tray table next to his recliner in front of a big screen TV. He's watching a game show with the volume muted.

"Let's talk, Bryan." The only time Colonel Langford calls me by my first name is when he's mentoring me.

He has aged since the raid in Iraq and it's taking him too long to recover from the injury.

POTUS will be here tomorrow. I was hoping it's to announce when Langford will be reinstated as Second Command. Looking at the man now, I highly doubt it.

Langford's lips start moving yet the words are stuck on his tongue.

"Is Mrs. Langford home? I want to thank her in person for the muffins she sent to the office."

"No." The one-word reply discourages any other questions about his wife's whereabouts.

I watch the game show and wait for him to gather his words.

Three contestants later, Langford finally speaks. "Do you know why the position is called Second Command?"

"No, sir."

"The man in the position is the second most powerful person in our nation. Not even the vice president has as much power as Second Command. It's not a position for just anyone. That much power *will* change even the most honorable man."

A seed of weighted responsibility is planted in my gut.

"Being Second Command, you will be forced to make difficult decisions. You'll never have a day off, even if you're at home. Vacations can't be planned because protecting the United States of America will always come first. Twenty-four hours a day, seven days a week, there's always some level of threat that needs to be assessed and handled by Second Command."

A sprout grows from the seed in my gut.

Where is he going with this?

"The minute I met you, I knew you were a leader. I just needed you to be a great leader. That's why I brought Chen back to work with you. You'll have to appoint a Lieutenant Colonel. Make sure it is someone strong enough to walk in your shoes if he's ever called to do it. It's tradition for the outgoing Second Command to facilitate the transition of the incoming Second Command. Colonel Murray died, and I had to learn the job on the fly. If there's breath in my body, I'm here for you."

Stomach acid is the food for which the sprout grows into a sapling.

"One thing you need to know: Phantom's headquarters must be in Boulder because trainings are held at the university and personnel can take classes and earn degrees. That rule can never be changed. It's how Woodrow Wilson set up the branch. Bryan…"

Don't say it, Langford. Don't you dare say the words. I can't be Second Command. I've got a baby mama who doesn't want the child so I'm going to be a full-time dad in a few months. My business is growing faster than I can keep up with because I'm doing your job *and* my job. And the woman who willingly gave up her virginity to me isn't speaking to me and that is messing with me on so many levels I can't begin to identify them. So please, do not say it.

"…I called you here because I wanted to be the one to tell you—I resigned effective today. President Nelson is coming tomorrow to officially appoint you Phantom's new Second Command. No one your age has ever held the position, but I know you can handle it."

Of all the questions I need to ask—should ask—the one on my mind has nothing to do with the position. "Sir, why did you tell Mrs. Langford Danielle is your granddaughter?"

His huff isn't humorous. It's victorious. "Because Danielle *is* our granddaughter. You were thorough with your background check on her. There were certain things that stood out to me, that wouldn't have to you. The biggest being the similarity of her name to the boy my daughter was involved with, Daniel Lawrence Tatum. She has his color of brown eyes. They don't run on my side of the family, nor Marie's side. Danielle is the right age if my Elizabeth was pregnant when they ran off. The last name on the birth certificate is Beaudry. That is Marie's maiden name. And I contacted the county hospital, it took some time and a lot of money, but I found a nurse who was on duty in the ER on Valentine's

Day nineteen years ago. Showed her a picture of Elizabeth. She remembered my daughter. I did the same with the city morgues and found out what happened to the boy. He and Elizabeth were using different names. I pieced together what happened and told my wife the truth."

"Are you and Mrs. Langford going to introduce yourselves to Danielle?"

"No. Family relations do not take precedence over protecting our country's biggest secret. You know what we do. And you know what will happen if that information gets out. It's up to you to bring down RAGS."

"Danielle isn't one of them, sir."

"She's the type they go after. Her husband was one of them. Just because you didn't find anything in the apartment that links her to them does not mean she isn't one of them."

I *know* Dani isn't RAGS. She's too much of an alpha to be a follower. Going back and forth with Langford about a granddaughter he's never had a conversation with is pointless.

He stands.

I do too.

Langford holds out his hand. "Congratulations, Bryan."

I don't remember agreeing to take the job, but I shake his hand anyway.

Feet dragging, shoulders slumped, head hanging lower than before, Langford leads the way to the front door.

I wait until I'm far away from his house to pull over. I need to process. Filling in as Second Command is a lot different from *being* Second Command.

My life is already in turmoil. Every day, Amelia threatens to give the baby up for adoption if I'm not in the delivery room. I was toying with the idea of having my attorney draw up the papers for Amelia to give up her parental rights, giving me sole custody. Now, it's no longer an idea, it's a plan of action. When I sign the contract for the position, I can't guarantee I'll be there when my daughter is born. I just need to come up with something to dangle in front of her to get her to agree. It has to be something big.

My friends helped me fake Amelia's death to stop RAGS from continuing their search to kill her. If she gives my daughter away, I know my friends will help me dispose of her body after I kill her.

Shit!

Then there's Dani. She's the granddaughter of my mentor. I owe it to her and the Langfords to clear her name and keep her safe. I want to give her the opportunity to know her grandparents.

Once I become Second Command, I'll have to give the assignment to someone else though. That person will do his best to get to know Dani in a way only *I* know her. My heart is on triple time and I'm breaking out in a sweat just thinking about it. The thought of another man touching her brings out the monster in me. I don't know what I'd do to a Ghost who dares to lay down with Dani.

I look upward. "What else you gonna throw at me?"

My cell phone buzzes and I jump in my seat. Grandma warned me not to play with *Him*.

"What did Langford have to say?" Tony asks when I answer.

"Fish Friday still on tonight even though Charly's in Vegas with her friends?"

"I let her fry fish *one* time and you guys can't let it go."

"My stomach still bubbles every time I think of that fish she made."

"Hey, my girl is studying to be a dessert chef, not a food chef."

"Hundreds of stomachs and toilets are thanking her for that." I laugh. "I'll tell you what Langford said over fish and whiskey."

"Ahh. I've got good news too."

"What is it?"

"I'll tell you over fish and the top shelf whiskey you're bringing."

"Make sure you have lots of red snapper."

"Will do. Later, Hawk."

"See ya when I see ya."

Langford's warning about Phantom being first and foremost stays with me for the rest of the day. I'm not even fully Second Command yet and I'm already leaving the office two hours late.

Our monthly fish fry Friday dinner started when we were college roommates. Once a month each of us took a day to cook for everyone. I cooked on the last Sunday of each month.

The minute I walk into Tony's condo, I open the whiskey and tell my friends about Langford resigning and Dani being their long-lost granddaughter. After the shock wears off, their excitement over me getting the position kicks in. And it becomes contagious.

I start to look at ways I can improve operations and still be a good single dad. With their input, I draw out an organizational chart and revamp the duties of each level. We come up with a story to explain the sudden appearance of my daughter in December. Ig suggests plastic surgery and a new identity as the carrot to dangle in front of Amelia.

Over our second glass of whiskey we come up with a plan for Dani that doesn't include me assigning someone else. Tony coughs "do-right-girl" in his hand and passes it on to Vin, who coughs "do-right-girl" too and passes it to Ig, who out and out says, "Do-right-girl."

We stand and salute with our third glass of whiskey to congratulate Tony. He's going to pop the question to Charly with a rare chocolate diamond he paid a year's worth of salary for. Over more fried fish and more whiskey, we help our friend come up with a unique way to ask *his* do-right-girl to marry him.

I am back at headquarters before sunrise to meet with Major Chen. An idea came to mind while I read reports at zero two hundred hours. I want to see how Chen feels about it before I tell the guys. He is vetting surrogate mothers and I don't want my plan to interfere with what he's got going on.

President Nelson arrives at twelve hundred hours. To my surprise Colonel Langford shows up dressed in a three-piece suit and clean-shaven with Mrs. Langford on his arm. I'm promoted to the rank of Colonel, then officially appointed Second Command of Phantom.

From that point on, I am nonstop.

I'm given the official Phantom personnel roster to review before I have a one-on-one meeting with them. I scout the downtown Boulder area for an office building that fits the needs of the Phantom I envision. I write and edit a two hundred-page operation plan I want to implement.

It seems like every hour I'm assessing threats and deciding if sending Field Operatives is necessary.

I go out on missions with Langford's ESO Team. I don't consider them mine because I didn't select them. But that will change once Tony, Vin, and Ig train with Chen.

I fly to Washington D.C. to sign government contracts for Hawkeye Personal Protection. President Nelson and I go over my plan for Phantom. He rejects eighty percent of it, but a few of the key items he approves.

The reports from Cooper and Watanabe are uneventful. Dani's car is down for good. She had a doctor's appointment. Met with a financial advisor. Had a long meeting with her educational advisor. Started the fall semester at the university.

Tony, Ig, and Vin leave for Indonesia with Chen right after we celebrated Tony's engagement. Helping him pull off the proposal was hard; Charly is nosey. My friend is the happiest I've ever seen him, and I'm happy for him. They will be back before my daughter is born in December.

Two exciting things happen on the last Friday in July, I purchase a nice piece of land I want to build a house on. The original house on the property I will keep as a guest house. And I pick up the keys to my new office building. I've already started drawing up the plans for a total remodel based on the security measures I designed.

The data center for the super computer I had down on paper is now under construction. It is an underground multistate project that is half the span of the Rocky Mountains that will take a year to get up and running.

Although Hawkeye Personal Protection is on the contract I negotiate with a big manufacturer, the cars and trucks purchased will be for Phantom too. A Denver based dealership will handle the shipments. Ricci will oversee the modifications.

I meet with the university's president to update the training space needed for Phantom. I am able to secure a building for Ig's medical projects, and a building for Vin's specialties. An offsite building is designated for what Tony needs.

RAGS has been quiet since the botched sell of information.

Amelia signs the papers and my lawyer files them. Because we embellished on the dates, I use my position to push them through. I'm going to name my daughter Emma Rose Hawk. That's the name my grandmother wanted to give her daughter, but she had three boys instead.

The second weekend in August and Dani is heavy on my mind. I've been keeping up with her via the surveillance cameras and reports from the three women watching her. She is searching for a cheaper apartment in neighborhoods I don't consider safe for her.

Dani spends a lot of time on a car manufacturer website. The car note on the luxury SUV she's researching is more than she can handle.

An idea pops into my head.

I find a dealership in Tucson, Arizona, and call the sales department. They have an SUV in stock that matches Dani's specifications. I purchase it over the phone. If I can convince Dani to accept the SUV, then she won't have to move to a cheaper apartment.

The salesperson is so excited about the sale, he offers to pick me up from the airport tomorrow afternoon and drive me back to the dealership to finish the paperwork.

I pack an overnight bag and fly to Arizona.

I am in and out of the dealership in thirty minutes.

Watanabe tells me Dani's new work schedule now includes Sundays. I get to the clinic right at the time Dani gets off.

From where I'm leaning against the front grill of the SUV, Dani can't see me when she walks out, plus she's talking to a coworker. It looks like Dani's put on a little weight, not much, but it looks good on her.

The two-women part ways.

Dani is walking away from the parking lot. It's a warm evening and a slight breeze brushes past me moving in Dani's direction. She stops and lifts her head higher.

I stand up straight.

She looks to the left then the right, then takes off her sunglasses and turns around.

Our eyes connect, immediately.

Dani doesn't frown, nor does she smile.

I take a tentative step forward. She doesn't step back or run away.

I approach her. "Hi."

"Can we talk?" she asks.

"Hey, that's my line." I laugh. "May I take you to dinner?"

"Can we pick up fried chicken from a soul food place that just opened up not too far from me instead?"

"I'll follow you there." I can't let on that I know about her transportation situation.

Dani bites her lip. "The wheels fell off. I'm on the bus until I buy a car."

"Then I guess I'm driving."

She nods.

We walk side by side to the parking lot. Her eyes light up when I open the passenger door to the gray Range Rover with a charcoal gray interior.

"Is this yours?"

"Bought it today." Technically that wasn't a lie. I did sign the papers that have both of our names on them.

Other than her giving me directions to where we're getting dinner, Dani doesn't say much. She's looking around the inside of the luxury SUV.

The restaurant is small, and the line is out the door. I understand why once we get up to the order counter. The food looks good. I let Dani order for us.

The portion sizes the server piles in the take-out containers are enough to feed four people. For dessert Dani gets two slices of pound cake and homemade vanilla ice cream.

I pay for our food and carry the brown bags back to the truck.

Dani stops me from opening the passenger door with a hand on my arm. "Can I drive?"

I hand her the key. The smile on her face chases away any anxiety I was feeling about this reunion. Dani is ready to talk to me. My weight just got lighter.

She sprints around the truck, climbs in and adjusts the seat and mirrors, then fastens her seatbelt. Dani takes a deep breath before she backs out of the stall and turns on to the street.

I don't comment on her taking the scenic route home. If driving this Range Rover makes her happy then she can take it as far as she wants.

We talk about how school is going. She tells me she added two classes to her schedule this semester because she's taking the spring semester off. But doesn't say why and I don't ask.

She pulls into her stall with the ease of someone who drives an SUV all the time.

I open the passenger door while Dani fiddles with the controls on the steering wheel and the ones for the sunroof.

"Push that button on the dash for the hatch," I tell her.

The door automatically lifts, and I get my overnight bag and close it. I get her backpack off the back seat. Dani turns off the engine. With a slight frown, she climbs out of the driver's seat. I follow her to the apartment.

She's stripping out of her clothes as she walks toward the bedroom. I put the ice cream in the freezer and get out the plates.

"Let's sit on the sofa and eat. I need to put my feet up and relax," Dani calls out.

While she's getting dressed, I dish up the food from the take-out containers.

Dani comes back into the living room wearing too short shorts and a wife beater. No bra. She's got a little stomach pouch, but she still looks sexy.

I carry our plates to the living room. She turns on the television and we watch the evening news.

The food is good, but I barely eat it and she's picking at hers.

"I miss you, Dani." It sounds convincing to my ears. Maybe because I mean it.

She sets her plate on the coffee table, picks up the remote, and turns off the TV. "I'm pregnant. I knew I was pregnant the last time you were here. I didn't tell you because…" She shrugs. "I don't know. I guess I wasn't ready for you to know. If you're going to leave, do it now."

Well damn, Hawk, when you decide to become a father you don't half-ass it. Two kids, back-to-back. Two baby mamas. But you knew this could happen since *you* didn't cover up when *you* were having sex with her. How will you explain this to your family?

I set my plate next to hers and take her hand, using my thumbs to draw circles around her knuckles. "Were you ever going to tell me?"

"Yes. But I can do this on my own if you don't want the baby. I have a plan."

"I respect the fact that you think you can do this alone, but I'm going to be a part of my child's life." The smile she gives makes me smile too. "It means I'll be a part of your life too. You don't get to push me away again. I *want* to take care of both of you."

"James left a hundred and fifty thousand dollars in a savings account. I'm investing some of it, putting some in a trust fund for the baby, the rest will stay in an interest earning account."

Whoa! I know I've been slacking in monitoring her accounts because I truly believe she's not RAGS, but this is big. That savings account didn't come up on any of my monitoring of Edwards's finances. When I get back to Boulder, I'll have to do a thorough search to see how I missed it.

"Open the trust account for my baby, but *I* will be the one putting money in it. You're not carrying his kid so don't use his money on *our* baby. And I'm putting you on my health insurance." I never had a reason to monitor her medical records, but I do now.

"I already have a health plan."

"I guarantee mine is better. I want the best for you and our daughter."

"What makes you think it's a girl?"

With the kind of luck I'm having, girls are all I'll have. "Father's intuition. When are you due?"

"February sixteenth."

CHAPTER TEN

DANIELLE

Colorado, Present Day

"MRS. HAWK, ARE YOU OKAY?" Someone knocks on the office door.

I look at the time on the clock on Bryan's desk. I've been here a while. "Yes, I'm fine." I quickly close out the files, log out of the computer and fold my notes, tucking the paper into my back pocket. I pick up some random papers off the conference table, slip my sunglasses back on, and open the door. "Sorry, I just needed a moment."

"It's okay, ma'am. Did you find everything you needed?"

"Yes, I did. Thank you."

He walks with me to the elevator and rides down to the garage too. "If there is anything we can do to help, do not hesitate to ask."

"Thank you…"

"Jansen, ma'am."

"Thank you, Jansen. My family and I appreciate the support."

He stands and watches me get into the car and back out of the stall.

I do not drive in the direction of the highway to go back to the Goldman Hotel and Resort. The public library is two miles south of here. I need to do more research.

On the way, I stop at a corner discount store and purchase a notebook, pen, and prepaid cell phone.

Today, there is an activity going on in the children's section of the library. I go to the second-floor resource desk. The librarian gets me set up at a computer. He leaves me to locate old periodicals with articles on Rebels Against Government Suppression.

While I wait, I find a website where people can research their family history and come across government census records dating back to the nineteen hundreds.

Based on the notes I took from the files on Bryan's computer, I am able to plug some of the holes in the information on Dominique Toussaint. Including the name of the unknown mistress, Henriette Dupree, and their son, Pierre Dupree. I suspect he is the same Pierre Marie told me was her fiancé. My grandmother is a better liar than Bryan.

According to the 1940 census record, Thaddeus and Bernadette Beaudry are listed as residents in the home of Dominique Toussaint. An old saying Mrs. Franklin once told me comes to mind: *when they went down to the creek, they didn't always come back with water.* Now I get the meaning. There is the possibility that Antoinette Marie Beaudry is Toussaint's daughter. Her mother lived in the same house as Toussaint.

The librarian sets a stack of old magazines next to me. "Start with these. I may have found some newspaper articles on microfiche. I will get the machine set up for you when you're ready."

"I really appreciate all your help."

The articles in the magazines are helpful. One published a copy of a handwritten letter from Toussaint outlining RAGS's purpose. His ideals showcased an extensive knowledge of the inner workings of a single political party dictatorship for a man with little to no formal education. He promised equality for every man, woman, and child no matter their race, religion, or wealth. I can see why the government felt threatened by him. He painted a convincingly gruesome picture of the privileged American.

Another article described the violent outcome of RAGS's presence at a rally for the gubernatorial race in Louisiana in 1940 that left Toussaint blind in one eye and several of his followers badly beaten or bludgeoned to death. Bernadette Beaudry was arrested. Thaddeus Beaudry is credited for taking the photos and writing an article that was published in a French newspaper. RAGS did not start the violence, the police officers did, and the supporters, along with RAGS members reacted with deadly outcomes.

At a different RAGS demonstration, Thaddeus Beaudry was killed for not following police orders to stop photographing the officers as they beat and shot those present listening to Toussaint speak. The salvageable photos from Beaudry's camera were published. One photo shows Toussaint using his body to shield a pregnant woman, who could pass for Marie, and a young boy.

On the computer, I do a search for Thaddeus Beaudry and find an interview published in an American magazine in 1931. He said his great-grandfather, a mulatto, escaped slavery with two other young men by convincing the captain of a French trade ship to let them work on board in exchange for passage to France. His great-grandfather married a French Creole singer and they had one son. Thaddeus's grandfather was a photographer and passed the skill onto him. His father, a wealthy entrepreneur, taught him tolerance and acceptance. Thaddeus said he's the youngest of three children, and the only boy. In the article, he talks about experiencing complications from the mumps virus when he was thirteen that kept him out of school for half the year. He describes the love of his life, Bernadette LaFleur, as the woman who opened his eyes to the ways of the world. Bernadette was heavily involved in a political activist group in college. The guest list for their lavish wedding included the elite of Europe. Thaddeus goes on to tell how Bernadette's father, the editor of the biggest political magazine in France hired him for a special assignment where he would live in the U.S. to photograph and document the inhuman treatment of Negro men, women, and children. Thaddeus says he knows his father-in-law chose him for the assignment because of his strong beliefs in equality for all. Their first year in the U.S. was challenging.

The last magazine article I read gives a timeline of RAGS-linked activities. The most interesting is that the radical group's deadly, deliberate confrontational attacks started after Toussaint's death. Prior to that, they were provoked into deadly actions.

I can't find any articles on Bernadette Beaudry, but in every picture of Dominique Toussaint I come across, she is standing slightly behind him. I study each photo, this time using my knowledge as a psychologist to write a profile on her. Her placement behind Toussaint. The look on her face. The clothes she wears. The position of her body. And the distance between Bernadette and Toussaint.

The microfiche proves to be useful as well. The older articles I read help me to develop a profile of Dominique Toussaint.

"Here you go, miss. This is the last magazine we have that references the organization." The librarian sets it on the desk next to me.

Its publication date is March 1974. On the cover of the popular magazine that has been around for nine decades is Dominique Toussaint in a three-piece suit that fits his body like it was made for him. Even the patch over his eye looks custom made. The tie clip is engraved with his initials *DET*. The Rolex watch stands out, but the gold pinky ring with the black onyx stone surrounded by diamonds stands out more. The photographer captured his commanding yet distinguished aura. Inside are photos of him behind the desk at home. Speaking at events. Hanging out at a bar. I smile at the one of him with a little girl running around the yard of his home and him laughing. It is hard to miss the love and joy between the two. I turn the page and gasp at the full-page color photo. The little girl has her arms around his neck. They are cheek to cheek staring at the camera. She has the biggest smile on her face. The jade dolphin charms on the bracelet on her wrist rest against the crisp white collar of his dress shirt. I pause because it's like I'm looking at a picture of me at that age. Her eyes are dark brown whereas mine are light brown.

I remember Marie said she looked for clues when they realized Elizabeth wasn't coming back. What could my mother have left behind that would make Marie search Elizabeth's bedroom? I stare at the picture. Study it. Memorize it.

A smile slowly spreads on my lips.

Mr. Brumfield said he stored my parents' belongings in the basement of his house.

Even though it's against hospital policy, I access my patient files from the public library computer. I jot down Mr. Brumfield's address, then double-check that I've successfully logged out of the hospital's patient information system. I return the materials to the resource desk and thank the librarian for his assistance.

It's almost one o'clock in the afternoon. I wonder how much longer Bryan is going to allow me to be off plan before he sends someone to take me back to the resort.

I stop at a fast food drive-thru and get lunch. Eating while driving isn't something I normally do, but time isn't on my side. My chicken sandwich and fries are eaten while I drive to the next place where I might get the answers I need to help my husband.

Mr. Brumfield is surprised to see me when he opens the door. "Why aren't you in Colorado Springs with your girls?"

"I need to see those boxes that belong to my parents." I brush past him into his living room.

"This is not the time to go through Daniel and Elizabeth's things."

"I think I know who the heir is."

He closes the door. "Who?"

"Elizabeth, but I'm still piecing it together. Please, Mr. Brumfield. If I'm right, Bryan will have something Willis and Marie don't have."

"What's that?"

"The power to strip RAGS of everything."

He leads the way to the basement door in the kitchen. Two big, scary looking dogs bark as they peer at me through the mesh screen door. "*Trankil,* Rainy *avèk* Stormy." He says in Louisiana Creole. Both dogs stop barking right away. They sit and twist their heads to the side. The identical twins stare at me with curiosity. They look like they could come through the door with very little effort if they want to.

"What breed are they?"

"Bullmastiffs. They're brothers. Found them in a box by the side of the road on a rainy and stormy morning a year ago. The other pups were dead. I took them to the vet to make sure they were okay, then brought them home. Very good watch dogs, those two are."

"Are they well behaved?"

"Rainy and Stormy know I'm the only alpha in this house."

Mr. Brumfield flips a light switch and opens the basement door. With the aid of his cane, he walks down the steps into a cool, organized basement. I follow him to a tarp tucked away under the stairs. He removes the covering. The initials DE are written on four medium-sized boxes.

"This is it?"

"Daniel and Elizabeth had to pack light in case a quick escape was necessary. What are you looking for, Danielle?"

"In the hospital, Marie told me the night Elizabeth and Daniel went missing, she went to Elizabeth's room to look for clues to their whereabouts. Whatever Marie was looking for, Elizabeth took with her. And I think it's the document that names Elizabeth as Dominique's heir."

"You do know ninety-nine percent of what she told you was a lie?"

"Yes, I realize it."

"Go set up that card table folded in the corner over there and I'll carry the boxes over. Elizabeth was adamant about not leaving her journals and jewelry box behind."

I do as he says and unfold the legs of the card table, standing it upright. He toddles over with the first box.

"Mr. Brumfield." I place my hand over his. "I need to know. Our therapy sessions, were they real?"

"Yes and no. I loved my wife. She was my best friend, but I am in love with George. We'd been together since high school. Back in our day, people like us had to hide our feelings. Once he married Katherine and I married Agnes, we respected our wives. The court ordered therapy was forged. Agnes died five years ago. With George's mind slipping away from me every day, I'm feeling the loss of another person who had my heart."

My eyes fill with tears. "George, as in George Franklin, my foster father?"

A lone, sad tear rolls down his cheek. He nods. "George and Katherine love you like you are their own. Agnes and I were blessed with children. But Katherine was unable to carry babies to term. Her last pregnancy almost killed her, so they stopped trying. You were a blessing to them and their marriage. Katherine had a funny feeling one day after talking to you on the phone. George flew to Tucson to check up on you. He was there that night that man attacked you in the parking garage. George followed him to the bar near your old apartment and stabbed that man in the bathroom."

"I know it's against the ethical guidelines for a psychologist, but I'd like to continue our therapy."

"I'd like that too. It's not a topic I can discuss with just anyone."

I take a deep breath and release his hand to rip the tape off the center seam of the box on the table and open the flaps. I do not have time to be sentimental about the contents. When this is over, and we are back in our house, I will have the boxes moved and take my time going through them.

"Have you ever opened them?"

"No. Daniel and Elizabeth never unpacked them, they added to them.

Inside the first box are framed pictures, small photo albums, and refrigerator magnets from different cities and states. In the second box I find an envelope filled with identification cards with their photos but different names, social security cards, and birth certificates to match. Another envelope holds bundles of cash. In the last envelope are two sets of passports banded together. In the third box, I count four dozen pastel-colored knitted squares, bundles of yarn, knitting needles, and the pattern instructions for a baby blanket. Underneath are twelve journals, a jewelry box, and Elizabeth's medical file. The last box is filled with a collection of crystal dolphins wrapped in aged newspaper.

I go back through the third box and pull out the jewelry box. There isn't much inside. Necklaces, bracelets, and rings. And the dolphin bracelet from the picture along with its matching necklace and earrings. It's a beautiful antique jewelry box with an intricate design of dolphins on the outside. Inside, gold calligraphy lettering that spell out Elizabeth Elaine Langford on black velvet satin. It's not like anything you would find today.

I pull out the journals. All are cream colored with various aquatic scenes painted on the front and back covers. I open the top one. Written on the inside cover is, "Happy 5th Birthday EEL." At the top of the first page the date is written: 3/10/74 and below it is a hand-drawn picture and Dominique's signature. At the top of the second page in a young child's handwriting is March 10, 1974. Underneath is a young child's drawing and Elizabeth's printed signature. Some letters are larger than others. Some are written backwards. And the spacing is off.

I open the next journal. On the inside cover "Happy 6th Birthday EEL" is written, and on the inside cover, Dominique wrote the date at the top of the page and drew a picture and wrote a special message to his granddaughter. That same day, Elizabeth wrote the date on the top of the second page and drew a picture as a reply along with a written message. Some words are misspelled. Up until his death, Dominique gave his granddaughter a journal for each birthday, then Willis took over. He kept the tradition of writing on the inside cover, writing the date at the top of the first page, and a special message to his daughter. She replied on the second page.

Elizabeth, at different ages in her life, filled the pages of the journals with writings, pictures, and mementoes that show her life.

I skim through a page where she'd written her fears. In another journal I glance over the pictures of the places she dreamed of escaping to and horror stories about the real-life monsters she faced every day. I don't have time to read each page in each journal, but I will, one day.

I open the last journal. Its cover is different than the others. It is pastel pink with dozens of sayings from women of history who are role models for ambitious young girls. The sayings were written by hand on the front and back covers, and not part of the original design. The journal was given to her on her sixteenth birthday. The date written on the second page is the same day Elizabeth and Daniel left Boulder and there, written in my mother's calligraphy lettering, is what Marie has been looking for.

I dump the jewelry out of the jewelry box and read the instructions my mother left.

Even with Mr. Brumfield's help, it takes two tries to get the combination correct and the bottom of the jewelry box lifts to reveal a hidden compartment.

Inside is the Last Will and Testament of Dominique Elian Toussaint.

Arizona, Nine years ago

I can tell Bryan is getting aroused from our back-and-forth banter over me allowing him to financially support me during the pregnancy. He wants me to cut back on school and work. He stands to adjust himself after I come back with a witty reply, having tweaked an old saying about a well-educated woman.

When he picks up our plates and carries them to the kitchen, I follow. The quips and comebacks roll off my tongue. Bryan is holding his own, and that smile he keeps giving me is fanning the heat between my legs.

He opens the freezer and takes out the container of homemade vanilla ice cream. I set two bowls on the counter. I have been craving this all week.

I put a slice of pound cake in each bowl. Bryan tops them off with two scoops of ice cream each. I open the refrigerator and take out fresh strawberries. I slice some and top off our dessert. Bryan picks up the biggest strawberry with his fingertips and takes a bite. Red strawberry juice leaves a wet shine to his lips. His tongue slowly cleans it away. He cocks a questioning eyebrow and holds the strawberry up to my mouth, using the chilled fruit to trace my lips. I part my lips for him to put what's left of the sweet strawberry into my mouth. The tip of my tongue flicks his fingertip.

Bryan carries the bowls back to the living room where the battle of witty quips resumes. I'm in the lead until a slight cock of an eyebrow, a suggestive slow lick of ice cream off his spoon, and a sexually charged stare into my eyes makes my grip on my spoon falter. A glob of cake and ice cream drop, then begin to ease down my inner thigh.

In one smooth move, Bryan leans over, licking the stream of ice cream between my legs, then sits up with a triumphant smile on his face.

My slippery fingers tip my bowl over.

Bryan doesn't hesitate. He sets both of our bowls on the coffee table. He spreads my legs wide with his hands, leans in and eats the dessert like a starved man.

My fingers slither through his thick brown hair, gripping the strands at the scalp. I guide him to the place I want to feel his mouth the most.

When the coldness is gone and all that is left is the heat from his mouth, I feel the crotch of my cotton shorts and panties sliding to the side.

At the first brush of his tongue on my clitoris, I come, pressing his face against me and calling his name.

"How did Edwards get the money?" His tongue tickles my opening.

"I… Don't… Know."

"How was it deposited?"

A euphoric fog suspends in the atmosphere of my brain. The throb of my heartbeat is everywhere. The cotton fibers of the wife beater unforgivably scratch against my super tender nipples. I've missed him. I've missed this.

"How, Dani?"

"Wired… day… left." Am I making sense?

"Where's the key?"

His skilled mouth and tongue bring me to the edge, making me feel warm and sexy and uninhibited. My head drops back. I hold him hostage between my thighs, my second orgasm closing in fast.

"You have it."

"Edwards's key to the laptop."

"What… key?"

"Dani, are you RAGS?"

"Huh? You need rags? Why? You're doing a good job with your mouth and tongue." Everything around me disappears.

"Do you belong to RAGS?"

"No, I belong to you." I come, the pleasure thrusting my pelvis forward. The air in my lungs expels with the cry of his name on repeat. My body feels like the release will never end on this ever-lasting pleasure rollercoaster.

I get Bryan undressed and on his back, my clothes piled on top of his. I mount him and ride him hard. Chasing my next orgasm.

His eyes are on me.

His hands grip my hips.

He's matching my every movement.

"Play with yourself for me, Dani."

His request fills me with a whole new level of sexual arousal. I lean back to give him a good view. My fingers reach between my thighs parting my nether-lips. The finger of my other hand circles the hood of my clitoris and I buck at the charge of energy that shoots through my vagina. I am slick and hot and this feels so good. I throw my head back. My walls tighten around him and I orgasm, heavily coating his penis with my wetness. The throaty sounds coming from him signal Bryan's there too. His grip on my hips tightens, stopping my movement. His abs contract, and his body strains beneath me.

"Mine," he whispers.

Bryan releases my hips and I stretch out on his chest, breathing hard and listening to his heartbeat. The fog dissipates from my brain and I remember our last debate topic. "I can't have you coming and going as you please. A heads up when you're visiting would be nice."

"Fair enough, but running my own security business makes it hard to pinpoint an exact date." He brushes my hair aside. "I don't want to tell you I'm coming on Monday, then something comes up and I have to cancel. I don't want to disappoint you. Ever."

I kiss his chest. "How about you call me before you board your flight? A couple of hours' notice is better than no notice at all."

"Deal."

"Thank you for the Range Rover."

He kisses me. "You're welcome."

Bryan and I shower together and go to bed early. He has an early morning flight and I'm driving him to the airport.

When the alarm goes off at three, I hit the snooze button. Bryan climbs out of the bed to get ready. I go back to sleep until he wakes me.

On the way to the airport Bryan sits in the passenger seat with his laptop. I dictate my information and Bryan inputs it. He's adding me to his insurance. Before he gets out of the car he reminds me to open the trust account for the baby. I kiss him and tell him to have a safe flight.

I go back home and climb back into bed.

At nine in the morning, I go to the bank and send him the account information, then go to school.

By the time I leave my last class, I have a text from Bryan with a confirmation number for the wire transfer of one hundred fifty thousand dollars into the baby's account and another confirmation number for the wire transfer of ten thousand dollars into my personal checking account.

When I get to work, the receptionist, Alice Watanabe, hands me a messengered envelope. Inside is my new health care card. Bryan isn't messing around with his "taking care of me" vow. But for how long though?

Under the new health insurance, I have a new OB/Gyn who I really like. At my prenatal appointment, I find out the sex of the baby. I'm not ready to share it with Bryan. Part of me is still waiting for him to pull a ghost.

During one of our nightly phone conversations, I tell Bryan my clothes are getting too small. The next morning, an overnight messenger delivers an envelope. Inside is a credit card and a note saying: *it's time to go shopping.*

The staff at work are surprised and excited when I confirm that I'm pregnant. The head of the clinic thought I turned to food for comfort after James died. For some unknown reason, I do not correct them when they assume the baby is James's. Part of the reason I shut Bryan out is because of the mixed feelings I have about carrying another man's baby, when my husband had just died. The other reason stems from my fear that if I get too close, Bryan is going to disappear, leaving me alone like James did.

It takes having an honest conversation with my inner self to get me to take a deeper look at my relationship with James. There are some hard truths I still need to work through, but I am on the right path.

I keep my pregnancy highs and lows to myself, but Bryan has an uncanny knack for calling me out of the blue. Just hearing the excitement in his voice about the baby makes me happy.

Other than a friendly hello, I don't have much else to say to my neighbors, so when Yvon invites me over for dinner and I accept, I surprise myself.

I finally work up the courage to call Mr. and Mrs. Franklin to tell them about the baby. When I got my first period, Mrs. Franklin tattooed in my brain: be exceptional and not the statistic. I was not prepared for their excitement. Mr. Franklin brings me to tears, he tells me how proud he is of me.

Today, my day is long and hectic and it's not over yet. I get together with my study group for three hours to prepare for a test at the end of the week. By the time I pull into the parking garage, all I want to do is fix a sandwich, shower, and climb into bed. I open my apartment door and freeze. Bryan is sitting on the sofa in the dark. I turn on the light. His tears and sad red eyes show the deep and unbearable pain he's in.

I drop my things on the coffee table, take his hand, and guide him into the bedroom. Bryan lets me undress him and put him to bed. I quickly shed my clothes and climb in next to him. I wrap my arms around him.

His breathing is shallow, and his body is tense. Bryan is fighting against letting go. And the emotional weight is crushing him.

I place his hand on my stomach. "We've got you, Bry."

My words are the push he needed. A sob tears through him, and his tears flow onto my chest.

I silently cry with him.

His sorrow is deep. The man I know is strong and giving. Always there for me when I need him. I bet he does it for those he loves too. But who carries his burdens when he can't? I will. I will take away whatever is hurting him like he did for me.

When his tears stop, I warm up spaghetti, garlic bread, and make a salad. We silently eat in bed. I give him the mental space to gather his thoughts; yet I keep constant contact through my presence and my touch.

I take the dishes to the kitchen, then climb back into bed and lean against the headboard with Bryan's head resting on my stomach.

"I buried my grandmother today," he whispers.

My fingers trail through his hair. "I'm sorry, Bryan. If you had called, I would have come to support you."

"I know, but I didn't want you traveling." His lips peck my stomach.

"Tell me about your grandmother. What was her name? What was she like?"

"Allison Jean Hawk. She was my advisor and cheerleader and the self-appointed mediator between Dad and me." He tells me how special she was to him. And the advice she gave him about me. How his friends called her grandma too because that is what she was to them. Allison was a registered nurse who cared for wounded veterans. He and his sister spent summers with her in South Carolina. When she retired, Bryan's dad moved her to Colorado Springs. Her other sons had long since moved to other states. She died peacefully in her sleep of natural causes.

When Bryan finally falls asleep, I lie awake thinking of a first name to go with Allison. This is the first time I've thought of names for my daughter. As I feel myself drifting off a name pops into my head.

"Kourtney Allison Hawk." It rolls off the tongue nicely. I'll surprise Bryan with the name the day she is born.

He reaches for me in his sleep. Pulling me close to him. In the tranquility of his arms, I dream of the three of us living as a family in a big house.

I am up at my usual time. Bryan never sleeps this late, but I guess he needs the rest. Grief can wear you out. Plus, I know he works round the clock to make a success of his business.

His cell phone is buzzing nonstop on the coffee table. Someone named Paul keeps calling back to back. Ricci too. Acosta calls twice every hour. Mom calls a few times. Dad a few times too. JP1 and Chen both call once.

I am tempted to take him the phone. These people care about him and must be worried; otherwise they would not be blowing up his phone. He must not have told anyone where he was going.

Bryan feels comfortable enough to let his guard down and be vulnerable in front of me. He let me be his shoulder to cry on and that makes me happy. Maybe I can drop my guard too and stop waiting for him to leave.

Since I don't have classes today, I call off from work to be here for Bryan. While I wait for him to wake up, I make breakfast, then pull out my books, sit on the sofa with my feet up on the coffee table and study.

A little after noon dark clouds block out what little sunlight breached the overcast sky. Bryan walks out the bedroom wearing nothing but boxer briefs. He uses the bathroom, then comes into the living room. His eyes are still a little red, but the unbearable pain is gone. He's going to be okay.

I hug and kiss him, then go pour him a cup of coffee. "Check your phone. You have a lot of missed calls."

Bryan picks up the phone and squints at the screen.

As if the caller knows he is awake, Bryan's phone starts to vibrate. He does not answer it though.

"I just need a couple more hours before I call anyone back," he says and the phone stops buzzing.

I hand him the coffee mug. "Take all the time you need. I can go to the school's library to study if you need the place to yourself."

"Thanks." He takes the cup. "I don't want to be alone, and I don't want to interfere with your studying either."

"You're not. Are you hungry? I made breakfast earlier. I can warm it up. It's a breakfast bowl with turkey sausage, smothered potatoes, cheese, and I'll scramble a couple of eggs for you, or do you want lunch?"

Bryan sets the mug on the table, then places his hands on my nonexistent waist and pulls me to him. He leans in and nuzzles that spot behind my ear that makes me melt.

"Did your doctor say it's okay for you to still be sexually active?"

I nod.

"Do you want to be sexually active with me?" His teeth capture my earlobe.

"Yes." The pleasure of his bite affects me in the most sensual way.

His lips move to my neck. I lean my head to the side to expose more of my neck to his lips and tongue.

"Show me, Dani."

I guide his hands to my breasts.

He palms them, rolling my nipples between his thumbs and fore-fingers through the cotton material of my dress. "Their heavier. I like that. I hope you're going to breast feed."

I nod.

Bryan lifts me off my feet, carrying me back to bed.

Our lovemaking is slow and easy, as if no one is waiting for him to return their call. We communicate through our eyes and our touch. This is the closest we've ever been with one another because it is more than the act of sexual gratification.

We lie in each other's arms watching my stomach twitch and flutter. Bryan asks if I have a dream house. I describe the one I dreamt about last night. It includes a sitting room. In my perfect world, I have lots of family and friends to invite over for dinner parties.

I fall asleep to the soothing sounds of an afternoon rain shower, dreaming of us and the family that makes me whole because it begins with the one Bryan and I create. We're happy. Bryan is standing in the picture window smiling. He's holding our daughter in his arms and I'm pulling into the garage waving at them. Anxious to join him and our daughter. As the garage door comes down, I climb out of the car. A dark shadow slips under the garage door before it closes all the way.

I become pinned against the car door by an invisible force. The stench of fish and old dirty socks surrounds me, making me gag. One of its hands gropes me while the other prevents me from yelling for help. I turn my head away from the smell. The reflection I see in the car's window is the leering gaze of Mr. Tucker conveying his intentions.

My feet dangle off the ground. I'm suspended in the air by skin-less fingers wrapped around my neck.

I want to fight him off, but my fingers will not ball into a fist. I cannot lift my arms. In desperation, I look down and see my fingers spread out over my swollen stomach, hiding my unborn child. "Bryan," I choke out. Mr. Tucker disappears, the shadow returns.

Fire in its eyes. Angry words spit flames from its invisible mouth. "I'll come back for you."

My eyes spring open. I can't get air into my lungs. I reach for Bryan.

He isn't in bed with me.

My heart drums hard and fast as I reach for the baseball bat on the side of the bed. It's not there. I don't sleep with it anymore because Bryan secured the apartment.

Where is he?

"Mom, I'm okay. I just needed to get away for a day. I will be in Colorado tomorrow night."

He's in the living room.

I roll out of bed, taking the sheet with me, and walk-run to the living room.

Bryan is sitting on the sofa in boxers with the television muted. One half of a piled-high sandwich and a bag of chips on a plate are on the coffee table in front of him.

When he sees me, lines wave across his forehead, and he cocks an eyebrow, asking a silent question. His gaze drops to the vicinity of my stomach behind the sheet, then back to my eyes.

I can imagine what I look like. Bed-hair, chest heaving, panic-filled eyes. On the brink of tears.

Bryan reaches a hand out to me. "I called them first."

I do not hesitate to go to him.

He guides me onto his lap. "A friend, Mom."

Bryan gives me a brief peck on the lips. I relax and rest my head in the crook of his neck.

"No, you don't know my friend."

Her voice is muffled, and I cannot make out what she's saying. His fingers trail down and up my back as he listens to his mother.

"I promise I'll call you in the morning, Mom."

His gentle fingers sweep my hair back and his lips brush my temple.

"Love you too."

Bryan tosses the phone onto the coffee table. "Dani, what's

wrong? Is it the baby?"

I shake my head and snuggle closer.

"Bad dream?"

I nod. I've never told anyone, except for James, about what happened with Mr. Tucker.

Bryan holds me in a way that's soothing, reassuring, and loving. "I'll always fight off the bad guys for you, Dani."

The promise in his words makes me cry.

Bryan stays with me for two days, then goes back to Colorado. He calls me every morning and every evening.

The week before Thanksgiving, my desktop computer goes out and I'd just finished a research paper I have to turn in after the break. I call Bryan, hysterical and crying. He shows up five hours later with a brand-new laptop. Somehow, he's able to retrieve all my files from the desktop and transfer them to the laptop.

I treat him to a neck and shoulder massage to work the kinks out. Afterwards, we lie in bed watching my stomach move.

Bryan presses his lips to my stomach. "Kick once if you're a boy, twice if you're a girl."

Our baby kicks three times.

"I guess, you'll have to teach her how to count," I whisper.

Bryan jumps out of bed dancing around the room singing, "I told you so."

I drive him to the airport in the morning. Before he climbs out of the Range Rover, he apologizes for not being able to come back to Arizona for Thanksgiving. I assure him I'll be okay. I did something I've never done before, I invited my neighbor Yvon over for dinner because this is her first major holiday as a divorcee and she told her son to go camping with his friends for the week.

On December 7th, I get a two-second morning phone call from Bryan telling me good luck on my last final and he will call me tonight.

I do not hear from him again until the next morning and he sounds exhausted.

Every morning and every night thereafter, he sounds like he is falling asleep on the phone. Our conversations get shorter and shorter.

The walls are starting to come up. Doubt settling in.

Is Bryan going back on his word?

Is he slowly phasing himself out of my life?

How could I have been so stupid to think he'd be different from those who father children and never see them?

How much do I really know about him?

He's from Colorado Springs.

He has a mom and dad and a big sister.

Once a month, money is deposited into the baby's trust account *and* my checking account, but I know nothing about how he is making this money.

When I research Bryan Kendall Hawk IV on the internet, I find stories dating back to 1930 about a small coastal town in South Carolina whose corrupt mayor, Bryan Kendall Hawk, ran a speakeasy and brothel. I read a 1965 article about another Bryan Kendall Hawk, a philandering lawyer from the same small coastal town in South Carolina, who was shot and killed in front of his office by an angry husband whose wife was carrying Hawk's child. And a 1968 article about yet another Bryan Kendall Hawk, high school valedictorian from the South Carolina town, who was barred from giving the valedictorian speech at graduation because of the history of the Hawks.

I can't find anything specific on Bryan Kendall Hawk IV.

Mrs. Franklin calls to let me know they won't be able to come to Arizona for the holidays as planned. Mr. Franklin had some kind of episode and his doctor advised against him traveling.

I call my boss to let her know I'm available. It's the holiday season and a busy time for the twenty-four-hour mental health clinic. She refuses to put me on the schedule, stating I need to rest while I have the time because once the baby gets here, rest is a luxury not a necessity. She has three children of her own.

With no one to celebrate with, I don't bother putting up any holiday decorations like my neighbors. Not that I have a lot anyway. James wasn't much on observing Christmas and New Year's.

I piddle around the apartment during the day in T-shirts that barely covers my big belly and panties, dancing and winter cleaning.

It's eight days before Christmas, and I decide to get out of the apartment. I go to the cemetery and leave flowers at James's gravesite, then go to the mall with intentions of window shopping. An electronics store is having a sale on digital cameras. I go inside and buy one as a Christmas gift to myself. The window display at a children's clothing store catches my eye. I go inside not to buy anything, just to look. I leave the mall hours later with three shopping bags.

I walk into my bedroom and stand in the doorway holding the shopping bags. I realize the bedroom is too small to fit a crib because of the king size bed. I sit on the edge of the bed and mentally rearrange the room, then change my clothes and get started.

Knock!

Knock!

Knock!

I look at the clock. It's eleven thirty at night. I am still up, emptying the dresser drawers. I creep to the door and peer through the peephole.

"Where's your key?" I start disengaging the locks.

"My hands are full, can you hurry up, please? I have to use the bathroom."

I unlock the security screen and step back.

Bryan swings the strap of a pink and black bag onto my shoulder, then carefully hands me a white blanket covered in mint green flowers. He rushes by, practically sprinting toward the bathroom.

"Danielle Lauren Tatum, meet Emma Rose Hawk." Bryan turns on the light in the bathroom.

The blanket squirms. I look down at it and peel back a corner.

Words fail me.

I'm holding a pacifier-sucking baby dressed in a pink infant snowsuit.

I didn't know I'd moved until Emma and I end up in the doorway of the bathroom. Bryan has his zipper down and is reaching for the toilet seat. I am throwing eye daggers at his back. Emma squirms again and grunts.

"Bryan, whose baby is this?"

"She's mine." The heavy sound of urine falls into the toilet water. Bryan sighs and throws his head back.

"How old is she?"

"Almost two weeks."

"Did you kidnap this baby? Where's her mother?"

"I did not kidnap my daughter. I have custody of her." His stream is going strong.

"Why did you bring her here? Why would you travel on an airplane with a newborn?"

"I drove. We didn't get out of the car. When I needed to feed her or change her diaper, I pulled into a parking lot and got in the backseat with her. I cleared it with her pediatrician. Emm and I are here to celebrate Christmas with you." Bryan finally finishes and flushes the toilet. He zips the zipper, then washes his hands.

"Tell me what's going on, Bryan."

"I will, but first can you change her diaper? I'm going to get the rest of her stuff out of the truck. And I'm double parked." He kisses my cheek, then rushes out.

I carry Emma across the hall to my room. With one hand, I clear a spot on the bed, unzip the diaper bag and pull out the changing pad. While I'm unzipping her winter suit, I hear sounds of Bryan's struggle to get through the front door.

He made sure Emma was warm. He dressed her in layers including a cap on her head and mittens on her hands. Bryan put her in mint green feet-in pajamas. I unzip it. He also put her in a white onesie with snaps and socks on her tiny feet that gap around her skinny legs.

Emma stretches her little body. I search the diaper bag for lighter pajamas. I free her from the layers of clothes and change her diaper in the process. Bryan has her in a cloth diaper with a Velcro covering.

She is too cute. Her little bald head has no signs of hair on it. The headbands I bought today will look adorable on her. I don't want anyone mistaking her for a boy. I'll handwash them in the morning, then take a picture of her wearing the headbands with my new camera.

By the time I have her dressed and back in my arms, Bryan has quieted down in the living room. I adjust the thermostat to turn up the heat in the apartment. With the extra pounds I'm carrying I'm always hot so I keep the apartment cool.

Emma and I stand by the sofa staring at a sleeping dad. At least he assembled the portable crib. I lay Emma on her side.

While Bryan snores sitting up and Emma closes her eyes, I unpack her things.

There is an insulated cooler with layers of dry ice packages in between layers of storage bags filled with frozen breastmilk. The emblem on the packaging is from a high-end human milk bank. There is enough to feed her for a month. I put the bags in the freezer.

In another insulated cooler I find four, two-ounce prefilled bottles with the date and time written on tabs on the tops of the bottle caps. If my calculations are correct, Bryan left Colorado at ten in the morning. I put the bottles in the refrigerator.

In the side pocket of her diaper bag I come across her hospital records and legal documents showing him as having sole legal custody of Emma Rose Hawk. No mother is listed on any of the documents. There is also a notarized paper giving me permission to make legal and medical decisions for Emma in Bryan's absence. All papers were filed in the state of Colorado.

I may not know everything there is to know about him, but I do know enough to trust Bryan. He has never given me a reason not to. And he's trusting me with the welfare of his daughter.

When I finish, I sit on the love seat, in a yoga position, and stare at them.

Of all the times Bryan has fallen asleep in this apartment, I have never heard him snore. He has dark circles under his eyes. Guess now I know why he sounded tired and was falling asleep on the phone. He wasn't pulling away from me. He was caring for a newborn. I really should stop waiting for him to leave; it's obvious he's not.

Around one thirty in the morning, Emma starts to cry.

Bryan stretches and yawns. "Hold on, Emm. Daddy'll warm your bottle."

"I've got her." I unfold my legs and go to the kitchen. I plug in the bottle warmer and get a bottle out of the refrigerator.

"I meant to put everything away, so it wouldn't clutter the living room. Thanks for doing it for me." He changes her diaper with the confidence most dads don't have this early in fatherhood.

"I liked doing it. Go take a shower and get in the bed. I'm on Emma duty for now."

I test the temperature of the breastmilk on my wrist as I walk back to the living room. Bryan grabs a burp cloth from the storage compartment of the portable crib, then lifts Emma and cradles her in his arms. He kisses me, then kisses Emma on her forehead. Bryan places her in my arms and lifts my T-shirt enough to expose my belly and presses his lips to my skin. He is creating a bond between the four of us.

It does not matter how he ended up with sole custody or how we are going to work this out. What matters is, Bryan just declared us a family. I will revise my plan to include him and this beautiful little girl.

Bryan rolls his suitcase into the bedroom. He pokes his head out of the door. "Winter cleaning?"

"Yeah, just shove everything to one side." I sit on the love seat and give Emma her bottle.

She and I get to know each other better and her little sister kicks and flips in my womb. They will be two months apart.

Every two hours, Emma wakes for a diaper change and a bottle. I move some storage bags from the freezer to the refrigerator and mark the date and time.

After ten hours of uninterrupted sleep, Bryan emerges.

I commit to memory the way his thigh muscles flex with each step he takes in his low riding gray pajama bottoms. His abs look even more defined than the last time I saw him shirtless. And he has a new tattoo on his arm. A crest.

I am sitting on the sofa reading to Emma. She just finished a bottle. I toss the burp cloth over my shoulder. Bryan sits next to us and finishes the story while I gently rub her back.

At the sound of his voice, the baby inside of me starts to move. I take Bryan's hand and place it on my stomach. He leans in closer, his lips practically pressed against my T-shirt covered belly, and finishes the story.

"Did you get any sleep?" He tucks a stray lock of my hair behind my ears. I put my hair up in a messy bun to keep it out of the way as I cared for Emma.

"About five hours. We stayed out here so we wouldn't disturb you."

"Let's go get a tree today. It's seven days 'til Christmas. We'll make it a family tradition."

"We're not taking her out. You took a big chance bringing her here."

"I wasn't leaving her home and I wasn't letting you celebrate the holidays alone. So Emm and I talked about it and decided to take a road trip."

"We don't need to decorate."

"This is Emm's first Christmas. We need to go all out."

His enthusiasm kickstarts my holiday spirit. Plus, there is no point in going back and forth with him on this. "How are we going to shop with a newborn? I'm not exposing her to a dusty tree lot."

"You get out first and find a tree while we stay in the truck. When you find one, tag it and come back. I'll get out and pay for it."

We get dressed and the three of us leave the apartment. Yvon is out in the courtyard adjusting the decorations on her door. Her son is down with the flu so she didn't leave town for the holidays like she planned. I introduce Bryan and Emma to Yvon. She goes nuts over the baby and says she's available to babysit if we need her.

Bryan and I use his switch off plan at the tree lot, and the super store where I fill a basket with decorations. I find a cute Christmas cookie cutter set. I'm in the mood to bake sugar cookies so Emma can leave some for Santa.

CHAPTER ELEVEN

BRYAN

Colorado, Present Day

"COLONEL? SIR?" FONTENOT'S CONCERNED VOICE fills my ears.

My eyes do not veer from the man lying at my feet.

He isn't dead—yet.

"Is my wife out of the building?"

"Yes, sir. Jansen escorted her down to the garage. No one is allowed to leave the building until she has a two-mile lead."

"Good thinking. Is she heading back to the resort?"

"No sir, Mrs. Hawk is still in the downtown area."

"Let me know where she ends up."

"Roger that, sir."

Hatchett's body jerks involuntarily, and he gurgles in his throat. Blood spews from his mouth coating his teeth red. His eyes plead with me to save his life.

I bend my knees and balance on my toes, hovering by his side. My arms cross at the wrist, my trigger finger resting alongside the barrel, ready to move and fire another shot. The satisfaction of being judge, jury, and executioner is food for my monster.

"Even if Chen were here, he wouldn't stop me from killing you like he did that day you stared at Danielle's ass. You are a traitor. You've been feeding information to the enemy."

Hatchett's eyes widen.

"I hope all manners of evil bend you over a desk and fuck you raw every day for the rest of your pathetic eternity in hell." I press the muzzle of the gun to his forehead and fire the fatal shot.

The life in his eyes slowly dims. His body completely relaxes.

I walk out of the cell closing the sliding door behind me. "Fontenot, are the stairs clear up to the fourth floor?"

"No, sir."

"Clear them and block the Watchers' view for two minutes."

"Copy that, sir."

I walk down the passageway to the door to the stairwell. Fontenot tells me she sent the Watcher up to The Nest. I use my keycard to unlock the door and take the stairs three at a time up to my office floor without being spotted. The fourth floor is locked down. Without the predetermined clearance, the floor cannot be accessed by the elevators on a locked down order.

When I open my office door, I immediately catch a whiff of my wife's scent. Although I know she's not here, my eyes still search for her.

The chair at my desk is pushed back; a sheet of paper and a pen are in front of the computer monitor. The contract I left on the conference table for the real estate broker to sell the apartment building on Kalmia Avenue is gone.

"Sir, your wife is at the public library."

"Do you know how to hack into security systems?"

"No, sir."

"Type in the command for Riley to find visual access to the library's security system, then follow the steps. Let me know if you have problems. I'm going to get out of this suit."

Shedding the fat suit won't take as long as it did to get into it. I grab a box cutter from my desk drawer, push the panel in the wall near the window to open the bathroom door, and stand in front of the mirror.

With the blade, I slice through the wrist, careful not to cut my own, then peel off the puffy hand and finger glove. I do the other wrist next.

Each piece of the fat suit is thermally sealed together. The front and back torso go on first, then a heat gun seals the two pieces together. The arms are next. It's like putting together a human body puzzle. My feet were saved from having to be enclosed.

Maneuvering the box cutter is easy now that I don't have to use it with fat fingers. I unbutton the uniform shirt and start slicing.

If Ig filled the hollow suit with fake blood, the bathroom would look like a scene in a horror flick where the killer hacks the victim's skin piece by piece.

Once I peel off the last of the suit I take a hot shower.

My attitude brightens as soon as I put on the black shirt, black cargos, and black steel-toe military boots. This is my super-suit.

I go to my desk and log in to my computer.

"I have a visual on Mrs. Hawk, sir. She's okay."

"You're doing good, Fontenot. When this is over, we'll do the paperwork to bring you into Phantom full time."

"Thank you, sir." I hear the smile in her voice.

I access the Phantom satellite and check the activity in Yemen. The team is two miles behind the convoy and closing in. I switch to infrared imaging and count four vehicles, each carrying three riders and one lookout. The vehicles are moving toward the southern areas of Yemen off the Gulf of Aden. The missiles are covered by camouflage tarps.

The bright orange ninja icon flashes on my computer screen. I tap it and the box opens. "Please tell me you have good news."

"She is supposed to deliver a message to President Hart. RAGS will give him two hours to hold a press conference telling the world about Phantom or they'll launch the first two missiles. She doesn't know what country is targeted."

"So if he doesn't hold a press conference about Phantom, then they'll force him to explain to the world why the United States is attacking another country without probable cause."

"That's it in a nutshell."

"Who's giving the orders?"

"Pierre Dupree."

"Marie's ex?"

"One and the same."

"Isn't he supposed to be in a supermax?"

"According to Owens, he served two years then Langford got him out. On the books, Pierre Dupree is a prisoner."

"Will Owens recover from your interrogation?" I already know the answer. It's so rare I get to see him in full Ghost mode.

"*She* chose to remain quiet for this long. She would be alive if she'd answered my questions the first time I asked." He steps out of view so I can see the lifeless body of Nora Owens, slumped forward in the chair. Max steps back into view. No remorse. No emotion.

"Any other cabinet members or White House staff we need to bring in?"

"She was the only one. You made it hard for them to infest and breed."

"Thank you, Max."

"You're welcome, Bry."

My screen goes back to what I was viewing before the video call.

I trust Maxim Li Chen-Snyder. At one of the lowest times in my life, he confided in me the real reason he retired from Phantom. It had gotten too hard to rein in his monster after the assignments Langford sent him out on. Max is a chameleon and an exceptionally talented extractor, but convincing someone to end their own life chips away at his soul. That is why it took so long to interrogate Owens. If we weren't in this state of emergency, I would never have asked him to interrogate her.

Max's family are immigrants from China who became naturalized citizens when Max was ten years old. His father knew his son was different and loved him so much, he packed up his family and fled their birthplace after the mafia learned of his son's abilities to manipulate the mind's perspective.

The drag-lingo is Max's covert way of communicating in front of non-Phantom folks. His flaming flamboyance enhances it. On the inside, Maxim Li Chen-Snyder is a beast that scares the Boogeyman. If he had it his way, he'd study RAGS's leaders in a controlled environment.

Now that we have the information from Owens, I start the tedious process of transferring U.S. military intelligence and security measures to a highly secured system that only I can access. My technological skills afford me the ability to transfer the data under the radar of the Department of Defense. I'm giving President Hart another option if it comes down to him holding a press conference. Willis Percival Langford will be the one to take the fall.

Jessi checks in via a secured email. She's at the hospital in Colorado Springs. A pediatric team is waiting for Solomon's arrival. Jessi and her team will take care of Selam. An OR is prepared. I didn't tell Edwards, but his wife is in pretty bad shape. We don't know the full extent of her injuries, but we will make sure she gets the best care possible.

Other than being a little undernourished, Solomon is stable.

I open the hidden floor safe, and shove supplies into a backpack, then leave out of the office.

"Fontenot, are the stairs clear down to the first floor?"

"Yes, sir."

"Block the view again."

"Copy that, sir."

———◆———

Arizona, Nine Years Ago

The few times I leave the apartment telling Dani I have to go back to Colorado for business, I am really across the street hanging out with Vin. We do fly to Boulder for Phantom business but come back the same day.

Ig and Tony are spending the holidays with their families.

Tonight is our last night in Tucson. Dani and I are lying in the new bed I bought her for Christmas watching a movie on the television I also bought for her room. There is a loud New Year's Eve party going on in the courtyard. Vin is hanging out with them.

I reach out and tuck her hair behind her ear, so I can see those pretty brown eyes.

"If I promise to build you your dream home, will you move to Colorado?"

"I work here. My whole educational plan is mapped out here. Why can't you and Emma move here with us?"

"I can't just up and move my brand-new company to another state. My clients will think the business is unstable and start pulling out of their contract."

"Then how do we do this?"

"I don't know. But I know I don't want to be a part-time dad."

"It's going to be another three years before I get my doctorate."

Even though we established an emergency plan that includes car service to the hospital, it will take me *hours* to get to her. The thought feeds the constant burn in my stomach when it comes to Dani. "It will take a little over a year to build the house. I'm sure we can find a doctorate program for you in Colorado."

Emm starts to stir. I get out of bed to get her, then lay her between Dani and me after I check her diaper. Outside and on the television, people are shouting the New Year countdown. Emm has a death grip on Dani's pinky finger and is looking up at her. Dani is smiling down at Emm. Something deep inside feels warm just watching them bond.

Five!

Four!

Three!

Two!

One!

"Happy New Year, Dani." I kiss her long and deep, then kiss my daughter's forehead. "Happy New Year, my big girl Emm." I lift Dani's pajama shirt and press my lips to her stomach. "2006 is your year, baby girl."

In the morning, Dani helps me pack up Emm's things and take them out to the truck. She sniffs and wipes her eyes a lot. My reason for bringing Emm to Arizona with me in the first place was to get Dani to be more open with me. Everything I've learned about her pregnancy and how she's doing emotionally and financially is because I've monitored her accounts and school records since I started the investigation of Edwards. And once she told me about the pregnancy, I hacked her medical file. The reports from Wright, Cooper, and Watanabe only back up what I already know.

My plan worked, but now I'm left with this emptiness as I pull away from the curb and make the block and pick up Vin around the corner. It's getting harder and harder to leave Arizona each time I visit.

We begin the twelve-hour drive back to Colorado.

Vin and I take turns driving. By nonverbal agreement, we only talk about Phantom or Hawkeye business.

Emm must be missing Dani. She whines most of the ride.

We stop at my parents' in Colorado Springs to introduce them to their granddaughter. While Mom coos over her first grandchild and fusses at me, Dad paces back and forth asking question after question. Most about Emm's mother. If my grandmother were still alive, she would be acting as moderator.

Vin is no help. He sits on the sofa watching television and trying not to be noticed.

Dad doesn't question the explanation of Emm's mother dropping her off on my doorstep then committing suicide. Mom, however, is on the fence. Even as adults it's still difficult for Jessi and me to get things by her.

Once Emm starts crying, Mom gives me a reprieve to go warm a bottle.

I step out on the patio and call Dani. I promised to call her as soon as we arrived.

"How did Emma do on the drive?"

"Fussy."

"You didn't pull over and put her in a bunch of clothes, did you?"

"No. I think she misses you."

"I miss her too."

"Just her?"

"I miss you too. And I know it's hard for you to understand, but finishing school in Arizona is important to me. After I graduate, I'll seriously consider moving to Colorado. I don't want you to be a part-time dad either. As a compromise, the baby and I can visit you and Emma when you guys can't come to us."

"We'll make it work somehow, Dani."

The patio door opens, and Dad steps out.

"I have to go. I'll try and come week after next."

"Send me daily pics of Emma, please."

"I will. Talk to you soon." I disconnect the call as my dad closes the door behind him.

"Emma Rose? Is giving her that name supposed to make up for your recklessness? You are better than that!"

"I gave my daughter that name because my grandmother loved it and she wasn't blessed with a daughter."

"How much did you really know about the girl you impregnated? How long were you guys together?"

"I am twenty-six years old. Spare me the safe sex lecture. Condoms are not one-hundred percent effective even if used correctly."

"Did you even use one or are you out there playing Russian roulette with your penis?"

Dani is the *only* woman I haven't covered up for. If anyone is playing roulette with their sexual health, it's her. I know she's healthy, I am her first and only. She's not mine, but I'm healthy. Ig checks us out regularly. Plus, I haven't been with anyone since that first time with Dani. But I can't tell my father any of that, so I use my eyes to tell him to fuck off.

"You're single. Your company is making money. And you were childless. All the specifications to make you a target for gold-digging whores."

"I don't need money to get laid."

"Are you sure that baby is yours?"

"Emma is mine," I hiss.

The skin over my knuckles tightens. My right shoulder leads to protect my dominant side. One more comment like that and I'll punch my dad in his mouth. I've been raised to respect my parents, but at some point, that respect needs to go both ways. Right about now, Grandma would step in. A wave of loneliness surrounds me. I close my eyes and take a deep breath and pray for her to appear because I don't think I can control myself if my overbearing father keeps it up.

"You have no idea what you're getting yourself into. Raising children isn't easy, even for a two-parent household. There are couples…"

"Why? Why can't you just be proud of the fact that I'm being a man? *I'm* taking responsibility for my children, unlike Bryan Kendall Hawk, Jr. And I'm certainly not out there screwing over people like the first Bryan Kendall Hawk." A tense calmness settles around me, as if my grandmother is standing by my side. "Look, I'm Emm's father and I'm going to give her the best life I can. Accept her. Don't accept her, Dad. I really don't give a damn." I brush past him and walk into the house.

I *was* going to tell them about my other daughter, so it won't be a surprise when she and Dani come to Colorado for the first time. I'm not ashamed of my children, but I'm not going to subject Dani and my girls to his rhetoric.

Vin looks over his shoulder, already in attack mode and waiting for my cue. I guess they heard us.

Mom transfers her granddaughter to her shoulder and starts patting Emm's back.

"It's getting late. We need to get home."

Behind me, the patio door closes. Mom's eyes cut in that direction. She stands. "Give me a minute to pack a few things. I'm coming with you to help you two get settled." Mom's words are for me, but she's glaring at Dad. She gently places my daughter in my arms.

I toss the burp cloth over my shoulder and shift Emm. "You really don't have to do that. Her crib is in my room until I get everything moved out of the spare bedroom."

"Then I guess I'll be clearing out the spare room for *my grand-daughter!*" Mom doesn't say another word. She charges up the stairs.

Emm lets out a juicy burp, which means she's spit up too. I wipe her mouth and ask Vin to put the changing pad on the sofa for me.

I lay my daughter on it and change her diaper. I feel my dad's eyes on me. He moves closer to the sofa.

"The first time I changed Jessica's diaper it took me ten minutes to figure out how to do it. She screamed at the top of her lungs and turned red. I broke out in a sweat. I thought I was hurting her. Your mother was too weak to get out of bed because of postpartum complications. I was teaching full-time at the high school and a night class at the community college. It was a lot for first-time parents. Mom took a temporary leave of absence to come stay with us." He comes around to the front of the sofa and scoops up his granddaughter. "I'll come to Boulder on the weekends and your mom will stay the weekdays to help you for as long as you need us."

My instinct is to tell him to go to hell, but my grandmother's presence is still with me, telling me to accept the peace offering.

Jessi and her girlfriend, Samantha, walk through the front door. They go crazy over Emm. When Samantha wrestles my daughter from my sister, I pull Jessi upstairs into her old bedroom.

"I need to tell you something," I begin and tell her all about Dani.

"You're shitting me, right?" She's pacing. "You better be lying, BK4. What is with you? How do you know she was still a virgin? Was there blood on the sheets?"

I nod.

"I taught you how to track a woman's period, so you wouldn't be in these kinds of situations. How could you screw her without a goddamn raincoat every single time?"

"She's not some random fuck buddy, JP1."

"No, she's the widow of the man you're investigating, BK4."

I have no words for that. My sister stops pacing and looks me in the eyes.

"I'm sorry. What do you need me to do?"

"I just wanted someone in the family to know about Dani and the baby in case something happens to me."

My big sister hugs me. "I'll look out for them."

"Thank you. Not just for this but for that thing with Amelia too."

"Bryan, I thought you needed to get home!" Mom shouts from downstairs.

"I don't think Mom is buying my story about how I got Emm."

"Yeah, good luck with that." Jessi laughs.

Turns out, I need my parents' help. Getting the office building ready for Phantom to move in is a long process. As the new ESO Team, my best friends and I train daily together. I'm also weeding out personnel who do not meet my standards for Phantom Ghosts. Having my parents and sister there to watch my daughter makes it possible. Charly, Tony's fiancée, steps in when everyone is super busy.

I submit my report to First Command clearing Dani of any involvement with RAGS along with strong, documented proof. President Nelson approves the report and Dani's case is closed, but the one for Edwards remains open until I retrieve the Phantom information.

Dani's nerves are starting to kick in; we're getting closer to her due date. I fly back and forth between Colorado and Arizona every chance I get. If Emm is with me I drive. Either Ig or Tony rides with us. Vin is back and forth to Italy. His grandfather is ill.

I plan my trips around the times the Langfords come back from Arizona. They watch their granddaughter from a distance. They think the baby is Edwards's.

I'm packing for my overnight trip to Arizona when Vin calls with news that Nonno Ricci passed away. I dump everything out of my small bag to pack for a trip to Italy. I'm also on my laptop checking for flights.

Emm is already in Colorado Springs with my parents. I call them to let them know there's a change of plans and I'm going to Italy.

The phone call to Dani I save for last.

"I know we're supposed to go pick up the things you'll need

after you have the baby, but my best friend's grandfather just died. I'm going to Italy for a week."

"It's okay, be with your friend. The staff at the clinic threw me a surprise baby shower today since I start maternity leave tomorrow. There isn't much I need to get. I'll go to the store. Maybe I can talk Yvon into going with me."

"No, wait for me to get back. One week, I promise."

"Okay."

Before Tony, Ig, and I board our flight, I assign an extra Ghost to Dani's detail, a male from level five Security. There has been a couple of incidents in the neighborhood lately.

The tension between Vin and his big brother Salvatore is volatile, and Paola, Salvatore's wife, is happy we're there to help her keep the brothers from tearing each other's heads off. The days leading up to the funeral services Tony, Ig, and I act as buffers between the two headstrong Ricci brothers.

Hundreds packed the cathedral to pay their respects to Alessandro Massimo Ricci, a businessman and humanitarian in the little Italian town two hours from Rome. The service is long and emotional. Nonno Ricci is laid to rest next to his wife and only daughter, in the Ricci family section of the cemetery.

The atmosphere of the gathering after the services is like two hostile countries about to go to war and Paola is caught in the middle. Once the mourners leave, the two Ricci brothers go to their respective wings of the historical winery castle.

I'm awakened by the constant buzzing of my cell phone. It's an urgent text message. Dani called the car service. She's in labor.

I jump out of bed and open my laptop to check flights to the States. The earliest one is late in the afternoon.

"Fuuuck!"

My phone rings. The caller ID flashing Dani's picture.

"My water broke," she pants. "And the contractions are close together. I'm waiting for my ride to take me to the hospital."

There's an eight-hour time difference between where I am in Italy and Tucson, Arizona. It took us sixteen hours to get here on a commercial flight and that was with a two-hour layover plus another two-hours to get to the castle.

"I'm trying to get on the first bird out of Italy. I'll be there as soon as I can, Dani. I'm so sorry I'm not there." Flakes of guilt start to rain down on my back. "I'm on my way, Dani." I toss my phone on the bed and check other airlines for flights.

The bedroom door opens. Tony stands in the doorway. "Get dressed. I'll find a way to get you in the air."

Vin stumbles up behind Tony. "I'll call the Prime Minister. His ass better pull some strings to get us on a private plane."

"You need to stay and get things settled with your grandfather's estate."

"Nonno already told us he split everything fifty-fifty. One can't do anything without the other. And neither one can buy the other out or sell their share."

Paola tiptoes down the hallway tying the belt on her robe. "Is everything okay? I thought I heard shouting."

The walls are thin, and sound carries throughout the castle.

Ig's door opens, he is already dressed. "Bry needs to get back to the U.S. right away." He drops his suitcases by the door and walks into my room to start packing my clothes.

Paola squeezes my hand. "I'll call my father. He'll arrange a government plane for you. Are you going back with them Vinny?" She looks at him. Paola wants the brothers to stop fighting over past mistakes and be a family.

The muscle in Vin's cheek twitches from him clenching his jaw. "There's nothing left for me here."

Even in the dim light we see the tears in her eyes. "I'll tell Salvatore to bring the jeep around." Paola turns around, wiping her eyes, and leaves us.

There's no sense wasting our words on Vin's deaf ears. He is sticking to his vow to never forgive Salvatore.

As soon as everyone is packed and dressed, we head out.

The jeep rocks and dips and speeds along the dark road toward an airport that is two hours away from the vineyard with Salvatore driving.

I try calling Dani, but her phone goes straight to voicemail. I leave a message letting her know I'm on my way.

My head hangs low and sways along with the rocking jeep. Desperate for information, I contact the people assigned to Dani. Wright doesn't have an update. She says Dani declined the offer to ride to the hospital with her. Cooper and Watanabe are at the hospital but can't get any information from the nurses on the labor and delivery floor. The security agent is on the floor, but in the family waiting room. My laptop is in the back with the rest of our luggage. I don't want to waste time by telling Salvatore to stop so I can get it.

My brothers place their hands on my shoulders and back. I close my eyes and listen as Tony prays for a safe labor and delivery for Dani and the baby. They were with me when Emm was born too, whispering the same prayer.

We reach the small airport. I thank Salvatore and tell him to let us know if he and Paola need anything. Vin doesn't acknowledge his brother. I'm informed that the pilot is on his way.

I pace back and forth in the airport's terminal for an hour, trying to get information about Dani and my daughter.

I'm informed that the pilot is here and doing the inspection check.

I pace for another forty-five minutes.

We board the fourteen-passenger private jet with Italy's flag on the tail. I've been toying with the idea of buying one for Hawkeye Personal Protection. Phantom have military jets, but they are not for personal use.

Sitting in the luxury leather captain's chair convinces me to compare performance stats for privately owned jets. I'll hire an ex–Navy pilot to fly it.

As the door closes, I get an update on Dani. My daughter was born at seventeen-zero-six hundred hours, Arizona time. Both Dani and the baby are good.

Shit! I wasn't there to see my daughter come into the world.

The weight of guilt settles on my back and I will carry it for the rest of my life.

Sixteen hours after takeoff. We touch down in Tucson, Arizona. A car is waiting for us.

I turn on my cell phone. Once it connects, it goes off from the text messages that came through while we were in flight.

My best friends try to cheer me up. We stop at the apartment, so I can shower and get the car seat before heading over to the hospital.

I walk into the private room just as the hospital's records clerk is reviewing the information Dani filled out for the baby's birth certificate.

Dani looks tired and beautiful. She barely glances my way.

I put the car seat in the chair and peek into the medical bassinet next to the bed. My daughter is dressed in pink and white feet-in pajamas with a headband to match. She has a head full of swirly black hair. A receipt from the hospital's photographer is tucked into the slot on the bassinet.

The white post card with pink bears on the front of the bassinet reads:

Baby Girl Tatum

February 11, 2006 5:06 p.m.

5lbs, 15oz – 19"L

She is smaller than Emm was.

The clerk gets my attention and hands me the form and a pen. I read it and fill in the blanks where my name and information go, then sign in the designated place.

I stare at my daughter's name before I hand it back.

My baby stretches and grunts. Her bottom lip pokes out and then she releases a big cry. *You don't know how lucky you are to be her dad.* I pick her up, cradling her in my arms. "Hello, Kourtney Allison Hawk. May I call you Kourt for short? I'm your daddy and I'm going to always love you." My fingertip brushes her cheek and she turns her head with her mouth open. I vaguely hear the click of the camera's shutter.

Two doctors and a nurse enter the room. I place Kourt back in the bassinet and step aside.

Dr. Housemen, Dani's OB/Gyn, pulls back the covers to examine her.

Dr. Wolfe, a pediatrician, undresses Kourt to examine her. My daughter cries that stuttered newborn baby cry and turns red, bawling her fists. I give her my pinky to hold and softly sing to her. She has a good grip. At the end of the exam, Nurse Linda gives her the HepB shot in her thigh.

I put Kourt back into her pajamas and cover her head with the cap I see in the bassinet. I pick her up and walk around the room trying to comfort her. She's hungry.

"The baby looks good," Dr. Wolfe says. "I'll see her again in five days."

Dani's doctor finishes with her, and she climbs out of the bed. She slow walks to the rocking chair. After she gets settled, Dani gestures for me to give her the baby.

"We've already gone over postpartum care," Dr. Housemen says. "I'll see you next week. Once the lactation nurse comes in and consults with you, I'll sign the discharge orders."

"Thank you." I shake both doctors' hands.

I pick up Dani's camera and snap photos of her nursing Kourt. Viewing them through the lens makes me realize something is missing. I should be in the picture with them. Emm too. As soon as we can, I'm going to have a professional photographer come to the apartment and take our first family picture. In the meantime, I set the camera on the mobile tray, make sure it's in focus, then set the timer and rush across the floor. I drop to my knees next to the rocking chair. The camera flashes, capturing a picture of us.

"She's beautiful, Dani. Thank you for giving her my grandmother's name." I kiss Dani's cheek.

The sight and sound of my daughter nursing from her mother's breast is mesmerizing. I can't not watch it. Theoretically I know a woman's body can sustain her child, but never have I witnessed something so amazing. And I get to experience it with my own child and her mother.

Once Kourt falls asleep, Dani lays her in the bassinet on her side with rolled up hospital receiving blankets behind her. Dani climbs back into bed and channel surfs until she falls asleep. I sit in the chair by the bed and nod off too.

Late in the afternoon someone knocks on the door. I wake Dani as a nurse walks in with a gift bag.

"Hi, I'm Grace. I'm the lactation nurse."

I watch and listen as the nurse goes over breastfeeding with Dani. This is all so fascinating to me. Before Nurse Grace leaves, she gives Dani the signed discharge orders for her and Kourt.

Dani swings her legs off the bed and stands. She slowly waddle-walks over to the closet and gets her overnight bag.

"Do you want me to change her diaper and get her into the car seat while you're in the bathroom?"

"Do whatever you want," she snaps.

"Whoa. Is that the hormones talking or are you mad about something?" I really wanted to be here with her through labor and delivery. Amelia elected to have a C-section so she wouldn't have to go through the process.

Dani doesn't answer me. She waddle-walks into the bathroom and shuts the door.

I change my daughter's diaper. I sing to her and take pictures of her on my phone and send them to the guys and Jessi.

Dani comes out of the bathroom and starts packing her things. She is not talking to me, nor is she making eye contact. I get Kourt strapped into her car seat and wait for Dani to finish.

Nurse Linda comes in with the wheelchair. I grip the handle of the car seat and carry my daughter out of the room behind Dani and the nurse.

A taxi is waiting at the curb for us. Dani insists on securing the car seat it in the backseat herself. She's being very quiet and reserved and I don't know how to get through to her.

My friends follow the yellow taxi, at an inconspicuous distance, to the apartment.

I get Dani and the baby settled in the bedroom and sit on the edge of the bed next to her.

Dani releases a stuttered emotional breath. She shivers and blinks back tears.

"You are not going to do this alone, Dani. I promise."

She shivers again. "The midwife had to pile heated blankets on me right after I had her. I started having chills."

The intensity of the constant burn in my gut gets stronger.

"All I could think was, I'm going to die and my daughter is going to be like me. A foster kid who knows nothing about her family history. Then I wondered if that's how my mother felt. Alone and abandoned by my father."

Dani starts to cry.

I kick off my shoes and lie with her. Holding her tight.

"I know you had to be there for your friend. I'm not mad about that. I'm mad at myself for becoming dependent on you."

A kick in the nuts would feel better. What can I say? In reality they are alone here. And after the way my dad reacted to Emm, I'm not sure I want to press the issue of Dani and Kourt moving to Colorado.

The front of my shirt is wet, but not in a place where it should be. I lean back and look down. "You're leaking."

Dani looks down at the front of her dress. Breast milk is causing the big wet circles. "I didn't think my milk would come down this soon. I need nursing pads."

"What else do you need? I'll go to the store."

Her cheeks turn a slight red. "Sanitary napkins."

The tips of my fingers trail down her cheek. "Don't be embarrassed. I grew up in a house with a mother and sister. Plus, I have two daughters now. It doesn't bother me to buy pads and tampons or anything else a woman needs."

She points to the list on the nightstand. I take it and the keys to her SUV and leave the apartment.

As I drive to the store, I notice the same black car that pulled away from the curb when I pulled out of the garage is still behind me. The driver is staying three cars back.

I change lanes and check the mirror. Two heartbeats later, the black car changes lanes.

I make a right turn at the corner. The black car also makes a right turn. I pull out my cell phone and call Tony. "I'm being followed."

CHAPTER TWELVE

MALINDA WILLIAMSON

Colorado, Present Day

THIS COFFEE IS HORRIBLE, BUT I continue to sip it from the Styrofoam cup anyway. Like the others, I too was fooled by the sign promising the best coffee in all of Colorado. After the first taste, I was tempted to throw the hot beverage in the barista's face, then reach in the register and get my money back. But I can't draw attention to myself. No one notices me because I went to great lengths to blend in with the people in the station either waiting to depart or waiting for an arrival. Me—the latter.

By now, Bryan is looking for me, so I must be mindful of the places I show up. Once my parents get here, we will spend the night at the hotel, then head to Canada. The passports I paid an old contact to secure for me are in my bag.

I check the time on my watch and look at the board. Drew and Harriet's bus is twenty minutes behind schedule. Flying them here would have tipped off Bryan to my whereabouts. I'm sure he has someone watching their ranch. It took a lot of fast talk to convince my parents to take the trip on the bus under aliases and without luggage. Drew and Harriet are retired RAGS trainers. Naturally they were suspicious of a stranger claiming to have information about their supposedly dead foster-daughter, Amelia Goodman. Harriet's mother-love is why they agreed to come all the way from Texas to Colorado.

My seat in the middle of the waiting area gives me a view of the entrance and exit doors, the status board, and the arrival doors. I take out my notebook to reread what I'd written.

Bryan's unexpected appearance had me on edge. At first I thought he was mad that I killed my hump-buddy. I had no choice, the guy started stalking me and acting possessive. He showed up at my job. Popped up at the same restaurants I was at with coworkers. Knocked on my door in the middle of the night demanding to come in to make sure I didn't have someone else in my bed. Then my hump-buddy's stalking turned into threats of harming me. Killing him was a form of self-preservation.

Lucky for me Bryan wasn't angry. He was in Texas on business and wanted to see how I was doing. Every attempt to get him to fuck me was shot down. I learned the hard way—you only get one shot to burn Bryan Hawk. He left before I woke the next morning. I was used to it. It's the kind of relationship we had until I did something stupid. I intentionally got pregnant, thinking I could use it to get him to join RAGS. What I got was a price tag on my head, thirty-eight weeks of misery, and plastic surgery that saved my life.

The job offer from the principal at Greystone Preparatory Academy was a shock. Dr. Barrett read the article in the national education publication about me winning Innovative Second-grade Teacher of the year from the Association of Private School Teachers of Texas. The salary and benefits alone were the best any elementary private school teacher could hope to get. When I told Bryan, he reminded me that I'm supposed to be living under the radar. If I had listened to Bryan and stayed in Texas, maybe I wouldn't be running from him now.

It started with seeing my ex-girlfriend Deidra for the first time in nine years. She's going by Madelyn Brooks now and was nowhere closer to collecting the millions than I was before my pregnancy. Watching her flaunt herself at Bryan awakened my competitive side, and it clouded my judgment. Then Danielle walked into my classroom. I didn't make the connection until I'd gotten a good look at her. The first month of school was chaotic. I was busy getting acclimated to my new job, the students, and flirting with Madelyn Brooks. Back to School Night was when I put names with faces. Dr. Danielle Edwards. Kourtney Edwards. James Edwards.

James lied about sleeping with her. The proof was a student in my class—in Boulder, Colorado. Danielle in the same city as Bryan was no coincidence. She was there to flip him and get the money, just like Madelyn.

I needed to see Danielle's approach to luring him in. Putting them together for the Halloween project was spur of the moment. I used it as an opportunity to observe Danielle. The constant flirting between the two of them made me angry. Bryan was falling for her. I wanted back in the race.

Snatching Danielle at the mall would have gone as planned if Emma hadn't followed me. I was forced back into observing Danielle until another opportunity came up. The way she and Bryan moved on the dance floor at the club was not like strangers getting to know one another. Their R-rated dance moves were like lovers engaged in a public display of foreplay. The club was too crowded for me to kill her and when she went to the restroom, she wasn't alone.

I tried a different approach to getting to Danielle. It was a good thing I had the chloroform. She might have beat me in a hand-to-hand fight even without the baseball bat. My shoulder was sore for a week from her ramming me into the wall. That was the second time Bryan warned me to leave Danielle alone.

I didn't heed the warning.

I hired a kid to run her off the road. The kid disappeared after he failed.

Madelyn's foolish actions made her a liability, especially after the news about Danielle and Bryan getting married. I wasn't at school the day Jacob and his followers bullied Kourtney. Madelyn denied encouraging her son to do it, but I'd gotten to know Jacob. He never would have called Kourtney those names on his own. None of those kids would have. Bryan didn't believe me when I said I had nothing to do with what happened that day. I got a third warning.

The overhead speaker crackles and the muffled voice of a female announces the arrival of the bus my parents are on. I store my notebook in my newsboy satchel and stand.

The arrival doors open.

Drew and Harriett are in the middle of the pack of people entering the station's receiving area. I hold up the white sign that I'd written their aliases on.

Drew is the first to see it.

I feel the smile on my lips spread as my parents weave their way toward me.

Too impatient to wait, I meet them halfway and lower the sign. "Hello Mr. and Mrs. Novak. Welcome to Colorado."

Harriett's fingers capture my arm. "You said on the phone you may have evidence that our Amelia is still alive?"

My eyes dart around to see if anyone is listening. "Yes, ma'am, but let's not talk here. It was a long ride. Are you hungry?"

"No." Drew holds up an insulated bag. "We packed for the thirty-hour ride."

I want to throw my arms around him and squeeze tight. I've missed his Texan talk and cowboy mentality.

"Then let's get you over to the hotel and settled in your room. We can talk in private over dinner." I lead the way to the exit.

The mid-afternoon sun shines bright in the cloudless sky. I tug on a baseball cap over the copper wig and slip sunglasses over my eyes. We walk the parking lot in silence. The used car I bought before leaving Boulder is parked in a stall at the far end of the lot.

Drew and Harriett comment on how fresh and clean the air is here in Buena Vista, Colorado. When Bryan brought me to this small town in Chaffee County to hide me from RAGS hitmen, I thought it was beautiful and promised myself I'd one day bring my parents.

Along the short route to the hotel, they ooh and aww at the sights.

When I pull into the hotel's driveway entrance, Drew leans forward. A distinct cowboy whistle escapes his lips. "We can't afford a room here."

"As I told you on the phone, your expenses are covered. I made sure you guys got a room with a view of the river."

I park and hurry out of the car and get the bags of clothes I bought them from the trunk. I lead them inside the nineteenth century-inspired hotel and up to their room.

Harriett opens the balcony's double doors. A light breeze blows the ends of the white curtains back into the room.

"I will give you some time to rest and get settled. I'll come get you around six for dinner. If you need anything, my room is just across the hall. Number two-seventeen."

I open the door to my room and peel the cap and wig off my head, dropping them on the made bed. I take out the notebook and pen and go sit on the carpeted floor just inside of the open balcony doors. This is how I spent most of my time here when Bryan brought me to this hotel. The beauty of my surroundings never gets old. I open the notebook and begin to read.

On the day of Bryan and Danielle's wedding, I sat by the fountain near the courthouse wondering why a self-proclaimed bachelor up and decided to get married. It couldn't be because she was pregnant. That doesn't work on Bryan. A man like Bryan doesn't fall in love. From that day on, he started ignoring me. I'd go to his building only to be told he couldn't see me. Phone calls, text messages, emails went unanswered. Bryan never ignored me. The only reason I could think of was because Danielle was closer to getting him into RAGS and getting that reward money. I decided it was time to take Danielle out of the picture. I rejoined Rebels Against Government Suppression as Malinda Williamson and officially put my name in for the Hawk assignment.

With a few manipulatively placed suggestions, I knew Madelyn would run with it. I needed a fall person and she was it. I had someone stick that guy in the movie theater while I stood on the side of a building across from the courtyard, out of view of the cameras, and waited for Danielle. I tracked Danielle from the scope attached to the sniper rifle. Finger on the trigger, then someone stepped out of the shadows and I shot Bryan.

I lay low after that. Plotting another way to take down Danielle. I thought for sure she'd come to the school after my exchange with Kourtney, but Bryan stormed into my house instead. I'd never feared for my life like I did in that moment. Bryan wasn't Bryan. The eerie reflection of fire in his darkened eyes made him look demonic. His last words stuck with me long after he left. My neck was so badly bruised that I had to use concealer and foundation to cover the fingerprints. And I couldn't get the taste of gun oil out of my mouth.

"What do you want with her?" an angry male shouts out.

It sounds like my dad.

I get to my feet. The notebook falls to the stone balcony floor. I run to my purse and grab my gun; the silencer is already attached.

The door to my parents' room is cracked opened. I use my free hand to ease it open wider and peek inside.

Just inside the door, a small red and black hole dots the center of Drew's head while a dark crimson circle spreads out like spilled paint on the white carpeted floor beneath him.

My eyes snap to the vicinity of the whimpering coming from the bathroom. Harriet cowers in the doorway wrapped in a plush white bath towel. Steam from the shower floats around her like cloud cover.

An auburn-haired woman dressed in dark jeans and shirt blocks my mother from escaping.

"Where's Amelia?" Her thick Russian-accented voice demands my mother to answer.

"I'm behind you, bitch," I respond for Harriet.

The gun-wielding woman whips around and smiles. Her eyes scrutinize my face.

"Who the fuck are you?" I demand.

The turned-up corners of her thin lips mock me. "Kimberly Baryshnikova-*Edwards*. And you're the dumb bitch that was in love with my husband." She gets off a shot—not at me.

My mother is dead before her body falls back on the white tiled bathroom floor.

I react.

The first shot wipes the smile off Mrs. Edwards's face. The other shots make her body jerk as I advance on her, my finger not letting up on the trigger.

Her back hits the wall and then she falls face first to the carpet. I put one last bullet in the back of her head.

Unsure if anyone else on the floor heard the commotion, I run to the door and close it, then sit on the bed and try to breathe.

With each labored inhale and choppy exhale, I breathe in the odor of gunpowder mixed with the angry scent of death. My eyes dance back and forth between my dead mother and dead father. And the dead Mrs. Kimberly Baryshinikova-Edwards.

Oh, this hurts like hell. They were not my biological parents, but Drew and Harriett were the only people in this world who loved me. And I was so close to getting them out of the United States and safely away from Bryan's reach.

I ease off the bed, getting to my knees. Slow as a turtle, I crawl over to Kimberly. Angry tears falling from my eyes get absorbed by the blood-splattered white carpet.

I summon the emotional strength to search Kimberly's pockets for clues as to who sent her. I find nothing in her back pockets. I shove her over and search her front pockets.

My fingers pull out a folded piece of paper from one pocket and car keys from the other. I drop the keys in front of me and unfold the paper.

It falls to the floor like it burned me as I scramble away until my back hits the wall.

A sob steals my breath. My body grows cold. I sit there staring at the paper next to Kimberly's body. It's the photo Dr. Eggenberger took after my last round of plastic surgery and my face had completely healed. One person outside of the Switzerland hospital had this picture. And that person knows how much I love Drew and Harriett. I have nothing left to lose. I'm ready to die.

Is Bryan ready for his wife and kids to die too?

CHAPTER THIRTEEN

DANIELLE

Colorado, Present Day

THE VALET OPENS THE CAR door. He is not the one from this morning.

"Do you need assistance with your bag?" He gestures to my backpack sitting on the passenger seat.

"No, I can handle it." I grab my backpack, unzip the small front compartment and take out some money from the bundle. I discretely pass him the one-hundred-dollar tip as I climb out of the car. "I do need a favor though. I'm in the north penthouse suite. If anyone else pulls in saying they're going up to the penthouse, call me on the suite's phone. To signal how many people are coming up, let the phone ring that many times, then hang up. Do you get what I'm saying?"

He is well trained. The tip goes into his pocket without a glance at the denomination. "Yes, ma'am."

The backpack is a little heavier than it was when I left with it this morning. The supplies Mr. Brumfield gave me are the cause of the extra weight. I walk through the lobby slipping my arms through the straps.

The elevator doors open three seconds after I push the button. I step inside. Once the doors close, the air in the cab becomes thick with unease.

"This is going to work," I whisper to myself.

While the elevator ascends to the penthouse, I slip my hand in my back pocket to make sure the note I wrote and the prepaid cell phone are still there, then I take the safety off the gun holstered at my side and adjust the borrowed men's button down shirt to cover the bulletproof vest I'm now wearing.

The elevator stops.

I take a calming breath and channel defiance.

The doors open.

"There she is," Marie croons. She rises from her seat on the sofa with grace, a bright smile on her face. She's changed clothes. "Elijah, this is my granddaughter, Danielle." Marie executes the perfect tone and grand gesture, with her one good arm, like a Southern high-society hostess, introducing guests at a soirée. "Danielle, this is my oldest and dearest friend, Elijah Hopper."

I drop the backpack on the end table as I approach them.

Hopper stares at me with a cold, blank, calculating face and reaches for my outstretched hand, enclosing it between his. The corner of his top lip curls and he forcefully yanks me closer. "If you don't mind, I need to search you for tracking devices."

I snatch away from him, balling my fists.

"Now, now, Eli," Marie sings. "My granddaughter is on our side. I made sure of it."

"That audio hypnosis stuff didn't work on her."

"Yes, it did."

"You just said she told you someone is translating through an earpiece. The command is in Creole. If she doesn't understand the language how could you condition her?" He waits for Marie to respond, but she doesn't. "Look, Antoinette, it's my job to protect your anonymity. Even though you went behind my back and trusted the wrong people, I'm still going to clean up this mess and get you out of here."

"I told my grandmother I don't speak the language, but *wish* I had a translator in my ear." My gaze shifts to Marie. I force the sweetest smile I can conjure up and drop my arms, so my body language makes my lie believable. "Do you even remember how you got to bed last night?"

Wrinkle lines mar her brows. "No."

I toss Hopper the "there you have it" gesture with my hands and create some distance between us. "The attempts on her life have obviously hindered her thought process."

Marie plops down on the sofa, rubbing her injured arm. "Maybe I misheard you. My brain is still a little fuzzy on what happened yesterday."

"There's nothing wrong with your hearing," Hopper roars. "Your granddaughter isn't on the up and up." He takes a threatening step in my direction.

"Don't think my stage of pregnancy or your age will stop me from laying you out on this floor, Eli."

He chuckles and bats away my words with a dismissive flick of his hand. "Little girl, I'm too old of a tomcat to be scratched by a kitten." He makes a move, reaching behind him.

I pull my weapon and fire a shot in his chest.

The frightened scream from Marie is muffled behind her hand clamped over her mouth.

Hopper falls to the floor at her feet. His eyes are open and locked on her. A bloody circle begins to grow on his baby blue dress shirt.

"This kitten's claws are very sharp, old man," I hiss.

He wheezes. Then his body slackens and his eyes close.

Heavy footsteps echo from upstairs. It sounds like a platoon is storming the penthouse. James reaches the landing. His feet are a blur on the stairs. Gun in his hand.

"We have to go," I tell him.

"Why'd you kill Hopper?" he demands.

"He's working with Willis."

James's body jerks to a stop on the last step like he ran full speed into an invisible wall. "What?"

Marie scampers away from the body at her feet, whispering, "No. No. No. Eli is my guy."

I holster the gun and cover the distance between us in five determined strides to grab her hand. "How long have you known Elijah Hopper?"

She is focused on the man on the floor.

"Look at me, Grandma. How long have you known him?"

"Years. He came to meetings. Worked his way up. When my father died, Eli made suggestions on how to hide me from the enemy."

"A RAGS meeting isn't the first time you saw Hopper."

She stares at his body. "Of course it is."

"Think back to that day in the bar in New Orleans. Who was with Willis when you argued with Pierre?"

Slowly her head turns in my direction, but her eyes are the last to follow. "I don't know."

"Yes, you do. You were taught to be observant."

Marie looks like a small scared child. I take her hand.

"Why did you go to the bar?"

"To stop Pierre from taking credit for my work. He was jealous because I did a job on my own and was about to make a million-dollar sell."

"How could you let your no good, lazy half-brother take away your sell, Antoinette?" I squeeze her hand until she cries out in pain. "What do you remember seeing, hearing, smelling?"

"A small jazz band playing in the corner. Catfish and shrimp and chicken frying. Fresh baguettes baking in the oven. Stale alcohol in the air. People eating and drinking and dancing and talking loudly. A bald man sitting by himself on the last stool at the bar, pretending to read the newspaper, but he's watching the room. Pierre sitting at Daddy's table in the back by himself."

"Whose table is closest to your brother's?"

"I don't know."

I didn't think it possible to squeeze her hand any tighter, but I do. "Yes you do, Antoinette."

She closes her eyes. Her head slowly shifts left to right, then stops, like she is reliving that exact moment. I ease up on the pressure of her hand a bit.

"The loudest ones are sitting at a table a few feet from Pierre's table. They're trying too hard to fit in, but it's obvious they're casing the joint."

"How do you know?"

"The glasses on the table are dry, yet the pitcher is half full."

"What are the men doing?"

"One is standing with one foot on the chair and he's leaning over with his arm on his leg. One has a walking cane hanging off the back of his chair. He's laughing the loudest. The one with thick wavy hair has a tattoo of boxing gloves on the inside of his arm. He's talking the most. There's a quiet one with a rolled magazine in his hand that he keeps hitting against the table."

Marie gasps.

"What did you see?"

"Elijah. Elijah is the one holding the rolled magazine."

"Danielle, what's going on?" James asks.

I reach for the backpack on the end table and start pulling out supplies. "We need to wipe this place clean, then get the hell out of here before Willis finds us." I pass out packs of premoistened disinfectant wipes and small bottles of bleach. "Pull the sheets and blankets from the bed. Put them in the tub. Turn on the water and pour the whole bottle of bleach in."

Marie looks lost.

"Grandmother. Go. Do it now. We can't leave any traces of us being here. I'll take care of things in here."

She nods and rushes to the bedroom with the supplies in the crook of her good arm.

"Have you completely lost it? Hawk is going to flip his shit."

I reach into my pocket, palm the squared piece of paper, and grab James's hand, pressing the note into it. "I need you to trust me, James. There is more going on here than Bryan realizes."

His fingers close around the note. He nods, then heads upstairs.

I bend down and check Mr. Hopper. The circle of blood on his shirt is still growing. He is completely still. His face and body are relaxed. As I stand, I notice the bright red light next to the tagline "bedroom" is lit up on the phone. I pick up my backpack and quickly walk to the dining table.

From the back compartment I pull out a gun and a roll of industrial tape out of the backpack, then sit in the chair at the head of the table with its back to the stairs. I do my best to measure the length of my husband's arms. I stand, take the safety off the gun and rack the slide. My teeth act as scissors as I unroll two strips of tape to secure the gun to the back of a chair.

Next, I count the number of stairs. Midway, I use one strip of tape to secure the second gun to a baluster.

At the top of the stairs on the last step I loop fishing line low around each newel post three times, tying it off like Mr. Brumfield showed me. A half-inch above it, I wrap another line. A half-inch above that, I do another line.

Blink. Blink. Blink. The tip of my finger flicks each line to make sure they are taut enough to trip up an unsuspecting pursuer. I stand back to make sure they are invisible. I test out the height to make sure I don't trip myself up running up the stairs.

When I hear the water running in the downstairs en suite bathroom, I hurry down the stairs and stash the backpack behind the curtain of the patio doors.

The water stops. Marie comes out of the bedroom. "I cleaned up everything that I could."

"James, let's go!" I pull my gun from the holster.

He charges down the stairs. When he's midway, I raise my hand, aim, and fire one shot.

James falls back. Motionless.

"Why'd you kill him?" Marie cries.

"If Hopper is working with Willis, then James is too."

Marie heads to the elevator and pushes the button. With her back to me, I reach in my pocket to get out the earpiece and put it in my ear. The bell chimes, signaling the arrival of the elevator.

The doors open.

A fair-skinned man with curly salt and pepper hair steps into the penthouse suite. He is wearing my great grandfather's gold pinky ring with the onyx stone surrounded by diamonds and the gold tie clip with the initials DET engraved in it.

"I'm h-h-here, l-little s-s-sis." Marie's half-brother, Pierre Dupree, stutters.

"Bryan needs to get here, now!" I whisper.

———◆———

Arizona, Eight Years Ago

The wedding band I still wear and my visits to the cemetery are the source of small arguments between Bryan and me. He says it's just a piece of metal, but Bryan doesn't understand that the ring symbolizes my connection to my past. Most of the time I forget I'm wearing it. I take flowers to James's grave because I miss my friend. After three weeks of face-to-face and cell phone confrontations, I call a cease-fire because the verbal punches are getting too personal.

I pack up a two-month-old Kourtney and drive to California to visit my foster parents. Bryan is waiting for us when we return home five days later. The fury in his eyes trickles down to his body language. He gets Kourtney washed up and tucked into her bassinet while I wait for him in the living room. Through clenched teeth, Bryan reprimands me for not letting him know I was taking *his* daughter out of the state. With balled fists, I remind him that *I* am Kourtney's mother and can take her anywhere I want *without* his permission. The calm façade is dropped, and the verbal tug-of-war begins, neither side conceding. Bryan brings up a good point: I should at least let him know my itinerary so if something happens on the road and I can't call for help, he'll know where to look if I don't make it to my destination on time. I promise to tell him about the road trips *before* Kourtney and I leave and give him a full itinerary. He promises to try and ease up with the overprotectiveness.

All the little arguments were just the prelude to a massive bomb that has been building between Bryan and me since we brought Kourtney home. I am fed up with him not giving me a valid reason for why Kourtney and I cannot meet his family. This time, I use sarcasm to shoot down his lame excuse. Bryan throws the sarcasm back at me and his words touch the wrong nerve.

In retaliation, I yell into the phone, "You're hiding Kourtney because she's your dirty little secret!" I hang up before he can refute the accusation.

Bryan calls right back.

I turn off my cell phone.

He calls the landline.

I unplug it and go to bed early, but I cannot sleep. Wondering what he'll do next makes me anxious.

In the middle of the night, my front door opens. I hold my breath and keep a half-cracked eye on the bedroom doorway.

Bryan walks in carrying a sleeping Emma. He lays her in the empty crib, then removes her jacket and hat without waking her.

He walks to my side of the bed where Kourtney sleeps in the bassinet and kisses her head.

I watch him shed his shoes and clothes with jerky movements, then walk around to his side of the bed and climb in behind me.

I kick the covers off and move to get out, but his arm clamps around my waist and drags me back against him—hard.

Kaboom.

Bryan rests his head on mine. Cheek to cheek. I don't have to see his face to know how angry he is. It's in the way he holds me captive. It's in the way the breath leaves his lungs to slam against my face. It's clear in the deathly calm timbre of his voice once he decides to address me.

"If you were trying to push a button, congratulations, you succeeded. But I don't give a *damn* how angry you are at me. Don't you *ever* refer to *my* baby girl, as a *dirty secret* again, Danielle."

Hearing him repeat my words make me realize how racially charged the accusation came across. That was not my intention. Before she was born, Bryan and I talked openly about our daughter's biracial identity and how we are going to raise her to embrace both races.

"Bryan, I'm sorry. I didn't mean it in that context…" His arm tightens around me, cutting off the rest of my apology.

"I already hate myself for not being there when she was born and only seeing her a few times a month; I don't need you piling on more shit. The first time I took Emma to my parents' house, I came close to punching my father. I can't guarantee I won't if he reacts to Kourtney the same way. *Both* of my girls are my life. I will protect them to my last breath and even then, I'll keep fighting for them. You and Kourtney will meet my family and friends but give me time to make it happen."

I wait several minutes for the mushroom cloud to settle before I turn over. The nightlight across the room is enough for me to see his face, but he keeps his eyes closed. I reach out to touch his face. He pulls away, turning his back to me.

"Being Bryan Kendall Hawk is a goddamn curse. I don't get why he gave me the name when he hated being Bryan Kendall Hawk the Third. I'll never saddle my son down with it. And in case you haven't already guessed, my dad and I don't have the best relationship."

I scoot closer and spoon him, pressing my lips into his back. "Bryan, I'm so sorry. You have to know, that's not how I meant it. If you had explained things to me the first time I brought it up, I would have stopped badgering you. I just want Kourtney to know that she didn't appear out of nowhere, that she has a family."

"Why can't the four of us be enough for now?"

"You don't know what it's like not to have roots because your family has always been a part of your life. I want that for our daughter."

"Have I ever given you a reason not to trust me, Dani?"

"No."

"Can you trust me to handle this my way?"

I exhale. "Yes."

"Thank you."

He keeps his back to me, but the anger that fueled him to leave Colorado in the middle of the night to come to Arizona slowly leaves his body. Once his shoulders relax and his breathing is slow and steady, I whisper, "We weren't expecting Kourtney to come a week early. What's important is that you're a part of her life. She'll know her father and her sister. She knows you love her."

Bryan and Emma are back in Arizona the following week. He and our girls are the loudest in the audience when I walk across the stage at the graduation ceremony. I now have my master's.

We find a way to make our unconventional family unit work without extended members. In August, he leaves Emma with me while he goes on a two-week business trip.

The fall semester starts and with it, a new set of educational pressures. I'm working toward my doctoral degree.

Yvon is a big help. She watches Kourtney while I am at work or in class or at the gym. And when Emma is here, she watches both girls. Yvon and I have an unspoken edict on discussing my unique relationship with Bryan. She never questions why the signature on the weekly childcare checks is not mine.

On Halloween, Emma, dressed in a pumpkin costume, lets go of my hand and walks from the dining table to the love seat. You'd think she ran a marathon and won from the way I'm clapping and jumping up and down. After that, there is no stopping her. Bryan and I rearrange and swap out some furniture to accommodate a walker *and* a crawler. We are outgrowing this one-bedroom apartment.

Coming home from putting red, white, and blue flowers on James's grave in honor of Veteran's Day, I run into the apartment manager in the courtyard. He asks if I'm interested in moving into a two-bedroom unit. I don't need to think twice about it, I say yes! We have two of everything squeezed into my small apartment because when Bryan and Emma are here, we need two of everything.

The security improvements he made in the one-bedroom apartment, Bryan does the same in the two-bedroom apartment while I'm at work. Except for the bed and television Bryan bought me for Christmas last year and Kourtney's and Emma's things, all of my old furniture and appliances are donated or tossed out. We buy new, coordinating pieces.

We celebrate Emma's first birthday—two days late—in the new apartment. Bryan couldn't make it to Arizona on her actual birthday. Emma is the sweetest one-year-old. She has expressive chocolate brown eyes. Her mousy brown hair is down to her jawline. She likes for me to put it in ponytails.

Emma and I cuddle when I read to her. I love Emma like she is my own. Her smile warms my heart. Our bond is stronger than a shared bloodline. I don't correct her when she calls me Mommy.

Kourtney refers to everyone as Dada now. She's a total daddy's girl. When he is around, Bryan does everything for her except nurse her. She is inquisitive and daring and the sweetest ten-month-old. Bryan sings to her all the time. Bedtime it's always "Baby Mine." When he wants to make her belly laugh it's his modified rendition of, "I Can Dream About You" while he dances around. Boy, do I hope our daughter has my dancing gene.

Traveling back and forth is wearing Bryan down. But he doesn't complain. He's made so many sacrifices for us, it's time I make some for him. I research doctoral programs in Colorado and find one that I can start next year. For Bryan and our girls, I will take some time off from school. I even find a job listing that I qualify for. Today I leave Bryan and the girls at the apartment and go to the post office to mail off a job application and resume for a position at the hospital in Boulder, Colorado. The head of the Behavioral Science Department, Dr. Jasper Stevens, is a renowned psychiatrist. Boulder is only an hour and a half drive from Colorado Springs. If I get the job, at least we'd be in the same state.

Last Christmas, Bryan said he wanted to start a tradition of getting our tree seven days before the holiday. This year we go to the Christmas tree lot when I get off work.

Emma was too young to remember her first tree and this is Kourtney's first time at the lot, so I bring my camera along and snap pictures.

The trip is fun for me and the girls. I can't say the same about their dad. He hasn't paid much attention to us, not even after carrying in the six-foot Noble fir Christmas tree. He has been on his phone.

After I get the girls fed, bathed, and into bed, I sit on the sofa and upload the pictures I took of this year's Christmas tree shopping adventure from my camera to my laptop.

Bryan plops down next to me on the sofa. "I see the holiday bug bit you. Every room in the apartment has holiday decorations." Bryan's phone buzzes again.

"I'm surprised you noticed." I shut down my laptop and set it on the coffee table.

His thumbs rapidly tap out a text message on the cell phone. Bryan has never been this preoccupied with his phone.

I leave him sitting on the sofa. I start undressing as I walk down the hallway to my bedroom, stripping all the way down to my panties and nursing bra by the time I make it to the bathroom. Standing at the sink, I stare at myself in the bathroom mirror while gathering my hair into a messy bun on the top of my head.

Even though I lost the twenty-three pounds of baby weight, my body is curvy in all the right places. Mrs. Franklin calls it my grown woman body. I did a modified boxing routine while I was pregnant. After my six-week checkup, I went back to my usual three days a week workout and twice a week kickboxing class routine.

Movement in the mirror catches my eye. Bryan is undressing in the bedroom and walking toward the bathroom. "I'll wash your back."

He stands behind me in just his black boxer briefs.

"Are you sure you can leave your phone alone long enough to do that?" I hope my comment sounds as snarky as I meant it.

"My phone doesn't leave scratches on my back and call out my name when she comes." Bryan stares at me through our reflection in the mirror. He intentionally wets his bottom lip, then drags his teeth across it while a heated gaze starts at the top of my thighs and prowls every inch of me like hands stripping away the barriers that hide my nudity from him.

The next sassy comment dissolves on my tongue. A sequence of sexual details that he is capable of unleashing on me are checked off a mental list.

Fleshy pleasures that live up to my sexual dreams in every way.

Uninhibited itch that only he knows where and how to scratch.

Carnal needs and desires acted out in the most intimate scenes.

Kisses in places only he has been allowed to penetrate.

Motions that drive the energy to a series of orgasms.

Erotic touches everywhere imaginable.

Bryan and I have explored each other's bodies in an assortment of sensual means. Our coupling is more than just intimate contact because sex isn't the only way we connect.

From somewhere behind him, a different ringtone sounds goes off—loudly.

"I'll meet you in the shower," he whispers, then leaves the bathroom, closing the door behind him.

I turn the knobs and test the temperature of the water with my hand. Once it's where I want it, I reach behind me to unhook my bra, then step out of my panties.

The door opens. From the look on his face, I know sex is no longer on his mind.

"Baby, are you okay with the girls by yourself for a couple of days? I need to go out of the country on business."

I try not to let the disappointment show on my face. "Yeah, sure. Yvon will watch them on the days I'm scheduled to work. When are you leaving?"

"I need to be at the airport in an hour."

"You want a ride?"

"No, I've got a car coming. But can you lay out a suit for me, baby?" He steps out of the boxer briefs and into the shower, closing the transparent door.

I put on my robe and leave the bathroom.

Bryan's side of the closet is equally as full as mine. I sift through his selection of suits and choose the charcoal gray one. I like the way it fits his body. I pick a crisp white shirt, a patterned emerald green tie and matching pocket hankie. The combination will complement the color of his eyes. I lay out everything on the bed, including a pair of cufflinks, boxer briefs, and socks. I unzip four shoe bags and set the shoes on the floor near the bed. It takes a minute, but I pick the shoes that go with the belt. Too bad he doesn't have a power watch, it would complement the look I put together. I put the other shoes back in their bags and back on the shelf in the closet.

Picking out what Bryan puts on his beautiful body is oddly gratifying.

He opens the bathroom door with a towel wrapped low on his hips. Wet hair slicked back. Face shaven. Wet chest hairs and line of pubic hairs lay flat on his body.

"Dada." Kourtney's sleepy voice calls out through the baby monitor on the nightstand.

I go across the hall to the girls' room.

Kourtney is standing in her crib. Arms reaching up.

"Hi, sweetie. Why are you awake?"

She whines and looks past me, no doubt looking for her dad. One chubby fist rubs her eyes.

"Daddy is busy right now. Can Mommy hold you?" I lift her out of the crib.

Right away her hand slips through the opening of my robe to my breast. I carry her over to a rocking chair and open the robe. Kourtney settles in my lap and latches on. She alternates patting and squeezing my breast with her hand as she nurses. I pick up the children's book about the curious bear cub that I found at a used bookstore and start reading it to her.

When I look up, Bryan is standing in the doorway fully dressed.

"Is everything okay?" he asks.

Kourtney pulls away at the sound of his voice. She smiles at her dad while streams of breast milk shoot from my nipple.

"Hey." He laughs and walks into the room. "You're wasting good milk, baby girl. If you're not going to drink it, I will."

She turns back to my breast and latches on.

He runs his fingers through her thick curls and he kisses her forehead.

Kourtney reaches out to grab his tie. She smiles with my nipple still in her mouth. I rescue the silk tie before she yanks it.

"I'll call you as soon as I can, Dani." He kisses me.

Bryan walks over to Emma's crib, kisses two fingers and touches her cheek, and then he's gone.

I slowly rock Kourtney and try not to feel resentful towards him for allowing his job to interfere with the tradition he started.

The tug on my nipple starts to slow down, then stops. Now that Kourtney has top and bottom teeth I don't let her fall asleep with my nipple in her mouth. I learned that after the second time I got bitten.

Kourtney's body completely relaxes. I lay her in her crib, check on Emma, and go to bed.

In the morning, my alarm goes off an hour earlier than I usually get up. I have to be at the clinic at seven because I'm leaving early to pick up the Franklins from the airport at four in the afternoon.

The landline rings. Yvon's name flashes on the caller ID. "Good morning, Danielle. What time are you bringing Kourtney and Emma?"

"How did you…"

"I saw Bryan leaving last night and Emma wasn't with him."

"You are a one-woman neighborhood watch team. When do you sleep?"

She laughs. That has been an ongoing joke since she moved into the building.

"I'll bring them over at six thirty."

"Don't worry about getting them dressed. I'll do that. And bring the double stroller. It's going to be a nice day. We'll get out for a little while."

That is code for patrolling the neighborhood for news, events, and gossip. Yvon knows what's going on in every apartment building on this block *and* the next five blocks. She could write a soap opera based on what she knows about the people in the neighborhood.

I get out of bed and begin my day.

The mental health clinic is always busy during the holidays. Now that I have my master's, my duties have changed along with a nice raise in pay. From the time I clock in to the time I clock out, I am in group sessions or case study sessions with the doctor I'm assigned to work with.

Traffic at the airport is crazy. Impatient car horns drown out the sounds of airplanes taking off and landing. Luckily, I find a parking spot on the first level in the structure.

Even navigating my way to the baggage claim area takes time. I snag a luggage cart and wait. According to the board, the Franklins' flight is already at the gate.

I don't have to wait long. I see Mrs. Franklin first. She is walking alongside the airport attendant pushing Mr. Franklin in a wheel-chair.

Last year Mr. Franklin was diagnosed with early stages of Alzhei-mer's. He's on medication. The last time I visited them, he seemed to be doing well, so why is he in a wheelchair?

"Look, Kat, Danielle's waiting for us." Mr. Franklin points in my direction. The strong man who taught me to stand up for myself consented to being pushed in a wheelchair in the airport. I know it must have taken a monumental amount of convincing to get him to agree to use one even for a short period of time.

Mrs. Franklin's smile is bright and welcoming, yet I can see the tiredness in her eyes once they reach the spot where I am standing.

"Where's bright eyes?" she asks.

"Kourtney is with the sitter. I came straight from work."

The sound of a goose using a megaphone echoes throughout the baggage claim area. The carousel starts turning and luggage starts rolling down the conveyer belt. It's not hard to spot their suitcases: bandanas are tied around the handles.

Once I get their suitcases on the cart, Mr. Franklin thanks the attendant and rises from the wheelchair.

They follow me to the parking structure.

The drive to the hotel is filled with small talk about what is going on in Los Angeles, and who in their group of friends has passed on. Despite his diagnosis, Mr. Franklin's mind seems to be sharp.

We leave their luggage in their room and drive to my apartment.

Yvon brings the girls home and when Kourtney sees them, she toddles straight into Mrs. Franklin's open arms.

"When did she start walking?" Mrs. Franklin hugs my daughter.

"A couple of weeks ago."

"Hello there, bright eyes," Mrs. Franklin sings to Kourtney. "I swear I've never seen hazel eyes quite like hers." She says that every time she sees Kourtney.

"She certainly didn't get them from that no-good James," Mr. Franklin growls and reaches for Kourtney. She happily goes to him. "How is Pop-Pop's little lightweight?"

I'm not ready to explain that she is a Hawk, not an Edwards. If Bryan were here, they'd know it without me telling them.

"Mommy." Emma pats my leg, then raises her arms.

I lift her up and kiss her sweet cheek and breathe in her toddler scent. She hides her face in the crook of my neck. I run my hand up and down her back to reassure her she is okay.

"Who's this?" Mr. Franklin demands.

"This is Emma. My friend had to go out of town on business and I'm keeping her."

"What kind of mother leaves her baby with a friend days before Christmas?"

"Her father owns his own business and had an emergency. I sometimes keep Emma for him."

"Him?" Mrs. Franklin smirks. "Are you already seeing someone, Danielle?"

In their day, the grieving period for a widow is a decade before it is acceptable to entertain male company. I wanted them to meet Bryan and together we could tell them Kourtney is *his* daughter.

"Are you up for helping me cook dinner, Mr. Franklin?" Yes, I'm deflecting her question for now, but I lived with Mrs. Franklin; I know the question will come up again before the night is over.

"Go to Nana." He hands Kourtney to his wife and stands.

Mrs. Franklin smiles and reaches a hand out to Emma. "Come on cutie-pie. Come to Nana."

It takes Emma a full three minutes and lots of coaxing from me before she goes to the older woman.

In the kitchen, Mr. Franklin and I talk boxing. He wants to know how often I go to the gym and what techniques I've perfected. I promise to take him to the gym where I workout and show him my progress. He tells me they want him to sell his gym but doesn't elaborate on who "they" are. I sense the thought of selling the gym really bothers him.

In the living room, Mrs. Franklin has Kourtney's hair bucket and is trying to tame the thick curls of my daughter's hair into individual plaited braids. Kourtney is batting at Mrs. Franklin's hand and dodging the comb. My poor daughter is tender headed.

Emma finds the exchange funny. She has the brush in her hand and is trying to brush Mrs. Franklin's salt and pepper hair.

Dinner with them feels like old times back in their home in Los Angeles.

After we eat, Mr. Franklin falls asleep on the sofa with the evening news on the television. Mrs. Franklin helps me get the girls washed up and ready for bed. She tells me that Mr. Franklin's knees have been bothering him lately and that's why she arranged for a wheelchair at the airport.

I sit in one rocking chair nursing Kourtney while Mrs. Franklin rocks Emma in the other chair. She reads a story aloud. Yvon must have tired the girls out today. Both Emma and Kourtney fall asleep right away.

"Emma's dad is more than a friend, isn't he?" Mrs. Franklin sets the book on the nightstand and takes the bottle out of Emma's mouth. She shifts Emma to her shoulder and stands.

I take Kourtney off my breast and stand too. There is no sense in lying. She has been all through the apartment. Bryan and Emma's presence is in every room.

We lay the girls in their individual cribs and pull the blankets up to their shoulders.

"Danielle, it's okay if he is. I know you're not a foolish person. Me and George just want you to be happy. That's why we're here. You and Kourtney have been weighing heavy on his heart."

I look up to see an understanding smile on her face and compassion in her eyes.

"I really want you guys to meet him."

She sits back down in the rocker. I follow her lead.

"I can tell he respects you."

"How? You haven't seen us together."

"I don't have to. All I have to do is look around. And look at you and those girls. You care about this man too?"

"Yes."

"But?"

I shrug.

"Child, if it's because of James, don't be a fool. George told me to stay out of it and let you live your life. Come to think of it, he's always said that where James was concerned. But you listen to me. That marriage wasn't going to last. Bright eyes is the only good thing that came out y'all's union." She stares at the wall across from her.

I know that look. Mrs. Franklin is about to share some real-world wisdom.

The second hand on the clock is on its fifth cycle when Mrs. Franklin stops rocking and turns her head to me. "Before I married George, my something old was advice from my Auntie Linda. She said the foundation of real love is unconditional trust because every relationship has its seasons. If there's a strong foundation, through it all, unconditional trust makes loving each other—

effortless. I didn't understand a word of what she'd said. As a matter of fact, my face probably looked confused like yours look right now. I tucked away her advice and went on to marry the man I loved. Boy, did we have seasons. Some more bitter than others. There were times when I felt like we were drowning in the waters of a rapid river and the only way to survive was to let him go. But something in me just wouldn't let me give up on him. Something stronger than love. Then Auntie Linda's advice made sense. I'm saying all this to say—if this young man is the one you're meant to weather the seasons with, you too will understand the advice."

I hear the front door open and Yvon calls out. Earlier, I asked her to come by around eight-thirtyish to watch Kourtney and Emma while I drive my foster parents back to their hotel.

Mr. Franklin is disoriented when we wake him. He calls me Elizabeth. It takes a minute for him to remember where he is and who I am.

Every afternoon when I get off work, I pick up Mr. and Mrs. Franklin from the hotel and bring them to my apartment. Mr. Franklin and I cook dinner. Mrs. Franklin is determined to plait Kourtney's hair while Emma brushes Mrs. Franklin's hair.

It's two days before Christmas and Mrs. Franklin wants to go shopping after I get off work. I'm just getting out of a group session when the receptionist, Shayla Cooper, tells me I have an urgent call. Kourtney's and Emma's faces flash in my mind and my heart pounds in my chest. I pick up the phone.

It's the front desk manager at the hotel. Mrs. Franklin told her to call and tell me to meet the ambulances at the hospital.

Dr. Blanchard, the clinic's director, is standing close by. I tell her I have an emergency with my foster parents. She practically pushes me out the door.

The hospital is four blocks away. I get there ten minutes before the two ambulances pull up. The back doors of the first one opens, and Mrs. Franklin's stretcher is pulled out. There is an ice pack on her forehead, one on her left knee, and another on her ankle.

"What happened?" I ask.

"George is having an episode. He keeps talking about his gym. Please make them understand what's going on," she cries.

The back doors of the second ambulance open. Mr. Franklin is thrashing on the stretcher and pulling against the restraints on his wrists and ankles.

"Miss, you need to stand back."

"The Franklins are my foster parents." I follow the EMTs through the emergency room doors, flashing my work badge to keep from getting put out.

Mr. Franklin is very agitated. I wonder what set him off?

An ER doctor approaches Mr. Franklin's stretcher.

"He was diagnosed with Alzheimer's last year." I begin to rattle off the list of medications he is on. Across the floor, another ER doctor is examining Mrs. Franklin.

I stay by Mr. Franklin's side as he's put through a battery of tests before he is given a sedative and falls asleep.

He has a urinary tract infection. The doctor says the discomfort caused by the UTI is probably why he is agitated, coupled with having his hands restrained.

Mrs. Franklin is being kept overnight because of the bump on her head. I request a private room, so they can stay together, which the ER doctor agrees to.

It's after eleven when I get back to the apartment. I'm tired, hungry, and my breasts are full, and they hurt. Yvon isn't the one sitting on the sofa when I open the door.

Bryan is wearing basketball shorts, a muscle shirt, and his bare feet are crossed at the ankle on the coffee table. His arms and legs are covered in fresh scabs and bruises. He's holding a plate piled with leftovers from yesterday's dinner in his hands.

"Damn, Dani. These are good. Why haven't you made them before?" He stuffs a chunk of hot water cornbread in his mouth.

"What the hell happened to you?!"

CHAPTER FOURTEEN

BRYAN

Colorado, Present Day

FROM THE SENSITIVE COMPARTMENTED INFORMA-TION Facility on the first floor of my building, I monitor activity in a Yemen coastal town along the Gulf of Aden. The town is heavily occupied by the Islam Liberation Army; it's no surprise the transporter erector launcher and radar vehicles stopped there. So far, there is no action to launch the Intercontinental Ballistic Missiles.

Fontenot is doing an excellent job of directing the ESO team to the location. With the team wearing body heat concealing combat uniforms, she is using the tracking devices in their military rings to keep up with them. It is zero-two-hundred hours in Yemen. Sunrise is about three and a half hours away over there. Paul, Acosta, Ricci, and Porter won't have the cover of darkness to sneak in, kill everyone, disarm the missiles, and be on their way home before the rest of ILA knows what's going on.

In the background, the local news station is playing on the flat screen television. The top of the hour story is still the collapse of the warehouse and the seven dead bodies recovered from the rubble. The names of the deceased are being withheld until the next of kin are notified. But I already know who the seven are, including the female I snapped pictures of while I was there.

Riley identified her as Faatima Yousef, the youngest daughter of Amir Mahdavi. And the most active of his children in ILA.

I look up from the computer monitor to see if the report about the American airplane that exploded over the mountain in Nepal is still running along the tickertape bottom portion of the station's broadcast.

The station is replaying the moment when Langford arrived at the scene.

"The owner of the business operating inside the warehouse has just arrived on the scene," the newscaster announces as he joins the other on-the-scene news personalities shoving a microphone in Langford's shocked face.

"Mr. Langford, was the building up to code?"

"What are the names of the employees who died in the building?"

"When were you notified of the collapse?"

"Why are you just now arriving to the site?"

"Sir," Fontenot speaks. "Rosemond and North just pulled into the building's parking garage."

"Make all elevators busy except for the one already down here. Send it up to the second floor." I jump to my feet, get the night vision glasses and utility gloves from my pack.

The elevator chimes twice, signaling the doors are closing.

I haul ass toward the cab, clearing the opening with my shoulders brushing the rubber door gaskets before they seal shut. Using my momentum, I Jackie-Chan-climb the cattycorner metal walls and push open the shaft panel in the process.

As the elevator starts to rise, I pull myself through the opening and set the panel back in place.

Lying face down, I ride the top of the elevator car.

It stops on the second level. The rogue Watchers enter the cab discussing the extra security to get into the building.

Rosemond swipes her keycard across the sensor.

The elevator doors close and it starts its rise to The Nest.

"How does Langford expect us to find Mrs. Hawk? It's too risky. If we had to go through all that just to get into the garage, I'm sure the computers are being monitored," North says.

"We have to figure it out. Like Langford said, there's no way she and his wife got out of the hospital on their own," Rosemond replies.

"You think Mills is gonna make it?"

"He's in pretty bad shape. If Acosta was still alive I'd say he has a chance."

I slip on the glasses and gloves and open the breaker box that controls the lights and pull the wires. The elevator passes the third floor and the interior lights flicker, then go out.

"What's going on?"

The shaft panel makes a soft scraping sound as I ease it open. Cool air from the dark shaft spills into the cab.

"Who's there?" North asks. She is the closest. Her wide-eyed gaze focuses on the top of the cab, but it is too dark for her to see me.

The monster does his best work in the dark.

Using my feet and legs as anchors to keep me in place, my arms and torso drop through the opening.

I strike.

Hooking an arm around North's neck, I press the heel of my free hand to the back of her head and lift her off her feet. She gurgles and struggles against me. Her hands and nails grip and scratch at the sleeves of my shirt that fully covers my arm.

"What's happening?" Rosemond quivers as she blindly searches the darkness.

North is in full panic mode. I reach around, grip her face, and twist. Snapping her neck. Her body instantly goes limp. I release her, and she falls to the cab's floor.

Rosemond screams and backs away, moving out of range, but she can't go far in the confines of the elevator. I stretch and reach with my left hand until I get a good grip on her hair, wrapping it around my fist.

Her fists pound and swing blindly at my arm while she twists and turns her body, trying to back away.

I yank her closer.

It's a struggle, but once I'm able to get my arm around her neck, I lift her off her feet and release her hair.

Rosemond blindly takes swings at me. Her energy to fight for her life is food for my monster. It gives me strength to use my ab muscles to rear back, lifting her higher off the cab's floor.

Suddenly she stops fighting. Rosemond inhales, grips my upper arms, and draws her knees up toward her chest all in one motion. I flex my boot-covered feet and use my thigh muscles to keep me anchored.

As Rosemond exhales, her body completely relaxes.

My feet slip. The full weight of her body is pulling me down. The metal edges of the panel's opening scrape my legs. I try to hold the position. My abs start to quiver and the energy to hold her up becomes too much. We tumble to the floor, landing on the dying North.

Rosemond scrambles to get away, but even in the fall, I didn't relinquish my hold on her neck. From my position on the bottom, I tighten my grip, then snap the third, fourth, and fifth cervical vertebrae in her neck.

"Fontenot, stop the elevator."

"Yes, sir."

The cab starts to slow down, then it stops.

"Send it down to the first floor and disable it. You can enable the other three elevators."

"Yes, sir."

I get to my feet and look down at both women. Rosemond gets a star for thinking defensively in the face of death, but in monster mode, I'm invincible. The two will be dead from asphyxiation in about four minutes.

"Sir, Mrs. Hawk put her earpiece in. She needs you to come to the resort right away."

"Did she say why?"

"No, sir. She took out the earpiece before I could ask."

"What about Edwards?"

"His earpiece is inactive as well."

The cold heat of adrenaline starts to flow faster through my veins. If Dani is summoning me then something is wrong.

As soon as the elevator doors open, I run to the SCIF, shove my laptop in my backpack with the other one, and leave the building through the passage.

The Tomahawk is in the bunker, but I have another fast motorcycle at my disposal. The resort is forty-five minutes away and I need to get to my wife in *five*.

I make a quick stop at the van to pick up an envelope and store it in the backpack.

I unlock the chains around the black tarp and toss them aside.

The bike's engine thunders. I secure the helmet and pull the straps of the backpack tight to keep it from sliding as I ride.

The back tire spins on the concrete, kicking up smoke, and my boot drags along as I whip around and head toward the exit.

Rush hour traffic is heavy at this time of the day, but I zip in and out of lanes and cross the double yellow lines to get around it. In the earpiece, Fontenot alerts me as to which streets to travel on to avoid law enforcement patrol cars. Not even Boulder's finest will delay me from getting to the Goldman Hotel and Resort. I swear Edwards is a dead man if Dani is hurt. He doesn't get to explain himself.

The highway entrance resembles a parking lot. I skirt the middle line between the two lanes of cars on the onramp and merge onto the highway.

Leaning in, picking up speed, I cross the white lines to get to the HOV lane. It is moving at the posted speed limit, but that's still not fast enough for me.

Minutes and miles pass and yet my heart does not have a pulse. My body is running on pure adrenaline. The nuances of rush hour traffic add to my tension. My imagination dreams up possible reasons neither Edwards nor Dani have their earpieces in. None of them good; all of them end with dead bodies.

Drivers allow me to briskly change lanes and exit. The speed of the bike does not slow down as I ride the mountain road. My knee sails just above the asphalt as I lean in to each curve. I fly past the sign for Hawk Mountain. It's only after I come out of the last curve that I start to slow down. The straightaway to the employee's lot and entrance to the resort is just ahead.

I pull in and stop in front of the door. Before I dismount, I unzip the leg pocket of my black pants and retrieve the all access keycard for the resort.

I enter and go to the service elevator and insert the keycard in the slot.

While the elevator rises to the suite, I give Fontenot instructions to notify POTUS of my whereabouts.

The door opens. I step into the back area of the penthouse.

It's too quiet.

I pull the firearm holstered at my left side. Keeping my back against the wall, I ease my way toward the living room.

My eyes survey the room and every reason I came up with for why Dani brought me here flies out the window.

I wasn't even close.

On the floor beside the sofa is the body of Elijah Hopper, blood covering the chest area of his shirt. Midway up the stairs to the second floor, Edwards's body is sprawled out. Seated at the dining table like stuffed life-size dolls are Marie, Langford, and Pierre.

Where's Dani?

Langford is the first to notice me. His eyes give nothing away, but I see he brought Edwards's laptop with him.

Of course, this could be a trap. I exercise caution and ease over to Hopper's body, squatting by his side. My index and middle finger check for a pulse.

The cold hard muzzle of a gun presses into the back of my head.

"The last time I saw yo' ass, you were running toward a goddamn burning car that exploded when you got to it." Her tone is cold. "Drop the gun and the backpack and slowly stand up."

"You know I can disarm you, Dani."

The stream of heat from the bullet leaving the barrel chamber brushes my ear and the scent of gunpowder drifts past my nose as the slug hits the wall to the side of me. The casing falls to the floor behind me. "Second rule of gun safety, never point your weapon at a muthafucker unless you're gonna bust a cap in his ass. I'm all for bustin' caps today, Hawk. So, drop the gun and the goddamn backpack and stand the fuck up."

I huff, a short, condescending sound. My monster wants to defy her, but she's piqued my curiosity. I don't immediately follow orders to see how far she's willing to take this.

"Sir, do I need to send help?" Fontenot's voice comes through the earpiece.

"No," I whisper.

The muzzle of the gun hits the back of my head. "Now, Hawk."

The straps of the backpack slip from my shoulders and it falls behind me. I set the gun next to Hopper's hand but keep my eyes on the cusp of his neck.

As I rise and turn around, my gaze shifts to Edwards's body in the shadow of the stairway. I can't tell what his injury is.

My wife keeps her eyes locked on mine for good reason. Hmm, her right hand supports the left one which is holding the gun, and it's not steady. She's keeping her trigger finger on the trigger guard instead of where we taught her.

"When the opportunity presents itself, I will disarm you, Danielle."

The smile on her face is as fake as it is daring. She cocks an eyebrow at me and lowers the gun to her side. "If I had to pick a number between one and one hundred, I'd say you can make it to the empty seat at the head of the table in eleven steps." The gun taps her thigh five times.

Keeping her in my sight, I take exactly eleven steps to the chair. The stairs to the second floor will be behind me. Before I sit I glance at Edwards.

"Hands behind your back, Hawk."

"Why aren't the others cuffed?"

"They aren't Krav Maga Don Masters *and* military-trained sharpshooters." Her lips press against my ear. "Only you."

I place my hands behind me. The others at the table watch me as the clank of the handcuffs locking sounds off.

The back of the cloth chair is smooth, but it's sticky and hard near my hands. I decide to ride this one out especially since Dani didn't handcuff me.

Her fingertips glide over my shoulder blades. She walks back over to where I left the backpack, then picks it up, and brings it back to the table. She drops the backpack a foot from my chair on the left side.

"Now that you're secured, let me introduce everyone."

The gun in her hand taps the back of the first empty chair five times as she passes. She places her gun-free hand on the back of Marie's chair. "This is my grandmother, Antoinette Marie Beaudry Toussaint Langford. Damn"—her laugh is humorless—"that was a mouthful. But in light of today's event, we'll just call her by the name the world has been burning to know: Antoinette."

Dani moves on to the man seated across the table from me. "This gentleman is Antoinette's older half-brother and my grand-uncle, Pierre Elian Dupree. Welcome, *unc,* I'm the daughter Elizabeth gave birth to before she died."

Pierre draws back his fist.

A growl rumbles from my throat in warning. "Handcuffed or not, I *will* get up from this seat and kill you if you throw that punch."

"Thanks for the backup, baby, but I don't need you to fight my battles." Dani places her hand on the man's fist and forces him to lower it. "Rear back at me again and I'll fucking break it. I am a strong, hardworking woman who eats alpha-males for dinner."

He sneers at Langford but speaks to Dani. "Careful grand-niece, every time Willis pulls one of these stunts, my little sister lets me kill someone he loves."

A single tear tumbles down Langford's cheek. My gaze follows its trail.

Dani moves on to Langford, locking eyes with me. He is seated to my right. She places a hand on his shoulder. "This is Willis Percival Langford. My grandfather."

His face takes on the look of a constipated man straining on the toilet. Dani has a death grip on the pressure point at the base of his neck.

"Too bad *mô pépé* condones that myth about the power of a man's penis."

"She called him, my grandpa." Fontenot translates.

Langford whines, shaking his head in denial.

"I heard you tell Bryan to fuck his way back into my good graces after we were released from the hospital."

"I only said that because it wasn't safe for you to leave."

If she doesn't let up on Langford's neck soon, the old man is going to pass out.

The corners of Dani's mouth turn up in a sexy smile. Not once have her eyes left mine. "If you knew anything about me, then you'd know I'd only give my body to the man who respects me."

Everything she's silently trying to communicate starts to sink in. This is the most I've heard her cuss in all the years I've known her. Profanity is not in her character. Dani's using her nondominant hand to hold the gun and tapping it five times. Vin made her practice using her left hand five times before she defiantly switched to her dominant hand. Lastly, how she introduced them to me.

I give a slight nod of my head to let her know I'm catching on.

Dani releases the old man and walks toward me. I take the time to scrutinize what she is wearing. Her baby bump is hidden behind the oversized, crisp white men's dress shirt. She must be wearing the special vest underneath. Dani stands behind me and places a hand on my shoulder.

Langford touches his watch. The pulse in his neck beating fast. His eyes sweeping the room and floor. No doubt plotting his escape.

Dupree keeps his eyes on Dani and the gun in her hand. His pinky ring taps a constant beat on the wooden surface of the table.

Marie's fingers grip the pendent on the gold chain around her neck while side-eyeing Pierre. A smirk of satisfaction on her face.

"Sir." Fontenot's voice shouts in the earpiece. "The team is under heavy fire. I'm patching it through."

Immediately I hear Paul's voice rattling off orders and the rapid fire of automatic assault rifles going off. Frontline experience tells me ILA is doing most of the shooting because they're panicked. The return fire from Phantom's Elite Special Operations Team is calculated and precise.

My blood chills when I hear the next message from Fontenot. "The missiles are hot."

———◆———

Arizona, Eight Years Ago

Rescuing Crown Prince Jawad bin Ali Al Omran from the men who are holding him captive is the first mission for me, Tony, Ig, and Vin as the new Elite Special Operations Team.

Ig shares his underground rap music to pump us up as we head to the Middle East.

Before we dive into the dark waters, Tony huddles us for a prayer.

Vin comes up with a strike chant off the top of his head.

We have been training together ever since they got back from Chen's boot camp, but this is our first opportunity to put that training to use.

We're coming in by water because the kidnappers are watching the sky and the roads leading to their camp.

The climb up the rocky cliff is challenging. We keep an eye on Vin because he's carrying the most weight.

Working together as one, we're able to extract Jawad with minimal gunfire. He is injured so we carry him out of the compound via the road to the beach, then tow him on a surfboard out to the military inflatable boat anchored offshore.

Paul gets the prince strapped down. Acosta assesses his immediate medical needs. Ricci handles the outboard motor. I notify

President Nelson that we've got him.

Considering we had little time to prepare, the four of us kicked ass out there. Prince Jawad's captors won't know he's gone until morning.

For now, he will be under our protection and stay hidden in the United States until the Saudi Royal Guard Regiment investigates how security was breached.

We get him settled in one of the bedrooms of the apartment across the street from Dani's with Tony, Ig, and Vin on watch.

The only way I can hide the bruises and scabs from Dani is to keep her blindfolded. Since that isn't happening, I have a lie prepared and photoshopped pictures of me rock climbing with a client to back it up.

"Dada," Kourt says as she slides off the sofa to wobble-walk to me.

"Daddy," Emm sings as she passes her sister.

I drop my bag by the door, stoop down, and open my arms. My girls are excited to see me as much as I am to see them. "Where's Mommy?"

"Danielle is at the hospital with the Franklins, sir," Wright says.

I scoop up my girls and carry them to the sofa, sitting them on my lap. Wright fills me in on why the Franklins are in the hospital.

"Are you sure you're okay with the girls by yourself, sir?"

"I'm good, Sergeant Wright. Thank you for keeping an eye on them. I know babysitting both of them isn't part of your assignment, but I do appreciate it."

"I don't mind. They're good girls."

After she leaves, I get the girls ready for bed. Emm is so easygoing. She and I have a nighttime routine of songs and numbers and colors and shapes and saying her name, Emma Rose Hawk. My big girl will never know the woman who gave birth to her did not want her. Emm will always know she is wanted and loved.

It is taking longer to get Kourt in bed. Her nighttime routine includes nursing, and I'm not equipped to give her what she wants. She keeps pushing the bottle of breast milk away. Four songs and two readings of that curious bear book and she still won't take the bottle. Man, is she stubborn. Not even a visit from Uncle Vinny can get her to settle down.

Vin likes her spunkiness and has already claimed the primary role of godfather. Tony is Emm's. Ig says he'll wait until I have a son because he already has five older sisters, and a dozen nieces, three of which are his goddaughters.

I wish my grandmother lived long enough to know her great-granddaughters. If she were around, I wouldn't have to find the right way to introduce my baby girl and Dani to my family.

Kourt and I sit in the living room and I hold her close until she stops fighting me and cries herself to sleep. Once she takes the stuttering-breath and her body relaxes, I lay a blanket on the sofa and ease her on top of it. Uncle Vinny goes back across the street.

Now that Kourt is down, I can eat. Dani always has something good in the refrigerator.

I find leftovers that I put on a plate and place it in the microwave to heat up. While I watch the timer countdown, I bite into a cold odd-looking bread. My taste buds orgasm. I finish it in two bites and go back to the fridge to get more.

If they taste this good cold, I know they'll be even better hot. I pause the microwave, toss in two, then press the start button.

I pour a tall glass of sweet tea and take it to the living room.

The timer beeps and I go back to the kitchen and retrieve my plate.

I pick up the remote, find a movie to watch, but keep the volume down, and dig in. On my third round of a fork full of food, Dani walks through the door looking like she's about to fall on her face. She's surprised to see me.

I ask her about the great-tasting bread.

"What the hell happened to you?" is her response.

At the sound of her mother's voice, Kourt's eyes spring open and she starts to whine. She rolls onto her stomach and climbs to her knees trying to see over the back of the sofa.

"Why are you still up?" Dani drops her keys and briefcase on the table near the door.

Kourt stands, reaching for her mom. I keep a protective hand on her so she doesn't lose her balance and fall back.

Dani kicks off her heels while shedding her jacket and unbuttoning her shirt. She walks around the sofa, unhooks a cup in her bra, and settles our daughter on her lap. She winces and hisses as Kourt starts sucking. Finally content, my baby girl bounces her foot and pats her mother's chest.

"The way she's guzzling down breast milk you'd think she's starving." I lean over and kiss my daughter's head. "She wouldn't take the bottle."

"Hopefully she'll want both breasts. They're full and sore. I didn't get to pump today because I was at the hospital with Mr. and Mrs. Franklin."

"I'll help you out if she doesn't."

Dani shakes her head and laughs. "Yeah, but your way of helping leads to sex and I'm too tired and hungry to be an active participant."

Careful not to drop food in Kourt's hair, I offer Dani a forkful of beans and rice. Which she accepts with a smile.

"You can just lie there. I'll do all the work." I offer another forkful.

Dani rolls her eyes as she chews. "How's Emma? Did she give you a hard time too?"

"Emm's fine. She went right to sleep." I feed Dani more food while my baby girl nurses.

"Rough business trip?" Her eyes give my body the once-over.

The prepared lie is ready to roll off my tongue, but I don't use it. "I'll tell you about it tomorrow. Tonight, let's talk about how I can help you with your foster parents."

I'm rewarded with one of her special smiles.

As it turns out, I don't need to lie about my whereabouts. Between work and visits to the hospital, Dani doesn't question me about the injuries. Wright pretends to be sick, so I stay home with the girls as an excuse for not going to the hospital to meet Dani's foster parents. After Amelia told me RAGS wants me, I've exercised caution when it comes to interacting with people outside of my circle. I wouldn't put it past RAGS to use the people I care about to get to me. I've already got a team watching my parents and Dani. For the Franklins' safety, I can't risk getting close to them.

The day after Christmas, the Franklins are released, and they head back to Los Angeles. Dani is disappointed that I didn't get to meet them before they left.

Once we ring in the New Year, Emm and I pack up to leave. This is the part of my visits that I hate the most. I never tell Dani and Kourt goodbye. I tell them, "See you later."

The guys—along with Prince Jawad—meet me at the private airport where Hawkeye Personal Protection's jet is waiting. Emmy shies away from the strange man.

When we land in Denver, Colorado, Emm and I head to Colorado Springs to spend a few days with Mom, Dad, and Jessi. The guys get Jawad set up in my old condo with a team of Hawkeye Personal Protection Officers on duty round the clock.

Over the holidays, movers packed up my and Emm's things and moved them to the four-bedroom house on the land I purchased in Boulder. Tony's crew will be finished with the pond by summer and then the construction company will start building Dani's dream house—with a few of my own tweaks.

Dr. Jasper Stevens emails me a copy of the application and resume Dani submitted for a position at the hospital. He said they did a telephone interview and she's in the top three. I reply: *send her a denial letter.* Although her applying for a position here in Colorado is a good sign, the house is still under construction. When she and Kourt move here, I want it to be in her house where it's safe and secured.

January is an extra busy month. Hawkeye clientele is growing, and Phantom work is non-stop. I don't make it to Arizona, but I call and video chat with my daughter and Dani every day.

For Kourt's first birthday, Emm and I drive to Arizona. The back of the car is full of presents from her uncles. Dani and I have a small party for her at the park. It is hard to believe that both of my girls are a year old.

There is some activity going on in the U.S. that the ESO Team needs to handle and Dani is disappointed that Emm and I can't make it back to Arizona for her milestone birthday. I send her diamond earrings as a gift hoping it makes up for our absence.

Presidential Primaries and Party Conventions are keeping Phantom busy too. As Second Command of Phantom I am being pulled in many directions. As the owner of a business with government contracts, I'm getting calls every day from campaign managers inviting me to fundraising events or asking me to give a public endorsement. Despite my personal opinions, I have to stay neutral—especially with the presidential candidates.

While going through my emails, I open an alert from the credit card company. There has been suspicious activity on the card I gave Dani. Three thousand dollars was charged to the card at a lingerie store in Arizona.

I call Dani's cell phone to see if she's been shopping. I don't mind. I just want to verify she's the one making the purchases. The call goes straight to voicemail. I call her job and I'm told she's out for the rest of the week. I call the apartment's landline; after the fourth ring, the call goes to voicemail.

I log in to the security cameras in the apartment. Every room is empty. But on her bed are four white shopping bags with symbols of long sexy legs of different hues and shapes.

I call Sergeant Wright.

"Sir?"

I skip the pleasantries. "Where's Dani?"

"She and Kourtney just left for California. I thought you knew. She always tells you when she's going to visit the Franklins. Permission to speak freely, sir."

"Go ahead."

"Danielle was looking forward to spending her twenty-first birthday with you. Kourtney and Emma were going to spend the night with me so that you two could have some real alone time."

"Sergeant Wright, despite what you see when I interact with Danielle, I am playing a role. This case isn't over until we've recovered that information." I can't believe I didn't choke on that lie.

"Yes, sir."

"Is there anything else you want to speak freely about?"

"No, sir."

"Good. Let me know when they get back."

"Yes, sir."

After my phone call with Wright, I can't stay focused. When Tony has to snap his fingers in my ear to bring me back to the meeting we're having, Ig asks what's distracting me. I tell them about the amount of money Dani spent in the lingerie store and what Wright said.

The jokes begin to flow like liquor at a frat party.

The following week I get another alert from the credit card company. Three thousand dollars was credited back to the account.

Prince Jawad likes hanging out with us so much, he stays in the U.S. even after the investigation is concluded. His father issues an ultimatum and Jawad is preparing to return to Saudi Arabia. As an extra security measure, he signs a contract with Hawkeye Personal Protection. I assign one of my best female PPOs to him. No one will suspect she is his bodyguard because of the long-standing tradition of men protecting the House of Saud.

Now that Emm is getting older, she and I do more daddy-daughter things together. Her little vocabulary is growing and she's also starting to parrot us. The guys and I turn to American Sign Language to converse when she's in our presence.

I hire Marie as a babysitter and housekeeper. It helps that Marie knows about Phantom and I don't have to make up excuses for those times the guys and I need to leave in the middle of the night. I haven't seen much of Langford.

Charly and Tony have been fighting a lot lately. The constant unexpected "trainings" is taking its toll on their relationship. Ig, Vin, and I have a bet on whether Tony and Charly make it down the aisle.

October 6, 2007 is a tough day for my best friend. Instead of giving the best man's speech at the wedding reception, we're completely wasted—in Paris, France—getting tattoos by one of the best tattoo artists in the world. This is how we're helping Tony cope with the woman he loves standing him up at the altar in front of family and friends.

Her actions just reaffirm my beliefs about love. I keep that to myself and use the thirty racks I collected from Ig and Vin to pay the ink artist.

The morning we return to Boulder, Tony starts the sheriff's academy.

POTUS summons me to the White House for a face-to-face update on the changes in the recruitment process for Phantom. He is a conservative president and has a hard time understanding the direction I want to take the organization in. President Nelson is standing firm on his "old ways" mentality: *if it's worked this long, change is not needed.* I can't tell First Command that the reason Phantom is stuck in the ordinary is because he refuses to grasp the possibilities of being extraordinary.

Wright tells me she thinks there is a pattern to the burglaries that have happened in the neighborhood and wants permission to use Phantom's resources to investigate. She assures me it won't interfere with her duties to watch Dani and Kourt. I tell her to go for it.

Since her birthday, Dani has been snappy and withholding sex of any kind. Emm and I spend Thanksgiving with them. When I come out the bathroom with a towel wrapped around my waist, Dani comments on the hawk tattoo that covers my back. That night, I get my all-access pass to her body *and* phone sex back.

Emm and Kourt are growing so much. It trips me out how, at their age, their personalities are distinctive. Emm is an introvert, while Kourt is an ambivert.

My mom is starting to question where Emm and I go when we leave Colorado, and why are we gone every December for two weeks. It's not easy to lie to my mother, not because I feel guilty or can't. My mom has some kind of super power that detects lies. With that in mind, I give her a modified version of the truth: work keeps me busy most of the year, so I block out time at the end of the year to hang out with my daughter. Is it really a lie if I don't indicate which daughter I'm blocking out time for? Mom buys it for now.

The old saying about how you ring in the New Year is how you'll spend the year must have some merit. My 2008 begins with an alert about Grigori Popov—a rogue Russian General—who has gone off grid. I send field agents to the country to get more information. I get another alert about a RAGS bombing near the home of Democratic candidate for the presidential race, Governor Emmerson Hart of Ohio. No one died, but dozens are injured. Hart is leading in the polls and is the only one running for office who openly speaks out against RAGS's existence in the United States.

The construction of Dani's dream house is finished. All that's left to do is the security system, but that can be done while we're living in it. Emm and I will move in first, then I'll move Dani and Kourt to Colorado. Marie is now my full-time live-in sitter and housekeeper. I have no idea how I'm going to explain to Marie and Langford my relationship with their granddaughter and why she and Kourt are moving into my new home.

Emm and I make it to Arizona to celebrate Kourt's second birthday. I have to leave Emm with Dani that same evening. The ESO team is being sent to Asia to instigate a hostile situation between two enemies in order to gain one as an ally.

Dani stands in the doorway of the bedroom watching me pack. "If you don't want a repeat of last year's birthday cold shoulder, you better go big with a gift this year."

As far as I know, she hasn't worn the diamond earrings I got her last year, so getting more jewelry is out. Then I catch her staring at my back and I get an idea for a gift. Before I walk out of the door, I kiss her like a hungry man devours a meal, then whisper in her ear, "I dare you to get inked. I'll have the guy who did my hawk come here to do it."

She leans back with the biggest smile on her face. Her pretty brown eyes are shining. "Can I get whatever I want wherever I want it?"

I nod.

"Then you're on, Hawk."

I make the call and text her the artist's information. She'll probably get something small that stays covered most of the time.

Our covert mission to Asia takes five days to complete. On our way back to the States, I send Dani a text to see if she followed through with the dare. Her response is a photo text message that makes my cell phone fall from my hands. I knew she'd go through with it. I wasn't prepared for the lady hawk taking up most of her side. It looks good on her beautiful skin tone. The image of her laid out on the bed in a black bra and panties makes my hawk stand in its nest.

Tony snatches up my phone and whistles. "Damn. Is that what cost eight racks?" He tosses my phone to Vin.

Vin nods approvingly. "It looks better than yours." He tosses my phone to Ig.

"We still at thirty racks on the do-right-girl bet?" Ig tosses me my phone.

We nod confirmation.

"I raise you another ten," he challenges.

The rest of the flight is uncomfortable, not because the guys pass the time with endless innuendos; my erection won't go down. I try jacking off in the restroom, but it only relieves some of the pressure. The cure for this hard-on is sex with the woman sporting the lady hawk tattoo.

The picture didn't do it justice. The talons stretch out toward her pelvic area and the tail feathers brush her ass cheek.

Dani makes me work hard for the right to get her naked and in my favorite position— her on top. But she is being exceptionally adventurous and vocal about how she wants me to please her tonight. If I had to rank all my sexual experiences, I'd say tonight is number two on the list. Number one is my first time with Dani.

All is right in my world until Vin knocks on the door with a package for the old tenant. It's a signal that something's up and they're checking it out. Ig is across the courtyard in Wright's unit, messing with the plumbing to give her an excuse to bring the girls back and stay with Dani while I help check things out. Tony is already out searching the area with Watanabe and Cooper.

Just like the first time I was followed, the perpetrator is in the wind before we can subdue him. Before I leave Arizona, I meet with Wright, Cooper, and Watanabe. Wright reports that the perpetrator seems to be most active around the times I visit. I was going to tell Dani about the house and ask her to move to Boulder, but if my visits are putting her and Kourt in danger, then being with me twenty-four seven in Colorado isn't a good idea without the security system installed in the house.

No one from Edwards's past has tried to contact Dani that we know of. It could be ILA. Until I get the house secured, Dani and Kourt will have to stay put, and I have to be more conscious about my visits.

Amelia calls me. She wants to come home because she misses her parents. I tell her no. RAGS is too active and I forked out too much money to have her face and body altered just to have her run back to them. She swears she's done with RAGS, but I don't believe her.

Dani and I ring in 2009 talking about her buying a house. Via an earpiece, Chen coaches me through the conversation. I need Dani to get on board with the idea without making it seem like I'm pressuring her to move. Even Chen agrees it's not a good idea to move them to Boulder yet, but it will be easier for me to secure her in a single dwelling structure than it is in this apartment building. Before Emm and I leave, Dani says she'll think about moving.

It is tradition for the outgoing president and Second Command to sit down with the incoming president after the inauguration ceremony to talk about Phantom. The 44th President of the United States, Emmerson G. Hart, requests a copy of my operation plan. It takes me a week to revise the now three-hundred-page document. Once I present it to First Command, we go over it, page by page.

He likes the direction I want to take Phantom in and wholeheartedly approves the plan. President Hart is a forward-thinking president. It helps that he unknowingly tested for Phantom back when he was a Navy fighter pilot but missed passing the written exam by two points in each category. I show him his scores and the average score of the men and women currently in the branch.

"Could the Elite Special Operations Team use a transportation expert?" he asks.

"Yes, we can."

He hands me a file containing information on Dr. Taylor Barrett. His certifications in military vehicle operation and engineering are almost as thick as my operational plan. I show the file to the guys and we all agree, Barrett is perfect for the job. We make his cover job principal of the prestigious Greystone Preparatory Academy: a private school in Boulder, Colorado. Emm is starting preschool there in the fall. The current principal is retiring at the end of the school year.

The morning I leave Arizona after a weekend visit, Dani goes to work, and Wright takes Kourt for a walk, someone gets into the apartment. The intruder uses a key to let himself in through the front door. He's covered head to toe in all black. Including the ski mask and gloves. He even thought enough to cover his shoes with surgical booties before coming in. He's only in the apartment for a minute, but he knows his way around like he's been there before. He goes straight to the bathroom and puts my toothbrush in a plastic baggie then lets himself out the front door and locks it before Cooper and Watanabe can get there. There aren't any cameras in the courtyard of the building, so they can't track which direction he goes. While Cooper and Watanabe are out searching for the intruder, Wright informs me that the police are pulling up to the apartment building across the street. The apartment next to the one the guys stay at when they go to Arizona with me is broken into. The renter was on his way up the stairs when he saw a man—in all black—leaving his apartment. He chased the intruder but lost him on the next block.

I finally say the words out loud, "My visits to Arizona are putting Dani and Kourt in danger."

Whoever the intruder is must be looking to ID me. Dani does not know someone got into the apartment, but I step up my efforts to get her to start looking for a house until she hires an agent.

The constant burn in my gut intensifies as I prepare for what must be done to protect Dani and my daughter. If RAGS can link me to them emotionally, RAGS will use them to wrangle me into their organization. As Second Command of Phantom, I can't let that happen. I'd die before I let Dani get dragged deeper into this RAGS stuff then she already is. Wright practically lives with Dani and Kourt and she is armed.

I purchase a three-bedroom home in a quiet neighborhood of Tucson, Arizona. I pay the company that built my home here in Boulder to send a crew to fix up the house in Arizona. When they're done, Vin and I install a state-of-the-art security system. It's nothing like the one I'm installing in the house in Boulder, but it will deter an intruder. Chen is vetting the neighbors. Anyone he can't get a handle on is offered double the value of their home to move.

I anonymously send the private quick-sale listing to the real estate agent Dani is working with. The asking price is a quarter of what I paid for it. Dani does a walk through and tells the agent to make an offer.

Once the sell goes through, I leave Emm with my parents and drive to Arizona. The miles help me clear my head and focus on why I'm doing what I'm about to do. But my equilibrium is off. I feel like I'm falling even though I'm sitting.

"Where's Emma?" Dani asks when I walk through the door.

"She's sick…" The burning pain in my stomach is so intolerable, I can't stand to look Dani in the eyes and finish the rehearsed lie.

Not even a round of hello sex can extinguish the fire in my gut or make me feel better about what's to come.

While Dani is asleep, I survey the packed boxes and mark the ones containing anything that belongs to me or Emm. They will get lost in the move—go back to Boulder with my friends.

I go through the boxes labeled photos and remove all pictures of me and Emm. I pack those in a different box and take them across the street.

The memory card in Dani's camera is filled with pictures of us. I swap it for a blank one. The last thing I do before rejoining Dani in bed is, I erase anything on her laptop that leads back to me or Emm.

We wake early the next morning and start the process of moving Dani and Kourt from the apartment to their new house. All day, I feel Dani watching me. I know I'm being uncharacteristically quiet and staying busy with the movers, who are really Phantom Sweepers.

By sundown, the apartment is empty. Another team of Sweepers are coming in to clean the unit top to bottom, removing any DNA traces of us.

The first room we get unpacked and set up is Kourt's room. My baby girl loves her new big girl's bed we bought her but says she's afraid to sleep in her new room by herself because it's ginormous. I have to put in two nightlights before she settles down and falls asleep. I discourage Dani from setting up Emm's room tonight.

While I wait for Dani to get out of the shower, I sit on the edge of the bed with a thick envelope in my hands. I'd never say this out loud, but Dani is the only woman who makes me second-guess my commitment to my job.

I smell her unique scent before the mattress dips when she crawls up behind me and starts massaging my neck and shoulders.

"That's a cute bear on the nightstand. He looks like the one from that story Kourtney loves."

"I thought so too when I saw it."

"Bryan, what's wrong?"

I inhale deeply, and exhale slowly. "Do you trust me?"

Her arms wrap around my neck and she kisses my cheek. "Yes, I do."

I shift so I can see her face, then hand her the envelope. "Dani, I need you to trust me more than you ever have before."

"You're scaring me, Bryan. What's going on?"

"Open the envelope."

She sits back on her knees in the middle of the bed. The hem of the night shirt she's wearing rests at the tops of her thighs revealing her pink panties. Dani's fingers squeeze the clasp prongs together, then peel open the flap.

I watch her eyes move left to right as she reads each line of every document in her hands. By the time she gets to the final page, her body is trembling.

"What the hell is going on Bryan? I never filed papers to change my last name to Edwards. Did you forge my signature? Why are there new social security cards for Kourtney and me? Why did you change *her* last name without my permission? Kourtney Allison *Hawk* is *your* daughter!"

"This is where I need you to trust me, Dani."

She throws the papers in my face and scurries back on the bed until the headboard stops her from going any further.

"Are you into something illegal? Is that why you're giving us new last names? Are the authorities going to come knocking on my door looking for you? Is my home going to be raided? Is that why you're able to transfer so much money into the two accounts each month?"

"No, Danielle."

"You called me Danielle. Tell me what's going on."

My words get stuck and I can't say it. Verbalizing it makes it real.

"Are you"—her voice cracks—"are you leaving us Bryan?"

The answer is in the look in my eyes.

The question—why?—looks back at me.

I gather up the papers and place them on the nightstand.

I stretch out on the bed next to her, opening my arms and waiting for Dani to join me. I count the number of times I inhale and exhale until Dani stretches out and lets me hold her—one hundred twenty-three.

My eyes close as I inhale, hoping her scent extinguishes the flames burning my gut. "I promise I'll keep you and Kourt safe, but you have to trust me and not ask questions."

Dani reaches out. The touch of her thumb along my bottom lip is different. It's painful and full of questions which I can't answer. I open my eyes and for this one night, I step out of the role of Second Command. I don't hide the turmoil I'm feeling. I do something I've never done with any woman except Dani; I let her in.

Everything I can't tell her I say with my eyes. I don't want this to be goodbye. I don't want to walk away, but if I keep coming around, the consequences could be fatal.

Our daughter cries out for me. Regrettably I untangle myself from Dani, I climb out of bed and grab the stuffed bear, and wipe away my tears as I go to Kourt.

"Hey, baby girl, what's wrong?" I drop to my knees on the side of her bed.

She looks so tiny in her big girl bed with the flowers and butterflies on the bedding. "Monsters in my room."

"Guess what? I brought a friend with me. His job is to keep the monsters away while you sleep. His name is Mr. Cuddles. Do you want to meet him?"

Kourt nods.

I hold up the bear. "Mr. Cuddles, this is my baby girl. Do you promise to always keep the monsters away while she sleeps?" I channel a deep bear voice. "I promise."

Kourt giggles and reaches for the bear. She tucks him into her arms and holds him tight. I sing to her until her eyelids get heavy and they don't open again after a sleepy yawn.

When her body relaxes, and she takes that deep breath that carries her to dreamland, I kiss her forehead, then whisper in her ear, "Please remember me. Remember I love you."

I'm counting on the timing of Dani's pregnancy to hide Kourt from the people who'd harm them to get to me. Me disappearing from their lives is the only way to keep them safe.

I tuck the covers around her and kiss her cheek one last time and leave the door cracked open as I leave her room.

Dani isn't in the bedroom when I return. She isn't in the bathroom either. I find her downstairs sitting on the sofa with a frosted bottle of clear alcohol and a shot glass. Tears trekking down her cheeks.

Dani tosses back a shot, refills the glass, and swipes her nose with the back of her hand while she glares at me.

"When I found out I was pregnant, I had a plan. I was prepared to do this on my own, but you said you'd always be here. And I trusted you'd always be here. But now you're leaving for reasons you can't or won't tell me, *and* you're asking for the ultimate level of blind trust. Am I right?"

"Yes."

I could not have hurt her more if I'd struck her.

She tosses back another shot, then refills the glass. "I can give you that if you do something from me."

"Okay."

"Leave me alone for the rest of the night."

I do as she asks and walk up the stairs, but I sit on the top step, out of sight. I could say I'm sitting here because I'm keeping an eye on Dani. But really, I'm sitting here because everything in me hurts and I could *not* take another painful step.

Dani's not a drinker, but for this one night, I watch her get wasted. When she stops refilling the shot glass and cries herself to sleep, I carry her upstairs to bed and hold her. I whisper in her ear promises of a reunion.

I tell her subconscious mind, "If I ever call you and tell you to run, grab Kourt and run. Don't look back, and don't worry about packing, just head straight to Boulder, Colorado, because that's where Emm and I will be waiting for you and Kourt."

I leave before sunrise.

The reason my friendship works with Tony, Ig, and Vin is because we are always there for one another—ride or die. When I look in the rearview mirror, I see them behind me. I pull over and Vin takes over driving. I feel off balanced and can't keep the truck on the road. The miles back to Colorado don't fill the hole in me; they make it bigger, deeper. *Oh god, I can't breathe.*

In May I finally give in and allow Amelia to come back to the United States. I create a new identity for her—Malinda Williamson—and send Hawkeye Personal Protection's jet to Switzerland to pick her up.

CHAPTER FIFTEEN

DANIELLE

Colorado, Present Day

"ELIZABETH WOULDN'T WANT YOU TO act this way."

"And how would you know, *granmé*? You and your mother mentally and physically tortured her because she refused to be molded into your evil image."

"Who told you such lies?"

"She did, in the journals she kept."

"How did you… Where did you… Those were just stories made up by a troubled child…"

"Shut up!" Willis slams the table with his fist. "Everything Elizabeth wrote in those journals was true."

"Elizabeth and that boy got what was coming to them," Pierre seethes.

His words set off Willis. The accusations and profanity are rolling off my grandfather's tongue.

Marie joins in, throwing verbal insults at Willis for being weak and the reason his ex-fiancée and his precious daughter are dead. And soon his granddaughter if he doesn't stop this nonsense. Pierre tries to join in on the shade throwing but Marie turns on him. She calls her big brother every name she can think of for a simple-minded man. Marie is not the same person who welcomed me the first time I visited Bryan's home. This person is Antoinette, the fierce daughter of Dominique Elian Toussaint and Bernadette Beaudry.

The twitching in Pierre's eye and clenched fists accompany the increased stutter of every other word he shouts at his sister. The disturbance in the fluency of his speech pattern as he defends himself is off. I didn't catch it at first, but I hear it now. In response to his little sister's name calling, Pierre stutters through describing how he mutilated Willis's ex-fiancée's body and left her for Willis to find, and how he tracked down Elizabeth and Daniel in California and killed them; a simpleton couldn't have done those things and not get caught.

The roar from my grandfather's chest would make a lion proud. If I wasn't holding a gun on them, I'm positive he'd jump out of his chair and strangle the life out of Antoinette and Pierre.

I look at Bryan. The hazel of his eyes is eclipsed by the darkest color. His body language is too relaxed. The rise and fall of his chest too even. Bryan is in Deathly-Dangerous-Alpha-Male mode.

I allow the argument to grow louder because today, right here, right now, we are going to spread all their secrets out on the table. Shine a light on their lies. And tell the truth. When my husband and I walk away from this table, I don't want any unanswered questions or loose ends following us for the rest of our lives.

"Dominique Toussaint was just the face and voice of Rebels Against Government Suppression." The trio stop their yapping and turn their attention on me. "The man couldn't read or write past a fourth-grade level, but when he spoke, people listened. Bernadette Beaudry was the trained dragoon behind the vision of RAGS. She coached Dominique through everything. But you know that old saying, 'beware of the hell you make, it will outgrow you'. Bernadette lost control over Dominique so she turned to her daughter. Call it your good fortune, Antoinette, or Willis's bad luck, but by the time Willis realized he'd been hoodwinked, he was addicted to the possibilities of the power of being Sovereign of a social democracy."

Every message Willis wrote to Elizabeth began with an apology for being a pitiful father who wants to protect her but doesn't know how to curb his thirst for being great.

I place my hand on Bryan. "The rhythmic click of the knitting needles along with that song Marie softly sang or hummed is the reason I dreamt of killing you, Vin, Tony, and Ig." I turn my sights on Pierre. "I'm guessing Bernadette used similar techniques on you when you were a child. Your speech impediment doesn't follow the normal patterns of someone diagnosed with the disability in childhood. The disturbance in your speech pattern only happens when you're speaking to your sister. You were conditioned to feel inferior to your little sister."

Pierre bares his venomous fangs.

"Dominique created a proprietorship called RAGS that actually sells rags. He hid the homeland terrorist organization's activities and laundered money through the legitimate business that made monetary donations to a dummy non-profit organization based in Opelousas, Louisiana. To ensure no one could supersede the company's control over Rebels Against Government Suppression's finances, Dominique hired a high-powered law firm to help him trademark the business name and draw up a will with a non-contestability clause. How could a man with a fourth-grade education accomplish all this, even the illegal stuff?" I pause for dramatic effect. "His son-in-law helped him."

"How do you know all this, Danielle?" Willis asks.

"I know Dominique made you a promise that he didn't keep, and it's gotten harder for you to cover your tracks. I know Antoinette locked up a resistant sixteen-year-old Elizabeth in the basement because my mother refused to tell her where to find Dominique's will." I fight to keep the emotion out of my voice. "I know Daniel came to you and told you Elizabeth was pregnant. And you told him if he really loved Elizabeth, he would get her out of Colorado and never come back. Then you gave him the plans for a RAGS attack on the White House and told him to take them to the only friend you trusted, Terrance Brumfield. And I know Dominique taught his granddaughter two important things: how to resist the conditioning of her mother, and how to unlock the secret compartment in the jewelry box he gave her."

I intentionally walk around the table until I'm standing between Pierre and my grandfather. I pull the laptop to me and rest my hands on top of it, switching the gun to my right hand. I stare at Antoinette and wait for her to make eye contact. "I know Dominique named Elizabeth Elaine Langford as heir. And while Elizabeth was on the run, she wrote her own will naming her first-born child as her heir. Since *I* am her only child, *I* control Rebels Against Government Suppression's three point eight billion dollars."

Marie huffs—sarcastically.

I return the sentiment with a humorless smile far more superior than sarcasm. "*Yè un shyin, piti.* Which dog do you want me to kill now, Grandmother? You or your brother? Because I'll defend my husband and my grandfather to my very last breath."

The penthouse phone starts to ring. Their eyes turn to the intrusive object like they can see the caller. The phone goes silent after the fourth ring.

Pierre wrestles the gun from my hand while jumping to his feet. His arm hooks around my shoulder as he presses the gun to my side.

Willis jumps to his feet. "Let go of my granddaughter, you son of a bitch."

I keep my eyes on Bryan. His eyes are no longer hazel. They are stone cold black. It's chilling to see him still-hunting his prey with the fierceness of a hawk.

Antoinette rises from her seat, lifts her chin, and looks down her nose at me. "Do you think I'd allow you to control what my mother built, Danielle?" The drawl in her voice clearly delivers the threat in her words.

I issue one of my own using my deathly-dangerous-alpha-female voice. "The phone transaction you thought you made was reversed. My great-grandfather's law firm contacted the bank on my behalf. Whomever you owe money to for the missiles is here to collect."

Antoinette looks faint.

"That's right. Recognize who's in control, Grandmother."

The elevator signals its arrival.

My elbow catches Pierre in the solar plexus as I grasp the hand holding the gun and point it away from me. The elevator doors open. Bryan is on his feet. Heat from a bullet warms my temple and Pierre is no longer holding me. The patio's glass doors shatter and Antoinette falls. Willis drops to the floor and scrambles for the gun Pierre dropped. Four well-dressed armed men step out of the elevator.

I don't wait around to see what happens next. I charge for the stairs just as James retrieves the gun taped to the baluster. Elijah Hopper has the gun I forced my husband to leave by his hand.

Gunshots ring out around the room.

Disembodied voices shout. Some with Russian accents.

At the top of the stairs I remember to jump over the trip lines. I run to the master bedroom. I close and lock the door behind me. Bryan and James won't let anyone up here, but just in case, James left the gun he had on the nightstand. I use the prepaid cell phone I bought to make a call.

"I'm secured in the bedroom."

"Copy that, I've got their six."

———◆———

Arizona, Four Years Ago

"Hi, Danielle." My doctor shakes my hand. "You want to remove the IUD? Are you experiencing any discomfort or are you trying to get pregnant?"

"I'm definitely not trying to get pregnant, Dr. Houseman."

She washes her hands at the sink in the corner, then covers them with examining gloves. "Do you want to try another form of birth control?"

"I haven't had sex in almost a year and I don't foresee having sex anytime soon. If I do become sexually active again, I know my options." I gesture to the rack of pamphlets and the posters on the walls.

She nods and begins.

Removing the IUD is one of three things left to do on my list titled: Retaking My Life.

The first three months after watching Bryan drive away were the hardest. I left a few voicemail messages, but Bryan didn't return my calls. I emailed him once; it bounced back "undeliverable". It was like he and Emma no longer existed.

Bryan couldn't erase my memories, nor did he take *every* photograph. The pictures I was going to use to make him a collage for a Father's Day gift were hidden in my safe in a file marked tax records.

Every day Kourtney asked to call Daddy and Ma. She, Mr. Cuddles, and I would lie in bed and I tried my best to explain things to her three-year-old mind. We developed a morning tickling ritual to start our day off with happiness and laughter. Her joy is how I made it through each day.

I put on a brave face for everyone, but I was merely going

through the motions of everyday life. Studying for the national exam and preparing my case study to present fell off. Poor Yvon didn't know what to say to make things better.

The clinic's director, Dr. Blanchard, pulled me aside one morning and we had a heart-to-heart talk. She said she'd recognized my grief because she'd gone through a difficult divorce a while back. She asked me to help her with her case study. Working with Dr. Blanchard helped me to accept that Bryan and Emma were gone.

At the sixth-month mark, I did some soul searching and faced some hard truths about myself, my relationship with James, and my life with Bryan. I realized I don't even know Bryan's favorite color. I put my big girl panties on and sat down to make my list. Number one on the list: genetic testing. It's my first step in discovering Danielle Lauren Tatum, single mother, independent woman, graduate student, and kickboxer.

Today is exactly one year since Bryan left and I've accomplished just about everything on my list. As I walk out of the medical building and into the sunlight, I put on my sunglasses and smile. I feel weightless. Even the drive to work is uncomplicated.

I clock in at the mental health clinic and start my work day. Dr. Blanchard isn't in her counseling room, so I go to her office.

"Danielle, great you're back early. I just got a call from the hospital board. I have to go to an emergency meeting. Can you take my sessions? I don't know how long I'll be gone." She's rushing around her office shoving files and notes in her briefcase.

"Are you sure you want *me* to meet with them?"

Dr. Blanchard stops mid shove of a file into the briefcase and stares at me. "Why not *you*? You know my research. You sit in on sessions with my patients. You ask questions during sessions that I don't think of asking. You give valuable input on the direction I should take with patients who are at the plateau stage of therapy. I wouldn't trust anyone but *you* to meet with my case study patients."

I take a deep breath and let it out. "Thank you, Dr. Blanchard, for taking me under your wing. I truly appreciate all that you have taught me. But I'd really like to get back to working with the foster and adoption case studies."

She sets her briefcase on top of her desk and gestures for me to sit while she eases into her chair. "When I interviewed you for the intern position, I admired your drive to help foster children. But I also recognized a spirit in you that could benefit so many. It's a rare natural gift that you have with counseling people that is going to make you a great doctor. I intentionally assigned you to different doctors and not just the ones who specialize in grief therapy because I didn't want to see you limit yourself to just one specialty." Dr. Blanchard opens the center drawer of her desk and pulls out a file and places it in front of me. My name is written along the tab. "The first patient will be here in an hour. That's plenty of time to prepare for the session." She rises, grabs her briefcase, purse, and car keys and walks toward the door. "Dr. Colby is on standby if you really think you need babysitting." She closes the door behind her.

I slowly open the file. The first sheet of paper is an evaluation written by my least favorite doctor to work with. Her words of praise and admiration are a shock. I turn the paper over and read the next evaluation. Then the next. And the next. Apparently after I complete a service assignment the doctor writes an evaluation of my performance. They go all the way back to the beginning. The last page in the file is not an evaluation. It's a job offer—post-graduation and results from the licensing board exams. I close the file and set it aside and prepare for my first solo session.

I end up having an empowering day. Before I leave, I input my notes into the patients' files myself instead of handing it off to another intern.

The weightless feeling I had when I left the doctor's office is still with me as I head to my old apartment building to have dinner with Yvon and Kourtney like we do every Friday evening. We're having homemade pizza a la Kourtney.

"Hi, sweetie. How was your day?"

"It was great! How was your day, Mommy?"

"I had a great day, too. What did you guys do in class?"

Her beautiful hazel eyes get really big as does her smile. "Mr. Mackey brought mealworms and grubs to school today. And he let us *touch* 'em." She uses her hands and arms for emphasis.

I'm excited that she is in his class again this year. Mr. Mackey is a great preschool teacher. And he is loved by all his students and us parents. He's a green earth activist and his classroom reflects it. If he had his way, the entire preschool would be environmentally friendly. Kourtney and I sign up for every green day or earth day event that she is old enough to participate in.

"What did they feel like?"

In between bites of pizza, she uses her four-year-old expressive and extensive vocabulary to describe the insects.

"Did you wash the mealworm and grub cooties off your hands before you made these pizzas?" I laugh.

"I made sure she did." Yvon laughs too.

Kourtney falls asleep on the sofa when I help Yvon clean her kitchen.

When we finish, I thank Yvon, and hand her this week's childcare check. The preprinted checks that come in an envelope without a return address every week I make her shred. Any money wired to my account I deposit the entire amount into Kourtney's trust fund account. Bryan left and *I'm* financially supporting myself and my daughter. I shredded the credit card he gave me; I have my own.

I carry Kourtney out to my truck and get her secured in her car seat.

"You two have a good night," Yvon says from the entrance to the building.

"See you tomorrow." I wave back and climb into the driver's seat.

As I head home, I peek at my sleeping daughter from the rearview mirror. When asked, she says her name is Kourtney Allison Edwards. She caught on after two weeks of constant coaching. I'm still getting used to being called Danielle Edwards.

Kourtney does not wake when I carry her from the car into the house and upstairs to her bedroom. She cracks her eyes open when I get her out of her school uniform and into her pajamas. I hand her Mr. Cuddles, turn on her nightlight, and kiss her cheek.

Before I climb under the covers in my room, I get my list from the drawer of the nightstand and check off the task I completed today. I stare at the task below it.

Without thinking, I pick up my cell phone and open my contacts. I changed his contact name to BK4. My finger hovers over the green symbol of a phone. Mentally I go back and forth about tapping it.

There are days when his scent will surround me in crowded places, and I'll look over my shoulder to see if he's there. I miss him.

I tap the symbol.

The call goes straight to voicemail.

"Hi Bryan, it's me. I don't know why I'm calling you now." I take a deep breath. "That's not exactly true. I do know why I'm leaving this message. I'm feeling a little sentimental. Tomorrow is my graduation. The final phase of my educational plans. I worked hard to get here, but it's nothing like how I pictured it when I was fifteen years old, entering college, and choosing a major. My life has changed so much since then. I lost my best friend, but I gained you, Kourtney, and Emma. The way I pictured this day changed too. You guys are supposed to be there to cheer for me as I cross the stage in my cap and gown, decorated with all my honors sashes. I accept that you and Emma won't be there. I guess this voicemail is my way of truly getting closure. Thank you for our beautiful daughters. I hope you and Emma are happy and thriving as well as Kourtney and I are. Goodbye, Bryan." I tap the red icon to end the call.

I fall asleep feeling accomplished. Tomorrow I get to cross off the last thing on my list.

Midafternoon, Kourtney sits in the backseat of the Range Rover playing with the hem of her dress. Yvon is in the passenger seat and we're on our way to the university.

We get here early enough for Yvon and Kourtney to find seats close to the stage. Once they are settled, I go line up with the other graduates.

The ceremony is long, but the speakers are encouraging. Row by row, graduates stand and line up to cross the stage. As the announcer speaks my name into the microphone and reads the dedication written on the card, for one heartbeat, I feel Bryan and Emma here to see me walk across the finish line. I hear the claps and whistles from fellow study group partners, and some unknowns, but what I hear above all that is my daughter shout out, "I'm proud of you, Mommy!"

I did it. Spring 2010 I'm Dr. Danielle Lauren Edwards.

After the ceremony, I drop Yvon off at her apartment, pick up a bouquet of flowers, and drive to the cemetery. I come here on his birthday, Memorial Day, and Veteran's Day. This is the first time I bring Kourtney with me. On the way, I tell her about my relationship with James and why I want to visit him today in terms she understands.

When we get out of the truck she immediately talks about how pretty the green grass is and how healthy the trees are. Then she notices how the headstones are lined up no matter which way you look at them.

She holds my hand as we make our way to James's grave.

"Hello, Mr. James. I'm Kourtney," she says and places the flowers against the headstone. "Mommy, may I go sit on that bench by the tree?" She points to the tree a few feet away.

"Stay where I can see you. We're not staying long."

I watch her run to the bench and sit. She places her hands on the trunk of the tree and looks up at the leaves on top.

"I did it, James. I have my doctorate in clinical psychology. I wanted to share today with you because you were an important person in my life who understood my need to go as high as I could educationally. I miss you, James. Even though you're not physically here, you will always be my friend." I stand there for a few more minutes, silently remembering the boy I met in middle school, the best friend whom I loved but wasn't in love with, and the man I married. "Come on, Kourtney. Let's go to dinner."

She runs to me and takes my outstretched hand. "Mommy, why does Mr. James have the same last name as us?"

"James Edwards is the man I married. He died before you were born. Since Edwards is my last name, I made it your last name too." God forgive me for the lies I tell my daughter. According to her father, they are necessary.

One day there will be no more secrets and no more lies…there will only be the truth.

I sign her up for summer day camp this year instead of her spending the summer patrolling the neighborhood with Yvon. I don't remember checking the box for her to take swim lessons, but she goes to the sessions every day. With things slowing down at the clinic, Kourtney and I go on lots of mini vacations and road trips.

We are super excited to see her name listed on Mr. Mackey's class roster for the new school year. This is her last year at the preschool. Mr. Mackey is getting them ready to transition to kindergarten next year. Kourtney comes home with homework every night.

The preschool has its annual holiday play in December. All

students are participating. Kourtney is nervous because she was chosen for a special part for her classroom. I assure her I will be seated where she can see me from the stage.

As the auditorium fills with parents, grandparents, and extended family members there to support and cheer on their preschool superstar, I can't help but feel alone.

Right before intermission, Mr. Mackey's class is announced. A cool breeze from the back of the room brushes my neck. It happens every time the auditorium's doors open. This time the breeze carries a familiar scent. Power. Strength. Spicy. Confidence. Soap. Comfort. Warmth. Sandalwood. I look over my shoulder toward the back of the auditorium. Searching for the source. All I see is a sea of parents and guests. I turn my attention back to the stage when the curtain opens.

Camera flashes go off. Including mine.

Kourtney, dressed in a red holiday dress, tights, and shiny red patent leather Mary Janes, gives a nervous little wave when she sees me sitting in the promised spot. I wave back, then wipe tears from my eyes. This is my baby's first solo. I hold my breath when my daughter steps up to the microphone and recites the poem Mr. Mackey tasked her with learning. It took her three days to memorize it. When she speaks the final word. I jump to my feet and clap. I'm not the only one clapping. There is the customary polite clap from everyone in the room, but I hear enthusiastic clapping from somewhere in the middle of the auditorium. Deep in my soul, I feel Bryan's presence here.

We keep the tradition of getting our tree seven days before Christmas, but last year, Kourtney and I started a new one with how we ring in the New Year. I cook our favorite food and I let her stay up to watch the ball drop in Times Square.

Year 2011 starts off good for us. Kourtney gets accepted into my first choice for a private school. The letter of recommendation Mr. Mackey wrote helped, but it was Kourtney's test scores that gained her a coveted spot. School starts in August.

After turning down many propositions from overly flirty men, I go out on my first date in the summer with a man who didn't use lame pickup lines to get my attention.

I change outfits three times before I settle on a flower-patterned jumper with spaghetti straps and open toe sandals.

Morgan and I agree to meet at the restaurant instead of him picking me up.

He is standing in front of the restaurant when I walk up. He compliments me on how I look. I compliment him too because he looks so much better than I remembered. Thick thighs and long legs fill out his jeans.

Morgan is the perfect gentleman. He opens the door and allows me to enter first. He keeps a respectful yet possessive distance between us while we wait for the hostess to show us to our table. We share an appetizer. The conversation is comfortable and easy. We don't talk about anything too personal. His stories about the high school students in his history class are funny. I can tell he really enjoys teaching.

After dinner we hold hands and walk the courtyard of the promenade and sit at a table eating frozen yogurt for dessert. The conversation between us continues to flow smoothly.

He walks me to my SUV and kisses my cheek before he opens my door.

I like him. He put me at ease. Not once did I think about Bryan while on the date or feel his ghost haunting me.

Morgan and I call or text each other every day for the next two weeks. He and I meet for lunch at a sandwich shop near the clinic. The more time I spend with him the more I like him, but I'm not ready to take things to the next level.

Kourtney cries when I get dressed for my third date with Morgan. She tells me I look ugly every time I ask for her opinion about what I put on. Yvon, on the other hand, gives an honest opinion. She is spending the night at the house to babysit Kourtney. The concert I'm going to with Morgan doesn't let out until one in the morning.

I settle on a lavender sleeveless blouse and lightweight denim capris.

Kourtney is so upset about me going on this date that she makes herself sick. After I get her cleaned up I pull my phone out of my purse to call Morgan and cancel. I do not feel right leaving my daughter upset like this.

"Don't you dare make that call, Danielle," Yvon scorns. "You are too young to be living your life like all there is to it is motherhood and a job. You need to get out and let off some steam with adult company. Find your own happiness. Kourtney will be fine."

I hesitate, but Yvon shoves my purse and keys into my hands and pushes me out of the front door.

The restaurant slash bar slash hotel where the concert is being held was built in the 1930s in the heart of downtown Tucson. The first of three opening acts is already on stage when I get there. The headliner isn't scheduled to go on until eleven thirty. Morgan is friends with two of the group members who gave him VIP passes.

Morgan is sitting at the bar when I clear the bouncer's screening. From the looks of it, my date is already on his fourth drink.

"Well hello, sexy," he says as he swivels around on the stool. His gaze starts at my breasts and goes down to my pelvic area, then back to my breasts. "What do you say we skip dinner, go upstairs to one of the dressing rooms and fuck until it's time for my boys to go on?" Morgan swings the VIP passes on a lanyard in my face.

"Excuse me?" *Did I hear him correctly?*

"Look, it's time you gave up the pussy." He captures my wrist and yanks me toward him. His arm clamps around my waist.

The bartender makes eye contact with me. I shake my head letting him know I don't need assistance—Morgan might.

I press my lips against Morgan's ear so only he can hear my threat. To ensure he hears every word, I press the tip of my truck key into a pressure point in his back. "If you don't take your hand off me right now, I'll break it."

He tries to kiss me.

In a blink of an eye, Morgan is cowering on the floor looking up at me with big, shocked eyes. I'm pretty sure I cracked his rib and he's going to need stitches for his busted lip.

The bartender is applauding as I walk away.

From the safety of my truck, I exhale. "Next time I'll listen to Kourtney."

The year comes and goes. My luck with dating doesn't improve. The guys I meet and go out with do not make it past the fourth date. They go from good, intelligent men to sex-driven adolescent boys.

Yvon keeps telling me to stick with it, eventually I'll find a guy who wants to be my friend before we become lovers.

One good thing that comes out of the year: Kourtney is becoming more open with me dating. I'm not introducing her to anyone until I know one hundred percent he is serious about being my friend first.

Kourtney's bedroom wall is filling up with certificates and awards. Her kindergarten science fair submission earns her first place at the school.

My Christmas cookie cutter collection has grown since I started it with my first Christmas with Emma. Kourtney and I bake and decorate lots of cookies for the holidays.

We ring in 2012 with a buffet of our favorite foods and watching the ball drop.

The clinic is experiencing funding problems. Five staff members are laid off and the clinic's hours of operation are reduced to twelve hours a day instead of twenty-four hours per day effective March 1st. Any afterhours mental health emergencies are sent to the hospital, which means the permanent licensed therapists are on rotation in the emergency room.

Kourtney and I adjust to my new work schedule. It's still flexible, but we're not able to go on a lot of mini vacations or long road trips. Anytime I'm scheduled to work at the hospital, Yvon spends the night at my house and gets my daughter to school in the mornings.

Yvon urges me to go on a date in the middle of April with a police officer I met at a community function put on by the mental health clinic.

We meet at an Italian restaurant. Zachary hands me a single red rose, and I force myself not to compare it to the one Bryan gave me the first time he took me to dinner.

Right away Zachary dominates the conversation with talk about his work as a police officer and community liaison. I do not see it as bragging or being cocky. He loves protecting and serving the community. It's actually nice talking to him.

There are no awkward silences or dull moments throughout dinner and dessert.

I excuse myself to go to the restroom.

After I relieve my bladder, I wash my hands and rinse my mouth out. I reapply the clear lip gloss.

As I'm making my way back to the table, I hear the sound of dishes breaking and a woman shouting. She is sitting in my seat across from a red-faced Zachary. Her blonde barrel curls bounce with every angry bob of her head.

I approach the table with caution. "Is everything okay?"

"I'm trying to have a conversation with my husband, if you don't mind." She's got that black-girl neck roll thing going.

"Not at all." I pick up my jacket off the back of the chair and leave the rose and the husband and wife to hash out their troubles in front of the rest of the diners. Dating is now off the table for a little while.

Needing to get out of Arizona, Kourtney and I spend Thanksgiving in Los Angeles with the Franklins. It has been awhile since we've visited them.

The responsibility of caring for Mr. Franklin is starting to show on Mrs. Franklin. She's ready to consider alternative living arrangements for him.

I help her find a round-the-clock facility that has a look and feel like home. Mrs. Franklin can spend nights with him whenever she wants. The place is expensive, and I set it up where I pay the balance of whatever isn't covered by Mr. Franklin's pension and social security each month. I want him to be comfortable. Mrs. Franklin puts the boxing gym up for sale.

On the drive back to Arizona, I explain to Kourtney what is going on with Pop-Pop. She doesn't want him to forget us and makes me pinky-promise-cross-my-heart to send pictures of the two of us every month.

Our 2013 starts off with Kourtney marking cities on a map of the United States that she wants to visit this year. I laugh when I see she has already included our annual February trip to Los Angeles, so I can get a birthday cake from my favorite bakery, Hansen's Cakes.

Today is my day off and I'm at the dealership for the Range Rover to undergo routine maintenance. While I sit in the waiting area, I reread the memo from Dr. Blanchard. There will be more budget cuts at the clinic, which translates to layoffs.

I open my laptop and begin typing questions I want to ask at the next small support group session. I'm working with mothers who lost their children to terminal illnesses.

"Excuse me, is anyone sitting here?"

I look up from my laptop at the gentleman pointing to the empty chair across the table from me. "No, it's empty."

"Do you mind if I sit here for about ten minutes? They promised my truck will be ready by then."

"Sure, have a seat."

The chair's plastic legs glide on the waxed tile floor. I go back to typing. My therapy session with the mothers is the day after tomorrow.

"I'm Conor, by the way."

I glance at him and offer a friendly smile. "Hi, I'm Danielle." My gaze drops back to the monitor. My fingers rapidly tap the keys to keep up with the questions that come to mind.

Conor's fingers drum a beat on the table top.

The constant *thump, thump, thump* is breaking my concentration. I glance up at him. His eyes are sweeping the waiting area. They land on me.

I arch an eyebrow.

He looks down at his hands then back up at me. "Sorry, I don't mean to disturb you."

"How long have you been waiting?"

"Four hours."

I frown. "What happened?"

"I wasn't exactly kind to my Rover on the drive here from Oklahoma."

"Is that where you're from?"

"Born and raised." His smile sets off the two cutest dimples in his beard-shadowed cheeks. "Are you from here?"

"No, I grew up in California."

A service clerk approaches the table with a stack of papers in his hands. "Mr. Wheeler, you're all set. Again, I apologize for the long wait. If you will follow me to the service desk, I can get you out of here."

Conor pushes back in the chair and rises. Immediately I check out his jean-clad thighs. He reaches across the table with his right hand. I reciprocate. His handshake is firm yet gentle and his palm is the right amount of rough.

"Thank you, Danielle, for letting me sit with you."

"You're welcome, Conor." I watch him walk away.

He has an easy, confident stride to his walk and a nice backside too. His thigh muscles contract behind the material of his jeans with each step. His polo shirt isn't loose, nor is it fitted, it hangs on his body like it was custom made.

A question for the focus group comes to mind and I quickly type it out, then others follow.

"Excuse me, Danielle."

I smile and tear my gaze from the monitor. Conor is standing beside my chair.

"Look, I don't know how to ask for your phone number without it coming off like some pickup line."

"Conor, I'm a single mother. A widow. A therapist with a crazy work schedule. I don't have sex on the first date or the fourth date. There's the possibility I won't ever have sex with you. Do you still want my phone number?"

"I married my college girlfriend. She cheated on me the entire three years we were married. Everyone knew about it except me. I found out after she gave birth to a baby that isn't mine. Messy doesn't even come close to describing my divorce or the child support battle I'm still going through. It took me a couple of years to date again. I can count on one hand the number of women who went out with me thinking I am an automatic money dispenser and the last woman I dated just finished her first year of a ten-year prison sentence for assault with intent to kill. You're looking at the victim. Right now, the only thing I can handle is friendship. Do you still want to give me your phone number?"

I reach for the receipt in his hand and quickly write down my phone number.

CHAPTER SIXTEEN

BRYAN

Colorado, Present Day

IF I DIDN'T KNOW OTHERWISE, I'd say my wife is trained in strategic offensive and defensive operations. The way she positioned us in the room is genius. The four men getting off the elevator don't have a chance.

Edwards is the lookout from his position up on the stairs. Hopper is frontline and using furniture as a shield. I'm positioned in front of the stairs, blocking passage to protect the rightful heir to RAGS. I don't know who Dani put on sniper detail, but whoever it is has a good view of the penthouse from outside.

Langford is the wild card. His position is neutral. He's either with us or against us. Dani is forcing him to make a choice.

The gunfire around the room stops.

I turn my gun on Langford. "Toss it, and you know what to do after that." I don't give a damn that he'll be lying on broken glass.

"Edwards, you and Hopper secure the room. Fontenot, open the communication between me and the team, then use Riley to cut off all access to the penthouse." I holster my firearm and grab my backpack. Two ballistic missiles were launched that have the potential of reaching an unsuspecting country in thirty minutes.

Edwards retrieves Dani's backpack from behind a curtain and finds plastic cable ties. He tosses some to Hopper, then crouches near Langford.

I set two laptops on the table and sit. Instead of saying my code out loud, I go through the manual identification process on one of the laptops. I'm praying I do not have to log on to the other one.

My laptop instantly connects with Phantom's network and satellite. The view on the monitor is grainy, but I count twenty-two orange outlines of body heat projecting off the insurgents near the transporter erector launchers and structures in the area. There could be more, most appear on top of each other. The ESO appear as white dots because of the tracker in their military rings. "Spread out. Form a protective scalene triangle around Paul."

Three dots move to make the shape with unequal distance between one another. One dot remains in the center.

Paul's field laptop connects to the network. I start two countdown clocks. The first one is for how long it will take the ICMBs to leave earth's atmosphere. The second is for how much time I have before the United States government realizes they no longer have control over the national missile defense systems.

"Crack the biscuit," I command.

Paul reads off the alphanumeric code listed on the credit card-sized plastic authentication card. Without physically being there, it's the only way to identify Lieutenant Colonel Anthony Jonathan Paul as the Ghost accessing the antiballistic missiles on board the USS Jashen, the US Navy destroyer in the Indian Ocean on a different assignment.

This wartime situation is the reason Paul is authorized to play video games. It's a form of his training: maneuvering interceptors to take down ICBMs. In the simulators, he has a one hundred percent success rate in every "engaging test" given.

But this isn't a simulator.

We don't get a do-over.

There's never been a situation where Paul has tested his skills for real. If he can't intercept the ICBMs before they reenter the earth's atmosphere, I am prepared to respond with an immediate counterattack. Yemenis will not have time to react and my team will not have time to get to a safe zone. This is one reason why Second Command is the second most powerful man in our nation.

Paul asks for numbers. I quickly do the math and rattle off the trajectory angle and the speed of the two missiles. The ICBMs will leave earth's atmosphere in three minutes.

A world map flashes on the screen with a country highlighted in red. Riley projected where and when the missiles will hit once they reenter the earth's atmosphere based on the numbers I recorded.

Paul asks for the next set of numbers. I give him the longitude and latitude of USS Jashen's location.

The background noise in the earpiece sounds like a serious gunfight going on. Ricci has taken over command and is directing Acosta and Porter. They are preserving ammunition by only firing when insurgents threaten to breach the parameter of their triangle. The shape shifts after each Ghost fires a shot to make the insurgents think there are more than four of them in the field.

My peripheral vision keeps track of the people in the penthouse. Hopper is checking the dead men. Edwards is lifting a wounded Antoinette off the floor and into a chair. Willis is quiet and reserved sitting in a chair. Dani has yet to come downstairs.

Paul launches the Kinetic Energy Interceptors onboard of the Navy destroyer. They are not weighed down by explosives so they're moving at maximum speed. I start a third countdown clock. If the ICBMs stay on their current path, the force of the interceptors' kinetic energy will obliterate them in six minutes.

Communications on board the USS Jashen are going crazy. I filter the military responses through Riley.

The first countdown clock on my monitor reaches zero. Both intercontinental ballistic missiles have left the earth's atmosphere and are releasing decoys. They are now in orbit. I start a fourth clock for how much time there is before the ICBMs reenter the earth's atmosphere, and Paul gets one final shot at intercepting them which is much more difficult at their rate of speed.

Math is as natural to me as inhaling and exhaling. Equations float through my mind as I analyze speed and projectile trajectory and relay the results to Paul so that he can prepare to launch a final round of antiballistic missiles from another Navy destroyer if the ICBMs do reenter the earth's atmosphere.

The skin along my jaw grows tight. Tension settles in my shoulders. I'm ready to give the command for the people on our lists to be taken out of the country. Then I'll clean up the last two RAGS loose ends—killing Antoinette and Willis—grab Dani and head back to the bunker.

The numbers on the clocks are changing faster than the eyes can transmit it to the brain. The battle on Yemen's coast is going strong. Ricci, Acosta, and Porter are keeping the enemy at a distance while Paul is focused on a different threat.

"Target one destroyed!" Paul shouts.

On my monitor the tracking image of one missile is gone, but another remains. According to the second countdown clock, we have forty-five seconds before I have to log on to the other laptop and launch a counterattack.

The lock signal beeps.

Three. Two. One.

The tracking image of the second ICBM is gone.

"Sir, I'm getting something," Fontenot announces. "It's faint…" Rapid clicking of keyboard keys. "I think"—more key tapping—"the last two ICMBs are warming up and so are the surface to air missiles. I have a lock on where the launch signal originated. One klick East of the team's location. Nine minutes 'til launch."

The only reason to launch SAMs is they are going to try and shoot down our interceptors when they launch the last two ballistic missiles.

"Too many ILAs for us to get there," Porter reports.

"Fuck me sideways," Paul complains.

In the upper right-hand corner of my monitor, I can see what Fontenot has on her screen. Paul can't move from his current position because he'll need to launch the interceptors. Ricci, Acosta, and Porter can't leave him behind because he can't watch his back and stop intercontinental ballistic missiles too.

"Need a little help?" the muffled voice of a female asks.

Fontenot and I respond at the same time, "Identify yourself."

"Lima. Victor. Echo. Seven. Nine. Zero. Three. Echo. Six." Captain Vanessa Larson's photo flashes in the upper left corner of my screen.

I smile. "You're supposed to be on an aircraft back to the States."

"First Command ordered me to stay and back up the team."

"What are you in?" I ask.

"Air Force attack helicopter."

"Why aren't we picking it up?" Fontenot asks.

"I'm honored to be the first Air Force pilot to test the stealth helicopter in a real combat situation."

"That isn't supposed to be ready for another couple of months," Paul says.

"Table the talk for now. Larson, take out those TELs, then clear the path for Ricci and Porter. Acosta, you stay with Paul and watch his six," I command.

The noise from my earpiece reminds me of movies with war scenes amplified by the surround-sound system in a movie theater. I don't have to be there to know how good of a fighter pilot Larson is. Her reputation in the US Air Force is one of many reasons she's a top Ghost today.

"Whoo-hoo!" Acosta cheers. "Larson is on *fire*."

"Thanks for the compliment, sir. Clear to advance." We can hear the smile on her face through her words.

"Roger that," Porter replies. "I got your right flank, Ricci."

"Copy that, Porter."

The two white dots move eastward.

"Paul, hold your position. We don't know if more ICBMs will be launched from other locations. Fontenot, do a worldwide search for activity."

"Hawk," Hopper says. "Those are Grigori Popov's boys." He gestures to the four dead men in the room.

"Popov? The rogue Russian General they've been searching for, for six years?"

"I had no idea she was in cahoots with him."

"Is that what you and Pierre were up to when you were pretending to be sick?" Willis asks.

"Paul, give me a second. I know a quicker way to find out if there's more missiles." I rise and take seven steps to stand in front of Antoinette.

Her wrists are bound together in front of her, fresh blood seeping from the gunshot wound in her shoulder. Although her eyes show no fear, her body language gives her away. She is slightly leaning away from the threat of my closeness. The monster smiles in pleasure. He loves it when the enemy fears him.

Without warning, I grip her injured arm. The pain meds wore off hours ago. Antoinette lets out a scream that would set most teeth on edge.

"Are there any more?"

Her lips press together to form a thin, tight line. I don't have time for defiance. My grip on Antoinette's arm tightens and I grab her hand. She screams again. This one giving the monster more energy, more strength to take over.

"Answer me."

"Bryan, I love you like a son…" The rest of her speech is cut off by a scream stuck in her throat. I've broken her index finger.

Leaning closer to Antoinette, the monster speaks. "You had your own daughter gunned down like a nobody on the street. Let me show you how a real monster successfully gets what it wants."

Any semblance of the man I am has completely disappeared. I've crossed the planes of existence into the vortex of darkness that the monster thrives in.

The military knife that was in the pocket of my cargo pants is now in the hand of the monster. The tip of the blade follows the line of black sutures in Antoinette's arm, slicing them. She tries to cower away, but there is nowhere to go. I'm everywhere she moves. Her lips part; they move like the words are strangling her. Her blood begins to seep through the newly reopened wound.

The monster is thirsty for more of her blood.

The knife's blade starts at the top, pressing deeper into the wound. Coaxing more of the dark red blood of the enemy to gush out. The sight of it is like heavy rain drops painting the white marble floor.

The blade of the knife cuts the plastic cable tie with little effort. And I flip Antoinette's hand over—palm up.

"The next sound out of your mutha-fuckin mouth better be what I need to know." The sharp blade presses into her wrist, the sun's light reflects off the six-inch stainless-steel blade. Just one quick swipe will open the veins.

"What do you need, Bry?"

The sound of Dani's voice makes a small crack in the dark tinted shield of the vortex. The monster doesn't break eye connection with the knife against Antoinette's wrist. But the energy of Dani's presence is pulling me to separate from it.

I don't want her to see me like this. The last time my monster appeared with her in the room, I had the presence of mind not to go too far. I'm not in that frame of mind right now.

"Get. Out." The harshness of my order sounds unreal in my ears. I have never, ever spoken to Dani in this tone. I realize my monster has complete control over me. He does not know or understand love. He will hurt Dani if she tries to stop him.

"No, Bry. Tell me what you need."

My wife's voice makes an even bigger crack in the shield of the vortex.

"Get. The. Fuck. Out. Danielle."

"Stand down, Hawk," Paul warns through the earpiece.

"Bry, let *me* help you," Dani pleads.

"No." The tone of the one-word reply should be enough of a deterrent to warn Dani to stay back. I am not the person she thinks I am in this moment. Even my best friend realizes that from thousands of miles away.

She places her hand over mine—the one pressing the knife's blade into Antoinette's wrist. Dani squeezes herself between me and the enemy.

The monster turns its sights on Dani. Her presence has replaced Antoinette. The monster now sees Danielle as the enemy.

Dani doesn't back down from the dark, cold glare.

I feel its anger. It's nothing like that time in the bedroom. The monster wants me to turn the knife on Danielle.

She faces the monster head on. No fear in her eyes. It wonders why? People we come face to face with fear him. What's so special about her?

My Dani remains steadfast in her stance. The monster sneers at the unconditional love in her eyes.

My Dani pleads with me to regain control. Not with words but through the cupping of my cheek and the brush of her thumb across my bottom lip.

That touch.

Her touch reaches my soul.

I release Antoinette and put the knife away and the eye of the vortex disappears. My monster retreats into the shadows of the cage, yet the door remains open.

"What do you need?" Dani whispers.

"I need to know if Islam Liberation Army has any more intercontinental ballistic missiles. And I need to know where Grigori Popov is."

Dani turns to face Antoinette.

She inspects her grandmother's injuries.

"James, can you give me the supplies from your backpack?"

Edwards does as she requests. He unzips the center, turns it over and dumps everything out on the table.

I watch my wife sanitize her hands, then put on surgical gloves and begin to carefully clean the open wounds. I don't feel bad about what I did. Antoinette is still the enemy.

"It's over," Dani says to her grandmother in a consoling tone. "There is nothing more you can do to keep RAGS going. But you can save yourself."

Antoinette shakes her head in denial. "With my guidance, you and Bryan can be the most powerful couple in the world. I can teach you how to be the strong woman behind the great man."

Dani stops cleaning and looks the woman in the eyes. "You may have been raised to be second to a man, but that's not how George and Katherine Franklin raised me. Bryan and I are already a powerful couple because we love each other. My husband doesn't have a strong woman behind him…"

"I've got a strong woman standing beside me."

The special smile the woman I love gives me makes my monster close the door on his cage because he's come up against someone who can look him in the eye and defeat him.

I was so close to hurting Dani, it scares me. Now I understand what Chen went through in the field as a Ghost and why it is so hard to keep control of the monster once it is out.

Dani opens several packages of sterile bandages and packs them in the open wounds. "I wasn't lying. Whomever you owe money to will come looking for you. The only person who can protect you needs you to answer his questions."

Antoinette just sits there.

"You and Willis are the only links I have to my mother. I don't want Bryan to torture you. But if you continue to refuse to tell him what he needs to know, I will put aside my love for you and let him do his job."

God, I love my wife.

Dani wraps her grandmother's arm with an elastic bandage, then layers ice packs on top and covers them with another elastic bandage. She slowly wraps tape around the broken finger, securing it to the one next to it.

"This is your last chance. Once I step away, I will not stop Bryan again."

Antoinette's shoulders slump in defeat. Her eyes fix on me. "There aren't any more."

"Where's Popov?"

"In Minsk."

I glare at Langford. "All that riding my ass to stay focused was to keep me thrown off?"

"No. I needed you to do something I couldn't do."

"Save your ass?"

"No! Be the better man. Protect my granddaughter and great-granddaughter because I couldn't protect my daughter or Carolyn. You don't know what it's like to come from nothing and be given a taste of something. You get greedy for it. I sold my soul just to get more and anytime I tried to curb my hunger, someone I loved died." The waterfall of tears starts, and he begs for forgiveness.

I sit at my laptop, tuning him out.

"Burn the village down, Paul," I command.

"Roger that, sir."

I start typing a secured message to President Hart, giving him an update.

"Sir, Instructor Hawk just notified me that Edwards's family made it to the hospital," Fontenot says.

"Let her know he'll be on his way after we wrap up here. Give me two hours then dispatch a Phantom Security Team to pick up the Langfords and have Sweepers clean up the penthouse."

"Roger that, sir."

Dani is watching me like she's gauging my mood. I open my arms and pull her onto my lap when she reaches my side. I hold my wife tight and breathe in her scent.

"What happens now?" she asks.

"You are going to get in the car with Edwards and go to Colorado Springs. He'll drop you off at my parents' house, then go to the hospital to be with his wife and son."

Dani kisses my cheek. "Okay."

"Okay?" I was half expecting a fight.

Dani scrunches her nose and gives me the innocent, wide-eyed look. "I'm too shaken to do anything other than what you tell me to do."

"Sir, someone did an override on the service elevator. They're on their way up."

I ease Dani off my lap as I stand, pushing her behind me. I grab my gun and relay Fontenot's message to Hopper and Edwards.

They arm themselves too.

The service elevator door opens.

I wait for the visitor to show himself.

At the first sight of the mahogany cane, I relax and holster my firearm. Terrance Brumfield strides into the room dressed in a military combat uniform, the strap of a rifle bag across his chest.

I look over my shoulder and cock a questioning eyebrow at my wife.

She shrugs nonchalantly. "The only reason he didn't make it into the Army is because of his knee."

I shake hands with Brumfield. "Thank you for having our back."

"Glad to help, son."

———◆———

Colorado, One Year Ago…

"Who is the hottie with the smoking gray eyes?" Chen gestures to the image on the screen by the conference table.

"Conor Wheeler?"

"You're vetting recruits this early? When do I get to interview him?"

"I thought Tom put a lock on you." I use the pen in my hand to point at his engagement ring.

"We're not married yet. And I'd never cheat on him, but that doesn't mean I can't appreciate a fine-ass—man."

I shake my head at his pun and write a note on the legal pad next to me. "I'm not vetting Wheeler. He and Dani are going out."

Chen falls into an empty chair. Unfortunately, it's the one directly across from me. He has been the most vocal about the unconventional conversations I have with the men Danielle dates. For the past two years, I've convinced those men it would be in their best interest to find another yard to piss in.

"You've moved on. Why can't Danielle?"

This is a different approach. Normally he goes straight for the jugular. Shrinking my motives behind the intimidations. "The women I fuck are just a means to let off stress. I don't lie to them. They can always tell me no and there'd be no hard feelings."

Chen cocks an eyebrow. "Maybe Danielle wants to let off stress too."

"She's not like that."

"Why do you care who Danielle lays down with?"

"Anyone she gets serious about will be a part of my daughter's life. And I'll be damned if *my* baby girl calls some lowlife, Daddy."

"Is that what this is really about? Kourtney acknowledging another man as Daddy?"

Part of it. "No."

Chen cocks an eyebrow. "One of these days, some guy is going to stand up to you because he loves Danielle and is willing to fight you for her. What are you going to do then?"

The constant burn in my belly spreads to my chest at the thought of another man's hands on her body. So far, every orgasm Dani's ever had, *I* own. Even the ones coaxed by her own fingers because it's *my* name on her lips when she comes. It's me she's imagining when she finger-fucks herself. I look Chen square in the eyes and answer, "Kill him."

"This 'if I can't have her, nobody can' mentality isn't healthy for her or your daughter."

"I never said nobody can have her." At least not out loud.

"You don't have to. Your actions say it." Chen leans back in his chair. No emotion on his face. "You haven't gotten over her. And she hasn't gotten over you. The house is secured, bring them to Boulder."

"Since I stopped being around them things have been quiet in Arizona. They are safe as long as I'm not in their lives."

"Why isn't Wheeler good enough for her?"

This isn't the first time he's asked me that question. Hell, I've asked myself the same question after watching Dani come home from a bad date with hurt in her eyes and disappointment in her body language.

"This guy's got a juvie record. And a shitload of baggage."

"Show me." Chen gestures for my laptop.

I pass it to him.

Right away, his eyes move left to right, reading every word on the screen. His finger taps the down key so the information in the file scrolls up as he reads.

While he's on my laptop, I go to my desk and open the email from the CEO of a multibillion-dollar telecommunication company in Texas. We're in the final stages of contract negotiations for Hawkeye Personal Protection. The guy needs a team of PPOs round the clock. I'm scheduled to interview men this morning for the team. I don't have to fly to Texas until the end of June to sign the contract, but I want Paul to put the team through exercises before they start on the first of July.

"How long has Danielle been going out with Conor Wheeler?"

"Wright said they've gone out several times in the past six months."

His eyebrows reach his hairline as his eyes widen. "How'd that happen?"

"Wright kept it out of her report. Saying Dani and Conor are just friends. And her instructions are to report romantic interests not friends."

"I bet the new one you ripped her is the size of a bowling ball."

"I couldn't. She was right, so I amended my instructions."

"He seems on the up and up."

"Are you shitting me, Chen? The man was charged with assault at the age of sixteen."

"He beat the shit out of the man who tried to rape his sister. You would have done the same. No, scratch that. You would have murdered the pedophile."

"It says his actions were excessive. Have you gotten to the photos of the man he beat? He did that with his fists. The guy was in a coma for a year."

"It also says the man was fresh out of prison from a molestation sentence and Wheeler's sister was not the only child he sexually assaulted that week. Wheeler served three months and completed a year of anger management therapy. He's been a model citizen ever since."

"Dani's letting him hang out with her and Kourt. I don't want him around my daughter. The baggage he's carrying is too volatile."

"Yeah, I see. His ex-wife is suing him for child support of a non-biological child. His past breakups were not amicable. And his last girlfriend stalked and tried to kill him. Yep, his baggage is volatile, all right."

Wait for it.

"Speaking of baggage, I hear Amelia, pardon me, Malinda Williamson got teacher of the year."

Chen never misses an opportunity to bring up my own shit.

I'm adding a visit to Malinda to my itinerary when I go to Texas. It's been two months since we've had a face-to-face conversation, but I do keep tabs on her in other ways. The unexpected visits over the past three and a half years is my way of keeping her off balance. RAGS's attacks on the United States have become more vicious. If she is involved again, I'll end the life I've created for her.

"Looks to me like Wheeler is better than the others, Bry. And cute too. I can see why Dani likes him. Thick thighs. Long legs. Strong shoulders and arms. Pretty eyes. If my fiancé didn't demand monogamy, I'd do Big Wheeler." Chen winks.

"Fuck you." I add the gesture for emphasis.

Chen laughs at my expense. "I'd love to fuck you, honey." Max does that twisted mouth smile with a sway of his head and shoulders thing. "I'm sure Thomas will make an exception since it's you. I promise I'll be gentle your first time."

"Why are you in my office, Max? Don't you have family and in-laws to entertain?"

"I need a break from the chaos. This fairytale destination wedding in Maui my future husband has cooked up is getting out of control."

"No one would ever think *you'd* be against the traditional wedding stuff?"

"I can turn-up with the best of 'em." He snaps two times.

I abandon the email and lean back in my chair. "For real, Max. Why are you working today?"

"I thought Tony could use some help interviewing that detainee. The guy's definitely high up in RAGS. People are out looking for him."

I sit up quick. "No. Max. No way. You're getting married this weekend. You need a clear head. Someone is sure to piss you off before the wedding and I don't want to have to send a team of Sweepers to clean up brain matter and bodily fluids because you convinced someone to eat a bullet."

His smile shows an immense amount of gratitude. He stands and walks toward the door. "I'm not going in the room. I'll observe and relay techniques through an earpiece."

"I don't know about that. You and Tony don't know how to

keep it simple."

"Since when have you done anything simple when it comes to protecting the country or the woman you love?"

He just had to get one last dig in before he walks out of my office.

"Sir, Marie Langford is on line one," Riley announces.

I put on the headset and push the button. "Hi, Marie."

"I hope I'm not disturbing you, Bryan. Are you busy?"

Her accent is thick. She's either mad or worried.

"No, I'm not busy. What can I do for you?"

"Some man named Mills is here saying he's filling in as Watcher. I didn't open the door. Usually you let me know who is covering while Willis is gone. He's not wearing a Watcher's suit. He's wearing a Security's suit."

"I apologize, Marie. Willis was supposed to inform you. Tell Mills to hold tight and Major Ricci will be there to give him instructions. If you're not comfortable with him being in the house, I'll call him and tell him to wait in the car."

"As long as you know he's here, I'll let him in."

I laugh. Marie is my overprotective second mother. She understands the seriousness of Phantom and keeps my house secure.

I reply to the new client's email, then go back to taking notes on Conor Wheeler until my first interviewee arrives fifteen minutes early.

At fourteen hundred hours, I shut down everything and pack up my briefcase. "Porter, I'll be leaving in five minutes."

"Roger that, sir. Larson and I are ready."

Since that intruder took my toothbrush from Dani's apartment, Tony *and* President Hart insist I have a security detail. In the beginning I hated it and I ditched the men and women assigned to tail me. It drove Tony crazy. This is Larson's first time on my security detail, which works out. Emm is too old for me to take into the men's restroom and I'm not comfortable with her going to the ladies' room by herself. This evening, I'm taking my daughter out to dinner to celebrate her last day of first grade. Larson can keep an eye on Emm in places I can't.

I make it to the school a few minutes before the bell rings and join a group of mothers standing in front of the entrance. I've known most of them since our children were in preschool together. Jennifer Hill is the director of Parks and Recreations for the city of Boulder. She tells us about the summer activities going on to keep kids busy. I'm hoping Emm will want to sign up for the art program this year.

Max joins the group and the conversation switches to his upcoming wedding. He turns up the flame. Inwardly I roll my eyes. He has the women oohing and awing about the location and decorations.

"Long time no see, stranger."

A chill strikes my spine. The hairs on the back of my neck stand at attention. Madelyn Brooks squeezes her plastic surgery-enhanced body between me and the woman standing next to me. I catch the sneer Madelyn tosses at the woman.

"I was thinking maybe you and I can get together over the summer"—she pauses to let the innuendo sink in—"with the little ones. My Jacob just adores Emma."

Her claw reaches for my arm, but I step out of her reach before it makes contact. Madelyn Brooks has been trying to get my attention for years. I prefer women who are naturally beautiful, not women who are surgically beautiful. I've tried being subtle about turning her down. I've tried avoiding her. My next move is to put her in her place.

Kids begin to storm the gate. Some faster than others. I spot Emm walking with Penny.

"Emm," I call out.

She looks up and smiles.

I open my arms and she runs into them. "How was your last day of school?"

"It was good."

I say goodbye to the parents and carry my daughter to the truck.

On the drive home, she tells me all about her day. Emm is excited about getting dressed up to go to dinner. Tonight, I'm taking my big girl to an upscale restaurant thirty minutes from the house, at the base of the Rocky Mountains. The view is nice year-round. Dani would appreciate the sight. One day I'll take her there.

Whoa, Hawk, where'd that come from?

A voice in the depths of my soul that sounds a lot like my grandmother whispers, "*You miss her.*"

The minute I pull into the garage, Emm is out of the truck and racing into the house calling for Marie. The two go upstairs to get her ready. I head to my office and review my interview notes then email Tony the list of men I want on the new client's team.

An hour before it's time to leave, I go up to my room to shower and change into a more formal suit, then wait for Emm at the foot of the stairs with a special surprise that Marie hid in the kitchen for me.

When my daughter comes down the stairs in her yellow dress with matching purse, I present her with a yellow rose. Marie fixed her hair with bouncy big girl curls. I offer Emm my arm and escort her to the garage. Since this is a special occasion, we're taking my new Chevy Camaro. Vin finished armoring it today.

The hostess at the restaurant flirts with me, and I quickly shut her down. She's making Emm uncomfortable. Someone else on the wait staff shows us to our table on the terrace. I pull the chair out for my big girl, then take the seat across from her.

"Dylan's mom told me that the park near the house is having art activities this summer. Should I sign you up?"

Emm drop her eyes to the table and shakes her head.

"Why not? I thought you loved to draw and wanted to learn how to paint."

"I do, but I don't want to do it at the park."

"You'd have fun. Kids you know from school will be there. I think Uncle Max and Uncle Tommy are putting Penny in the dance program at the park. Do you want me to sign you up for dance?"

Her long brown curls swish across her face as Emm vigorously shakes her head.

If Dani were still in Emm's life, I know my daughter would be more outgoing. What the hell am I going to do when she reaches puberty? I know Jessi, Mom, and Marie will help Emm through it, but I really wanted the woman she called Mommy to guide her to womanhood.

"Okay, we'll stick to what you've done each summer before now." It's hard to plan a vacation getaway, but I will do all that I can to make it a fun summer for my daughter. Maybe I'll see if one of the art teachers will do private lessons for Emm at the house.

The head chef is an old high school buddy. He steps out of the kitchen to come say hello. He takes the menus from our hands and tells us he'll fix us something special. This brightens Emm's mood. From that point on, I don't mention summer activities and just enjoy this time with my daughter.

Emm can't stop talking about being a flower girl this weekend. She asks why we can't drive to Maui. Emm doesn't like to fly. I promise to hold her hand the entire plane ride.

Before we leave the restaurant, I take my daughter out on the dance floor. I'm not a good dancer, but it doesn't matter to her. We dance for a few songs, then head home.

I help her put her rose in a slender vase and set in on the nightstand next to her bed. We change out of our clothes and kick back in our pajamas in the family room watching one of her favorite kids shows.

Wednesday morning, we fly commercial to Hawaii. Mom, Dad, Jessi, and the guys travel with us. As promised, I hold her hand from the minute we board to the minute we deboard the plane.

One of my duties as Max's best man is to throw a co-bachelors' party with Tom's best man—his younger brother. Austin and I put our heads together to come up with something appealing for the gay and the straight. Once the alcohol starts flowing, the shindig takes on a life of its own.

Late Saturday afternoon, everyone is sober and in attendance for the sunset wedding of Maxim Li Chen and Thomas Carlton Snyder.

The guys and I stand on Max's side. Thomas's brother and frat brothers stand on his. Emm and Penny steal the show as flower girls.

At the reception, Ig and I stand at the bar watching Max and Tom dance for the first time as husband and husband. He jabs my ribs with his elbow. "Still think love is just a four-letter word people use to explain that animalistic need to fuck as much as they want without judgment?"

I sip my drink, knowing I'm about to tell an unbelievable lie. "Yep."

He pats my shoulder. "It's up to fifty grand, right?"

I nod.

"I raise you ten." Ig walks away sipping his glass of expensive whiskey.

That night I dream of Dani and the life I had with her in Arizona. It's not the usual dream I have about her. This one magnifies a feeling deep in my soul. It's something I've never felt so I can't identify it.

Monday afternoon we are back in Boulder and Paul starts working with the PPO team for the new client in Texas. I continue digging into the life of Conor Wheeler.

Every day I'm haunted by the unfamiliar feeling sparked by the dream I had of Dani.

At the end of May, I go to Arizona to tell Conor Wheeler to back up off the mother of my baby girl, but he is out of town. So that it's not a wasted trip, I go to the park where Kourt attends day camp and watch her from afar.

She has grown so much in the past few months. I snap some pictures of her, then head over to the clinic to see Dani. I sit in a corner in the cafeteria where no one notices me and I watch Dani eat lunch with coworkers. If she were to look over her left shoulder, I'd be in her line of sight.

"I miss you, Dani." The whispered words slip from my mouth before I can stop them.

Dani sits up straight. *There's no way she heard me.* Her chin brushes her left shoulder as her eyes search the room. I lift the book in my hand to cover my face and keep still. This isn't the first time Dani has looked in my direction over the years. It's like she knew I was there; she just couldn't see me.

I count to one hundred and slowly lower the book. Dani is dumping her trash. I wait until she leaves the cafeteria to escape through the exit door in the back. As I walk to the parking lot, I have a name for the unknown feeling—loneliness.

Since I got back from Arizona, Langford has been asking me for updates on the RAGS case. Phantom Field Operatives came across some intel that there may be a power struggle going on within the organization. We haven't been able to confirm the information.

On 29 June 2013 the PPO team is ready. I fly with them on the company's private jet to Texas. The client is disappointed that there aren't any females on his security detail. One of the reasons people like to do business with me is because I don't sugarcoat the facts. I point out how his very public booty-calls with random females would bring too much attention to any female PPOs, putting their safety in danger. He stops whining and signs the contract.

My next destination is Malinda's.

She is genuinely surprised to see me. I take her out to dinner to catch up on what she's been doing. I remind her that she is supposed to be living under the radar. Winning Innovative Teacher of the Year isn't living under the radar, and neither is killing a lover who turned stalker. But I let that one pass. The guy was becoming dangerous.

Not once, during the course of our evening, does she ask about Emma. It would shock me if she did.

Malinda is extra flirty tonight. On the ride back to her apartment, she offers to give me a blow job while I'm driving. She goes as far as reaching over the center console to unzip my pants. I capture her wrist in a vise grip and throw her a warning look.

When I pull into the spot next to her car in the garage, I decide to spend the night in her guest room instead of heading over to the hotel. I grab my overnight bag and briefcase from the back and follow Malinda inside.

I've spent the night at her place before.

I set my overnight bag and briefcase in a chair and sit on the sofa and turn on the news. Malinda disappears into the kitchen.

I don't look away from the television when Malinda walks back into the room, but she gets my attention when she passes in front of the TV in her panties and bra. She's carrying two glasses and a bottle of wine.

She sits on the other end of the sofa, pours wine into both glasses, and settles back. "It's been a while and I really need to fuck."

I huff. "Do you really think I'd touch you after what you did to get pregnant?"

She guzzles down her glass of wine, then reaches for the one she poured for me. "Is that the only reason you won't fuck me, Bryan?"

I cock an eyebrow. "It's not the only reason, but it is in the top two."

"What's the other reason? Is it somebody else?" She downs the glass of wine and pours more into both glasses. Malinda turns her body toward me and throws one leg over the back of the sofa. The center of her shiny black panties is wet. The scent of her arousal floats in the air. She puts a hand under the waistband of her panties and starts to finger herself.

I rise to my feet and grab my briefcase. "I'll make you breakfast in the morning."

I leave her masturbating on the sofa and escape to the guestroom. I wasn't going to sit there and watch her. Any sexual attraction I had to her went away the day she confessed to purposely getting pregnant. No one gets a second chance at burning me.

If there were a lock on the guestroom's door, I'd use it.

I set my briefcase next to the bed and put my cell phone on the nightstand and go to shower. After I undress and am standing under the showerhead, I realize I left my overnight bag in the living room. I wash up and get out. The towel I use to dry with, I wrap around my waist and climb under the sheets.

Sleep does not come right away. I relax my body. Clear my mind. And focus on drifting off to sleep.

My dream features Dani cat crawling onto the bed and up my body. She smiles down at me, then leans in for a kiss. Her tongue pushes past my lips into my mouth. This kiss feels too real to be a dream. Something isn't right. Dani's mouth tastes like wine.

I frown and turn my head away.

My body becomes alert before my mind.

Someone is under the sheet with me.

My eyes open right as Amelia loosens the towel around my waist. The moonlight casts enough light that I can see her naked body. I reach down, grab her shoulders, and flip her onto her back.

A wrestling match begins on this full-size bed.

I haven't forgotten how agile Amelia is. Consuming an entire bottle of wine gave her the courage to pull this stunt, but it also inhibits her abilities. I get Amelia in a hold that she can't get out of. I keep her captured until she settles down then falls asleep, her arms and legs tangle around me.

I'd like to get back to the dream I was having about my Dani, but I can't allow myself to fully sleep with a horny Amelia in the bed with me.

On 30 June 2013 0345 hours my world changes.

That inexplicable pull to be near Dani and Kourt is triggered and it's stronger than ever; Riley's automated voice confirms why. Army Sergeant James Andrew Edwards—the man I shot and killed eight years ago—escaped Israeli custody.

Plans start formulating in my mind like mathematical equations. The answers are all the same. Move Dani and Kourt to Boulder, and to keep an eye on Malinda, she's moving there too.

After I hang up with President Hart, the next call I make is to Sergeant Wright. She promises to call as soon as she gets to Dani's house.

My cell phone rings. "What's up, Bry?" Tony yawns on his end of the phone.

"Edwards is alive!"

"I'll pull some strings and have law enforcement patrol Danielle's neighborhood until we get there."

"Have Larson stay in Texas to keep an eye on Malinda. Porter will stay with me. Tell Ig to arrange the exhumation of the body in the grave for James Edwards."

"How soon are we moving Danielle and Kourtney?"

"As soon as I can get her laid off from that clinic and get Jasper to hire her at the hospital in Boulder."

"It's about time you brought them to Colorado."

CHAPTER SEVENTEEN

DANIELLE

Colorado, Present Day

"DANI, WAKE UP," BRYAN WHISPERS. My hair is brushed off my face. "It's time to go."

Reluctantly I open my eyes. The real Bryan sits on the side of the bed leaning over me. I can tell he knows I was dreaming about him from the cocky smile he is giving me. I know we do not have time for anything more, so I steal a moment of intimacy to reconnect with my husband. I reach up, cup the back of his neck, and guide him down to kiss me. As always, my husband does not disappoint.

"I waited as long as I could before waking you. The Sweepers will be up in fifteen minutes. They can't see me yet, and I don't want them to see you either." He moves aside and helps me get out of the comfortable bed. Bryan pulls me into his arms. "Are you and the baby okay?"

I inhale his scent and let the warmth of his embrace set in my soul. "We're fine."

"Are you sure? Jessi has someone on call if you need to be seen."

I reach behind me to take his hands and place them on my stomach. "We're fine, Bry."

"Let's get out of here." He helps me put on my shoes, then picks up my overnight bag. I follow him out of the room.

As we walk down the stairs, the first person I see is my grandfather staring through me. No light in his eyes. No life in his body. A trail of dried tears runs down his cheeks. I want to go to him. Comfort him. Willis is a man in mourning.

I glance at my grandmother sitting in the chair, quiet yet tense and alert. Her eyes sweep the room. She thinks no one notices her, but *I* see her—clearly.

Mr. Brumfield and Mr. Hopper are already gone.

Death and defeat smother the room. I'm happy to be leaving.

Bryan leads me to the service elevator where James is waiting inside of the cab, an envelope in his hand. He looks solemn. James nods in greeting once Bryan and I are inside and takes his finger off the button that held the doors open.

I look back at my broken grandfather before the door closes.

"Will I be allowed to visit him?"

"That depends on how much he cooperates." The timbre of Bryan's voice fails to hide his disgust for the man he once considered his mentor.

"How long before you're able to join us in Colorado Springs?"

"I need to take care of some things and meet with President Hart. I can't give a definite date."

"Can I stop by the house? The girls and I need clothes."

"Jessi already packed clothes for you guys and dropped them off at Mom and Dad's. But if you guys need something else you and Mom can always go shopping."

The door opens on the first level.

We exit the building.

The red four-door Chevy I left with the valet is parked in front of the exit. Bryan sets my bags on the backseat. James walks around to the driver's door.

Bryan kisses my cheek. "You won't be able to contact me, but there is a team of PPOs watching you guys."

This seems all too familiar.

Bryan cups my cheek with one hand and places the other low on my baby bump. "I'm not disappearing, Dani. Where I'm going is top-secret. But I need you to stick to the protection plan. No going off on your own."

"I promise to be good while you're gone."

To prove I'm telling the truth, I hold up my pinky. This draws a big smile from Bryan. He hooks his pinky with mine and follows it up with a kiss that says he will hold me to my word.

Bryan goes over what I can tell his parents or our girls—which pretty much is nothing—when I get there. He gives me my cell phone back and the contact number to the lead PPO assigned to us.

"I'll be home as soon as I can."

Bryan waits until I've secured my seat belt to close the car door. I watch him walk to a sleek, black and silver motorcycle and put on the helmet. He swings his leg over the seat.

That knot I felt in my stomach when I stood in my bedroom window and watched Bryan drive away all those years ago is coming back. And it hurts.

James stuffs papers back into the envelope, then wedges it between the driver's seat and center console. He starts the car just as Bryan starts the motorcycle's engine. James drives toward the exit. From the sideview mirror, I see Bryan behind us. Behind him is a black SUV.

The motorcycle stays on our bumper with the SUV following at a safe distance as James navigates the downward slope of the twisting road. My fingers grip the door handle and my butt cheeks tighten on each curve. My son kickboxes in response to the anxiety I'm feeling. James isn't the best driver. I should have insisted on driving at least to the bottom of the road; then he could have taken over.

My body relaxes, and the blood flow returns to my fingers when we reach the four-way stop sign at the base of the road. We make a left and continue to the highway's on-ramp. James merges into the lane to take the entrance toward Colorado Springs.

Bryan pulls alongside of us. He points to his chest, then makes the heart symbol with his fingers, then points to me.

The knot in my stomach goes away. I mimic the sentiment and add two fingers at the end.

Bryan waves, then flies past to take the entrance heading back to Boulder.

The black SUV stays with us.

I crane my neck to watch my husband speed down the highway for as long as I can.

Traffic isn't bad for this time of the evening. It is pretty much a straight shot to Colorado Springs. I don't have to worry about James's less than stellar driving form.

I retrieve my sunglasses from the center console and cover my eyes. I lean the seat back and get comfortable. According to the

GPS's automated voice, it will take us an hour and forty-two minutes to reach the Southwest side of Colorado Springs where my in-laws live.

Twenty minutes into the drive, James has yet to utter a word or turn on the radio. I glance over at him. The skin over his knuckles is tight from his grip on the steering wheel.

"What's on your mind?"

"How do I explain this to my wife and son?"

"Start with the truth. There's been too many secrets and too many lies. It's time to tell the truth."

"I've lived a lie for so long, I'm not sure what the truth is."

"The truth is everything that wasn't a lie."

He chuckles, and his fingers relax on the wheel.

"What's in the envelope?"

"Dual citizenship and other documents for Selam and Solomon to stay in the United States. Hawk got me a real birth certificate, social security card, school records and documents for Nathaniel Andrew Edwards."

"Why did you keep your middle and last name?"

"Hiding in plain sight. No one would expect it."

My friend grows quiet. He's gripping the steering wheel tight again.

"Look, I have truths to tell too, so I know what you're going through. The best you can do is reassure them that you love them, they are safe, and they're under the protection of the U.S. government. Tell your wife when she's ready, you'll answer all her questions, honestly." I pause to take a good look at his appearance. "But in that getup, you look like you're still running from the bad guys. There's a mall not too far from my in-laws. We'll stop there, get you a change of clothes and something to eat."

I take out my phone from my pocket and send a text to the lead PPO to let him know we're stopping at the mall.

"Marie said your parents are missing. Is that the loose end Bryan has to take care of?" I asked.

"Hawk had them moved."

"Where are they?"

"I don't know. Let me rephrase that. I don't want to know. Hawk said they're safe. They're together. And they're still confined like prisoners, but no one can use them against me ever again."

"Don't you want to get to know your parents?"

"No."

"Why?"

His short, humorless laugh expresses two decades of pain. "It's because of Leroy and Bertha Mae Edwards that my brother and I ended up in a system of treachery that shaped us to be cunning. Our parents' thievery had no boundaries and unfortunately the trait was passed down to my twin brother."

If a small part of him didn't care about his parents, he never would have contacted the prisons after reading that article on the internet.

"What did your brother do?"

"Jamal had his own agenda. He moved the money we'd collected to an offshore account without my knowledge. He planned to take the money and run and leave me to face prison for treason."

"How did you come to that conclusion?"

"There was a letter found on Jamal that was in the box of belongings that was shipped back with his body. It wasn't like the ones he and I used to pass between us. The letter read like it was written to you. Jamal basically called me a fool for believing in anyone but myself and I deserved being locked up for the rest of my life."

When he stops talking, I lift my sunglasses and lift an eyebrow.

James takes a deep breath. "He said before he disappeared, he was going to go back to Arizona to fuck you, then slit your throat."

"Was the letter really from your brother?"

"The first line confirmed the date, location, and time of the exchange between him and Islam Liberation Army."

"Islam Liberation Army?"

"Yep. We were dealing with dangerous people, but they had the kind of bread we needed to top off our stack of money and live the rest of our lives in hiding."

"Thank you for the money, James."

"I wanted to make sure when you graduated you wouldn't be buried in student loan debt."

"When did you find out about the letter?"

"Last night. Hawk came to my cell to tell me that his team extracted my wife and son. I offered to help him corner and trap Antoinette and Willis. He showed me a copy of the letter. And I unscrambled it for him."

We spend the rest of the drive telling me about how he and his twin exchanged information.

James parks the car in the lower level of the parking garage. The black SUV pulls in to a spot next to us. Only two PPOs exit the vehicle; the driver stays behind.

We go into the first men's store we come across. All these years and nothing has changed—James complains about the numbers on the price tags. Even though I have the cash to pay for the clothes, James refuses to shop in the store.

One of the PPOs points us in the direction of a discount department store at the far end of the mall.

While James tries on clothes, I go to the pharmacy section and pick up toiletries and an electric razor for him. By the time I get back to the dressing room, James is coming out. We pick up shoes, socks, and underwear before going to checkout. After I pay for everything, I send him to the restroom to get changed and tell him to meet me at the food court.

Unsure of the protocol for dinner for one's personal bodyguard, I text the lead PPO and ask. He replies not to worry, that they have a company credit card and a system for breaks while on duty.

James sits down in the chair across from me with a thankful smile on his face. I ordered him a loaded wet burrito with an extra side of guacamole and sour cream. He finishes his food in record time and snags one of my asada tacos.

We head back to the car.

The automated voice of the GPS system gives turn-by-turn directions to my in-laws' house. The clock on the dash reads nine fifty-nine when James turns into their driveway. The front door swings open, and Dad charges down the steps. Mom right behind him.

The passenger door is jerked open and I'm pulled into Dad's arms. "You're late. Where have you been?"

"We made a stop at the mall…"

Mom sandwiches me in. "You stopped at the goddamn mall instead of coming straight here? We were worried about you. Where the hell is that son of mine?"

"Mom. Dad. I can't breathe."

They ease up on the embrace but do not let me go. I wiggle and squirm until I find a hole and escape. Might as well get this out of the way. "Bryan still has some things to take care of. He didn't tell me what they are or how long it will take. The girls and I will be staying here with you until further notice." James walks around the back of the car carrying my overnight bag and backpack. "This is James Edwards…"

"Your dead husband James Edwards?" Dad shouts, then looks around as if remembering we're outside.

"Yes, but he can't stay. He has to get to the hospital. If you two will excuse me for a minute to see him off, we'll go inside and talk."

Dad snatches my bags from James, eyeballs him, then he and Mom walk toward the house.

"Call me if you need me to come to the hospital."

"You call me if you need rescuing from Hawk's parents."

I laugh and glance at them waiting on the porch like overprotective parents waiting to ground their child for missing curfew.

"I may take you up on that." I exhale slowly. "Is it selfish of me to not want to say goodbye? Every good childhood memory I have includes you."

"I don't know where Selam, Solomon, and I will end up, but you and I will keep in touch. You can definitely hold me to that."

I hug my friend, then stand in the driveway watching him back out.

The minute I walk through the door, Mom and Dad are on me.

Dad fires question after question while pacing in front of the sofa. At the rate he's going, he'll wear a hole through the rug and floorboards.

Mom uses language I never thought I'd hear come from her mouth. She isn't holding back on expressing her displeasure at being in the dark about her son's military career, and me running around like I'm some vigilante. I'm guessing the girls told them about what happened at the house.

My head bounces back and forth between bad cop and badder cop. Every vague answer I give only incites them more, so I stop answering and let them talk.

After a good hour of nonstop interrogation, Mom takes me up to Bryan's old room. She says Kourtney didn't want the room this time.

I see my suitcases in the corner. I shower and change into pajamas, then go check on my girls.

Kourtney is asleep but wakes because Trevor barks his greeting when I walk into the guest room. The bedside lamp is on and Mr. Cuddles is now Trevor's bedtime buddy.

"Hi, sweetie." I hug my daughter as tight as she holds me.

"I missed you so much. Where have you been? Why didn't you fly on the helicopter with us?"

"There were some things I needed to help Daddy with before I could come here with you guys. We can talk more about it in the morning. I just wanted to check up on you and Emma and Trevor before I went to bed."

She yawns. "Okay, Mommy."

I reach to turn off the lamp. Kourtney stops me. "Leave it on, please."

"Are you scared to sleep in here by yourself? Do you want me to sleep in here with you?"

"I'm okay. I just like for the light to be on."

I kiss her cheek and scratch Trevor behind the ears, then leave.

Across the hall, Emma is sound asleep. I pull the blanket up around her shoulders and kiss her sweet cheek. On the nightstand are drawings of us at home in the yard or in the family room sitting on the sofa.

I go back to Bryan's childhood bedroom and check in with James. He says his wife is still in surgery and his son was happy to see him. He sounds overwhelmed. I offer to come sit with him, but he says he'll be okay.

The nap I took earlier was enough to rejuvenate me, so I'm not sleepy. I wander around Bryan's old room. I find his high school yearbooks. From freshman year to senior year, I view his physical transformation. If our son takes after Bryan, he'll be a handsome man just like his dad.

My stomach rumbles and I look over at the glowing red numbers on the digital clock. It's a little after midnight.

I close the yearbook and go in search of food. Careful not to make any noise, I tiptoe down the stairs and find my way to the kitchen. When I walk through the swinging door, I catch Dad standing at the stove with a spatula dangling over a small frying pan.

"Hungry?" he asks.

I nod.

"Grilled cheese okay with you?"

I nod again.

Dad lifts a small plate from the countertop and uses the spatula to scoop the hot sandwich out of the frying pan. I take the plate to the table and sit.

He drops a sliver of butter in the pan. The sound of it sizzling adds to the awkward silence in the room. Streams of white smoke rise from the center toward his face. Dad drops a slice of bread in the pan and covers it with slices of three different cheeses, then tops it off with another slice of bread.

He walks to the refrigerator and opens the door. I can't see what he's doing, but when he closes the door, he's balancing a carton of milk on top of a clear container of watermelon chunks.

Dad brings everything over to the table, then grabs two glasses from the cupboard, and two forks from a drawer. He sets a glass in front of me and hands me a fork. "Eat before it gets cold."

He goes back to the stove and flips his sandwich over.

The elephant in the room is growing bigger by the minute. His silence worries me.

"Is everything okay, Dad?"

At first, I don't think he intends to answer.

"My family is from a small town in South Carolina." He turns the knob on the stove; the fire under the frying pan goes out. He uses the spatula to place his grilled cheese sandwich onto a plate, then joins me at the table. "Being Bryan Kendal Hawk in that small place is a curse. The first Bryan Kendal Hawk was unethical and immoral, *and* the mayor. If you research him, you'll understand what I'm talking about."

I open the milk carton and pour some into our glasses. He seems to need to talk openly about this, so I remain quiet.

"My dad is the legitimate first-born son of Bryan Kendall Hawk Sr. He loved being a junior. He used the Hawk name to con his way into many women's beds. He also used the Hawk money to pay for many illegal abortions and silence. But in small towns like the one I'm from, everybody knows everybody's business. I'll never understand why my mother, a sweet and loving woman, would marry such a loser, and stay with him even though he was the town's Tomcat."

I dish up watermelon chunks and continue to actively listen.

"I am their first-born son and therefore the name passed on to me. I learned early on about the weight of being Bryan Kendall Hawk in South Carolina. It made me determined to get out from under it. My two younger brothers didn't understand because there were no negative stigmas associated with their names. No one openly discriminated against me, but I felt it. It's the reason I wasn't allowed to give the valedictorian speech at my high school graduation. A major newspaper publication got wind of the school board's decision to not let me make the speech. Instead of shedding light on the injustice, the Superintendent of Schools gave an exclusive interview detailing my grandfather's criminal activity and the circumstances of my father's murder. His son was the man who killed my father. I bet you're wondering why I gave my son the name I hated so much, and why I want you to give it to my first grandson."

"I get it. You're rewriting the narrative."

"My son, Bryan Kendall Hawk the Fourth, is out there right now, preventing a world war and no one in that town will ever know about it."

"Dad, you are a strong, honorable family man. And your son is just like you. I know you want to shout in their faces, 'I am not those men,' and we'd all stand beside you, shouting too. But what do *you* gain by doing it? How does it change the narrative of the first two Bryans?"

A sheepish smile crosses his face. "Well, when you put it that way, it doesn't. I'll still be the son and grandson of two nefarious men."

I compliment him on the grilled cheese sandwich. And he changes the subject.

Several days pass.

I try not to let my worry about Bryan's absence show. When Kourtney isn't in the yard helping Grandpa, she's campaigning for us to move back to Arizona.

Emma and I watch videos on the internet to learn how to sew a quilt by hand for her bed at home. Mom tells us there is a quilting group at the convalescent home where she volunteers three days a week. If we want, she'll talk to the group and see if it's okay for Emm and me to sit with them in the sunroom.

I go to the hospital for an unofficial prenatal checkup. Jessi understands why I won't let her make it an official one—Bryan isn't here to be a part of it.

James introduces me to Solomon. He is a handsome, energetic little boy. Selam is being kept heavily medicated to keep her unconscious so her body can heal from the injuries she sustained while being held prisoner for almost a year. My friend looks like he is barely keeping it together. He and Solomon have a room at a hotel across the street from the hospital.

To make James and his son more comfortable in the hotel room, the girls, Mom, and I go on a big shopping trip at the mall, with four PPOs following us.

Cold compresses over my eyes in the mornings cannot hide the fact that I cry myself to sleep at night. I watch the news for anything that can tell me what Bryan is doing. I stay busy by helping Mom cook and clean and I go with her to run errands. The day the girls and I go to the convalescent home with Mom, she introduces me to the feisty gentleman she's paired with.

Dad is busy at the district office closing out the school year and preparing for the new school year. He and I have a standing appointment to meet up in the kitchen for a late-night snack.

Nine long days and nights and I haven't heard from my husband. Today is harder than the others. Mom is called to go to the convalescent home. They are short of volunteers. After lunch, the girls invite the triplets over to play in the backyard. I sit in a lounge chair in the shade reading a book, but really, I'm keeping an eye on Stuart. I heard he tried to kiss my daughter. Trevor sits at my feet watching the children run around. He's still recovering from the poisoning. The vet says he should be back to his old self by the end of the month.

At three o'clock the triplets go home, and the girls and I go inside. I hear a car pull into the driveway. I run to the door hoping it's Bryan, but Dad climbs out of the driver's seat with his briefcase.

"You're home early."

Dad walks through the door. "I'm taking you and the girls to the stables."

"For real, Grandpa?" Emma asks.

"Yes, for real. Go get ready."

"Dad, I don't think…"

"I've already cleared it, Dani. We're leaving as soon as I get out of this suit and into some jeans. Now go get ready."

Kourtney and Emma race each other upstairs with Trevor right behind them. He will have to stay home. I drag my feet but go change too.

We leave a note for Mom, then head out.

The ranch that houses the stables is a fifteen-minute ride from the house.

The owner, Robert Banks—no relations to Tristan and Stephanie Banks—greets the girls with smiles and high-fives. He and his young ranch hand, Ian, help the girls get Cuddles and Sweet Pea saddled. I was expecting little ponies, born in the spring. The girl's ponies are two years old, and already broken in. Robert climbs onto his own horse and the three of them trot off on one of the easy riding trails.

Dad and I find a walking trail that isn't too vigorous for me. We have one of our heart-to-heart talks while we stroll the path. Dad's real reason for the nature walk is he wants details on what Bryan does for Phantom. This is one of the topics my husband was adamant about me not discussing.

When we return from our two-hour walk, the girls are in the small stable at the far end of the ranch where only their ponies are boarded. My stomach rolls and I cover my nose and mouth with my hand. There is a strange, pungent smell in the air. It's not the normal scent of horses, hay, and manure.

"This stable is a mess. Where's Robert?" Dad asks.

"That's the same thing he said when we got back," Kourtney answers. "He went to find Mr. Ian a little while ago. We've been waiting for him to come back and help us get Cuddles and Sweet-Pea put away."

"If you're talking about that old man and that kid, they're dead."

I turn around at the sound of her voice. She stands just inside of the doorway, blocking our only way out. A gun in her hand; the other one is hidden in the front pocket of her black jeans.

Protectively, I step in front of my girls, shielding them with my body. It just occurs to me that I didn't notice the PPOs following us. My gaze sweeps the stable for anything I can use as a weapon. I spot something in the corner to my left.

Dad throws his arms out wide as he steps in front of us. "Who the hell are you?"

"Nobody, that's who the hell I am. Thanks to *your son*, I am nobody." She starts to walk forward.

One calculated step at a time.

Dad doesn't recognize her, but I know exactly who she is. She died her hair the same color brown as Emma's and cut it in a masculine style. Not even the androgynous clothes she is wearing throw me off. Her familiar chocolate brown eyes are throwing eye-daggers at all of us. I know who she really is. *Amelia Goodman aka Malinda Williamson. Emma's birth mother.*

The girls and I take synchronized steps back to keep the space and opportunity open for me to adjust to any form of defense I need to use to protect them from this woman.

Dad stands his ground. He takes a defensive step forward. "That isn't saying much."

"Judging by your daughter-in-law's reaction, she knows who I am."

"Mommy?" Emma cries.

A pretentious smile appears on Amelia's lips. "I'm right here, baby."

I stop creating distance but gesture for the girls to keep moving back. "My daughter was talking to me."

"Who is this person, Dani?" He keeps his eyes on her.

"She's nobody, just like she said, Dad."

"You bitch." Amelia charges.

Dad forges ahead too.

I turn and point to the ladder. "Stay together. Find somewhere to hide."

The struggle going on in front of the stable door is spooking the ponies. They whinny and pound the hay-covered ground with their hooves.

I run to the corner and lift the pitchfork off the hook. Just as I turn around, Dad grunts, and falls face first to the ground. The hairs on the back of his head are darkening. The collar of his yellow polo shirt is growing red. Amelia stands over him holding a shovel. The gun she had is gone.

"There is nowhere in this world you can hide where Bryan can't find you if you hurt one of his girls."

Amelia reaches in the front pocket of her jeans. She flicks the top back on the object in her hand. The red and orange flame dances in front of her face.

Lighter fluid. That is what I am smelling. I look down at the hay-covered ground then back up at her. My heart sinks. The hay is saturated with lighter fluid.

"I'm not going to hide from Bryan. He'll find my charred body along with yours and his precious girls."

Scared beyond words, I watch Amelia toss the lit lighter toward the hay-covered floor near the ponies.

Over and over and over the flame flips until the lighter lands on the bundle.

I scream.

The flames catch quickly. The ponies buck and rear back. They race for the stable door. Unfortunately, I am in their path. The pitchfork falls from my grasp as I shuffle, sidestep, and dance to keep from getting injured by the panicked ponies.

Amelia slips past me. She's climbing the ladder. The same ladder I just had my girls climb.

———◆———

Arizona, Eleven Months Ago…

"How did the interview go?" Yvon asks after I slam the front door behind me.

"A waste of my time. One hour, one way for them to say, 'We really want someone with more experience, but we'll keep your information on file.'" I kick off my heels and join Yvon on the sofa. I put my feet up on the coffee table and huff.

She picks up the remote and mutes the late morning talk show she was watching. "It's only been two days since you were laid off from the clinic. The right job is out there."

"Yes, and it's working under a world-famous psychiatrist, a flexible work and holiday schedule, three times as much as I was making at the clinic, and paid moving expenses." When Dr. Blanchard handed me my layoff notice, she called Dr. Stevens while I was still in her office and put him on speakerphone. She proceeded to tell him I am in need of a job.

"Tell me again why you didn't take it?" Yvon asks.

"It's in Boulder, Colorado. Arizona is our home. I don't want to uproot Kourtney."

She folds her arms across her chest. "Your hesitation doesn't have anything to do with Conor, does it?"

"No, of course not. I don't allow a man to dictate what I do."

"Okay, then forgive the cliché, but home is where you make it. And I bet if you talked to Kourtney about it, she'd be open to moving."

"She's open to it."

Yvon smacks my arm. "When did you talk to her?"

"This morning. I had a strange dream about running to Boulder. I woke up toying with the idea of calling Dr. Stevens to see if he filled the position."

"Your dream was a sign that you should take the job and not waste your time on interviewing for positions here."

I go get my laptop off my desk and rejoin Yvon. Once I log on, I connect to the internet and click the search history. Two websites open. One is for apartments for rent in Boulder. The other is for Greystone Preparatory Academy, an innovative private school with exceptional test scores. I turn the screen toward Yvon.

"The soaps start in thirty minutes. Plenty of time for you to call that Dr. Stevens fellow and I'll call the school to see if they still have space in the second grade."

She grabs the house phone. I get my cell phone out of my purse along with the paper Dr. Blanchard gave me where she'd written Dr. Stevens's contact number.

Dr. Stevens is happy to hear from me. He hasn't filled the position yet because he was hoping I'd call. By the end of our conversation, a letter from the hospital's human resources department, outlining everything he and I discussed, is emailed to me along with a Psychologist Application Checklist and the link to the online Endorsement Application for the state of Colorado.

The verification documents I need to submit with the application are in my portable safe upstairs in my closet. I mime to Yvon—who is on the phone with someone from the school— that I'm going upstairs.

I put in the combination to the safe and open it. When I lift the files marked Education and Professional Documents, pictures spill onto the closet floor. I gather them up and take a moment to look at them. These are the pictures Bryan didn't know I had.

Both happy and sad memories surround me. My thoughts of my other daughter, Emma, bring tears to my eyes. If Kourtney and I move to Colorado, I will make it a priority to find Emma.

"Danielle," Yvon calls from downstairs. "The office manager wants to know if you can email a copy of Kourtney's birth certificate, shot records, and school records so she can save the spot. She said she'll overnight the enrollment packet to you and you can return it once you guys get to Boulder."

I wipe the tears from my eyes with the back of my hand and drop the pictures back into the safe. "Yes, I can." I grab the files marked Kourtney Health, Kourtney School, and Kourtney Edwards. Hidden at the bottom of my safe under other files and documents is an envelope marked Kourtney Allison Hawk. Inside is her real birth certificate and social security card.

Yvon sets the DVR to record the soaps—I never watched them until she moved in with us. There was an electrical fire in the unit next to hers. The common wall was damaged. She's waiting for the all clear to move back.

At my desk, I scan then email Kourtney's records to the office manager. She replies to confirm receipt. Next, I click on the link the hospital sent and fill out the licensure application. Yvon sets a platter of vegetables next to me to snack on as she looks over my shoulder to make sure I do not miss a question on the application. I scan and upload my documents as attachments, then click submit. An application number is sent to my inbox that I forward to the hospital's human resource department. Two minutes later, I get a notification that I have a new email in my inbox. It's an offer and acceptance letter from the hospital. Dr. Stevens's signature is already on it. I print and sign it, but do not send it back.

"What are you waiting for?" Yvon demands.

"I need to talk to my daughter one more time before I send it."

Yvon smacks her lips, rolls her eyes, and takes the plate away right when I was reaching for a carrot stick. She plops down on the sofa and takes the TV off mute.

I shut down my laptop and join her on the sofa. "Kourtney's opinion about this move matters to me. We make important decisions together."

"She's already told you yes. Why are *you* hesitating?"

"I want to make sure Kourtney fully understands that it will be a permanent move."

Yvon holds the plate out to me. I grab a carrot stick and turn my attention to Bill, the handsome bad guy on our favorite soap.

Kourtney is super excited to be going to her favorite restaurant for dinner tonight. Yvon declined the offer to join us, claiming she'd do everything in her power to persuade Kourtney that moving is the best thing for us.

Over appetizers, I tell Kourtney I got the job offer from the hospital in Colorado and found a school for her, but I want to make sure she is fully aware of what this move means.

"Your opinion matters to me, sweetie."

"I know, Mommy. And I know we will be leaving our house, and the school, and Yvon, but I want us to move."

"Will you tell me why?"

"You said with this new job, you can pick the times you work. That means we can go on more fun vacations and go to fun places."

"You're not afraid?"

"A little. Are you afraid, Mommy?"

"What scares me is moving to a new city."

"Why?"

"Because we won't know anyone. And we've lived here for a long time. Sometimes moving away from what you know is scary."

"Well, you always tell me to turn my fear into courage."

Leave it to Kourtney to repeat my words of advice to her. I do what she would do in this situation and exhale dramatically. "Okay," I sing. "I'll turn my fear into courage. You and I will leave Tucson, Arizona, and make Boulder, Colorado, our new home."

We clink water glasses.

"Can we drive there, Mom?"

"You and I *are* overdue for a road trip."

"Can I pick the places we stop to see?"

"How about we do it together."

The server places our meals on the table in front of us. Kourtney digs into her mini cheeseburger sliders and fries. She's happy about moving and that makes me happy.

I start on my chicken fajitas.

"Mom, did you know that Boulder, Colorado, is at the foothills of the Rocky Mountains? And it's a twelve-hour drive from the center of Tucson, Arizona, to the Center of Boulder, Colorado?"

Sounds like she did some research in the computer lab at day camp today.

Everything she's read on the internet is discussed over dinner and dessert and the ride home and as I kiss her goodnight.

Before I go to bed, I scan then email the signed acceptance letter back to the hospital's human resources department.

I dream of the day I married James. After we were pronounced husband and wife, and we kissed, he pulled me into his arms and whispered in my ear, "Don't ever take off the ring." I wake up to the feel of me twisting the ring around my finger.

After breakfast I drop Kourtney off at day camp, then go to the office of the real estate broker who helped me find the house. I tell her I want to put it on the market. When I tell her I'm moving to Colorado, she accesses listings for apartments that only real estate brokers are privy to. The unit I really like is central to the school and the hospital. And there is a park within walking distance. She contacts the listing agent. They fax over a credit check application. I fill it out and she faxes it back. Ten minutes later, they fax over a one-year lease agreement.

As I'm walking out of her office, my cell phone pings from a new email alert. I open it and see it's from an Application Specialist in Colorado. They have reviewed my Psychologist Endorsement Application and verified the documents I submitted. My license is approved.

I wasn't expecting for it to be processed so quickly.

I forward the email to the hospital.

Everything is falling into place as if by design.

I take my Range Rover in for servicing. Although it's not time for it, I want to have it looked at since Kourtney and I are driving to Colorado. I troll the lot admiring the new models while I wait. A voice in my head whispers, *New state. New home. New job. Why not a new luxury SUV?*

I ask to speak to the sales manager.

Two hours later, I'm driving off the lot in a white, 2013 Range Rover.

Kourtney and I spend the last of our time in Tucson mapping out our road trip and packing. One week after signing the employment acceptance letter, the moving company the hospital hired confirms the moving date.

I contact the apartment owner and am assured the on-site man-ager will let the movers into the unit.

Tonight, Kourtney, Conor, and I go to "movie night under the stars" at the park. This is the second time I've allowed Conor to hang out with us. He is not someone I am romantically involved with, so it's okay.

While the three of us sit on the blanket watching an animated children's movie and munching on a big bucket of popcorn from the concession stand, I'm distracted by the feeling of being watched.

I look around at the people near, but no one is paying attention to us. Then a rare cool summer breeze brushes my cheek. With it comes a familiar scent that settles in my nose. I climb to my knees and search the sea of faces as best I can.

"What's wrong?" Conor asks. "Is everything okay?" He too is on his knees.

I squint and strain my eyes to find him. I feel Bryan's eyes on me. "Danielle. Are you okay?"

"It's nothing." I turn around and sit back down.

After the movie, Conor drives us home. He tells us to have a safe trip and to remember to call him at every checkpoint or else he'll come looking for us.

The morning before moving day, the apartment manager calls Yvon to let her know she's all clear to move back in. She's so anxious to get back into her own place, Kourtney and I help her move that afternoon.

We stay for dinner and say our tearful goodbyes there because tomorrow will be a busy day.

When Kourtney and I get back home, I double check that she labeled her boxes. She double checks mine. We load my truck with snacks for the first leg of our trip, and our suitcases, then spend our last night in our home camped out in the living room.

Our day starts at eight in the morning when the people from the charity I'm donating clothes, toys, and appliances to knock on the door.

The moving company arrives at nine thirty. They are efficient and quick. The entire house is empty in three hours.

I stand in the middle of the spacious living room. The memory of the day we moved in plays through my mind like a short film. I can't fight back the tears.

Kourtney wraps her arms around my waist. "Why are you crying, Mommy?"

I lift her up into my arms and hug her tight. "I'm remembering the day we moved here. And all the happy moments you and I have had, not just in this house but in Tucson."

She leans back to smile at me. Every time I look into her eyes, I'm reminded of Bryan. Her eyes are the exact shade of hazel as his.

The pull to call him overcomes me. It's so strong that I can't breathe.

I set Kourtney on her feet and swipe my tears away with my fingers. "Sweetie, can you do me a favor and take one last look upstairs to make sure we're not leaving anything behind."

"Okay, Mommy. I'll do a good job of checking."

"I know you will."

I watch her run up the stairs one last time. When she turns the corner, I pull out my cell phone. I don't know if it's still his number, but before I lose my nerve, I press the call icon.

Ring.

Ring.

Ring.

Ring.

"Leave a message." It's his voice.

"Hi, Bryan. It's been a while. I just wanted to tell you that if you came looking for Kourtney and me you won't find us in Tucson anymore. I was laid off from my job, but I got another one at the hospital in Boulder, Colorado. It would be nice if you and I could meet somewhere between Boulder and Colorado Springs, so you can see how much Kourtney has grown. And I'd really love to see Emma." I bite my lip to hold back the sob. "Kourtney and I are road-tripping it to Boulder, but we're stopping in Los Angeles to see the Franklins first, then go to Las Vegas for a few days. From there, we're driving through Utah. Yvon has our full itinerary."

"Mom, your room is the last one I need to check."

I pull my mouth away from the phone. "Okay, sweetie," I answer her, then finish my message. "I have to go. Bryan, I hope we… I miss you." I touch the icon to end the call.

Kourtney slowly comes down the stairs with her hands behind

her back.

"Did you find anything?"

She shakes her head.

"All set to go?"

Kourtney nods.

We walk out of the door together.

CHAPTER EIGHTEEN

BRYAN

Colorado, Present Day

THE LOOK ON THE GHOSTS' faces when the ESO Team strolls into the conference room as if we were not believed dead is priceless—they were expecting POTUS. The applause is loud. I announce that Phantom is officially off special protocol and it will take every man and woman to finish the final part, so we can close the books on the RAGS case.

Finding someone in Minsk who is an expert at hide-and-seek isn't much of a challenge for the ghosts of Phantom. In seventy-two hours, President Hart is sending Russian officials proof of Popov's plot to kill their president along with confirmation of the death of Popov and those in the Russian government who aided and abetted him. In a public appearance, Russian President Nikolai Kuzmich, expresses his sincerest gratitude to the United States for saving his life—in other words, he owes us.

My debriefing with President Hart lasts three days. We go over every aspect of the RAGS case to ensure all loose ends are either tied up or dead.

Langford is being cooperative. Antoinette, on the other hand, is convinced her granddaughter will rise up and revive Rebels Against Government Suppression. The two are Chen's lab rats. As long as they are useful to the experiment, I'll let them live.

While I was in D.C., the law firm handling Dominique Toussaint's will mailed me some papers. Dani transferred ownership of the trademark RAGS to my company, Hawkeye Personal Protection. I laugh to myself. My wife was busy when she deviated from the plan and went out on her own that day. Dani is making sure no one can revive the homeland terrorist organization under its trade name. I sign the paperwork and send them to my Phantom lawyer.

Edwards will be happy to know that Riley located the account his brother moved their money to. It's not the millions he thought was in it, but there is enough for him and his family to live off for a while, longer if he sells the island his brother bought. It took a whole lot of soul searching to let him keep the money considering how he got it.

Now that I've officially closed the RAGS case, I call Isaac, the lead PPO assigned to my family, to let him know I'm on my way; he and the team can head back to Boulder before returning to their regular assignments. I pack a bag and get on the road.

Traffic is heavy on the highway, but it gives me time to mentally prepare myself to come face to face with my daughter. It will take me over two hours to get to Colorado Springs.

Mom's car is the only one in the driveway when I park in front of the house. My bags can wait. I've been away from my wife and kids too long. I sprint from the truck to the front door and use my key to let myself in.

"I'm home," I sing.

Trevor's enthusiastic barking answers me back. He rounds the corner at a dead run. Tongue out. Ears back. The force of his happiness pushes me back a step and he jumps up, then stands on his hind legs, placing his front paws on my chest.

"Hey, boy. How ya feeling?" I scratch him behind the ears. "I missed you too."

His tail is a blur of back and forth whips.

I look up just as Mom appears in the entryway with frown lines around her mouth and squinting lines around her eyes.

"Hi, Mom. You look good today. Where—"

"Your dad took them to the stables," she interrupts.

Pleasantries never worked when she looks at me like that. I don't know why I even tried it now.

"You and I need to talk." She does a one-eighty and marches to the living room.

Trevor drops to all fours, tucks tail, and creeps off in the opposite direction.

I silently follow my mother, wishing I could switch places with

Trevor.

When Mom is like this, it's best to let her get it off her chest. I sit on the far end of the sofa. She perches on the other end. Physical distance isn't a good sign from Nancy Fleming-Hawk. It means she's so angry she's liable to hurt you if she were any closer.

Mom is the youngest of six kids and the only girl. She learned at an early age how to fight.

"Jessica told me what happened between you and Kourtney at the hospital. What I can't understand is why you and Danielle haven't told that child the truth."

My abs contract. Jessi wouldn't betray my trust.

"What truth are you talking about, Mom?"

"Do I look like a fool, little Bryan?"

Uh-oh, she called me little Bryan. Ultimate bad sign.

"It's bad enough you and Dani have kept up the lie this long, but I know the truth."

From what I can tell, she's known for a while. Mom is so angry she's at the point where feigned ignorance will drive her to strike. If Jessi had told her, Mom would never have called me little Bryan. "How long have you known about Kourt, Mom?"

"Since Christmas morning."

My mouth drops.

Mom scoots closer, and the squinty lines near her eyes have softened. "The Fleming Family hazel eyes, son. Our shade of hazel is rare. Her hair coloring is identical to yours." Mom nudges me in the ribs with her elbow. "She's left handed like you, me, my brothers, and my mom. And her middle name is Allison."

"Dani did that on her own. I didn't know Kourt's name until I signed the paperwork."

"Your grandmother told me about Dani."

"What?!"

"Oh, calm down. Allison only told me you were in love with a girl named Dani and too blind to know it. I didn't believe it until I saw you two together Christmas morning." Mom reaches for my hand. "When you disappeared after your grandmother's funeral you were with Dani?"

"Yes."

"You were at peace when you came home. Was it because of her?"

"Since the day I met Dani, she's made me feel things inside that I didn't know existed. She centers me."

Her fingers tighten around mine. "You just described love, son."

"I know that now."

"Why haven't you two told Kourtney the truth?"

I drop my head back and stare up at the ceiling. "It's complicated."

"The longer you wait, the harder it's going to be."

"I'm afraid she's going to hate me."

"Why?"

"Because I left them, and I can't tell her why."

"Can you tell me?"

I look at my mom and feel the comfort to bare my soul like I used to with my grandmother. The words spill from my lips. Starting with the day I first met Dani.

Mom listens without judgment.

I'm vague when it comes to the top-secret stuff, but forthcoming with the things I can be open about. My story ends with Kourt's angry words to me at the hospital. "She accused me of not wanting her and not loving her. My daughter called me by my first name and a liar in the same breath. What hurts the most is that she said she doesn't want me. If I tell her the truth, I'm going to lose her forever. Mom, I won't survive being hated by my own child."

"I bet it won't be as bad as you think. That little girl loves you too much to hate you. *Talk* to her, Bryan, then *listen* when she talks to you." Mom leans over and kisses my cheek. "I need to go finish preparing dinner. And you need to go to the stables and have a conversation with your daughter."

I get to my feet and start for the door, stop, turn around, and go back and hug my mom. "Thank you for listening."

She squeezes me like she did when I was little. "Anytime, BK4."

Trevor tries to run out of the door with me, but I make him go back. If Kourt left him behind to go to the stables, then it was for a good reason.

My thumbs drum the steering wheel in time to the music playing on the radio as I drive through the tree-lined streets of the Southwest side of Colorado Springs. Everything is green and fresh and peaceful. The day's temperature is cooling.

Buzz.

Buzz.

Buzz.

Unknown Caller flashes on the cell phone mounted in the holder on the dash. I start to ignore the call, but my number isn't accessible to just anyone. I press the connect button. "Hawk."

"You sent that woman to kill me and my parents," Malinda cries. "You don't know what it's like to lose the people you love most in this world. But you will today."

In the background I hear the unmistakable laughter of Emm and Kourt.

"What are you doing?"

"I'm burning your world to the ground."

She hangs up.

The gas pedal presses into the car's floorboard. One hand on the horn. The other almost breaks the steering wheel with its grip.

"Speed up or get the hell out of the way!" I swerve into the gutter lane to get around the slow driver who ignores my horn.

Tailgating. Weaving in and out of lanes. Crossing double yellow lines. I do it all to get to my girls.

A cold sweat starts to break out all over my body. Images of the many ways Amelia can hurt my wife and daughters plague my mind. My stomach convulses at the thought of their lifeless, mangled bodies laid out for me to find.

My world does not exist without them.

I don't exist without them.

How did you miss checking up on Kimberly's progress with finding Amelia?

I pound the steering wheel.

I dropped the goddamn ball again. Now my daughters and wife and dad are with an insane woman.

This is on me.

I blow through a red light, leaving a sea of car horns behind me.

Ten more blocks.

Ten very long blocks.

It might as well be ten thousand blocks.

The road seems to elongate the closer I get.

I fly through the open entrance gates. The tires of the Suburban grip the gravel as I stomp on the brake. My eyes search the area for my family's whereabouts.

There, to the far right, smoke is spilling out of the door of a two-story stable.

I turn the wheel at the same time I press the gas to the floorboard. The back end of the SUV fishtails, sending gravel spraying the air behind me. Defensive training kicks in. I get control of the truck and speed down the road toward the stable.

Screams for help touch my ears even though the SUV's windows are rolled up.

The Suburban rocks from the force of me shifting into park. I shoulder bump the driver door open.

Two panicked horses bolt out of the stable's door as flames dance on one side of the doorway. It won't be long before the entrance is fully engulfed.

I open the back-driver's side passenger door, flip the switch to slide the bench seat back and out of the way. From the storage compartment in the floorboards, I grab the fire safety kit backpack.

Years of running the incline of the mountain roads is how I train to run fast on flat land.

"Dani! Emm! Kourt! Dad!" I call out as I approach the entrance. The heat projecting from inside is enough to make a sane man pause before entering.

I'm not that man. I cross over—into hell.

Right away I spot an unmoving body lying face down in the hay-covered ground. The person is too big to be my wife or one of my girls. One side of the building is completely overtaken with flames. The scent of an odorant burns my nose.

My girls' screams grow louder—more urgent.

"Dani!"

She looks over her shoulder at the call of her name. Fear and tears and determination to climb the ladder to save her children is in her eyes. I get to her in twelve long strides.

Dani tries to shove me away as I lift her off the ladder. "No! Get Dad. I'll get the girls."

"I'll get them, but I'm getting you out of here first."

With her cradled in my arms I run out of the stable and put her on her feet a safe distance away.

"Go to the truck, call 911. Stay inside and lock the doors. I don't know where Amelia is."

"She's inside with the girls."

Her words send a chill through my bones. I haul ass back to the stable.

The opening is slowly narrowing.

The flames are low underneath the loft of the stable. I quickly weigh my options. I cough from the smoke and scent of the accelerant. Dad needs the most help because he is unconscious. For now, the girls are okay.

Some male stands at the landing of the ladder. *Why isn't he getting my girls out of here?*

I bend and catch Dad under the arms as I rise. He is deadweight. I scoop him up and carry him out on my back, fireman style.

"What about the girls?" Dani rushes toward us with my cell phone in her hand.

"I'm going back to get them." I ease my dad onto the ground.

Dani drops to her knees and starts checking him, and relaying information about his condition into the phone.

I run back to the stable, the fire safety backpack bounces on my back.

Dense smoke fills the stable, causing my eyes to water and my lungs to contract making me cough. I forge ahead, feeling my way for the ladder. The movement above makes me look up. She drastically changed her appearance and she's holding a half-filled water bottle in her hand.

Kourt is standing on one side of the loft. Emm on the other.

"You sent Kimberly to kill me and my parents."

Her dead tone worries me.

"I didn't send anyone to kill you and your parents." I step up on the rungs of the ladder.

"Liar! I found the picture in her pocket." Her tone went from dead to murderous.

She sweeps her hand side to side, spilling liquid from the bottle onto the floor of the loft. It drips through the cracks in the floorboards, feeding the flames below.

It's lighter fluid.

"Madelyn brought a bunch of RAGS people to my house. Someone must have found the picture." I climb higher.

Kourt has been slowly sidestepping the whole time. It seems she's trying to get to Emm. A floorboard squeaks, alerting Malinda. Kourt freezes.

Malinda tosses me a lip curling, evil smile and raises her bottle-wielding hand. She takes a step in Kourtney's direction.

I rush up the rungs to head her off.

My sudden appearance at the top of the ladder startles Amelia. I catch her by the arm and pull her toward me. The momentum throws both me and ladder off balance. I tighten my grip on Malinda's arm. The bottle falls from her hand. As the ladder and I barrel toward the floor, I drag Malinda down with me. My last sight of the bottle is it rolling toward Emm, spilling its contents and making tiny waterfalls pour through the cracks. The flames reach up to welcome it.

I prepare myself for impact and let go of Malinda. The angle of her fall is away from me and the ladder.

"Umph." My left shoulder takes the brunt of the fall. Any pain is muted by the tip of the ladder's stringer clocking me in the head. My vision blurs in my left eye, but I can still see clearly out of the right one. A tornado of tiny lit particles of hay floating in the air, drudged up from the force of our fall, touch the streams of liquid pouring from the cracks in the floorboard and ignite the underside of the loft on Emm's side. My big girl screams. Flames taunt her like orange-red talons ready to strike. She slowly backs up. My heart stops beating, but the rest of my body continues to function.

I struggle to stand and struggle harder with getting the ladder upright.

In that short amount of time, a wall of fire now separates my girls.

Both are watching me.

Desperation and fear in their eyes.

The thickness of the smoke causing them to cough and the heat making them sweat. My girls are depending on me to get them out of here unharmed.

The fire safety kit doesn't contain anything I can use to fight a fire cause by an accelerant. There is only one option to make. I move the ladder close to Emm's side.

As I climb the rungs, I glance at Kourt. Everything in my daughter's eyes triggers a memory of an important conversation. A promise made.

"Like say there's a fire and I'm in my room and Emmy's in hers. Who would you save?"

"Baby girl, I would fight the fire. Stop it from getting to you and your sister. I wouldn't stop fighting it until I put out every flame that tries to harm my girls. I would never choose one over the other. I choose both of you."

The higher I climb to get to Emm, the more I see Kourt pull away from me. I have no other options—Emm's danger is more urgent than Kourt's.

With both feet on the marked safety rung I swing the backpack off and unzip the middle compartment. "Kourt, put the hood on first, then the mask." I rip the packing off the items and toss them to her. I reach back into the backpack and grab a glow stick. It cracks on the first bend. I shake it until its ultra-glow shines bright yellow. "Wave this so I know where you are when I come back for you." I toss it to her.

"Daddy," Emm screams. She's backed into a corner, flames five feet from her.

I tuck the second glow stick into my back pocket, then rip open the packaging on the heat resistant blanket and step onto the weakening floorboards of the loft. Shaking out the blanket, I wrap it around me and rush through the flames. Despite the thickness of the soles of my boots, I feel the heat of the fire on my feet.

I unwrap the blanket, help Emm climb onto my back, then wrap the heat reflective blanket around us. The ends don't meet in front, but I don't care, my daughter is completely covered.

"Hold tight." On a run, I rush through the flames once again.

The climb down the ladder is made difficult by my sweaty palms, but I manage it. I turn and rush through the entrance. Dani is standing near, but far enough to be safe. She rushes toward me as I unwrap me and Emma.

"Oh my god!" Dani cries and points.

I turn around and let loose a string of cuss words. The entire entrance is engulfed in flames that fast.

Dani takes off running for the stable, calling for Kourt. I catch up to her.

"I'm going back for her."

"How? That is the only way in." She shoves against me.

The tips of my fingers lift my wife's chin. I stare directly into her eyes. "Dani. I *promise*. I'm going to get our daughter out of there, alive." The sounds of emergency sirens are growing louder. "Stay here."

My feet pump faster than ever. As I run, I wrap the heat reflective blanket around me. I know I'm not completely covered—and I really don't care.

"God, please get me through this."

I tuck my head into the blanket and breach the wall made of intimidating flames.

Fire isn't supposed to have a sound, but I hear it. The whoosh and low howl and mocking crackle. I pass through it all.

With my head covered I can't judge how far past the entrance I am. I keep running though.

Three steps.

Four steps.

Five steps—I trip over something.

My elbows and knees take the brunt of the fall. Quickly, I unwrap my head and look around. The density of the smoke clouds everything inside of this burning stable.

I reach in my back pocket for the second glow stick.

The bright yellow glow gives me some visibility. It highlights black sneakers, black jeans, black shirt, sharp metal tynes of a pitchfork protruding out of a chest cavity, pale white face, dead brown eyes fixed on the smoke-covered ceiling, and the flames three centimeters from her buzzed cut hair. Amelia Goodman aka Malinda Williamson is dead.

"Kourt!" The strain of yelling causes a violent wave of coughing. I try calling out to her again as I get to my feet, but her name comes out hacked.

I search for the yellow glow of the stick I gave her. Red-orange flames now cover ninety percent of the underside of the loft's floorboards and it's sprouting through the cracks on Kourtney's side.

There it is, the yellow glow I seek.

I throw the blanket off and rush to the ladder.

Even though the top three rungs are on fire, I shift it over to my daughter's side and climb.

"Kourt, answer me!" My throat is dry and irritated. I'm not very loud.

I get within fingers' reach of the ledge of the loft, then lean to the side off the ladder. I get my forearms anchored on the floorboards to support my weight as my feet leave the ladder. Dangling from the edge of the loft, I use upper body strength to pull myself up.

There are no words in any language that can describe the feeling that passes through me. The glow stick, mask, and hood lay where they landed when I tossed them to Kourt and she is nowhere to be found.

"Kourtney Allison Hawk! Answer me right now!" My lungs protest in the form of coughing.

The crackle of fire embedded in wood is all I hear.

A breeze cools the sweat on the back of my neck. I turn around. I run to the small opened window in the back wall of the stable's loft.

"Kourt!" Only my head, one arm, and part of my shoulder fit through the opening.

My daughter is plastered against the wall, her feet on the drainpipe that runs along the building. Fire trucks are now parked in front of the stable. The red and white spiraling lights bounce off Kourt's frightened yet determined face.

"Give me your hand." I stretch as far out of the window as I can. My fingertips brush the leg of her pants.

"No." She takes a slide-step away. I see what she is trying to get to. A fixed ladder mounted to the back side of the stable.

"Kourtney Allison Hawk. Give me your hand so I can pull you back inside."

A coughing fit rips through her.

I push and shove and push and squirm and try to find the leverage with my feet that gives me the super strength to break through the small window. I strain to get a grip on my baby girl.

The drainpipe jerks downward and Kourt loses her balance.

"Nooo!" My cry echoes.

Helplessly I watch my baby girl fall. Arms and legs flailing in real time—not slow motion. Her small body hits the unforgiving dirt. Hard. Landing on her left side.

Hands grip my arm. Another pair of hands grip my ankles. I'm pulled back inside.

Nothing else matters to me except getting to my baby girl.

How do I get from the loft to the smoke-covered floor?

I don't recall. But I did it on my own.

How do I get out of the burning stable?

I can't say. But I'm outside and running around to the back of the stable.

I drop to my knees at my baby girl's side.

Every fiber in me wants to touch her. Lift her into my arms. Be her pillow instead of the dirt and dead grass, and god knows what else.

Dani's on her knees next to me, crying, calling for Kourt.

We wrap our arms around each other and together we pray for our daughter as the paramedics work on her.

Things happen fast.

They call in a medical helicopter.

They get her strapped to a backboard.

I help the paramedics lift my daughter off the ground and strap her to a stretcher.

In a nearby open field on the ranch, the medical helicopter lands.

I turn to Dani and press my lips against her ear. "Call Jessi first. Then call the guys and Mom. Don't give a statement until Vin is with you. Don't let Emm out of your sight."

I release her to take hold of the stretcher.

We quickly move across the grass and through an opening in the fence to get to the medical helicopter. No one questions when I climb in and help them strap down the stretcher. No one raises an eyebrow when I strap myself into a seat, then place my hand on my daughter's chest. A mixture of dirt, sweat, and hay are plastered to my baby girl. The left side of her face is bloodied from a big gash above her eye. A dull white foam brace around her neck. She lies unmoving on the stretcher. Eyes closed. But breathing on her own.

The rotor blades pick up speed.

The pilot communicates with the tower.

An EMT is on the phone with the emergency room, relaying my daughter's medical stats.

The air bird begins to lift off the ground. Soon, the people on the ground and swirling lights of the emergency vehicles grow smaller.

The helicopter ride to the hospital isn't long, or maybe it is, and I've just lost all sense of time.

Jessi is among the team of doctors and nurses waiting on the helipad.

My sister finds the words to get me to let a team member take my place with the stretcher and agree to sit in a wheelchair. She takes over pushing it into the elevator and maneuvers the chair so that I'm next to my daughter.

Once we reach the emergency room floor, Kourt and I are separated. No amount of cussing, threats of bodily harm, and uncooperative behavior get me into the room where a team is assessing my daughter's injuries.

Realization settles in when Jessi pushes the wheelchair in front of the reflective glass and stops. Although my vision is blurred in both eyes, I now know why no one said anything about me getting on the helicopter. Most of my hair is singed. The big knot on my head is still oozing blood. I have no front to my shirt, only a back. All of the hairs on my chest and abs are gone and my torso is a deep red. My right shoulder is distorted. The legs of my jeans are burned up to my knees, and my legs are a nasty deep red and also hairless. The outsoles of my boots are burned down to the midsole layers. I can't stop coughing.

"BK4, adrenaline and determination blocked your body from telling your brain you're injured. There's nothing you can do for Kourtney right now. The ambulances carrying Dad, Dani, and Emma are ten minutes out. I can't be there for them if I have to babysit you. I promise, the best doctors in this hospital are taking care of Kourtney. Plus, Ig is already logged in and waiting to consult. Barrett is filing the flight plan to helicopter the guys out."

I stop resisting and a hospital wristband is placed on me. I'm admitted to the emergency room as a patient.

The ER staff are friendly and helpful. I try to be on my best behavior considering Jessi works here periodically. I'm given the VIP treatment because of my sister.

Now that the adrenaline rush is gone, my torso, arms, and legs sting like a muthafucker. The doctor says he'll give me something for the pain, but I decline.

The diagnosis for the large burn that covers my entire abdomen is a superficial burn. The ones on my forearms, ankles, and calves are mild second-degree burns. There is some blistering.

A registered nurse tries to distract me with small talk—he does most of the talking. I've been away from Kourt for three hours too long. After he fits my arm in a sling, he hooks me up to the portable oxygen machine. I sit in a wheelchair and he takes me to Kourt's room. She's been admitted into the hospital.

My baby girl looks small and helpless in the big hospital bed with a nasal canula in her nose. A gauze bandage covers the cut over her eye. The steady beep of the heart monitor does not bring me the comfort it should. It hurts me to see her like this.

"Hi, I'm Dr. Sullivan, head of the Peds Department." She was one of the docs who met us on the roof. "I've known your sister for years. When she called and said her niece was being helicoptered in, I turned around and came back to the hospital."

"Thank you, I appreciate that." I shake her hand.

"Mr. Hawk, your daughter is a lucky little girl." She points to the x-ray image on the computer monitor. "Kourtney fractured her left radius and humerus bones. The pediatric orthopedic surgeon viewed the x-rays and determined surgery is not needed. We have a splint on it for now, but once the swelling goes down, we'll put a fiberglass cast on it. She has bruised ribs and a bruised hip bone all on the left side. Her length of unconsciousness is a concern, so I had a neurosurgeon in for a consult. She ordered an MRI and ruled out a brain bleed. She will continue to monitor Kourtney closely throughout the night. I put three sutures in the cut above her eye to close it. The other scrapes, scratches, and bruising don't require any treatment. They will heal on their own in time. The good news is, your little girl is breathing on her own, and there are no signs of internal organ damage or bleeds. I only have her on oxygen because she inhaled smoke from the fire."

A load would be lifted off my shoulders if Kourtney would just open her eyes.

Jessi walks into the room with her hands in the pockets of her lab coat. Nothing in her face gives me cause for concern.

"Hey BK4. You look one hundred percent better. You scared the shit outta me when you got off that air bird."

"Did I look that bad, JP1?"

"You looked out of your mind crazy."

I cough and laugh. "How's Dani, Emm, and Dad?"

"Dani and the baby and Emma are fine. I put her and Emma in a room together. Both are on oxygen. Vin is with them. He cussed out a detective so bad the man looked like he wanted to cry. I've been giving Dani updates on you and Kourtney as I got them. Dad had to get five stitches and he's got a concussion and will have to stay over night. But other than that he is fine and wants to go home. Mom made him settle down. Ig is viewing your and Kourtney's medical records and reporting it to President Hart. Tony's getting your truck and dealing with the police."

"Tell Dani and Emm I love them. And I'm sorry I'm not there with them. But I need to be with Kourt."

"Dani knows this is where you should be. She told me to pass along a message. Talk to Kourtney even though she's unconscious, she will hear you."

———◆———

Arizona, Eleven Months Ago…

It took some creativity to orchestrate the layoff and expedite the approval of Dani's Colorado psychologist license. Getting her hired by the hospital, the leasing of an apartment in the building I just purchased and saving Kourt a spot at Greystone Preparatory Academy was easy.

Dani and Kourt pull out of the driveway. We give them a thirty-second head start, then pulls away from the curb. The guys and I are following them to Los Angeles. Edwards hasn't resurfaced. Phantom Watchers are working overtime to locate him. Field Operatives are on the ground trying to track him.

Dani and I will have to act like strangers meeting for the first time. I doubt she'll be on board with it without a reason. All I can tell her is it's for their safety. I can never tell her the real reason I knocked on her door eight years ago, but I've already made up my mind to find a way to ease them back into my life where I don't have to hide them. I'm hoping I can regain Dani's trust.

Sticking to their itinerary, Dani and Kourt stay with Mrs. Franklin for two days. They leave late afternoon for the drive to Las Vegas.

Vegas is the easiest place to trail them because we blend in with the crowd easily. Every leg of their sightseeing road trip to Boulder, Colorado, we follow them.

When Dani and Kourt finally arrive at their new apartment I

breathe a little easier. From afar, I watch them get settled into the city.

On the first day of school, I stall to give Dani time to get Kourt settled and leave before I walk Emm to the classroom. I don't want today to be our family reunion.

With the girls sitting next to each other in class, I'm keeping my fingers crossed that my daughters will become friends before Dani sees us.

Kourt peeks at me when I pull out Emm's chair, then push it forward. I hold my breath and wait to see if recognition fills her eyes.

When it doesn't, I kiss Emm's cheek. "Have a good first day and make new friends. Remember I love you."

"Okay, Daddy."

Kourt has this wide-eyed shocked look on her face. Unfortunately, Malinda Williamson chooses that moment to speak to me. I turn away from Kourt and greet Malinda—only because I don't want to appear rude.

I feel three sets of eyes following me out of the room. One pair belongs to Madelyn Brooks. She's not just following me with her eyes though, she's also trying to catch up with me. I wave to Max, Tom, and Penny and leave the classroom.

I stop by the school's office to have a quick meeting with Greystone Preparatory Academy's new principal, Dr. Barrett.

"I set up the classroom so Emma and Kourtney are seated together." He points to a memo addressed to the staff. "Ms. Williamson is aware that it is my policy to make unannounced visits to the classrooms. She shouldn't be suspicious of the true reason for me stopping in her classroom often. My firearm is hidden at all times. Rest assured Kourtney is safe on this campus."

"Thank you, Dr. Barrett."

I stand and shake his hand.

On my way to the parking lot I come upon Madelyn Brooks holding court with a handful of other moms. Captain Holly Valentine is one of them.

Holly is supposed to befriend Dani and feel out the other parents. I give her a slight nod as I pass the group.

CHAPTER NINETEEN

KOURTNEY

Colorado, Present Day

MOMMY CAN'T SEE ME SNEAK the picture I found out of Mr. Cuddles's jacket to look at again. Daddy and daughter meet for the first time. February 12, 2006. That's what Mommy wrote on the bottom. I'm the baby, so that man holding me is my daddy. I can't see his face.

"Out of state California," Mom laughs.

I jump and hide the picture under my leg.

"No fair, Mom. You were supposed to say something when we were getting close."

"I did, sweetie. You were looking down."

I look out the window. We crossed the state line. We're in Nevada now. I see a big truck. "Outta state Oregon."

"Good catch."

Me and Mom are playing the license plate game on our road trip to Colorado. I won from Arizona to California. The game started over when we got on the freeway in Los Angeles. Mom is in the lead now, but we're not at the hotel yet. I can still catch up.

I keep watching for license plates until I see the colorful bright lights and tall movie screen-like signs up ahead. "Wow, everything is so bright."

Mom laughs. "Welcome to Las Vegas."

There are lots of cars. Lots of people. Lots of lights. And the sun hasn't set yet. There is too much to look at all at once and if I blink, I might miss something.

I sneak the picture from under my leg and hide it under Mr. Cuddles's jacket again.

"Mommy, may I roll down the window?"

"Go ahead, sweetie."

I press the button and the window quietly rolls all the way down. Mom turns off the air conditioning and rolls down the other windows halfway.

The air is dry and hot just like Arizona's. It smells like food, car exhaust, cigarette smoke, and people. I've never seen this many different people in one place. You can't see the sidewalks and curbs because people are walking or standing.

"We'll get checked into the hotel, eat dinner, then walk the strip," Mom says.

"Can we go to that candy store over there?"

"Of course, we can. Do you see that big hotel on the corner right there?"

I lean as far as the seat belt will let me. "You mean the big green one?"

"Yes, that's where the restaurant with the tropical forest theme is."

"Really? Can we have dinner there tonight?"

Las Vegas is going to be fun.

We see sharks and white tigers and dolphins and lions and go to a magic show and play games at the carnival on the top floor of a hotel. I talk Mom into getting on a roller coaster high above the strip. She screams so much and so loud she's hoarse afterwards. We go to a place in Las Vegas where we see desert ecosystems and learn the history of the Mojave Desert.

The license plate game starts when we get on the highway heading for Utah. Me and Mom are tied.

In Utah, we go to national parks where we take lots of pictures. My favorite is Arches National Park because of the natural arches in the rock forms. They give me ideas for a science project I want to do.

Mom won't sleep in a tent, but the compromise is that we walk the nature trails and I use her camera to take pictures.

Each night of our road trip, when Mommy takes a shower, I take out the picture of me and my dad. Did Mommy tell him we're moving? What if she didn't and he goes to Arizona to see us? If I tell Mommy I want to go back to Arizona she'll want to know why and then I'll have to tell her I found the picture.

Beep.

Beep.

Beep.

What's that beeping? Is that what woke me up?

No.

Somebody is talking to me, but they sound far away. I'm not in the fire anymore because I can breathe without coughing and it's not so hot my face feels like it's burning. But my head hurts. I hurt all over.

"Baby girl. I'm here. You're safe. I love you."

Where's my mom? I want my mom. I want to open my eyes and yell at him to get away from me. He left me in the fire just like he left me in Arizona. But I can't make my eyes open and I can't make my mouth work.

"The first time I held you was at the hospital. I got there after the hospital's photographer had finished taking your picture. I remember looking down at this tiny person I helped make and saying to myself, "You don't know how lucky you are to be her dad." And when I picked you up I said, 'Hi, Kourtney Allison Hawk, I'm your daddy and I'm going to always love you.'"

The back of my hand is rubbed against something scratchy.

I want to snatch my hand away and tell him I don't love him.

"Do you know why your middle name is Allison? It was my grandmother's name. She died before you and Emm were born. Mommy kept it a secret until I read the paperwork for your birth certificate."

I want to yell I'm tired of the secrets and lies!

"I've always loved and wanted you, Cuddles. Come back to me. Please, baby girl. Open your eyes."

No! It hurts. I want to go back to sleep! Nothing hurts when I'm asleep.

The night before the first day of school I can't sleep. I ask Mommy to lie with me. We sometimes do this when we talk. But I don't feel like talking. I just want her to cuddle with me.

I've been thinking about that picture and why Mommy never showed it to me. And why she didn't have pictures of me and my dad on the walls. She put lots of pictures of me and her up.

In the morning, Mommy and me do our tickle game.

She goes back and forth between her room and my room getting dressed and checking to make sure I am too. Mommy has a lady-hawk tattoo on her side that she hides under her clothes. I like the way it moves when she walks.

Mom comes into my room and sits on the side of my bed. This is the part of the morning I don't like, getting my hair combed. I hate it more than I hate waking up in the mornings. Mom tries to be gentle, but it still hurts. I used to hide the comb and brush and say I couldn't find them but then

Mom bought a set that she keeps in her room.

Since this is the first day of school, she makes a big breakfast and we talk about having a good school year.

I get my backpack and lunch bag, Mom picks up her briefcase and purse. We leave the apartment and go down to the courtyard. Like every first day of school, I have to stand and smile and look excited while Mommy takes a million pictures of me.

When she finishes, we get in the truck and she drives me to school.

"I bet you can't wait to get into that science center."

"I think I'm going to do a photosynthesis project for the science fair." Last year I won the first-grade division at my old school and went to regionals. Another first-grader from another school made it to the state level. This year I want to make it to state, maybe even nationals, and one day, the world.

Mom parks in the parking lot and walks me to class. My heart beats a little fast. This school is bigger than my old one. I hope I don't get lost finding the restroom.

Dr. Barrett is in my classroom. I met him when me and Mommy went on a tour of the school. My new teacher is talking to other parents, so Dr. Barrett shows me to my seat.

Mom kisses my cheek. "Will you be okay with getting your desk set up on your own?"

"Yes, Mommy. I know how to organize my desk."

"Okay, sweetie. Have a good day. I'll see you after school. I love you."

She is going on a tour of her new job this morning. Dr. Barrett walks out with her.

"Hi, I'm Ms. Williamson. Welcome to my second-grade class." The teacher stands in front of my desk. She smiles real big and holds out her hand.

"I'm Kourtney Edwards."

Her hand is soft, and her nails are painted a light pink. I like her already.

"Sorry I missed meeting your parents. Everyone has lots of questions for me this morning. I'll make sure to meet them after school."

"It's just me and my mom."

"Then I'll meet your mom after school. I read in your file that you love science and made it all the way to regionals last year. Congratulations. Are you going to enter this year?"

I peek over at the science center, then look back at Ms. Williamson. "I really want to do a photosynthesis project that shows how plants and trees are needed to preserve our environment."

Her eyes crinkle when she smiles big.

"I also read that you were a green planet ambassador at your school. Maybe you and I can start a club and get our school to do things the green way." She leans in like she's going to tell me a secret. "Finish setting up your desk, then go explore the science center until the bell rings."

Ms. Williamson is so nice.

More kids walk in with their parents, and Ms. Williamson goes to meet them.

The chair next to mine is pulled back. I look up and see the girl who I share a desk with.

"Remember I love you…"

My mind shows me my bedroom at our old house. "Please remember me. Remember I love you."

Beep.

Beep.

Beep.

"I'm fine!" Bryan shouts.

Can you stop yelling? You woke me up and it hurts when I'm awake.

"Bryan, you really need to get some sleep. You've been by her side for two days. Go home with Mom and Dad. Sleep in a bed."

Mommy sounds sad.

"I'll stay with Dani. We'll call you if there are any changes."

That's Uncle Vinny.

"You've been right here for two days too. No one is telling you to leave."

Bryan sounds real close to me.

"Dani is sleeping and eating and taking a break from sitting in this room. And taking time to be with Emma."

That's Grandma.

"At least step out of the room for an hour to let Ig properly care for the burns on your body. You can eat a good meal. Get some fresh air. See Emma outside of this hospital room."

I'm in the hospital? Grandpa just said so. Is that why everything hurts?

And Bryan is hurt too?

Someone sniffs and something wet drops on the back of my hand. Then more wet drops fall on my hand.

"I can't leave my baby girl. Not until she opens her eyes."

Bryan sounds like people who cry and try to talk at the same time.

"BK4, you're tired. You're barely eating. And you really need to let Ig take a look at those second-degree burns before they get infected. If you hadn't discharged yourself the nurses would be dressing them."

Aunt Jessi is here too.

"You guys don't get it! I need to be right here."

"I get it, Bry," Mommy says. "You want to be the first person she sees when she wakes. We're all okay with that, but you are allowing guilt to overrule what's good for your health."

"Why is it so important that you be the first person she sees?" Grandpa asks.

"Kourt is my daughter."

"I know, I was there when you legally adopted her."

"No, Dad. I'm her biological father."

He said it. He finally said it.

I'm tired now. I need to go back to sleep.

"Kourtney, are you ready to go?"

"Yes, Mommy." I lay Mr. Cuddles on my pillow, grab my backpack, and leave my bedroom.

Mom is standing at the door holding my lunch bag and her briefcase. This is our routine on school and work days. Today she's wearing a green dress. Her curly hair is down.

I wait until she's driving to ask a question that I've been thinking about a lot. "Mom, who do I look like?"

Her eyes look at me in the rearview mirror, then go back to the road. "You are a combination of me and your father."

"How?"

"You have my nose and mouth and his forehead and ears."

"What about my hair?"

"Well, your hair curls like mine, but it's thick like his and the same color."

"Who do I get my eyes from?"

"Him."

"Exactly like his?"

"Yes, you have the green, gold, brown eyes exactly like him. I've never seen hazel eyes quite like you and your dad's."

That is the first time she's called him my dad. It's usually father.

"Is that why Nana and Pop-Pop call me bright eyes?"

"Yes, the golden color makes your eyes shine naturally."

"What about my skin color? Who do I get that from?"

"Remember that book I used to read you about beautiful Black people in all shades and shapes?"

"Yes."

"And remember we talked about you being biracial because your dad is White and I'm Black?"

"Yes."

"The color of your skin is a beautiful mixture of your dad and me. Always remember this sweetie, it's not the color of your skin that matters, it's the person you are on the inside that defines you. Be proud of your African American roots and be equally proud of your Caucasian roots. You do not have to choose one over the other."

I stare out of the window in front of me, but I see Mommy take her hand off the steering wheel and wipe her eyes.

"Does it make you sad that I'm asking you about my dad?"

"No, sweetie. Sometimes I get a little sad when I think about him. But I will always answer any questions you have about him."

She pulls into the parking lot.

"Mom, can you drop me off at the curb? I want to walk to class by myself."

"I don't know, Kourtney. I like making sure you get to class okay."

"Please, Mom. I promise to go straight to the classroom."

I can see her thinking hard about it. She reaches back with her pinky. I hook mine to hers. We shake, then cross our hearts. This is what we do when we make a promise we can't break.

She gets in the line with the cars pulling up to the curb. When a space opens, she pulls in and a parent volunteer wearing a bright yellow vest opens my door. I unhook my seatbelt, lean between the two front seats and kiss my mom's cheek.

"Have a good day, sweetie. I'll see you after school. I love you."

"I love you too. Have a good day, Mom." I get out and walk through the gate.

When I get to the hall where my classroom is, a tall man walks out of the door. The sun is shining bright behind him. I can't see his face, but I see his outline and the way he walks.

I remember something, a dream I used to have when I was afraid at night. In my dream I'm in my old bedroom and I'm crying. He always comes when I cry.

I blink. The man in the hallway gets closer, the sun shines on his brown hair. I know his walk. When we pass each other his bright greenish-gold and brown eyes look in mine. He smiles.

I remember another dream.

I'm in the bathtub with the brown-haired girl. We're laughing and splashing water at Mommy and he's singing a funny song and taking pictures with Mommy's camera. I remember his smile.

Beep.

Beep.

Beep.

"You started walking on November 25, 2006 at 6:17 p.m. You want to know how I know? I wrote it down, so I would never forget the date and time. I walked through the door at the apartment carrying Emma and you were standing at the coffee table. When you saw me, you let go of the table and walked all the way to me. You didn't stumble or fall. You kept your eyes and smile on me."

Something soft presses the back of my hand real quick.

"Come on, Cuddles, it's been four days. You can do this. Just like you did that day you started walking. All you have to do is let go and come to me. You trusted me then and you can trust me now."

Something touches my cheek.

"If you can't open your eyes, then squeeze my hand, or wiggle your ears. Just do something that says you hear me. We miss you and want you to come back to us."

I concentrate on my left hand and tell my brain to make a fist. Nothing happens.

I tell my brain to move my left foot.

"Hey, you guys, look," Uncle Iggy says.

"What's happening?" Mommy asks.

"Look at the EEG monitor. Her brain activity picked up. Look at the number of spikes."

"That means she can hear me?"

"I would say, yes."

"Hi, baby girl."

I hear a squeaky door open.

"Ig says Kourtney can hear us," Mommy yells.

Lots of footsteps are coming fast.

"What's going on, Ig?" Uncle Tony asks.

"Her brain activity has been in a dream state since I hooked her up to the EEG. But just now, Bry told her to do something that shows she can hear him, and her brain activity spiked."

"You mean my granddaughter can hear what we're saying right now?" Grandpa asks.

"That's exactly what I'm saying."

"Sweetie," Mommy cries. "We're right here." I feel lips on my forehead.

It makes me sad to hear my mom crying. She used to cry at night when I was little. She doesn't know I heard her.

I try really hard to try to make my fingers move, but when I do, everything starts to hurt really bad. I need to go back to sleep so it doesn't hurt anymore.

"Her brain activity is starting to level off."

"It's okay, baby girl. I'm not going anywhere. I love you, Cuddles."

Every day, I remember more of my dreams. I still haven't seen the face of the man in my dreams though.

Me and Emma and Penelope are friends. We eat lunch together every day. Emmy doesn't have a mom, but she has four uncles who aren't related to her and a grandma and grandpa and an Aunt Jessi and Willis and Marie and lots of older uncles and aunts and cousins who live in other states. Penny has two dads and one grandma and two grandpas and a bunch of uncles and cousins. They know I have a mom and a Nana and a Pop-Pop and Yvon.

Ms. Williamson lets me spend class free time in the science center. My project was approved by Dr. Barrett. Ms. Williamson has been working with other teachers and the principal to do green activities at the school.

Mommy and Ms. Williamson keep missing each other, but they will meet tonight at Back to School Night.

We go home to change our clothes. I'm in the kitchen eating a snack. Mommy says we'll go out for dinner after the meeting. Her phone pings. She's in her bedroom getting dressed. I get her phone and look at the screen. It's a text message from BK4 that says: follow my lead and I will explain later…trust me. I take Mommy her phone and go grab my jean jacket from my closet.

Ms. Williamson is standing at the door smiling and saying hello to the parents as they walk in with their kid.

Me and Mommy get in line. When it's our turn, Ms. Williamson stops smiling. Her eyes look Mommy up and down in a not so nice way.

"Good evening. Welcome to Back to School Night. My name is Malinda Williamson. I'm your child's second grade teacher."

I've never heard her sound mean to a parent before. Why is she being like that to my mom?

"Good evening, I'm Danielle Edwards, Kourtney's mom." Mom is being friendly like she always is to people.

"It's nice to finally meet you, Dr. Edwards." She looks away from us and talks to Dylan Hill and his parents.

I don't like the way Ms. Williamson treated my mom.

I take Mommy's hand and show her around the classroom. I rush through the boring sections and take her over to my area in the science center where I get to work on my experiment. Her smile goes all the way up to her eyes. She's proud of me.

Ms. Williamson tells everybody it's time for the meeting.

Mom turns around and sucks in air real loud. She's frozen like someone shot her with a freeze gun. Mom's eyes are super big. She's staring at Emmy and her dad.

Why is Mommy looking like that?

I take her hand and lead her to my desk. When we get there, I introduce Emmy to my mom.

Emmy is shy around new people at first. She just waves. But Mommy has tears in her eyes. Then Emma's dad stands and speaks to me first. He looks at Mommy and winks.

I start to feel like I'm on a merry-go-round.

Christmas tree lots. Christmas mornings. My birthdays. Ma's birthdays. Mommy's belated birthdays. Daddy's birthdays. Picnics at the park. Playgrounds. Nights in front of the television. Me and Ma's bedroom. Dinner at the table. Dinner at restaurants. Family pictures. Daddy hugging Mommy. Mommy kissing Daddy. Daddy sleeping in Mommy's bed. Mommy chasing Daddy because he messed up her hair after she got it pressed and curled and him laughing and apologizing. A bird pooping in Mommy's hair while we're at the park and Daddy washing it out of her hair when we get home. I see his face now. I know his laugh. I hear his voice. He has a big bird on his back. I've traced it with my fingers.

Beep.

Going to the Play 'n' Fun Center and hearing Mommy say angry words to Daddy about not returning any of her calls and how long he's been in Boulder. And him telling her now is not the time to have this conversation, that they have to pretend to be strangers. Mommy and Daddy don't see us standing at the video game near the table. Playing tag in the junkyard. Daddy making me breakfast on Halloween. Him hugging me when Mommy hit her head on the table. Staying at Daddy's house. Daddy holding on tight until I felt safe to ice skate on my own. Daddy fixing my hair after Dylan pulled my bow out. Daddy wiping my tears because I didn't want to go back to the party.

Beep.

Beep.

"Keep singing, Bry," Uncle Iggy says.

Daddy singing to me on the phone. Daddy yelling at Grandpa Christmas morning. Building a snowman with Daddy and my sister. The way Daddy hugged me on New Year's Eve. Daddy and me planning my birthday party. The way Daddy hugged me tight and cried because those kids kept calling me the N-word and other mean things.

Beep.

Beep.

"She's coming around, Bry. Don't stop singing."

Daddy's face when I pushed Emmy. Starting the butterfly garden with my dad. Helping my dad not get in trouble with Mommy. Mommy paying me ten dollars to kick and scream louder when Daddy does my hair. Yelling at Daddy at the hospital and calling him Bryan.

Beep.

Beep.

"Kourty, can you hear me? Please open your eyes. I miss you."

My sister is here. Emmy is okay.

"Baby Mine." Daddy used to sing it to me all the time.

Come on, eyes, open. I need to see my Dad. I need to tell him I'm sorry for thinking he doesn't love me. I need to tell him and Mommy about the picture.

My fingers move.

"She squeezed my hand," Daddy says.

People start shouting: Grandpa, my uncles, my sister. It's making my head hurt, but I concentrate real hard by telling myself I can do it.

My eyes blink.

I try again and this time they open a little, but the light hurts my eyes. I close them tight.

Mommy starts singing with Daddy.

I do it again. I open my eyes. This time the lights don't hurt and Daddy's standing right where I can see him.

My mouth feels dry, but I have to tell Daddy something really important.

CHAPTER TWENTY

DANIELLE

Colorado, Present Day

BRYAN IS ASLEEP WHEN I get back to the hospital. He found a middle ground that satisfies our need for him to sleep in a bed and his need to stay by his daughter's side. He had a chair brought in that breaks down and reclines at different angles or lays flat. As long as he can lie down and relax his body I'll accept his compromise. I sleep on the couch over by the window.

President Hart ordered Phantom's Secret Service to keep us secured. A mini command center is set up in a room across the way. Tony is in charge of the day-to-day operations of Phantom and Hawkeye Personal Protection and consults with Bryan when needed. Phantom's Delta Team is covering for the ESO Team.

It hurts me to watch Bryan let his guilt eat at him. Kourtney has been unconscious for five days. The longer she lies, unmoving, in the bed, the more Bryan slips into depression. I love him too much to let it continue.

I've never used my profession in personal relationships, but for my husband and children I am about to. That is why I enlisted the help of my daughter, Emma, and my mother-in-law. They soaked a pot of kidney beans overnight for me. This morning, I left the hospital to prepare my husband a home-cooked meal. I also inter-viewed the people he's close to. Maxie recognized what I was doing right away even though we were talking on the phone. I wasn't trying to hide my intentions. He explained, in detail, how he broke down the cocky kid and rebuilt him into an elite Phan-tom Ghost. For ethical reasons, there were certain areas of Bryan's primal human needs that Max left untouched because he didn't want to create an immoral monster.

I leave a small duffle bag on the couch and set an insulated bag on the mobile table, then push it across the room. The wheels roll silently on the tile floor. I stop in front of Bryan's chair bed.

I unpack our dinner from the insulated bag and dish up the food on paper plates that I'd packed along with napkins, utensils and cups. I made enough for Vin, Ig, and Tony.

"Bryan," I whisper. There's no need to talk any louder, he's not in a deep sleep.

His red-rimmed eyes open, unfocused. He's not wearing contacts and his glasses are on the other mobile table next to him.

"You cooked?"

"I was tired of take-out and I had a taste for red beans and rice, cabbage, and hot water cornbread."

His body jerks upright like something stabbed him in the back. I drop my head to hide the amused smile. Oh, the many ways in my arsenal to get my husband's attention.

While he is in the en suite bathroom, I pour the sun-kissed sweet tea and set my notebook of handwritten notes beside my plate. I'm not hiding the fact that this is a therapy session.

Bryan comes out of the bathroom drying his hands on a paper towel. Instead of going right to his seat across the mobile table, he comes to me. The tips of his fingers lift my chin as he leans down. His chapped lips brush mine. The gratitude behind the kiss is felt deep in my heart.

"Thank you for cooking my favorite dinner."

"I had some help, but that's all I can tell you. And you're welcome."

He cocks a questioning eyebrow.

"I promised my helper she could tell you."

He kisses me one more time, then takes his seat. On the first taste of red beans and rice, the aura of restored energy surrounds him.

I wait until he's had four good spoonfuls in his stomach to start our session.

"You have a lot of trophies, medals, and certificates in your old bedroom. What got you interested in sports and martial arts?"

He drinks down some tea and wipes his mouth on his napkin. "I was kind of energetic when I was little. Dad signed me up because he said I needed to learn discipline and focus." As he recounts his childhood, I actively listen.

Bryan does genuinely enjoy sports and Krav Maga. He excelled in them. I mention the pictures of different girls still on the corkboard in his room. He tells me a synopsis of his high school dating life. I ask how often he keeps in touch with the people he grew up with. His answer does not surprise me. There are three friends from high school who still live in Colorado Springs. He sees them when he's visiting Mom and Dad, but other than that, there is no contact with them.

The friendship between him, Tony, Ig, and Vin is unique because of the balance each one brings to the table. No one person's opinion is superior to the others. Even on the battlefield, they fight as equals. When they argue, they do not exploit each other's weakness. They like to bet on things in each other's lives. Bryan lost a good sum of money after he married me. Seventy-five thousand to be exact.

I move to his relationship with his sister. I ask what his gut reaction was to his sister coming out. What I learned from Jessi was that she came out to him first and he stood by her when she told their parents a year later. Without prompting, Bryan reveals that he was ready to pounce if his dad had reacted negatively. He adores his mother and has nothing but funny details about their relationship. I already know about his closeness with his grandmother.

"You once told me that you didn't have a good relationship with your dad. Where do you see the relationship now?"

Bryan's lips turn up in an amused, knowing smile. It brings a shine back to his faded green-gold-brown eyes. Before he answers, he refills his plate and pours more sweet tea for both of us. That's a good sign.

"It's gotten better since we had that talk Christmas day."

"How?"

"It wasn't a father-son type of conversation. It was one father talking to another father."

"How much of his reaction to meeting Emma for the first time played a role in your decision to take a different approach to talking to your dad Christmas day?"

"That was the reason I said the things I said. And they weren't polite words, so I'll spare you the monologue. Emm was a baby when she first met her grandfather. All she's ever known him to be is a grandpa who loves and helps take care of her. Kourt, on the other hand, was old enough to pick up on the BS he was spitting and he was upsetting her with his overbearing attitude toward my life. He needed to understand that my love for Kourt is just as strong as it is for Emma."

"He needed to see that, or Kourtney needed to see that?"

"Both."

"They did not know they were granddaughter and grandfather. All he saw was a woman and her child, that no one in the family had ever met, playing house with his son."

"Bottom line: my kids are my life and I will do everything in my power to protect and defend them no matter who, no matter what." He picks up his tea.

"So will your father for his own children."

The tea he was about to drink stops inches from his lips.

I gather from the double cocked eyebrows, it never occurred to Bryan that his own father feels just as strongly as he does about his own children. And the two of them want the same thing—to shield their children from anyone or anything that has the potential to harm them.

"How much of your past relationship with your father remains part of the relationship today?"

"To be honest, I think this whole experience with Kourt being in the hospital has brought us closer than we've ever been. But it took us a while to get here."

"Why do you think it took so long?"

"I guess because he spent so much time riding me about being responsible and making good decisions. Working hard to get what I want instead of taking it for granted that it will be handed to me or thinking I can manipulate it from people. Drilling into my head: the importance of family, understanding why it is my duty to protect those who mean something to me, being respectful—especially to women, honoring commitments because a man is measured by the value of his word. The true meaning of loyalty, being monogamous and practicing safe sex, knowing there are consequences for every action good or bad."

I let him get more food in his stomach before I verbalize two important observations.

"You listed all the things he did that put a strain on your relationship, but you didn't list yours?"

Bryan chuckles. "I rebelled as much as I could."

"And how did that work out?"

"It didn't. That's how I ended up in sports and martial arts."

"Bryan, all those things you listed are characteristics you have that made me trust you the first day I met you. They are the reason I'm in love with you more than I ever thought humanly possible. Everything you named as the reason you had a strained relationship with your father, are the very reasons you, Tony, Ig, and Vin have a strong brotherhood. You think you rebelled, but because Bryan Kendall Hawk the Third was steadfast in his rearing of Bryan Kendall Hawk the Fourth, you are an exceptional dad, a loyal brother and friend, an honorable man, a protector of the citizens of the United States, my first, my last, my husband."

He stares at me.

"If you had the power to go back to the evening of the fire, would you do anything differently?"

The brightness in his eyes is magnified by the answer. He doesn't want to verbalize it because it makes him face a hard truth. But Bryan needs to say it out loud, so he can start shedding the weight of guilt on his shoulders. I know Bryan has asked himself this question every day and every night since the fire.

"I weighed every option before I made a decision. Every option, Dani."

"Would you have done anything differently?"

Tears form in his red-rimmed hazel eyes. "I used the same logic that I do when I'm out on a mission."

He doesn't need to convince me, he needs to convince himself he did what's best for our daughters. In order to do that, he has to say it out loud and stop playing woulda-shoulda-coulda in his mind.

I ask him again, "Bry, would you do anything differently?"

The answer is right there. He just has to say the word and he'll be free. I won't touch him. If I touch him, the next time he makes a hard decision that involves the girls he'll look to me to say it was okay. So, I keep the distance by sipping sun-kissed sweet tea yet lend my support through constant eye contact.

"No," he whispers.

I let the verbal confession soak in for a minute while I finish my food. Positive results through therapy do not happen overnight, nor does it happen in one session. I know it will take an unbiased therapist to help him cope with the decisions he made in the fire, but this is a start. We're all going to do therapy—individual and group. Due to the sensitivity of what Bryan does, Max and Tony brought in Dr. Stevens. It would be easier to talk to Maxie, but he is too emotionally close to be objective. I was shocked when Tony told me Dr. Stevens is on Phantom's payroll. Emma and Solomon, James's son, are already working with him. Once Kourtney regains consciousness, and she is cleared by the neurologist, she will work with him too.

"Kourt once asked me if there was a fire and she was in her room and Emm in her own room, and I could only save one of them, who would I choose. I told her I would never choose one over the other."

"That was an unfair and impossible question that children ask their parents. Naturally we give a neutral answer, which is wrong on our part because in a real-life situation, with unforeseen variables, the answer we give may not always be the action we are able to take. Every loving parent will lay down their life for their children."

"I'm trained to adjust to the unknown."

"And when you do, you have everything you need to make that adjustment work in the situation. You had a small backpack and you did the best you could. If we were at home where there is a sprinkler system and fire extinguishers, yes, you would have fought the fire until it was out and you saved both girls. But this one happened at a place you don't control."

I see the contradiction on his lips and I cut him off before he can voice it.

"Bryan, if you take a moment to think about what she was truly asking, you'd see you fulfilled it and then some."

"What was she really asking me?"

"Does she matter to you? And you proved that by running through fire for her."

He looks over his shoulder at our daughter.

"There's one more thing I want to talk to you about, Bryan."

His gaze returns to me. "I've been waiting for you to bring it up."

"You went to such a dark place. I was afraid you'd hurt me for getting in between you and Antoinette."

"I never wanted you to see me like that after what happened in the bedroom."

"Who you were that day in the bedroom was a hatchling compared to who you became in that penthouse, Bryan. Your eyes weren't even hazel."

He finishes the last of the food on his plate and wipes his mouth with the napkin. Bryan inhales. "I call it my monster. It's the part of me that can get the Phantom job done in the most unthinkable ways and still be able to look myself in the mirror. Usually I'm in control of it, but what happened in the penthouse was different. It had more energy than I could control. I'm going to be honest with you, Dani, I was afraid I'd hurt you too."

"Why were you that angry?" I'm careful not to acknowledge the monster as "it."

"The enemy was in my camp and I didn't see it. Even now, when I look back on my interactions with them, there was nothing indicating they were RAGS. The trust I gave them..." He shakes his head. "I get why you shut me out when you found out about Phantom. That level of anger has no description. Even Chen is dumbfounded by their ability to deceive even him, and that is his specialty." Bryan stands and gathers up our plates and utensils.

"I didn't think I could get through to you." I help him put things in the small trash can.

"Your touch. Your love. Your voice." He reaches for my right hand, then presses his lips into my palm. Bryan places my hand over his heart. The steady thumping speaks the words before they pass his lips. "You don't even know the power you have over me. It's stronger than the monster." Bryan pulls me into his arms.

The brush of his lips on mine makes my soul feel loved. I open my mouth to him. The first intimate touch of his tongue reaffirms our connection. Our arms tighten around one another strengthening our bond.

"Whatever happens when Kourtney wakes, we'll face it together." Behind me, the hospital room door swings open.

"Sorry, I can come back," Tony says.

"No, you're fine. I know it's time for your meeting with Bryan. I brought you guys dinner. Everything you need is in the insulated bag, and there's sweet tea in the beverage container."

"You don't have to leave," Bryan says.

"I told Selam I'd try to braid her hair. I won't be long. Mom and Dad are dropping Emma off. She wants to spend the night here."

I retrieve the small duffle bag from the couch, swinging the strap over my shoulder. On my way out the door, Ig and Vin come in. Right away, they unpack the insulated bag, and Bryan takes his place by his daughter's side.

Two Phantom Secret Service Agents follow me to the twelfth floor of the north wing of the hospital, one male, one female. They are quiet and observant.

The first time I met Selam, I was nervous. James had already told her about me—well, as much as he could tell her. What he forgot to tell her about was my pregnancy. I walked into her room wearing a summer dress that does not hide my belly and Selam's eyes watered.

When she and Solomon were abducted, she was pregnant and didn't know it. Due to the harsh conditions they were being held in, and the fact her captors hit and kicked her, breaking ribs, she miscarried and did not receive medical care. An infection set in. By some miracle, Jessi was able to save Selam's uterus, but she will not be able to carry another baby. In consideration of her feelings, I said I wouldn't visit again, but Selam asked me to come back.

Now when I visit, I wear a big, lightweight sweater that some-what hides my pregnancy even though she always asks how we're doing.

Yesterday, I used a technique for bedridden people to wash and blow dry Selam's hair using spray bottles, lots of towels, and hair clips. Mom showed me how they do it for the men and women at the nursing home. Today, I'm going to moisturize Selam's hair, then braid it in big cornrows.

She is already lounging in a chair instead of the bed when I walk in. Selam looks up and smiles, tucking her bookmark inside of the bible she's reading.

Selam has the most expressive wide, almond-shaped brown eyes and distinctive facial bone structure that pays homage to her Ethiopian roots. Her big, naturally curly hair accentuates her slender face. Her terra-cotta brown-red skin is regaining a healthy shine. Selamawit Bahta-Edwards, her legal full name, is a stunning woman.

"Is there any change with your daughter?" she asks.

I blink back tears and drop the duffle bag on the mobile table near her chair. "No change."

Selam reaches for my hand. "Stand strong in faith. Your little girl will come back once her mind is at peace. I am praying for her."

A kaleidoscope of emotions clogs my throat. "Thank you."

"How are you and the baby doing? Are you eating and resting?"

I can see why James has changed. His wife is a genuine person who has a natural healing soul that is driven by her life-long religious convictions. Not even almost a year of captivity can shake her.

"We're doing well. And yes, with an OB/Gyn who is also my controlling sister-in-law, I have no choice but to rest and eat properly. How are you feeling today?"

"By the grace of God, I'm getting stronger. And having the same tenacious OB/Gyn as you, I'm healing."

The experimental procedure Jessi performed to save Selam's reproductive organs has only been done five times in the U.S. and Jessi's the one who performed them. My sister-in-law is well known in the gynecology and obstetrics field and belongs to an international organization dedicated to the reproductive and sexual health of all women worldwide. It also helps to be highly connected to the U.S. government. Petitions for medical trials bypass red tape and are decided on immediately.

"Do you feel up to getting your hair braided? I know yesterday's hair washing tired you out."

"Oh yes, I'm up to it. I've never had cornrows. I'm curious as how they will look on me."

"It's been a while since I've done them, so don't get your hopes up too high." I open the duffle bag and lay out the hair moisturizer, edge control, combs, and hair clips. Standing behind the lounge chair, I begin to section off her hair. "What adventure did Solomon take you on today?"

She laughs. "Nathaniel took him hiking. I think my son took pictures of every creepy bug—dead or alive—he came across with that kid's camera Emma got him."

It will take some getting used to hearing people refer to James as

Nathaniel and calling him by that name myself.

For the next hour, I braid Selam's hair and listen to her retell her son's hiking adventure and the progress he's making with his therapy sessions. Right now, his sessions are every other day, as are Emma's. Hopefully by the middle of the summer the sessions can be reduced to once or twice a week.

Selam is pleased with how her hair turns out. The cornrows do not look too bad. I wait for the nurse to help Selam back into bed before I pack up and leave, promising I'll be back tomorrow.

On my way to Kourtney's room in the south wing of the hospital, I meet up with Emma, Mom, and Dad getting off the elevator followed by their Phantom Secret Service Agents.

"Mommy." Emma runs into my arms.

"Hi, sweetie. Daddy loved the dinner you helped me make."

"Really? Did you tell him I made the sun tea?"

"No. You said you wanted to." I cup her cheek in my hand. "Did you have another good talk with Dr. Stevens today?"

"Yes. He wants me to bring my sketch pad next time."

"Sounds like fun. I see you brought Mr. Cuddles with you."

"Yeah." She frowns, her gaze falling to the beige tile floor. "Maybe Kourty will wake up if Mr. Cuddles is with her. She told me once, it's his job to watch over her while she sleeps."

"I'm sure she'll thank you when she wakes up."

"Mom, do you think Kourty will be mad that Mr. Cuddles kind of smells like Trevor? I had to trick him to get the bear away from him. I was going to ask Grandma to wash his jacket, but Kourty told me to never take it off him."

"I'm pretty sure Kourtney won't mind. Come on, let's go see your sister."

"Dani, can we talk for a minute?" Mom asks.

"Of course." I turn to my daughter. "Go on inside with Grandpa. I'll be there in a minute."

Mom and I walk over to the sitting area near the windows that overlook the hospital's botanical garden. We sit in the swivel armchairs separated by a small round wooden table.

Worry lines crease her eyes. "How did your talk with Bryan go?"

Why does he not see how his self-imposed sentence to stay by his daughter's bedside is affecting the people who love him?

"It went well. I think it helped him some."

"Is he coming home with us to sleep in a real bed?"

"I doubt it, Mom."

"I don't get it. You're okay with leaving the hospital for a few hours. Why does he find it so difficult?"

"Actually it kills me every time I walk out of that room. I hate being away from both my daughters. I hate that I couldn't stop that woman from setting fire to the barn. I hate that the man I love is drowning in guilt and second-guessing how he handled things. I hate this whole situation!" All my pent-up frustration comes out at once.

"Oh, Dani, I'm so sorry. You're being so strong for everyone else, I forget you're just as worried as the rest of us. Maybe you should start your sessions with Dr. Stevens now instead of waiting until Kourtney regains consciousness and is released from the hospital."

"I just want things to go back to normal. The kind of normal we had when we were a happy healthy family. A time when I was oblivious to his lies, and we didn't have this big secret hanging over us." My tears are plenty. I haven't cried since I watched the helicopter lift off the ground and fly off with my daughter and husband on board.

Mom reaches across the table for both my hands. "I knew Kourtney was Bryan's the day I met her."

"How?" Then I remember how she stared at Kourtney that morning. "Her eyes and hair."

Mom nods.

"Why didn't you say something?" I ask.

"My husband was acting such an ass that day, I didn't want to add more stress to an already awkward meeting."

"But after that, when we went shopping. Why didn't you say something then?"

"I figured you and Bryan would tell us when you were ready."

"Kourtney squeezed Bryan's hand," Dad shouts from the doorway.

Mom and I stand like a bolt of lightning simultaneously struck the seats of our chairs.

My feet move faster than my brain. I leave Mom behind and almost plow into Dad as he stands back, holding the door open.

Bryan is on his feet holding Kourtney's hand. He's singing that lullaby he used to sing when he put her to sleep.

Emma is standing at the foot of the bed cradling Mr. Cuddles and touching her sister's leg.

Ig is studying the EEG monitor while Tony and Vin stand beside Bryan, chanting for him to keep singing and for Kourtney to open her eyes. They step back and make room for me to squeeze in next to Bryan. My protruding belly brushes the edge of the bed.

My daughter's eyes twitch. And hope fills me.

Slowly her eyes crack open, then quickly close again. Vin reaches out and dims the lights over her bed. I hear Ig on the phone talking to Dr. Sullivan.

A second passes and Kourtney's eyes twitch.

Jessi barrels through the door wearing scrubs and a lab coat.

Bryan clasps my hand and I begin to sing with him. My voice is no match to his.

Our daughter's beautiful hazel eyes finally open and lock in on Bryan.

CHAPTER TWENTY-ONE

BRYAN

Colorado, Present Day

"I REMEMBER YOU, DAD." MY SWEET baby girl says.

The sound of her voice brings back the memory of how I felt that day in the hospital when I first held her. The love I felt back then is much stronger now.

I don't have time to ask her what she means. Dr. Sullivan and the neurologist converge on the room with a swarm of nurses and interns. They check my daughter. Ask her questions. Kourt keeps her eyes on me. I doubt she notices her mom standing next to me or the rest of her family in the room.

The process is frustrating her, it's starting to show in the downturn of her mouth and the tone of her voice when she responds to the same questions worded differently.

"Just a few more minutes, Kourty Bear, and we'll leave you alone," Uncle Iggy promises.

The bed is adjusted to an upright position and Kourt cries out. The nurse who did it quickly readjusts the bed and apologizes.

Beside me, Dani's patience is wearing thin too. She's tapping her foot and shifting side to side.

"Why don't you sit in my chair until they are finished with Kourt?"

The look my wife throws me can only be translated as: You've parked your ass in that seat for five days and now you want to offer it to me?

I raise my hands in surrender.

One by one the team leaves the room until only Dr. Sullivan

remains.

"So far, everything looks good. Kourtney's lucid. Her pupils are responsive. Her lungs are clear. She has a slight headache, so we'll continue to monitor her. But other than that, Miss. Kourtney Hawk, you are doing well."

"Thank you, doctor," Dani whispers.

Dr. Sullivan steps out of the way so we can surround Kourt's bed. I catch the brush of shoulders that transpires between the doctor and Jessi. The eye connection is a giveaway. They like each other.

Dani sits on the edge of the bed, leans over, and kisses our daughter's forehead. "Hi, sweetie."

"Hi, Mommy."

Dani succumbs to the tears she's held in for days. Kourt's eyes fill too. The tears spill over, traveling across her temples to wet the pillowcase beneath her head. I don't think anyone in the room has dry eyes.

A soft sniff from the foot of the bed gets Kourt's attention. She lifts her arm and reaches out to her sister.

Emm moves closer and they touch fingertips.

"Hi, Emmy."

"Hi, Kourty," Emm cries. "I brought Mr. Cuddles. Sorry he smells like Trevor."

Kourt takes the bear. "That's okay. I kind of gave him to Trevor." She hands me the bear. "Dad, can you unbutton Mr. Cuddles's jacket please?"

I push the first button through the hole, then the second one, then the last one.

Kourt reaches over and peels back the flaps. "I remember you, Dad."

Dani gasps and I feel like I'd just been punched in the gut.

Harbored inside of Mr. Cuddles's jacket is the picture Dani said was missing from her safe. It's the original to the image that appears on my computer monitor when I tap the hawk's eye, and the one I kiss and keep next to my heart on each mission.

"How long have you had this, sweetie?" Dani asks.

"Ever since we moved from Arizona."

I catch my wife before she slips off the bed. The room has grown quiet. The only sounds are the machines my daughter is still hooked up to.

Kourt shrinks into her pillow.

After I get Dani settled, I take my baby girl's hand and wipe away her tears with my thumb.

"Why didn't you tell your mom you had the picture?"

Her small shoulders brush the starched pillowcase as they rise and fall. She looks to her mother like she's waiting to be yelled at.

"Sweetie, do you know the combination to my safe?"

She shakes her head slowly.

"Then how did you get the picture?" I ask.

"I found it in Mommy's closet when she told me to check upstairs before we left our old house."

"My closet was empty."

"It was stuck between the baseboard and the wall. I thought it was just a piece of paper until I turned it over." She lifts the picture. "Daddy and daughter meet for the first time. February 12, 2006," she reads.

Dani is shaking her head like she can't believe what's going on. Her hand visibly trembles when she retrieves the picture from Kourt.

"Is this what you mean by you remember your dad?"

"Am I in trouble?"

"No, sweetie. Of course not. We're trying to understand what you mean, that's all."

Dani keeps calling her sweetie as a way to reassure Kourt.

"I used to dream about a tall man with a big bird on his back," she begins. Kourt recalls the times Emm and I spent with them in Arizona.

I look to Ig and sign "*impossible.*" Ig signs back "*it's very possible.*"

How could she remember things when she was a toddler? But everything she tells us really happened. When Kourt describes the night I gave her Mr. Cuddles, the hairs on the back of my neck prickle. She recites the last words I spoke to her verbatim.

"Kourtney?" Dani holds up the picture. "Is this why you've been so angry? Because you knew your dad and I were keeping a secret from you?"

She slowly nods. Her gaze shifts to me. "Daddy, I'm sorry for saying those mean things to you." She starts to cry again. Her body jerks from the sobs.

"Heyyyy," I sing as I cup her face with my hands. "It's okay, baby girl. Now that we know, we can talk about it. Nothing can make me stop loving you, not even your angry words."

It takes a minute to get her calmed down.

Dr. Sullivan steps closer to the bed. "Do you think you're up for some food?"

"May I have chicken strips and French fries and apple juice?"

"You need something soft on your stomach. I was thinking, chicken broth, mashed potatoes, and spinach."

"Nope, I'm not up for food."

We laugh.

"How about this? My sister owns a swanky bistro. She makes the best chicken noodle soup. Sometimes I get some for my patients and they love it. You want to try some?"

"Does it have yucky peas and carrots in it?"

"Nope, but she does make it with a fresh vegetable base roux and broth, no fats."

"Do I still have to eat a vegetable?"

"Not if you promise to eat the whole bowl."

"Okay, I'll try it. Can I still have the apple juice?"

"I'll go for that."

"This soup sounds good, doc. I think I might want some," Dani says.

"Me too," I chime in.

Then everyone in the room is suddenly hungry even though we've already had dinner.

"I'll place the order and have someone from the hospital go pick it up. I keep telling my sister she should hire a delivery person."

"No need to send someone, I'll pick it up. Just tell me where," Dad says.

"I'll go with you, Dad."

You'd think I just announced I'm really a cyborg from the wide eyes, open mouths, and arched eyebrows on everyone—including Kourt.

"Haven't you guys been hounding me about getting out of this room?"

Dani recovers first. "We're just shocked you're actually going to do it."

I kiss my daughter's forehead. "Promise you won't tire yourself out while I'm gone."

Kourt raises her pinky. "I promise."

I hook mine and we shake then cross our hearts.

Dr. Sullivan gives us the address, then makes the call to her sister. Dad and I leave the hospital room to the sounds of claps, whistles, and cheers. And Vin telling Tony and Ig to pay up the five racks they owe him—yeah, we bet on stupid stuff.

The awkward silence in the elevator is suffocating. I inhale deep and exhale slow and count the seconds until the door opens.

It takes my eyes a minute to adjust when we step out of the hospital's lobby doors into the fresh air. The transition lenses of my glasses help.

Three Phantom SUVs are waiting at the curb for us. Dad and I climb into the back seat of the middle one. One of the Phantom Secret Service Agents who rode the elevator with us climbs into the front. The others ride in the front or rear vehicles.

Dad shifts in his seat and pulls at the collar of his shirt. I tilt a vent toward him and turn on the air at the same time. Then I push the button for the privacy window to slide up.

"Are you mad at me, Dad?" I realize I sound like I'm five years old again.

"I'm trying to wrap my head around why you hid my grand-daughter from us for eight years. I understand about the job—that I can accept. But you purposely hid Kourtney from us. Your mom says it's because of how I reacted when you brought Emma home the first time. Is that true?"

I shift as much as the seat belt allows to face him. "I was struggling to understand the strong feelings I had for Dani and knew I couldn't explain it to you in terms that would go along with how you raised me. Grandma would have understood and helped me convey it to you. By the time I was ready to bring Dani and Kourt to Colorado, things happened and it was safer for them to stay in Arizona and for me to disappear from their lives."

"No matter how much I tell my granddaughter and daughter-in-law I love them, their first memory of me will always be the ugly way I acted when I first met them."

"Trust me, you'd know if my wife and daughter were holding a grudge."

"Dani lied to me."

"How?"

"She told me Kourtney's father is the only man she'd been intimate with and she was nineteen at the time. She waited until after she got married to have sex."

I smile. "Dani didn't lie. She used the way the brain processes words to tell the truth. Your brain's recorded experiences filled in the rest on its own. She married James when she was nineteen. Dani and I had sex *after* we thought James was dead. I *am* the only man Dani has been with."

"She and James didn't…"

I start shaking my head before he could finish the question. "They never had sex. Don't blame Dani, Dad. I told her we had to act like strangers."

"Why?"

For the rest of the ride I tell my dad about how RAGS wanted me to join them and why I walked away from Dani and Kourt. I don't tell him the leader of RAGS lived in my home. The SUV stops in front of the bistro. Dad and I get out and go inside.

Dr. Sullivan's sister walks through the swinging kitchen doors carrying a cardboard box. The scrumptious smells in the open floor plan space make my mouth water.

Dad relieves her of the box while I hand her my credit card.

She waves me off. "I owe Colette so much. Giving her patients and their families a free meal is how I pay her back. She always recommends my chicken noodle soup to the kids because it's made with one hundred percent liquefied fresh vegetables. I dish it up so they get their recommended portion of protein and vegetables in one bowl."

"So, that's why Dr. Sullivan told my daughter she had to promise to empty the bowl."

Dad shifts the box to balance on one hand. "At least let us leave a tip."

"No, sir. But if you like my soup, come back one day and try something else on my menu and recommend me to family and friends. I'm open for lunch and dinner."

We thank her and head back to the hospital. On the way Dad asks about my military career. I tell him as much as I can, but consciously leave out the specifics. I even tell him that the woman in the stable was Emm's biological mother. What I don't tell him is why she came after my family.

Dad stops outside the door to Kourt's room and faces me. "I know I don't say it enough, but I'm proud of you, son. And I love you."

"I love you too, Dad."

We have family dinner in Kourt's room until she falls asleep. Mom and Dad go home and the guys go back to the mini command center. Emm takes the chair-bed. Dani curls up on the couch. I sit in the armchair with my laptop. The number of emails in my inbox does not surprise me.

I kick up my heels and start the tedious process of getting caught up with Phantom and Hawkeye.

Before I know it, the sky is brightening, and I put a nice size dent in the work that had piled up. I look at the clock across the room. I log off my laptop and set it aside.

"I feel like running today." I stretch my arms above me and immediately wince and grip my shoulder. It's still a little tender.

I send a text to the guys and get my bag out of the small closet, taking it with me into the bathroom to change. I stand in the mirror to survey myself. The guys teased me when they first saw me because my hair was singed. Vin went out and bought hair clippers and gave me a buzz cut fade. I kind of like my hair cut short. Thanks to the ointment Ig gave me, my torso isn't tomato red any more, but spots are starting to peel though. My forearms and calves are still wrapped because of the blisters, and there will be some scarring. None of that bothers me because my wife, daughters, and Dad did not die in that fire. The way I see it, the scars are my badges of honor.

I put on a dry-fit shirt and jogging pants. Since my eyes are no longer dry and irritated, I put in my new contacts.

Before I leave, I wake Dani and let her know I'm going for a run.

When I walk out of the door, my best friends are suited up and ready to run too. We stretch right there in the lobby, then ride the elevator down to the first floor.

The air is crisp and fresh. I strap my phone to my arm, put in my earplugs, but do not turn on any music. I just want to mute the distracting sounds of the outside world. This run isn't for clarity. It's my time with God.

Tony, Ig, and Vin fall in place. We jog at a laid-back pace.

As my feet hit the pavement at a rhythmic beat, my eyes stay on the clear blue sky. *Thank you for the extraordinary woman you brought into my life and the amazing daughters you have given us and the son who will be here in a few months. The four of them are my light in the darkness and my peace in the chaos. Thank you for the love and support of my mom and my big sister. And thank you for my dad. It took the guidance of a good woman to give me the hindsight to the methods of a determined father to raise an upstanding man. Now that my eyes are wide open, let us continue to rebuild our relationship as father and son. Please let my sister find the same completeness I've found in my life. It is time for her to know what love truly is. Thank you for the brotherhood I have with the men I call my best friends. Without them, I wouldn't be where I am today. Let our bond remain strong and unbreakable. Remind Tony of what real love brings to his life. Help Ig find the words to reach the ears of his soulmate. Give Vin the understanding of what it means to forgive and to be forgiven. Let Max remain quiet within his inner storm. Let the wounds of the past heal for James and his family so they can move forward in their lives. And thank you, God, for the courage, the determination, and the strength it took to save the lives of the people I love. Amen.*

By the end of my spiritual run we are back at the hospital.

Kourt is awake and watching cartoons with the volume turned down low. Dani and Emm are still asleep.

"Will you be okay with just Mom and Emm here? I want to go to Grandma and Grandpa's to take a shower and sleep in a real bed. But I'll be back later."

"Dad, can I ask you something?"

"Sure, baby girl."

"How did you get back in the stable? The fire covered the doorway as soon as you carried Emmy out."

"I ran through it."

"What?! Why?"

"Because I love you more than my own life, Kourtney Allison Hawk. You matter to me. And plus"—I take my stance with my imaginary cape flapping in the wind behind me—"I'm Super Hawk, remember. I fly in and save the day."

"I love you too, Dad."

"I know you do, Kourt."

I turn to leave, and I see Dani watching us. She smiles, blows me a kiss, then closes her eyes.

Mom and Dad are not in the kitchen when I get there. Both

cars are in the driveway. I do find Trevor hiding under the kitchen table.

"Hey, boy, where's Mom and Dad?"

He whines and a chill pricks the back of my neck. I grab my gun from the side pocket of the duffle bag and go in search of my parents.

Trevor follows me from room to room. Nothing seems out of place downstairs.

As I approach the stairs, I take note of a faint, unusual sound. Trevor blocks the stairs with his body.

"Move, boy," I whisper.

He whines and bumps his head into my thigh like he's trying to push me back. I take hold of his collar and move him. Trevor crawls under the table by the door, resting his head on his front paws. If he could talk, I'm almost certain he'd say, "Suit yourself."

Gun leading the way, I keep my back against the wall as I climb the stairs one step at a time.

The sound becomes more pronounced the closer I get to the landing. I stay calm and alert, prepared for anything. Maybe my parents are bound and gagged and using their feet to kick the wall as a way of crying out for help.

I get to the top of the stairs and turn in the opposite direction of their room. Since I know where the sound is coming from, I need to check the other rooms to make sure no one is hiding in them.

Jessi's old room is the first one I check and clear. The guest room is the next place I check and clear. I saved my old room for last because it is the closest to my parents' room. It's empty.

Their bedroom door is cracked opened. I take one step in that direction and stop. The reflection in the mirror seen through the crack matches my dad's words. "Mmmm, damn, Nance, this feels so fuckin' good. Don't stop."

"Aww. Hell. No!" My eyes shut, and I turn away.

"Who's there?" Mom asks.

I'm already blindly running for the stairs. I don't open my eyes until I get to the bottom where Trevor greets me with a round of barking I translate as, "I told you so."

"Bryan, is that you?" Mom is leaning over the banister, belting her robe.

I run to the kitchen, grab my bag, and lock myself in the guest bathroom off the laundry room. Lucky for me, Dad had a shower put in when they had it remodeled.

I undress and don't properly cover my gauze-wrapped arms and legs before I stand under the waterfall from the showerhead. Nothing in my vault of memories can overpower the one of what I saw in the mirror's reflection. No one was in distress like I thought, unless the fit of the harness was too tight for Dad. Ugh! No one wants to think of their parents as being sexually active.

I don't recall the last time I'd been in their bedroom, but I do know I would have noticed suspension hooks in the ceiling. This is Dani's doing. She turned my mother on to those books. Now my parents are into BDSM. Ugh!

I get out of the shower and slather ointment on my burns. It's a struggle, but I get them covered, then put on a loose-fitting shirt and sweatpants. Hopefully I've been in here long enough for them to finish and Dad leave for work.

My good fortune has run out. He and Mom are seated at the kitchen table eating breakfast. I put on my imaginary blinders and I walk through the kitchen.

"At least you know it's in your DNA for your pipe to still work when you get to be my age." Dad laughs as I pass them by.

He's not that old.

My old room is my sanctuary. I lie on top of the bedcovers and force my brain to shut down. Without the weight of guilt on me I can relax and fall asleep. My dreams aren't plagued by fires and the threat of war. They're happy dreams about the days I spent in Arizona.

I might have slept all day if my cell phone hadn't awakened me. The secured message is the reason I get up and go back to the hospital in the late afternoon.

On the side of Kourt's bed are flowers, a teddy bear, and a get well balloon bouquet. Both girls are lying in the hospital bed reading books. Kourt is wearing her eyeglasses—one of the drawbacks from having the Fleming Family's hazel eyes. Kourt's and Emm's hair are in a bunch of square braids.

Dani walks out of the bathroom drying a hairbrush with a towel. "You look much better."

"I feel better."

The room door opens, and three Secret Service agents come in.

"What's going on, Dad? Who are they?" Kourt asks.

"You have a special visitor."

We watch them check the room.

"Who is it?" Emm asks.

"You'll see."

The agents leave the room.

First Lady Vivianne Hart enters the room carrying a basket filled with activity books, travel-size games, and healthy snacks. Behind her are Emerson Jr. and Everett, each carrying a bag.

"I understand the future Ms. President is awake and feeling better," President Hart jokes as he enters carrying boxes of pizza.

"No. Way," Kourt shouts.

CHAPTER TWENTY-TWO

EMMA

Colorado, Present Day

TODAY, MOMMY AND DADDY COME with me to talk to Dr. Stevens. The doctor starts by telling me the difference between a biological mother and an adoptive mother. Daddy shows me pictures of a lady that has brown eyes like mine and brown hair like mine. Daddy says the lady is my biological mother, but he had sole custody of me. Dr. Stevens explains what custody means.

Mommy shows me pictures of me and her when I was a little baby. She says she's my adoptive mother, but she loved me ever since the day she met me.

Dr. Stevens tells me it's okay for me to ask questions about my biological mother. I ask if she liked to draw or loved horses like I do. Daddy tells me she grew up on a ranch that raised horses. But he thinks I love horses so much because of the books Mommy used to always read to me when I was a baby. I ask what happened to her. Daddy tells me she died not too long after she had me.

Next Dr. Stevens tells me to ask my mom any questions about herself. I ask her what it was like growing up without a mom and dad. Mommy tells me that was a very good question. She says she felt lonely because she didn't have anyone who was blood related to her. But she did have two people in her life that cared about her. Mr. and Mrs. Franklin, her foster parents. Dr. Stevens explains what foster parents are. Mommy shows me a picture of her foster parents and I'm in the picture too.

We talk about how long Mommy and Daddy have known each

other and how Daddy is Kourty's biological father. And me and her are real sisters. We just have different biological mothers.

"Does that mean Kourty is my little sister?"

Mommy, Daddy, and Dr. Stevens laugh.

"Well, technically yes," Daddy says.

Dr. Stevens asks if I want to share with Mommy and Daddy what I've been drawing in my sketchbook. At first I'm afraid, because the ones I drew when Kourty was asleep all those days are pictures of just me, Mom, Dad, and the baby. Then Daddy tells me whenever I'm ready to show them the drawings, they'd be happy to look at them. I open the sketchbook.

I started off drawing Mommy and Daddy as superheroes fighting the evil bad guys, then things about the fire, then the ones without Kourty.

"Emm, I'm sorry that I didn't pay much attention to you when Kourt got hurt. But that doesn't mean I love you any less. If you were the one who had gotten hurt, I'd sit by your bed until you woke up too."

"I know, Daddy. Me and Dr. Stevens talked about it. But I was sad when I drew those."

"Do you still feel sad?"

"No, I feel happy because my sister is okay, and you're not sad anymore. And Mommy has always loved me."

"We've talked about a lot of things today, haven't we, Emma?" Dr. Stevens asks.

"Yes."

"How do you feel about the things we talked about?"

"I feel good."

"Is there anything else you want to ask your parents?"

"Yeah, where's Marie and Willis?"

"Marie is really sick and had to go to a special hospital. Willis is with her. They won't be living with us anymore," Daddy tells me.

"Is she going to be okay?"

"We hope she gets better, but where she is, it's the best place to help her," Mommy says.

"Do you have any other questions?"

"No."

"Danielle, how do you feel about the things we talked about today?"

"I am proud of my daughter for being open and honest with her dad and me." Mommy looks right at me.

"Bryan, how do you feel about what we talked about today?"

"I'm proud of Emm too, Dr. Stevens. But I also admire her for having the courage to ask questions." Daddy holds my hand. "And I want you to know, Emm. I loved you before you were born and I will love you forever. You are my first born."

Mommy and Daddy take me to get lunch at the restaurant with the good chicken noodle soup.

"Emm, do you feel like Trevor is your dog too?" Daddy asks.

"Kourty is the one who wanted a dog."

"Do you want a pet of your own?" Mommy asks.

"No, but I really want to draw a big picture of Sweet Pea on my wall, then paint it in."

They look at each other and say, "Okay."

I thought for sure they would say no. I might as well ask for the other stuff now too.

"Can I get a sewing machine? Ms. Abernathy from the quilting circle told me she'd teach me how to sew but she didn't have a machine."

"There's a store in the mall we can go to this weekend and find you a basic machine for now. Then if you're really interested in sewing, Dad and I will look into getting you a more modern machine."

"Emm, just because Mom and I are agreeing to these things now doesn't mean we wouldn't have agreed to them later. Mom and I like that you're into art and sewing and quilting and whatever else you'd like to do that is positive. We support you no matter what."

"Thank you, Daddy."

The waitress sets my plate of ravioli in front of me and I start eating. Daddy tells Mommy about the things the people are doing at our house. I miss sleeping in my room. I ask when we're going home. Dad says when the house is finished.

After we eat, we go back to the hospital. They walk me to Kourty's room, then go take Ms. Selam the soup they bought for her.

I get my box of markers out and carefully climb on Kourty's bed.

"What are you going to draw today?"

My sister likes the pictures I draw on her cast. I didn't want to be like everybody else and sign it.

"Us."

She closes the book she was reading. "Guess who came to see me?"

"Who?" I start drawing.

"Mr. Ian."

"Really? Why did he come see you?"

"He said he wanted to tell us Sweet Pea and Cuddles are settling into their temporary stable."

"I heard Daddy tell Grandpa that Uncle Tony and Uncle Vinny are finished looking at the old one, so it's going to be torn down and a new one built."

"Why did Uncle Vinny and Uncle Tony have to look at the burned stable?"

I shrug. "Maybe because it was Ms. Williamson who started the fire."

"Mr. Ian said Dad is paying for the new stable because he wants it to be special for our horses."

"Today Dr. Stevens talked about biological mothers and adoptive mothers and nobody said anything about Ms. Williamson being my biological mom. Dad showed me a picture of my biological mother and she doesn't look anything like Ms. Williamson."

"I told you, Emmy, Mrs. Brooks is a mean person. She lied to you about Ms. Williamson being your mom. And she lied about James giving Mommy something that Daddy wanted. Me and you *are* sisters."

"Yep, best sister friends. Hey, I should make us pillows that say that."

"And paint it on a rock in the butterfly garden." Kourty moves her arm and I mess up.

"Be still."

"Sorry, my back itches and I can't scratch it."

"Where?"

"On the right side."

"Sit up," I tell her.

When she slowly sits up her face scrunches like it hurts to move. I reach back and start scratching, but not too hard.

"Thanks, Emmy." She sits back.

"Did you like talking to Dr. Stevens this morning?"

"It was okay.

"Dr. Steven does what Mommy does but different because he can give people medicine and Mommy can't."

"Yeah, he told me they are doctors who take care of the mind."

Kourty gets quiet and stares at the ceiling.

I stop drawing. "Did you guys talk about it?"

"A little bit."

"What did he say?"

"He just said we may never know why she started the fire. He thinks she did it because she was so sad that her mom and dad died that she didn't want anybody else to be happy."

"Yeah, he told me the same thing. Did you tell him she said Daddy sent somebody to kill her and her mom and dad and that's why she wanted to kill us?"

Kourty finally looks at me and nods.

"Did he tell you Daddy would never do something like that?"

Kourty nods again.

"Do you believe him?"

"Yes. Daddy is a good guy. Not a killer."

I switch markers and start coloring in the outline I drew. "Kourty, will you get mad at me again if I do stuff with Mommy like cook and bake and sew without you?"

"Emmy, I wasn't mad at you because you did things with Mom without me. I was mad because that's all you wanted to do. Me and you like getting our nails and feet done. We like the same movies and TV shows and music. But you only wanted to be with Mommy."

"I'm sorry Kourty."

"I'm sorry too, Emmy. I was being really mean to you."

"I want you to do stuff with Daddy by yourself. Since you guys like sports, maybe you guys can go to games together or something."

We look up when the room door opens.

"Does anyone want a mini succulents garden?" Uncle Max walks in.

"And brownies?" Penny's behind him.

"And ready to take lots of pictures?" Uncle Tommy lifts his camera to his eye.

Penny runs to the bed with the clear square container in her hand. She put the brownies on the moving table, then climbs in on the other side of Kourty.

"Ow." Kourty scrunches her face.

"Be careful, Penny. Kourty is still hurt."

"Sorry, I forgot. I'm just so happy to see you guys."

"It's okay, just don't make me move so much."

"Can I sign your cast after Emmy finishes?"

I hand her my marker box. "You can do it now." I point to a spot with no writing.

"Can Penny have a sleepover with me and Emmy tonight? I go home tomorrow."

"You mean sleep here? In your hospital room?" Penny asks.

I stop drawing. "The nurse said it's movie night in the lobby and they're serving pizza and veggie-butterflies and caterpillar grapes." I point to Daddy's chair. "Me and you can sleep on that. It turns into a bed."

Penny turns up her nose. "What are veggie-butterflies and caterpillar grapes?"

I laugh. "Aunt Jessi said they are carrots and snap peas put together to look like a butterfly, and a cantaloupe ball with red and green grapes on a stick to look like a caterpillar."

"May I sleepover?" Penny asks her dads.

"We'd have to check with your mom and dad"—Uncle Tommy looks at Uncle Max—"but it's okay with us."

"We'll go find Bryan and Danikins."

"They went to see Ms. Selam."

"Penny, do not leave this room," Uncle Max says.

"I won't, Daddy."

Once the door closes Penny leans in close to whisper. "What's going on? Daddy bust through the door one night dressed like the men on TV who are special cops. He told me to get Bella in her carrier and wait for them in the living room. Then he dragged Dad upstairs. I heard doors slamming and them stomping around. When they came running down the stairs, they had black bags. Daddy put earplugs in my ears and told me not to take them out until we got to the airport. He started the kids' music app on a cell phone I've never seen and turned it up loud. We left in Uncle Bry's truck. While Daddy was driving he and Dad were talking. It looked like they were yelling at each other. Daddy was driving really fast and every now and then he put his wrist up to his mouth to talk. When we got to the airport four guys took our bags and Bella's carrier. Two guys had guns. Daddy left us with them and ran the other way. The men surrounded us and walked us through the airport. We didn't go through security and we were the only ones on the airplane. Dad looked really sad, but he kept telling me everything is okay. When we got to New York he told me I couldn't tell Grandpa about Daddy leaving us at the airport."

Most times me and Kourty don't believe what Penny says because she wants to be on TV and in movies so she's always practicing by making up stories. Like that time she told the kids at school she was really from another planet and during the day she studied humans, then at night went back to her planet to teach other aliens how to act like humans so they can take over our planet. But this time I believe her because Uncle Max was dressed like that the night Mrs. Brooks came to our house.

Kourty looks at me and I look at Kourty. Mommy said we can't tell our friends about what happened at the house, the hospital, or the stable. But Penny isn't just our best friend, she's our cousin too. If we tell her it's a secret, we know she won't tell anyone.

Kourty nods.

Together me and my sister tell Penny what happened. I start with when we went to the stables for spring break and Mrs. Brooks told me her friend was going to hurt Mommy. Then Kourty tells her about the night I screamed and Trevor ate a plant that made him sick. Penny's eyes get really big as she listens to us tell her about Mommy hiding us in the secret room under the stairs. She sits up straight when Kourty tells her how Daddy and our uncles came in dressed in black and shooting guns. Penny almost falls off the bed laughing when I show her while Kourty tells her how Kourty jumped on Mr. Bond's back and pounded him with her fist because he was trying to take me out of the room.

"My daddy taught me a safe word too. It's *binti*, it means daughter in Swahili."

Penny leans in. "I think Daddy, Uncle Bry, Uncle Vinny, Uncle Tony, Uncle Iggy, and Auntie Dani are spies for the government."

Me and Kourty bust out laughing.

"Our dad runs a company that protects important people. Even people in the government." Kourty laughs.

"His company could be their cover," Penny says. "Why else would the President of the United States *and* the First Lady *and* their sons, who are so cute by the way, come to visit you? I'm serious, you guys. They're spies."

We laugh harder.

"Daddy said he knows President Hart because of the government contracts his company has," I tell her. "And EJ is so cute in person."

All of us agree.

"Think about it," Penny says. "We have safe words. You guys have a secret room in your house. I bet we do too. I had to take an airplane to a safe house and you guys took a helicopter to a safe house. And they have guns." She raises her hands up to the sky, then lets them fall back to the bed.

My stomach hurts from laughing. "Grandpa taught Daddy and Aunt Jessi safe words when they were little. That's why my dad gave me and Kourty one."

"Mommy said because of Daddy's job, he has to have cameras in every room and that's why we have a secret room in the house." Kourt's holding her stomach to stop from laughing.

Penny crosses her arms over her chest and pouts because we won't stop laughing. "If they're not spies, then why do all of them have the same ring that they wear on the same finger on the same hand?"

This time when the door opens the adults come into the room. I look at the right hands of my dad and uncles, then look at my sister. She must have done the same thing because her eyes are really, really big.

We look at Penny.

"I told you."

EPILOGUE

BRYAN

AN HOUR BEFORE SUNRISE, DANI and I parked at the base of the trail. We got out and started walking up the path at a slow and easy pace. We were not in a hurry. Now that Rebels Against Government Suppression and Islam Liberation Army are no longer a threat, everything seems to have slowed down.

We have time to be a couple.

We have time to be a family.

Dani had been up since two in the morning because she started having contractions. They were nowhere near close enough for us to go to the hospital and walking was part of her birthing plan as long as it was safe for her and the baby.

When we reached the destination, I stood behind my wife, wrapped my arms around her, and looked out as the sky began to brighten. I put my lips to my wife's ear and whispered, "This is why I built your dream house in Boulder, Colorado."

I felt the moment when the sight affected her.

We stood there until the sun's light touched every inch of our beautiful city. We weren't in a rush to get back home. Mom and Mrs. Franklin were taking turns staying with us, so we knew our girls were being cared for.

Now, I watch my wife lose the fight to keep her eyes open. Our family just left. Everyone was anxious to meet the newest member.

Theoretically I know how babies are born, but seeing a vaginal birth up close gives me a new appreciation for what women go through to bring a child into this world. Dani was in hard labor for six hours. She did it naturally, no medication. I was right there with her.

I peek over at our newborn son asleep and swaddled in the medical bassinet. The place card on the front reads:

Baby Boy Hawk
September 9, 2014 9:27 p.m.
7lbs, 5oz - 19"L

Mrs. Franklin called it at the baby shower, when she said, "You'll have that baby under the first full moon in September."

Tonight, there's a full yellow moon in the sky. Tony owes her a grand. He said the baby would be born on his birthday, which is two weeks from now.

I insert the crochet bookmark into the journal Elizabeth wrote in at age eleven. I was reading it to Dani before she fell asleep. A soft snore escapes my wife's mouth. She's exhausted.

The room door quietly slides open. My sister comes in carrying a take-out container. Dr. Sullivan is with her.

"I want to introduce Collett to my nephew and check up on Dani." Jessi hands me the container. "Is she still having postpartum chills?"

"The warm blankets helped." I open the container. Pastrami on rye. Toasted. Light mustard and an extra pickle. A small side salad with ranch and the homemade chips. I smile.

My sister snags a chip from the container. "There are notes in her records from when she had Kourt. That's why I made sure the blankets were on hand here in the room, but if it gets worse have me paged. I'll be in the on-call room."

"Should I be worried? I wasn't there when she had Kourt so I don't know how severe the chills were."

"It's common, but I'm going to monitor her temperature for the next few hours."

"You'd tell me if something's wrong, right? She wants to wait two years then try and get pregnant again, but if this chills thing puts her in danger, I'll get a vasectomy before I let her go through labor and delivery again."

My sister squeezes my shoulder. She cocks an eyebrow. I know she wouldn't hide it from me if it was serious. The minute Dani walked out of the exam room nine months ago my sister was blowing up my phone. When I finally answered I was every dumbass she could come up with. I was cussed out for never using condoms with Dani to begin with.

I do something out of the ordinary. I set my food aside, stand, and hug my big sister. "Thank you, JP1. I love you."

The waterworks start. My sister is an emotional person. Through heavy tears and sobs, my sister tells me she loves me too.

◆

DANI

Bryan steps out of the room after receiving a phone call. I pick up my mother's journal and open it to the page where Bryan set the bookmark Emm made me. The first three journals were drawings from a young girl who didn't know how to spell some of the words needed to describe her life. It doesn't take a child psychologist to decipher Elizabeth's tale of her loving relationship with her grandfather and father. And the abuse inflicted upon her by her mother and grandmother. At age eight, the big words are written phonetically and there are fewer pictures.

Experiencing this with Bryan is bringing us closer on another level. I think he is starting to understand why I want to visit my grandfather. Bryan is even starting to warm up to the idea of us hosting a sit-down meal with my side of the family.

I reread the last passage I remember listening to Bryan reading before I fell asleep last night.

I'm hiding under my dad's desk to write this. He is out of town again, so that means Bernadette and Antoinette are not going to let me eat or sleep until I recite the RAGS creed without messing up. The last time they made me stand out in the snow without any shoes or socks on. I do not call them mother or grandmother in here. This is my safe place. Granddad promised one day they will be bowing down to me.

Bryan has a strange look on his face when he walks into the room.

He sits on the edge of the bed and takes both of my hands in his. This can't be good.

"I promised you no more secrets and no more lies."

"What's going on, Bryan?"

"Remember I told you there were two more people on your security team you didn't get to meet?"

"Yes."

"I know this isn't the best time to do this, but we're kind of on a time crunch. There's one spot left at Greystone for third grade and Ig's girlfriend wants to reenroll her daughter…"

I cut him off. "What does her daughter being at the school have to do with me?"

"You guys can come in," he calls out.

Speechless is just one word to describe my lack of ability to speak when three people enter my hospital room. The two women come bearing gifts with anxious smiles. Ig stands behind the one I assume is his girlfriend.

Bryan moves to stand beside the bed but still holds my hand. "Let me formally introduce you to retired Captain Holly Valentine and Sergeant Yvon Wright."

If I had the strength to crush the bones in his hand I probably would without knowing. I can't decide which one to address first.

"That thing in the parking lot of the school with the gun and me talking you down, that was an act?" The accusation in my tone is intended.

"It was not my first choice. Suicide is a serious matter that should not be taken lightly or fabricated."

"The intensity of your turmoil felt real."

"Major Chen was coaching me through an earpiece. He was parked in the lot where you couldn't see him."

"Unbelievable." I shake my head. "The insults and innuendos I had to endure were part of some act you were putting on for what purpose?"

Ig places a hand on her shoulder. "Captain Valentine's assignment was just to befriend you and other mothers in the class. But Madelyn Brooks instantly targeted you and it threw up a red flag. The focus of her assignment became Brooks."

"Bottom line, Danielle, this was the first time Colonel Hawk has asked me to work an assignment because I have a child the same age as yours. He made it perfectly clear that at any point if it became too much for Melissa, I could pull out. Madelyn was becoming suspicious about my marital status and I didn't want to bring in a fake husband. There were no boundaries Madelyn wouldn't cross. When she questioned Melissa about her father, it was time I exited, but it had to look believable."

I imagine myself in Holly's shoes. She is a mother before she is

Phantom. I respect her for that.

"I know the sincerity of your words to help someone in mental pain came from the heart. And when you said your friends call you Dani, it made me wish you and I really were friends. Melissa was doing really well at Greystone and she misses Emma, Kourtney, and Penelope. I could use a real friend too. And someone who knows about Phantom but isn't Phantom. Someone who understands what I'm going through when the man in my life is on a blackout mission and it can be days or weeks before I hear from him."

I untangle my hand from Bryan's to reach out to her. "Hi, I'm Danielle Hawk. My friends call me Dani. Emma and Kourtney Hawk are my daughters."

Holly approaches. "I'm Holly Valentine. Melissa Valentine is my daughter."

We shake hands.

The next person to approach the bed has a big smile on her face. I try and fail to scowl at her.

"Sergeant Yvon Wright, Phantom Watcher, applying for the position in your home, ma'am."

"Cut the crap. Give me a hug."

Yvon wraps her arms around me and together we laugh.

"I can't believe you're Phantom."

She stands up. "That's the only thing you didn't know about me. After my messy divorce I was going to retire. Colonel Hawk proposed an alternative option that gave me the opportunity to be closer to my son."

"Do you want the position?"

"Yes, I do." The smile in her eyes is genuine, reminiscent of the woman I knew as neighbor and babysitter.

My newborn son cries out, loud and demanding. Part of my birthing plan was to put him on my breast as soon as he emerged from my womb. Since then, he's nursed every hour and a half and refuses to take a pacifier or a bottle.

"How soon can you start?" I ask.

BRYAN

When she first discussed a Tatum–Langford family gathering with me, I thought she was taking on too much, too soon. But then I helped her plan it because I remembered how much she loved the impromptu family reunion my family had in South Carolina when my dad was asked to give the commencement speech at the high school graduation. His brothers and their families came to support him too.

Tonight, Dani's big happy family dinner is going well considering the palpable tension between Willis Langford and all of the Tatums. How the evening will end is still too early to call. My wife is bringing out the appetizers now.

She went to great lengths to get me to allow Langford to be here this evening. He thinks an electrical charge from the ankle bracelet will flow through his body and incapacitate him if he ventures too far from me, Tony, Ig, Vin, or Max. I don't trust that he won't try to escape, and his word don't mean shit to me anymore. Even if he does manage to slip out unnoticed, Ig implanted a chip in his neck that will give off a signal that Riley can detect from any distance above or below ground. I made it perfectly clear to my wife that if I have to go after Langford, he's a dead man.

Emm and Kourt are warming up to Dani's side of the family. They introduce their best friend, Penny, to their new cousins. It took a while for the girls to understand how, for twenty-eight years, their mother didn't have a family and now, all of a sudden, she has grandparents, aunts, uncles, and cousins. Dr. Stevens helped us tell them a heavily modified version of the truth.

Three-month-old Five was being passed around from person to person so much, he started to get irritated. His godfather, Uncle Iggy, now has Five swaddled in a baby wrap and attached to him. If I have to explain one more time why we call my son Five, I'm going to spray paint it on the walls: Bryan Kendall Hawk *V*. His big sisters started calling him Five for short and it caught on. Dad thought I'd object to carrying on the tradition. I'm proud to have my first-born son carry on the name.

When Dani goes back to work at the beginning of the year, Five will go with her. He won't take a bottle, so Dani is forced to stop what she's doing to tend to his hunger. With him at the hospital's daycare center, she can continue to nurse him while she's at work. An anonymous donor—me—gave the hospital the funds—from the RAGS money—to open and operate a twenty-four-hour day-care center for hospital employees.

My wife is working the room like a seasoned hostess. She's trying to bridge the gap between the two families. Preparation for this gathering started last month. She's using the same company I use for my company's holiday party to serve, but Dani did all the cooking.

Tony's girlfriend, Tiffany, offered to help Dani in the kitchen. It didn't take long for Tiffany to bolt out of the kitchen.

I count twenty-five people in the house this evening. Most of them Tatums. Dani's father is the middle child of the three Tatum children. In addition to his mother and father, both of his siblings are here with their spouses and their own children. From Langford's side, his half-brothers and sister are here with their spouses. Dani also invited Mom and Dad, Katherine Franklin, Terrance Brumfield, Elijah Hopper, Jessi and her date Colette, and Max, Tom, and Penny. We were hoping George Franklin could come, but the nursing home reported that he was agitated this morning. Dani and I will take the kids to visit him tomorrow. Even if he doesn't remember them, they seem to make him happy when we visit.

I hired Tom to capture candid shots that will go into a special photo album I'm making Dani for her birthday; Emm is helping me.

Vin gets my attention while Penny is standing next to him. The guys and I are feeding into the girls' sleuthing scheme to uncover hardcore evidence that we're government spies. We do Hollywood spy type stuff in their presence just to mess with them. We're planning something big for New Year's Eve.

Dani announces dinner is ready and everyone gravitates to the dining room.

Since this is my wife's party, I defer the seat at the head of the table to her. The girls sit at the other end with the rest of the twelve-and-under group.

Daniel's older brother is the first to acknowledge Dani's efforts to honor her mother and father. Langford's half-sister adds to that by recognizing that Daniel and Elizabeth's legacy lives on through their beautiful daughter. I can somewhat relax now and enjoy experiencing this with my wife.

———◆———

DANI

I thought for sure Bryan would say no to me having a few extra minutes with Willis before Vin and Ig take him back to wherever he and Marie are being held. The rest of tonight's guests have gone.

The first thing I do is hug my grandfather. The light has not returned to his eyes. He is still that defeated man I saw sitting at the table in the penthouse. Some things are easy to fake, but when grief touches your soul, there is no faking that.

"How are you holding up?"

"The only way I know how, adapt to survive each day.

"Bryan and I have been reading my mother's journals. The notes you wrote to her are so different from the man people say you are. On my birthday I saw a glimpse of the father my mother loved. I'm going to keep pressing Bryan to let me see you."

"Why?"

"Reading Elizabeth's journal and getting to know you is as close as I can get to knowing my mother."

"Bryan's not going to allow it to continue. I'm surprised he allowed me to come today."

"I'd like to think my powers of persuasion are the reason he let you be here tonight, but I know otherwise. My husband doesn't do anything he doesn't want to do."

"Bryan is a good man. A man who can be trusted to do the right thing. I'll spend the rest of my life regretting not telling him the truth that day in my den." He laughs humorlessly. "I guess he proved me wrong. He can be Second Command and a family man."

"That's because of the woman in my life."

Willis and I turn to the doorway of the family room where Bryan stands, holding Five up on his shoulder.

"Your ten minutes are up. Time for Langford to leave."

"Am I allowed to walk him out or do you and Tony have to do

it?"

"You and I can do it together."

I hook my arm around my grandfather's and together we walk to the foyer. I pick up his coat and help him into it. I hug my grandfather one more time just in case I don't get to see him again.

He steps out of my embrace and looks at Bryan. "I was wrong about something else too, Bryan. I told you being Second Command changes even the most honorable of men. It didn't change you."

"I was raised by an honorable man who didn't expect anything less from his son."

Five starts to fuss. I take him from Bryan. When I look up, there are tears in my grandfather's eyes.

He crosses the threshold onto the porch. Vin and Ig are standing by the back passenger door of the black SUV idled in front of the steps, the interior lights shining bright.

"It's cold out. Get my great-grandson out of the doorway," Willis says before he climbs in and scoots to the middle seat.

He keeps his eyes focused on the windshield.

Bryan tries to turn me away from the door, but I remain where I stand and cup the back of my son's head with my hand as if it is enough to keep the cold air from touching him.

What's going on?

Ig walks around the front of the car; the winter coat flaps open revealing the holster strap and the gun. The front of Vin's winter coat is unbuttoned too. The wind blows it open as he climbs into the back with Willis, exposing his gun and holster. The back driver's side door opens and Ig climbs in.

Why are they sitting in the back too? Who is going to drive?

Then I understand.

The shiny metal of the chains and handcuffs catches the light.

First Willis is secured in the center seatbelt. The chains protruding out of the seat go around his waist. Ig handcuffs his wrists while Vin cuffs his ankles. The contraption connects with a padlock in the center.

I can't watch any more of this. I turn away and carry my son upstairs.

BRYAN

Tony waves his hands to get my attention. I'm watching Vin and Ig taking Langford into the facility on my monitor.

"Did you hear any of what I just said?"

"Yeah, I heard you. You're wondering if it's a good idea to take Tiffany to LA with us."

"What should I do? I mean, when we first got together I told her I wasn't looking for something serious. She said she just wanted to have fun. The sex is good. At times it's fucking mind-blowing." He leans back in the chair with his fingers interlocked behind his head and stares up at the ceiling. "I don't want to mess up what we've got going on."

"Why did you bring her to that birthday thing Dani and the girls gave me if you're not getting serious with her?"

"She was with me when Dani called. I had the phone on speaker because I was driving and didn't have my earpiece. Tiffany started talking to Dani like they were longtime friends. Dani invited her. Dani invited her tonight too. I wasn't expecting Tiffany to help out in the kitchen as a way of saying thank you for the invite."

I try not to laugh. "What is with you and women who can't cook?"

"Hey, Charly could sling some bomb-ass desserts. Tiffany will burn water."

I can't hold it, I laugh until my stomach starts cramping. The first time Tony came to work after Tiffany cooked him a "morning after" breakfast, he spent most of his time in the bathroom. It was coming out of both ends. Ig ran tests to make sure Tiffany didn't poison him.

"Does she know about Charly?"

"She knows I had a fiancée. She doesn't *know* it was Charly."

"There's too many ways for them to cross paths, Tony."

"Right now, Tiffany and I are just friends. There's no need for me to cross that bridge. If Charly's added, she's just the job. Nothing more. Nothing less." He stands.

What Charly did to him was wrong and I hate to put my best friend in this position. Tony has been hurting for a long time, he's overdue from some peace, love, and happiness. I think he's on that path with Tiffany and I don't want anything to come between them. But with important foreign dignitaries and our vice president confirmed to attend the competition in October, Tuck 'N Strut Productions had to come to Hawkeye Personal Protection because their World Drag Queen Competition is receiving threats from extremists from all over. Which means Tony's past may come face to face with his present.

We bro hug and I walk him out.

"Riley, lock up my house," I call out.

The downstairs lights start to dim and the digital locks on the doors and windows activate.

Before we moved back in, I installed a real time interactive home security system that is filtered through Riley. I started designing it when we were staying with my parents. There are a few kinks that need to be worked out, but the new system surpasses the previous one. It operates independently from the electrical source to the house. Even if someone cuts the power, the security system will work.

It's time for me to make sure the girls are in bed, then go face my wife. I saw the look in her eyes when she watched Langford get shackled. I'm happy she left before he was injected with a sleeping drug.

I climb the stairs and turn right at the landing.

Kourt is a night owl, and with them being on winter break, she's been putting in extra hours on this year's science project. The habitat she designed and created will definitely get her to nationals. Tony looked over her plans before she started building it and gave her suggestions on the best materials to use to get the kind of results she wants to prove her hypothesis. I'm so proud of my daughter.

I knock on her door, then open it when she doesn't respond. Kourt is already in bed and asleep. Trevor raises his head from his spot at the foot of her bed.

Kourt's laptop is on the pillow next to her. Her screensaver is a slide show of the pictures from the memory card I took from Dani's camera years ago. I kiss my daughter's forehead and pull the covers up to her shoulders.

"Night, Dad. I love you." She turns on her side, snuggling down under the covers.

"Night, baby girl. I love you more." I close the laptop and move it to her nightstand next to Mr. Cuddles, then turn off the light and leave her room.

Across the hall, I knock on Emm's door. She's asleep with the quilt she made pulled up to her chin. The lamp on her craft table is still on and the project she's working on is spread out. On the wall behind her bed is the painting she did of her horse. I'm happy Dani and Dr. Stevens support my decision to not tell Emm the real identity of Malinda Williamson. That's one truth that needs to remain a lie.

I kiss my daughter's forehead and leave the room.

As I walk to the other side of the house, the lights dim and the track lighting turns on.

Dani and Five are already in their pajamas. She's sitting in the rocking chair reading him a book while nursing him. His normal bedtime routine is, I bathe him and get him ready for bed, Dani nurse him, and I read the story. Tonight, Dani didn't wait for me.

I go straight to the bathroom to shower. As I stand in front of the mirror, I check myself out. My chest and stomach hairs grew back in fuller. And the color of my skin is back to normal. The new tattoos on my ribcage look like a Sumerian scroll that now includes Dani, Emm, and Five below Kourt. The burn scars on my arms and calves don't look too bad. Mrs. Franklin made me a body butter that keeps my burned skin moisturized.

When I come out of the bathroom in my pajamas, Five is in his crib asleep and Dani is sitting on the couch in front of the fireplace.

I join her.

"I know how important family is to you. And I get why you want to spend time with your grandfather. But at the end of the day, he is a criminal in custody and will be treated as such. I don't trust that he won't use you to break free. I'm not going to sugarcoat things. I love you more than I can explain, and it would bother me if this came between us. But you don't get a say in how your grandparents are treated."

"I was high on the success of tonight and for a moment I let myself get caught up in the fairytale. Seeing him being cuffed brought me crashing down."

"You can never let your guard down around him or Antoinette

or show any weaknesses. They will pounce. I don't care if Langford is crying crocodile tears, if you can't maintain the alpha role I won't allow you to see them."

"I understand. So, does that mean I can see my grandparents?"

"Let's start with Langford once a month for thirty minutes and see how it goes. Antoinette needs a lot more reconditioning before you can see her." Dani knows Chen is working on her grandmother.

She leans in and kisses my cheek. "Thank you. I talked to Nathaniel and Selam today. Selam is off the walker. She now has a walking cane. Solomon likes his new school. And Nathaniel's home based business is picking up."

"It's good to hear things are working out for them." I take her hands in mine. "Dani, I've always wanted to ask you something, but I'm afraid of the answer."

"I love you, Bryan. You can ask me anything."

I look down at our hands and our matching wedding bands. When I look up at her, I read a mixture of emotions in her questioning eyes.

"Why me, Dani?"

She cups my cheeks in her hands. "Mrs. Franklin once told me a story about relationships, love, and marriage. She said: the foundation of real love is unconditional trust because every relationship has its seasons. You and I have had our seasons and I know we'll have many more. But if you look at the things we've weathered so far you'll see how something stronger and bigger than our love is why we survived and how we will continue to survive. It keeps our head above water when waves come crashing down. You want to know why you?"

I nod.

"Because trusting and loving you is—effortless."

Her thumb traces my bottom lip and just like the first time she did it, I feel her touch in my soul.

"Danielle Lauren Hawk, you're my do-right-girl."

"What do you know about a do-right-girl?"

My reply is a kiss from deep within my heart.

"You once asked me how strong is a relationship that is built on lies? I never answered because I didn't know the answer then. Ask me again."

Dani climbs onto my lap, straddling my thighs. "Bryan, how strong is a relationship that is built on lies?"

"It isn't. Despite the reasons I knocked on your door nine years ago, *our* relationship began with unconditional trust and that's why we've survived the lies."

The End

DEAR READER,

Thank you for sharing your valuable time with me by following Bryan and Danielle's journey through the web of secrets and lies. Their truths were always there for you to see in the books *Necessary Lies* and *Lies You Tell*. I hid them behind the way the brain processes words—I'm sneaky like that. Go back and see if you can spot the hidden truths in books one and two.

We must leave Bryan and Danielle to walk the path of Happily Forever alone, but you can catch glimpses of them in the stories of the other members of Phantom's Elite Special Operations Team. Where we leave Bryan and Danielle's story behind, Tony's love triangle begins.

Join me for the next journey. A spicy series about a fixation with cheating, the destruction of obsession, and the love it takes to let go and forgive. Can Phantom's Lieutenant Colonel Anthony "Tony" Jonathan Paul put aside his contempt for Charly—the woman who left him at the altar—to capture the vindictive person hell bent on killing her before she walks down the aisle to marry another man? But helping Charly puts a strain on Tony's growing relationship with Tiffany—the woman who makes him believe in love again.

Best,

Jacki Renée

BOOKS BY JACKI RENÉE

MEN OF PHANTOM SERIES

Necessary Lies – Book One of Lies Trilogy
Lies You Tell – Book Two of Lies Trilogy
Secrets and Lies – Book Three of Lies Trilogy

———◆———

For information about giveaways, upcoming books, and
appearances follow me on:

twitter @iamjackirenee
facebook /iamjackirenee
instagram /iamjackirenee
goodreads /goodreadscomJacki_Renee